Hollow Kingdom

Hollow Kingdom

A Novel

Kira Jane Buxton

GRAND CENTRAL
PUBLISHING

NEW YORK   BOSTON

Copyright © 2019 by Kira Jane Buxton

Jacket design and illustration by Jarrod Taylor
Jacket copyright © 2019 by Hachette Book Group, Inc.

Hachette Book Group supports the right to free expression and the value of copyright. The purpose of copyright is to encourage writers and artists to produce the creative works that enrich our culture.

The scanning, uploading, and distribution of this book without permission is a theft of the author's intellectual property. If you would like permission to use material from the book (other than for review purposes), please contact permissions@hbgusa.com. Thank you for your support of the author's rights.

Grand Central Publishing
Hachette Book Group
1290 Avenue of the Americas, New York, NY 10104
grandcentralpublishing.com
twitter.com/grandcentralpub

First Edition: August 2019

Grand Central Publishing is a division of Hachette Book Group, Inc. The Grand Central Publishing name and logo is a trademark of Hachette Book Group, Inc.

The publisher is not responsible for websites (or their content) that are not owned by the publisher.

The Hachette Speakers Bureau provides a wide range of authors for speaking events. To find out more, go to www.hachettespeakersbureau.com or call (866) 376-6591.

Print book interior design by Thomas Louie

Library of Congress Cataloging-in-Publication Data

Names: Buxton, Kira Jane, author.
Title: Hollow kingdom / Kira Jane Buxton.
Description: First edition. | New York : Grand Central Publishing, 2019.
Identifiers: LCCN 2018034444| ISBN 9781538745823 (hardcover) | ISBN 9781549113482 (audio download) | ISBN 9781538745816 (ebook)
Subjects: LCSH: Crows–Fiction.
Classification: LCC PS3602.U9825 H65 2019 | DDC 813/.6–dc23
LC record available at https://lccn.loc.gov/2018034444

ISBNs: 978-1-5387-4582-3 (hardcover), 978-1-5387-4581-6 (ebook)

Printed in the United States of America

LSC-C

10 9 8 7 6 5 4 3 2 1

For Jpeg,
who taught me how to fly

Hollow Kingdom

It is just like man's vanity and impertinence to call an animal dumb because it is dumb to his dull perceptions.

—Mark Twain

CHAPTER 1

I should have known something was dangerously wrong long before I did. How do you miss something so critical? There were signs, signs that were slow as sap, that amber lava that swallows up a disease-kissed evergreen. Slow as a rattlesnake as it bleeds toward you, painting the grass with belly scales. But sometimes you only see the signs once you're on the highest branch of realization.

One minute everything was normal. Big Jim and I were playing in the yard. We live together, you see. It's a platonic relationship with a zesty sprinkle of symbiosis. I get the perks of living with an employed electrician in a decent neighborhood of Seattle, and he gets his own private live-in funnyman. Winner winner chicken dinner, which so happens to be a favorite of mine.

So, Big Jim and I were in the yard. He had a Pabst Blue Ribbon beer in hand—classic Big Jim—and was stooping intermittently to yank out a weed the size of a labradoodle. Things grow heartily in our state of Washington: emerald moss, honey crisp apples, sweet cherries, big dreams, caffeine addiction, and acute passive aggression. We also legalized pot to which Big Jim likes to poignantly screech, "Fuck yeah!"

Where was I? Right. A summer evening glaze of gold varnish coated our yard with the fat frog fountain and that shitty little smug-faced gnome that I've been trying to sabotage since I moved in. And then Big Jim's eyeball fell out. Like, fell the fuck out of his head. It rolled onto the grass, and to be honest, Big Jim and I were both taken aback. Dennis, on the other hand, didn't skip a beat, hurling himself toward the rogue eyeball. Dennis is a bloodhound and has the IQ of a dead opossum. Honestly, I've met turkeys with more brain cells. I'd suggested to Big Jim that we oust Dennis because of his weapons-grade incompetence, but Big Jim never listened, intent on keeping a housemate that has zero impulse control and spends 94 percent of his time licking his balls. Dennis's fangs were within a foot of the eyeball as I snatched it, balancing it on the fence for safekeeping. Big Jim and I shared a look, or sort of three-quarters of a look, because now, obviously, he only had a single eyeball. Whilst making a mental note to add this to my petition to get Dennis evicted from our domicile (surely once you've tried to eat your roommate's eyeball, you gots to go) I asked Big Jim if he was alright. He didn't answer.

"What the fuck?" said Big Jim, as he raised a beefy hand to his head, and that was the last thing I heard him say. Big Jim retired indoors and didn't finish his Pabst Blue Ribbon beer. Again—signs. He spent the next few days in the basement of our house where the PBR fridge is and also the freezer with shitloads of meat in it. Then he didn't eat. Not one of the delicious ducks or deer he lovingly shot in the face. Things seemed even more severe when he missed the Monster Truck Show he'd been crowing about for weeks. I tried to reason with him, tried to get him to eat part of a banana—I took care of the moldy bits because he's picky about those—some of the Doritos I'd helped myself to, and even some of idiot Dennis's kibble. Nothing. Then the pacing started. Big Jim started to traverse the periphery of the basement, shaking his head to a melancholy tune like the sloth bear at the Woodland Park Zoo. Initially I assumed Big Jim was trying to wear a circle into the basement for conduit installation, which he is very proficient in. But his one eye was now staring into oblivion and he had stopped talking to me and his drooling became worse than Dennis's, which is really saying something.

I'd like to note that during this time, a time of great emotional duress and general uncertainty, Dennis did absolutely nothing except whiz all over the La-Z-Boy® and yarf on the carpet. I did my best to clean it up, but really he's not my responsibility.

The earlier signs were more subtle, only seen with the hindsight spectacles that Big Jim yearns for after every Tinder date. Before the eyeball evacuation, Big Jim started to forget things. He forgot a few appointments, then his wallet, and even his house keys, which he blamed me for because he thinks I'm a "giant klepto." Hey, I'm just a fella who likes to build on his hidden collections. Who doesn't enjoy the finer things? He told me that some of his words were stuck, that they had fused to his tongue. When I offered to orally investigate, I was largely ignored. He became lethargic, a subtlety that perhaps only I would have noticed, seeing as Big Jim has the physical motivation of a taxidermic sloth. But I know him well, and I saw the difference. He stopped walking Dennis, which had disastrous consequences for the couch cushions, may they rest in peace.

The runaway eyeball signified a turning point in our lives. I cached the eyeball in the cookie jar in case he could use it later. But Big Jim was never the same again. None of us were.

I hesitate to go on for fear that you will judge me and not want to hear the rest of my story. However, in the interest of full disclosure, I feel a duty to tell you the truth about everything. You deserve it. My name is Shit Turd and I am an American crow. Are you still with me? Crows aren't well liked, you see. We're judged because we are black, because our feathers don't possess the speckled stateliness of a red-tailed hawk's or the bewitching cobalt of a blue jay's, those stupid fuckers. Yeah, yeah, we're not as dainty and whimsical as hummingbirds, not as wise as owls—a total misnomer by the way—and not as "adorable" as the hambeast-bellied egg timer commonly known as a penguin. Crows are harbingers of death and omens, good and bad, according to Big Jim according to Google. Midnight-winged tricksters associated with mystery, the occult, the unknown. The netherworld, wherever that is— Portland? We make people think of the deceased and super angsty poetry. Admittedly we don't help the cause when we happily dine on fish guts in a landfill, but hey ho.

So, the truth—my name is Shit Turd (S.T. for short) and I'm a domesticated crow, raised by Big Jim who taught me the ways of your kind whom he called "MoFos." He gave me my floral vocabulary and my indubitably unique name. He taught me to say some MoFo words. Because of the aforementioned Tinder misadventures, Big Jim and I spent quality, or rather quantity, time together and I have an array of tricks under my plume. I know about MoFo things like windows and secrets and blow-up dolls. And I am the rare bird who loves your kind, the ones who walk on two legs and built the things you dreamt of, including the Cheeto®. I owe my life to you. As an honorary MoFo, I'm here to be utterly honest and tell you what happened to your kind. The thing none of us saw coming.

CHAPTER 2

❧

WINNIE THE POODLE[*]
A RESIDENCE IN BELLEVUE, WASHINGTON, USA

W innie the Poodle sat on the ledge, allowing the outside tears that streamed down the windowpane to saturate her tiny, broken heart. She pressed her petite muzzle onto her front paws and let out a woeful sigh, thinking of what she had the very most of in this world: wait. She had lots and lots of wait. Wait when she woke up, then wait some more, finding snacks, then more wait. Stay and wait. Good girl.

The skitter of claws on marble pricked up her ears. A side glance across the floor revealed what she suspected—lunch had arrived. She would see to it later. For now, she followed it briefly with her sad, sad eyes and sniffed it with her sad, sad, perfect poodle nose.

Loneliness itched her skin. Would they ever come back?

The worst of it? The guilt. Guilt that wriggled in her heart like an army of white worms (she never had any of these worms for

---

* Winnie was raised to talk about herself in the third poodle

really, of course, but had seen them in the commercials with
the uglier dogs in them). Lunch skittered into the next room.
With seventeen rooms, sometimes it was utterly exhausting to
track down lunch.

Winnie's guilt came from two things. The one thing was that
she hadn't waited the whole time they'd been gone. Because
she was Winnie the Mini Poodle, she could squeeze herself
through the cat's escape. She had done it a few times to see if
they were in the yard, waiting for her. Or by the big fountain.
Or by the stables. The big pool. The small pool. The bright
yellow ball and net place. By the shiny cars. They weren't there.
Only horses were there. Some breathing. Some inside out.

The second guilty thing was that she had spent most of her
life with the Walker trying to escape the home. She had done
a pretend go-potty and barked at the sliding doors to be let
out into the yard and then back in to the home. And then out
and in and out and in and out and in and out until she was
told to lie down and stop being an insufferable Q-tip. She had
even run away from the Walker several times, sprinting down
the never-ending path, confectionary pink tongue tasting the
manure-laden flavor of freedom, velvety ears streaming behind
her, kicking up gravel in the face of propriety.

"Poodle doodle doo!" she had cried, wild and free and
obscenely beautiful, like a moonbeam with teeth. Once, she
actually managed to escape her Walker captors and Butler put
pictures up of her everywhere followed by signs like this $$$$$
and many, many, many of these 000000000. She was found
within a half hour.

There was a third guilty thing. Her adopted brother. She
hadn't always treated him very nicely, but that was because he
was a fat moron who was petrified of his own farts. Guilt nipped
at her for this thought, though it was very truthful. Spark Pug
had not been able to stand the quiet of the big home when the

Walker went away. He had gone wet-cat crazy, barking at the walls, snorting up a storm and nipping at Winnie the Poodle's exquisite corkscrew coat. It was perhaps Winnie the Poodle who had planted the suggestion of the cat escape and against all odds, with a waist like a Glad bag stuffed with cat litter, Spark Pug squeezed himself through the small flap with bulging eyeballs and a fart you might expect from a Clydesdale. Amidst snorts, Spark Pug, bagpipe of the canine world, barreled down the pathway to oblivion, no doubt looking for his squeaky lobster, Jean Clawed, whom Winnie had buried in the yard.

Winnie thought of the day that the Walker left. It wasn't a day of picnic and being carried in purse and Veuve Clicquot. It was a day of screaming. The Walker couldn't suck in air fast enough, with sad, red eyes and runny nose, she yelped into her phone. Winnie had tried to comfort her, but was pushed aside. The Walker opened the door, Winnie ran after her, *NO, WINNIE, NO GIRL*, and Winnie barked and the Walker wouldn't let her, *STAY, WINNIE, WAIT! GOOD GIRL!* and she made the door bang hard as she staggered into the big potty world all alone without her Good Girl Winnie.

And then Winnie did her wait.

What had she done wrong? If only she could do it all again. If only the Walker would come back through the door with a new Seahawks jersey for Winnie and she wouldn't even struggle while it got put on or secretly pee under the bed anymore.

Winnie had a lot of wait and a lot of guilt. She stared at the door with what she presumed were perfectly breed-standard eyes that sparkled like the diamond collar around her neck. She was often told that she was very, very beautiful and perfect and asked who the good girl was, which seemed pathetically rhetorical. Obviously she was the good girl. How she missed those days. If she was honest with herself, she even missed Spark Pug's seizure-inducing snores.

She would wait here. Stay. Be good. Continue to poop in strategic piles all over the home so that, upon her return, the Walker could resume her compulsive collecting of it. Winnie held worry in her tiny pink lungs—she was long overdue for nail shortening and the salon must be wondering where in the potty world she was by now. She missed the Walker's toasty lap, her salty face, and the honeyed sounds she made from soft red lips that were just for Winnie. She missed being a part.

The sadness had her by the neck now like a chew toy and she no longer had the energy to fight it off. Winnie the Poodle laid down her head and said a quiet goodbye to the home and the potty world around her. She would not hunt down lunch again. She had waited long enough. She succumbed to a last tremble-making thought of Spark Pug tearing around the big potty world all on his own. With no Jean Clawed. No friend. And no flea protection.

CHAPTER 3

✿⟊ ⟊✿

S.T.

THE SMALL CRAFTSMAN HOME IN RAVENNA,
SEATTLE, WASHINGTON, USA

In the days after Big Jim's eyeball rolled out of his head, it became clear that I was going to have to pick up some of the slack. All of the slack, in fact. Since Big Jim was so busy jabbing his finger at the basement wall and doing a stellar impression of a rabid raccoon, I took on even more of the household chores than I normally do. I put clothes in the laundry machine and dealt with Dennis's not-so-subtle hints at dinnertime when he pummeled his food bowls as if *they* had castrated him. Filling his water bowl proved tricky for me, so I escorted him to the porcelain throne which was fruitful and utterly revolting. Honestly, the toilet wand has more dignity.

In the mornings, I waited for the young MoFo with the red headphones to hurtle past on his bike faster than a toupee in a hurricane, for him to use his black-and-white projectile to decapitate another hydrangea flower head. He never came. Neither did the car dealership mailers or the Amazon pack-ages or our *Big Butts*™ magazine subscription. It was curious. Curious enough for me to contemplate tuning into the goat rodeo that is *Aura*. Something you might be unaware of—in the natural world, there is an Internet. In English, it would roughly translate to *Aura* because it is all around us. It's not the same as MoFo Internet with YouTube crabby cat videos and sneezing infant pandas, but it is similar in that it is a network, a constant flow of information at your disposal, if you can be bothered to tune in and listen. Information streams daily via the winged ones, the judicious rustle of the trees, and the staccato percussion of insects. I can't tell you the number of times I've heard a MoFo claim, "Listen to that bird's mating song!" writing off the feathered kind as licentious horndogs (they are not squirrels for shit sakes). In fact, the birds are delivering information through melodic verse, releasing intricate notes much like how the trees whisper their slow secrets into the wind on the wings of leaves. A torrent of warnings, stories, adages, poems, threats, how-tos, real estate info, survival tips and non sequitur jokes are available for those who tap in. Everything talks, you just have to be willing to listen.

There certainly is a social dating service element to it, but not as much as most MoFos believe. Of course, there are those who refuse to tap in. Like yours truly, who had access to the real Internet and didn't feel that there was anything to be gained from all the twitter. You know who else never listened? Roadkill. There has never been an excuse for roadkill. *Aura* sounds with constant stories and statistics about cars and the perils of nearing the great white lines. Warning calls ring through the stratosphere—from green stinkbug to glaucous-winged gull—and still, the idiots who don't heed end up as curbside tortillas. Sometimes I have the thought that a lot of species are hardwired to refuse to listen to warnings. And that's how they end up extinct.

I braved *Aura*. Silence. An *Aura* silence can be cause for alarm. Either there aren't enough birds or participating trees around to spread the scuttlebutt. Or everyone is hiding from a nearby predator. A flight around the neighborhood confirmed that the roads around our house were eerily still—no cars zipping below like frenetic jewel weevils. It was as if a Sunday morning had flown in and made a permanent nest. This is when I started to get shivers that felt like an army of mites scurrying through my plumage, and dread spread a dull, hollow ache through my bird bones.

If I'm honest, I had a feeling that something was happening beyond our russet-brown front door, beyond our sleepy neighborhood. Something big and ominous and probably quite shitty, but I didn't like to leave Big Jim and I needed to lock things down at home and wait until he was feeling better before we decided to face the world together—always together. I checked on Big Jim hourly, bringing him bologna, Funyuns®, and the two Cheetos® I was willing to spare. I even rolled a Monster energy drink down the basement stairs for him. He showed interest in nothing but drooling and scraping his bloody finger across the wall. I brought the keys to his beloved gunmetal-gray Ford F-150 with the KEEP HONKING, I'M RELOAD-ING bumper sticker to see if a ride would perk him up. The silver keys caught his attention for a brief moment, but then he snarled, snapped at me (not verbally, with his actual teeth), and resumed dragging a finger at the concrete. Whatever was wrong with him was serious. When, after several days of this basement weirdness, he hadn't masturbated or mentioned the state of the economy, I declared a state of emer-Jim-cy.

Big Jim was in the grips of a medical crisis and it was up to yours truly to make things right again. I felt confident I knew what to do, an innate, natural instinct thrumming inside me. First, I had to make sure that Dennis was preoccupied. After watching him shit into the sound hole of Big Jim's guitar and then run full steam into the kitchen door, I felt reassured.

Exacting his revenge on the doorknob for the attack was taking precedence over anything else. It seemed unlikely that Dennis would venture down to the basement for a while, given his level of focus and typical chokehold on a grudge. Besides, ever since Big Jim's eyeball fell out, Dennis had steered clear of him. Man's best friend indeed. More like man's neediest parasite that would trade you in for a bull-penis dog chewy at the drop of a hat.

I flew out the kitchen window, over the yard, and up into a wolf-gray sky above the evergreen line to spy on the general situation. Though Seattle is a city thirstier than most, on this day, the rains stayed up high. Usually, Big Jim and I ride all over Seattle in his truck as he works on various houses and their electrical shitstorms, and we spend a lot of time at Home Depot and the feed store, but I never venture far alone. Today, I had to. This was a mission for Big Jim.

From the highest branch of a Douglas fir, everything seemed quiet except for the prattle of squirrels that I tried to block out (much of what they say can't be unheard, which is unfortunate since squirrels are five-star sexual deviants). As I neared my destination, I was distracted by an odd scene. Inquisitiveness grabbed me by the beak and wouldn't let go—if you think cats are curious, try being an enlightened crow. I craned my neck to get a better look and honed in on a topsy-turvy vision. Ten wheels suspended in the air. A rainbow of gasoline, pools of black oil. My mind took its time unraveling the twisted mess in front of me. Green where there should be yellow, yellow where there should be green. I swooped down closer to find an up-turned King County Metro bus. The bus had plowed into the side of the Blessed Sacrament Church, smashing right through the red brick ribs of the enormous edifice. When Big Jim has had too much Pabst Blue Ribbon and elects to take an open-mouthed snooze, the TV often spits out religious programs, which is how I know about churches and pyramid schemes. I wait until he's snoring to change the channel to the History Channel, Discovery Channel, CNN, the Food Network, the Travel Channel, and sometimes Bravo TV, which is how I know a great deal about the superlative ways of MoFos. Big Jim claims to be a deeply religious man, maintaining that his religion is primarily whiskey and women. I saw the connection between the two—most of his relationships were on the rocks.

I landed on an upside-down wheel and gently rapped my beak against the hubcap for comfort. I needed it—something felt very, very off. I peered below. All the windows of the bus were smashed and smeared with red. If there is something to be learned from Big Jim's horror films, it's that you should never insert yourself into a precarious situation, especially if you're a scantily clad blonde with breast implants or a MoFo with black skin—but again, crow, so on I marched. I entered the bus and a heavy foreboding pressed down on my wings. Sanguine smells held the fetid air captive. There were no MoFos in the bus, but I found two purses, a wallet. The shivers came back. MoFos don't leave their wallets. Up until recently Big Jim went bat-turd bananas without his. A huge clump of hair was stuck to one of the bus seats that hung in rows from the ceiling, and I found a ripped piece of a MoFo's shirt and an intact fingernail lodged between two seats. The wallet had a shiny gold cop badge in it that brought on an urge to cache that was hard to suppress. I found a paycheck in an envelope, a pacifier, and a book called *Don't Let the Pigeon Drive the Bus*. It looked like someone might have done just that. I left the creepy bus, exiting through the glassless front windshield and into the belly of the church.

The house of worship was cavernous, a vast space with a spire and enormous arched doors. Silence. When I hopped, my feet clicked and tapped on wooden floors, the parts that weren't caked in the beginnings of moss or rainwater puddles. I was careful to avoid stepping in rat droppings; that shit spreads disease.

"Hello?" I asked, committing the number one horror film faux pas. "Is anyone there?"

The inside of the church was damp; water had collected in pools on the floor, let in by a hole in the roof. Moss and weeds were elbowing their way through hairline cracks. I could hear the near-silent screams of bustling termites devouring the bones of the place. Peeled plaster had fallen like snow in piles on the damp ground. White poop spackled the cracks, though I couldn't hear the inane gibberish of a single pigeon. They had long since flown the coop.

A fake MoFo in a loin cloth stared down at me from a wooden wall. He had a headband made of barbs that looked fairly uncomfortable. Even though I knew he wasn't real, I gave him a nod of solidarity, wondering what crime he'd committed to deserve being stapled to plywood.

Then a smell found me. The unmistakable smell of death, acrid and ripe. Tension clouded the air, the kind that follows eruptive violence. The kind that's too heavy to drain itself. I found the source of the smell. Draped across the wooden benches ahead of me was a bull moose. His gargantuan bough of antlers weighed down a blocky brown head that hung over the edge of a seat row, half a tongue lolled from a permanently open mouth. His fur was sticky with red and something had eaten most of his entrails and removed one of his legs. A quick scan confirmed that the missing leg wasn't in the church.

"Hello?" I asked again, before realizing I was literally asking to join ranks with the moose and the hole-punched MoFo. There was a predator nearby. One that hoards moose legs. Fight or flight is sort of a rhetorical question for me. I took to the air, soaring above the benches and unlit candles,

whizzing past stained glass windows and through the hole
the bus made. MoFos clean up after themselves. They don't
leave holes in churches and wallets and baby MoFo stuff in
upside-down buses. They don't allow moose (mooses? meese?)
in churches. Or predators. If Big Jim knew there was a
predator near a house of worship, why, he'd grab Sigourney
Weaver and *track down that sum-bitch*. Sigourney is his Marlin
Model 336 lever-action rifle, named for its sexy streamlined
appearance and no-nonsense attitude. I steadied my breathing
and flapped my wings harder, determination propelling me to
finish my mission.

The Yoshino cherry tree I sat on to scope out my destination
provided little comfort. I was feeling unnerved, on edge, and
a tremble seized my legs. I couldn't shake the shivers as well
as they were shaking me. Walgreens looked much as it always
had, but lacking its harried hubbub, the tumult, the purr of
automatic doors. And a feeling wouldn't leave—the feeling of
a glassy fishbone lodged in my throat. The feeling that I was
diving into danger. I was preparing myself to do a flyby of
Walgreens when—BAAAAP!—a mighty force smashed into my
left wing, punching me from the cherry tree. I cried out. Free
falling, I shook my head, spread my wings, and caught a pocket
of air, righting myself and launching back upward to face my
attacker. He stared at me with beady black eyes and let out a
succession of warning calls from the back of his ebony throat.
He lunged, snatching at my wings. I darted in the air to avoid
him, his horrible screeches clawing at my brain.

Shit. A college crow.

Since they never travel alone, I was immediately accosted by
this crow's turd waffle of a wife who dive-bombed me, yanking
at my flight feathers. She perched in my cherry tree, unleashing a verbal assault. I won't repeat what was said because,
frankly, even Big Jim might have blushed.

"Leave me alone!" I yelled at Bonnie and Clyde. They continued spitting hideous insults at me, calling me a traitor. The male pelted a bottle cap at me before taking off, laughing, into the tree line. At this point, I was feeling for Tippi Hedren and could've really used a beer. Big Jim is always talking about boundaries, about sticking to your own kind and keeping everyone out of your business. I often fantasized about erecting a giant aviary over our house to keep all the pests out.

The college crows are the largest murder of Seattleite crows, and they roost nightly on the east side of the University of Washington's Bothell campus. They are also a giant troupe of swamp donkeys. UW Bothell is essentially an enormous frat house for a bunch of elitist toot cabbages. Every night from fall to late spring, the sky pulses with blue-tinged midnight wings as thousands of crows head over to meet on the UW buildings and then roost at the campus's neighboring wetlands together. MoFos find this fascinating and mystical. I think it's rude to take up all that airspace, but there you have it. I've never been to the campus since I'm unwelcome, so I can't tell you what goes on there. My guess? Preening, bragging, and beer pong. Generally, when I go about my business, I'm ostracized by the local crows—the "real" crows—and called an asshole for my close affiliation with a MoFo. Name-calling happens through *Aura*, sticks and stones are thrown at me and my mother is described in colorful ways. Mostly, I let it slide off my feathers, but when I'm physically attacked for just being who I am? Sometimes that really bothers me. No one seems to understand that your species is an accident of birth. No one understands that I should have been born a MoFo.

With my tormentors out of sight, I focused on plucking up the courage for my mission. I inhaled a deep breath and took wing, levitating over the empty parking lot before lowering down to the automatic doors of the Walgreens. They whirred open. Fluorescent glare illuminated the aisles. I perched on top of a Dos Equis man cardboard cutout to survey the scene. As in the church, everything was far too quiet. Too still. A low growl rumbled, reverberating through my feet. I hopped nervously on one foot, craning to find the source of the growl, thinking of the moose's missing leg. Another low growl sounded out, startling me. I flew up and perched, straddling Lucky Charms and Special K, and from there I could see the culprits. Four MoFos were gathered around a blood pressure machine, swaying and drooling. An ad for the shingles vaccine hung nearby. I immediately recognized the greenish tinge to their skin, the odd twisting of their joints, the pouring sweat, red raw eyes and bloody drool. They all exhibited the same craned-forward neck, like curious vultures, hunting for satiety. Blackened fingers repeatedly jabbed at the screen. They too had whatever was ailing Big Jim.

I decided to conduct an experiment, fear be damned.

"Hello!" I squawked in perfect English. No response. "Hello there!" A goddamned talking crow and not even a raised eyebrow. Seriously? The world had gone to shit. They continued staring at the glow of the inbuilt screen, which was playing a movie about heart wellness. Obviously, they missed healthier days.

Listening for any change in their actions, I got back to my mission, picking up a plastic grocery bag, swooping behind a ransacked counter under a sign that said "Pharmacy" and filling the bag with the medications I thought sounded helpful to Big Jim. E-Mycin, Keflex, Lasix, Prilosec OTC, Monistat, Sally Hansen Airbrush Legs, and Summer's Eve all sounded effective and surely a combination of them would cure Big Jim. Walgreens had come through for us before. I felt positive, important—a fella with a purpose.

Lifting the plastic bag proved very difficult, but by flapping in determined, energetic strokes, I was able to take a low flight. I lifted up over the ailing MoFos, above the red and pink aisle of Valentine's candy, heading toward the automatic doors. Just as I neared the glowing green exit sign, my plastic bag tipped and the Summer's Eve box slipped out, clattering down onto the cashier's scanner with a loud beep. And then all fucking hell broke loose.

The four MoFos by the blood pressure machine let out a skull-shattering scream. I heard them pounding the ground, running at full tilt toward the cash register. Two MoFos I'd missed in white lab coats vaulted from behind the pharmacy, sprinting like racehorses from the flaming hot cheese-hole of hell. Necks craned, fingers pointed, blood drool flying. And I, partly in panic and partly because I have butter claws, dropped the damn plastic bag. My medications—Big Jim's lifeline—exploded across the cash register with a spidery clatter. I dove down, flicking the pill bottles back into the bag. One, two, three, Lasix, Prilosec, No7 Lift & Luminate Triple Action Eye Cream…The MoFos' screams were nearing, their feet hammering the ground; one knocked over a Seahawks display, sending beer sleeves, slippers, Russell Wilson figurines, and mugs airborne. Porcelain flew, shattering against the rows of wine bottles, which burst and bled across white tile. The doors whirred. Two more MoFos wearing green Taco Time aprons stood in the pharmacy doorway, raising craned necks to the ceiling. They emitted a brain-bursting primal screech, their hands twisted like the branches of winter trees. Keflex, Paxil, Monistat. The two new MoFos started to run. The four blood pressure MoFos rounded the end aisle, seconds away, eyes like a forest on fire…

Gas-X, Dulcolax, stretch mark serum, Summer's Eve. That's it! I hoisted the plastic bag into the air, narrowly missing swipes from the Taco Time MoFos, who lunged, their mouths freeing strings of blood that whiskered the register in sticky crimson threads. I huffed it higher into the air above the commotion, as below eight unhealthy MoFos clamored and writhed over the top of the cashier scanner, jabbing at it with their fingers and saucer eyes. Then, in unison, they raised their gnarled arms to the ceiling. I flinched, almost dropping the bag again. They formed a circle around the scanner that beeped. Simultaneously, they began smashing their heads onto the scanner. *Bash, thump, smack,* harder and harder. Blood and pulp spurted, brain bits flew. The bashing continued.

I battled through the doors and away from the unpredictable MoFos, seeking refuge and a break in a nearby evergreen. With one plastic bag handle safely looped over a branch, I settled and took stock of how close it had been, how I was nearly snatched from the sky. No MoFo had ever shown any sign of aggression toward me before. What would they have done if they'd caught me?

What was happening to the MoFos? Hopefully, the answer was in my bag of goodies and I'd start with Big Jim, nursing him back to health with all my Cheetos® if necessary, and then we'd jump in his Ford F-150 with the Glock and the weed in the glove compartment and we'd set to fixing the other MoFos in the neighborhood who weren't feeling well. We'd fix it alright, because what would a world without MoFos be? The thought made me nauseous, gave me goose bumps, which is a stupid expression because geese are a crass bunch of douche McGoos.

From my vantage point, I saw someone I recognized at the base of the evergreen. That unmistakable blue rinse of curls and the polka-dotted rolling shopping bag. Thank heavens! It was Nargatha. Nargatha—whose mother must have had acute indecision, christening her after a bonkers blend of Agatha, Margaret, and Narnia—lived three doors down from Big Jim and me. She was eccentric and so old the Seattle Fire

Department was once called to put out her birthday candles, but she'd always been good to me. Sure, she talked to me like I had irreversible brain damage, but countered this by always having a sampling of animal crackers on hand. Big Jim liked how she always brought us Fireball whiskey if the Seahawks won. Looking down at the tiny figure with the pearly blue curls and the tennis ball–yellow trench coat, I felt a pang of relief, my chest filling with warmth. I darted my head side to side to get a better look. Closer inspection revealed that she was eating Triscuits.

Triscuits is her miniature schnauzer.

My stomach did a loop de loop. I watched from the evergreen for a few moments, hardly believing what was happening, until it became too much to stomach. No one deserves to become an hors d'oeuvre! Least of all her loyal and beloved Triscuits! Reeling, I accidentally let out a caw of horror.

Nargatha's searching eyes were the color of a cardinal. Scarlet wet strings hung from her mouth. I watched in horror as her head twisted 180 degrees. Then a bone in her neck cracked like the sharp snap of a branch, and her cranium inched its way around to 360 degrees. She looked up at me, drooling blood and her noggin dialed all the way the fuck around like a goddamned barn owl. Nargatha screeched like a desperate raptor, causing three squirrels to silently scatter to safety. Panic squeezed my trilling heart. Squirrels are never silent, those smutty nut-goblins. They are only quiet when their lives depend on it.

Triscuits. Nargatha was eating Triscuits. The next thought I had made me regurgitate a Cheeto®. Nargatha had what Big Jim had. Nargatha was eating Triscuits.

Dennis. I snatched up the plastic bag, pointed homeward bound, and flapped like hell.

CHAPTER 4

GENGHIS CAT
A HOME IN CAPITOL HILL, SEATTLE,
WASHINGTON, USA

There has been a change in the order of things that I can't quite put my claw on. My observations:

1. It's quieter out there. This makes the game more interesting.
2. There are no sprinting cars to compete with over squirrels.
3. There's a *lot* more to hunt.
4. There are plenty more hunters to fight it for. Hunters of *all* kinds.
5. There's decidedly less cheese available.

Perhaps it's due to a shift in the lunar light, a cosmic spell, or because I have finally mastered my innate feline sorcery. One thing that hasn't changed—my Mediocre Servants still never seem to leave the home. I believe, if it's at all possible, that they have devolved. According to my calculations, they now spend 186 percent of their time growling at the wall. But I have always known them to be a lower life-form, no better than slug-tongued, alopecia-stricken bears with epically shitty balance. They are eggs on legs with no discernible senses and the reflexes of a bugle stuffed with brine shrimp.

I have watched, with my unparalleled vision and laser-pointer focus, as my Mediocre Servants jab at the wall repeatedly with their fingers (or what's left of them). Up to down, up to down. Both are overdue for a thorough grooming, which their own mothers wouldn't attempt at this point. Today—

WAIT! HOLD EVERYTHING WHILE I GROOM MY INNER THIGH.

Today, my Mediocre Servants—the girl one with the long mane and the girl one with all the skin drawings who both liked to stay at home and talk about chemistry science until the coffee ran out—smell like a microwaved litter box. No longer do they turn on their silver lap boxes, which is characteristically selfish of them because it is a classically renowned nap location. The warm spots—silver lap box; top of tall, cold food house; winter bed blanket; top of their sacred "wine fridge"; Mediocre Servant's thighs while she's on the white seat that roars—have been confiscated. They appear to be staging some sort of feeble protest by refusing to replenish my dehydrated niblet stash. I have conducted experiments using techniques that used to be fairly effective—knocking over the French press, unraveling their shoddy knitting, chewing the covers of every book in the library, shitting on pillows, shredding the couch, eating all the Ethernet snakes, and pissing all over bed blanket—but they seem to no longer be concerned. Admittedly, I'm impressed. I respect the negligible number of shits currently being given. Case in point: one of my Mediocre Servants left her arm in the living room, which I believe speaks to their general ineptitude. I played with it momentarily, but found its pungency off-putting and resumed licking my anus. My instincts were always right—they were never to be fully trusted.

For a while, I persisted with this ill-fated relationship by bringing them mice, moles, rats, sparrows, finches, robins, wrens, and chickadees, and something new and exciting: a tuxedo-wearing bastard that called itself a Humboldt penguin before I assassinated it. I presented these offerings to them, as always, to remind them of their inadequacy and rub my hunting prowess in their faces, those dildo-nosed potatoes. But I am not an unreasonable creature; I also share my offerings to ensure the thighs of my Mediocre Servants are adequately padded for my sitting pleasure. When I offered up the black-and-white eggplant of a bird, which was heavy as fuck, by the way, the Mediocre Servant with the skin drawings tried to bite me, ocher nubby fangs narrowly missing my tail. I did what was necessary—bit her back, severing a finger. Then I attempted to bury it in the carpet by covering it up like a rogue turd.

I will no longer bring them offerings, exotic or otherwise. I will not grace them with my presence. Should have known it was all over when they stopped summoning the requisite number of boxes from the Amazon for me to cavort in. No. I made my decision to leave the home. It's true that I shall miss the toasty laps and the dehydrated fish blobs and ambushing their bulbous toes under the bed blanket and how they used to worship me. Most especially, I will miss the cheese. But not as much as they will miss me. I am incredible.

So once I'd systematically eaten all the contents of Aquarium, I left through the Flap Of Cat to the great outside, never to return to the home. Besides, I'd yarfed on every square inch of the place. There was nothing more to decorate. Before I left, I made sure I'd unrolled all the toilet paper.

Life on the outside is unpredictable, requiring vigilance and innate brilliance, both qualities I possess in numbers higher than I can count. I hunt and prowl and observe and fuck with shit. Also, my collection is growing. So far I have infiltrated four hundred homes and pillaged every sock I can find. I cannot explain my fascination with these delightful foot blankets, I can only tell you that it pleases me to carry them around while yowling like my fur is on fire.

Something of interest: Yesterday, I was minding my own highly important business around one of my territories—my newly acquired mosque. It's enormous and gold, sublimely spiritual with rainbow windows that let those rascally light beams in. I was busy chasing a light beam that had no business running up my damn wall when, out of nowhere, this asshole walks in. To *my* mosque! My urine smells stronger than hydrofluoric acid; I'm not sure how my territory could be made any clearer. Who doesn't respect boundaries like that? You know who? A gigantic piliferous orange, that's who. He just waltzes in like some big shot. I let out a viperous hiss, warning him that I collect femur bones. He seemed startled and then I asked him what the fuck he was because he didn't seem like a local Seattleite, and he said he was looking for his home, and then I'd just about had it with this mouthy tool running off his mouth, so I chased him out of my mosque. I was all talon and bite; I was a tricksy light beam of silver and brown and black, the power of the sun in motion if it were more kickass. He got the message alright. He loped off, not sure how to comprehend such an omnipotent ninja. But I'm worried he'll be back because he caught a glimpse of my sock stash, or perhaps the eggs I've collected from the nest raids, and I'm marginally concerned that he'll plan an ambush. It is a legitimate worry since he's the size of a wine fridge.

I can't complain. I'm living the good life. I've hunted and pillaged and fathered 130 kittens—that I know of—with twenty-six different mousers and none of this shit interferes with my sixteen hours of daily sleep.

You can fuck off now. I have nothing more to say to you.

CHAPTER 5

I burst through the kitchen window, dropping the plastic bag at the last second. The bottles containing Big Jim's life sustenance bounced off the window ledge, rolling onto the grass below. I dove through the kitchen, the living room, and shot down the concrete stairs to the basement, forgetting to inhale. Big Jim was up close to the wall where I'd left him, swaying as he dragged his nub of a finger. He'd have to replace that when he felt better. Relief rippled through me. No sign of Dennis. I took off in search of that lumpish codpiece.

Dennis was in the laundry room. He was lying on a pile of Big Jim's soiled boxers, head on black-padded teddy bear paws. The copious copper skinfolds of his forehead hung low, obscuring his eyes, facial wrinkles splayed on the laundry room floor. His hideous turkey-neck wattle, which normally looks like a water buffalo's testicles, now resembled a discarded pancake. Dennis lifted an eyebrow and a mountain of skin, exposing the melancholiest of melancholy chestnut eyes, then resumed his carpet impression with a chesty sigh. He pretty much stayed that way for days. And then Dennis stopped eating. This signified another major change in our already topsy-turvy lives. I'd known Dennis since he was a rumpled dumpling who tripped over his own ears, back when he still had hope of mental evolution and keeping his balls. He'd always been a clay-brained barnacle, but I'd never seen him like this. I suspected that even a visitation from the UPS man—the sworn enemy of canines everywhere and Dennis's archnemesis— couldn't have roused him. Dennis had succumbed to his own ailment. He'd been ambushed by an invisible assassin, which had blown into his body uninvited and was slowly eating his heart from the inside out. It drank his hope and anesthetized his feelings. Depression.

When you're depressed, where do you want to go? Nowhere.

Who do you feel like seeing? No one.

Depression hurts in so many ways. Sadness, loss of interest, anxiety. Cymbalta can help.

Big Jim listened to that commercial on repeat one day whilst downing Malibu and Coke before he drunk dialed his best friend's wife, shit his pants, and passed out on the lawn. I recall that we made two separate trips to Walgreens for Pepto-Bismol the next day.

For a while after the eyeball incident, Dennis had taken up redecorating the house, and against all odds, I found myself missing his demolition days, like when he tore the linoleum out of the kitchen and the time he helped himself to a jumbo bag of prunes from the pantry. This was only marginally less messy than when he drank a gallon of oil and yarfed up an Exxon Valdez–sized spill on the dining table.

Now Dennis—like Big Jim—was in crisis. He missed Big Jim so much it was killing him. I got to work immediately, pushing pills as close to Big Jim as I could without him sampling my thighs. I attempted dive-bys, launching individual tablets into his mouth midair, but the all-important swallowing part never happened and he just drooled out my precious pills in thick globs of blood. I launched heartworm chews and coffee and Snickers bars, I offered him old issues of *Big Butts*™ magazine and the photo of him with sunburnt knees when we caught the big Chinook salmon—still nothing. I Summer's Eve'd the crap out of him, sifting the white powder all over his twisted joints and ganja-colored skin. None of it seemed to help.

The sadness started to get to me too. And listen, I'm an eternal optimist; "plucky" is how I'm often described and I won't argue with it. Big Jim says that I'm a smart aleck, too brainy for my own good and a "fucking opportunist" (he grossly underestimated my love for coinage). I am well-read, have watched countless hours of educational and, thanks to Big Jim, reality television, and I tend to see the good in things. Generally, I believe the best is yet to come, but this? This was hard. A sadness crept under my skin like an army of termites, nibbling away at my resolve. At times, my heart felt like the fruit that shriveled and grew fur on the kitchen counter, bruised and rotting, fodder for flies. It made my legs feel heavy, made flight a chore. But while my sadness was temporary and healable— the makings of a scar—I knew, sure as I molt, that Dennis's was terminal. He was dying from sadness.

So yours truly embarked on two projects. Project Wellness and Project Happiness. I started using what I'd learned as a fledgling from Big Jim, when he first took me into his home, when the treat training was so successful that I began to resemble a monster truck tire and he had to mitigate the rate of reward. But Dennis's hunger strike was legitimate. Even when I brought him kibble, piece by piece, he wouldn't leave the laundry room or Big Jim's rancid skivvies. So, I was forced to bring in the big guns: Cheetos®, those delectable, radioactive poofs. Using my beak, I broke them into small chunks and placed a piece just out of Dennis's reach. I watched his spongy nose twitch and a forehead fold lift to expose an inquisitive eye. He sniffed again and unrolled a carpet of pink tongue to lasso the Cheeto®. As Big Jim had done when I was a chick, I placed the Cheeto® lures just out of Dennis's sight. At first I got more sniffs. Then a twitch of the paw. Then—eureka!—I got a tail wag. Finally, Dennis lifted his hulking mass of skin off the butt huggers, drove his snuffer to the ground, and snarfed up my lures like a champ.

I thought about the Cymbalta commercial. Since I didn't have any Cymbalta and wasn't willing to risk another foray to Walgreens—for your info, none of the medications there work anyway, they did diddly-jack for Big Jim—I thought about what the people and the dog that looks like a homeless Sammy Hagar were doing in the commercial. They were *frolicking*. That's exactly what Dennis needed: a frolic. Exercise. So, I implemented playtime, where I'd yank his tail and he'd chase me across the yard. I cached Cheetos® and Funyuns® and kibble and beef jerky and chunks of Hungry-Man frozen dinners around the house and yard, watching Dennis and his uncanny schnoz track down every last morsel. Against all odds, I enjoyed it. I worked on perfecting my whistle and replicating how Big Jim called for Dennis, "ZzzzZZZt! Dennis! Here, boy!" rewarding Dennis for answering my calls. I practiced the words in my best Big Jim from the back of my throat, "Dennis! Sit!" and marveled as Dennis parked his keister on the grass below my branch, waiting for me to toss him a bright yellow Peep. And would you believe it, the old Dennis started to come back. There he was with his rudder of a tail, plodding perkiness, that lumbering bloodhound bulk with more wrinkles than a cat's ass, and dare I say it, when I mimicked Big Jim's throaty calls of "Good boy!" I even saw Dennis smile, puffing clouds of salmon jerky into the night air. I like to think he believed I was just like Big Jim. That I was a MoFo.

When I wasn't working on Dennis's disposition for Project Happiness, I was in the basement, spitting pills down Big Jim's gullet. How long did this go on for? Can't say for sure—I've never fully grasped the concept of time—but I can tell you that I tried to follow Big Jim's Big Boobs Hot German Girls calendar and that we got through one month (two whole German boobs). I know what you're thinking. Why didn't I leave our home, fly out beyond our Ravenna neighborhood in search of help and medical assistance? Your question is valid and only slightly annoying. I made a choice, you see. I chose to stay close to Big Jim and keep to the nest because of the noises. During our forays into the yard, Dennis and I would hear sounds, sounds that were like fireworks and gunfire but louder. For a time, the sky was empty of birds like during war or the Fourth of July. We heard haunting shrieks we'd never heard before. Worst of all, we heard screaming. One evening, a crane fly—all gangly legs and drunken flight—landed on top of our fence. After catching his breath and stabilizing the quiver in his diaphanous wings, he called out to me.

"Stay inside!" he warned in a voice like the brittle rubbing of sticks. I ignored him as I'd always ignored insects and the constant babble of *Aura*. "Listen! Listen! Ghubari says you must stay inside!"

My skin pebbled into hard bumps. Ghubari. Ghubari knew I didn't listen to *Aura*. He had sent a warning anyway. I trusted Ghubari. It was enough for me. Dennis and I both now knew something very big was happening and I wasn't willing to throw us into whatever it was that ripped apart a silent night, toward whatever it was that snapped an evergreen in half. Call me naive or a coward and I'll show you a crow who is here to tell you the goddamned story. After all, the best way is always to look out for numero uno. Despite my efforts, Big Jim stayed in the basement, wearing down much of his arm against the concrete wall while smelling like a keg of sautéed cat pee, but whenever I started to feel sorry for myself, I thought of Triscuits.

In the middle of our Project Happiness month, the first tenacious buds began to kiss the air around them and the strange sounds finally stopped. Dennis and I celebrated by spending more time in the yard, chasing one another and working very hard at our happiness. Dennis even chased off taunting college crows and the salacious squirrels intent on tea-bagging the garden gnome. Some nights, Dennis would run to the fence, barking himself into a slobbering frenzy, smacking the panic button. As he'd raise his rubbery lips to the sky to let out a hound's bellow, I'd summon him inside.

"ZzzzZZZt! Dennis! Come inside and have a Twinkie!" It was my best attempt at instilling a sense of preservation in Dennis, and I'd lecture him from Big Jim's armchair about how in order to better one's survival odds, one should never be a hero, while he lay on the couch and licked his peeper. Confession time: I stored the Twinkie pieces in the cookie jar and may or may have not accidentally treated Dennis to Big Jim's eyeball. I have apologized to Big Jim profusely but honestly, he doesn't seem to miss it. Anyway, *mea culpa.*

Dennis's kibble ran out, but thanks to Big Jim's ursine appetite and predilection for a bargain, there were enough pantry staples to keep Dennis's heart afloat and his bowels permanently volcanic. This meant that I got to stay close to my nest and, apart from the odd recon flight, steer clear of the great unknown, of predators and meese and the den of horror that is Walgreens.

And then one morning, I found Big Jim's cell phone. I was hunting for Dennis's KONG and discovered it underneath Big

Jim's camouflage-duvet bed where he must have left it before the eyeball incident. A rush buzzed through me. Big Jim's cell phone! This would surely perk him up; he loved that thing. Yes! An opportunity to call for help! 911! I pressed on the power button and miraculously, the cell phone lit up, bright screen aglow with a welcoming chirp. A chiming melody.

And then hell broke from its fucking chains again.

An unearthly scream ripped through the house. Dennis hit the panic button, coughing out distress in booming barks. The scream stopped. Breakneck crashing of footsteps shook the house. Big Jim was fucking leaving the basement. The footsteps thundered up the stairs at lightning pace, full tilt, and I knew—a corvus knowing—he was coming straight for me. My eyes darted around his bedroom, looking for somewhere to hide. Half open closet? Drawer of the clothing cupboard? Could I open the ammo trunk? No, he'd find me. The phone chimed again—fucking software update alert—and the house filled up with a dreadful, skull-splintering scream. My god! Where was Dennis? Where did I see him last? Where did I leave him? I thought of Triscuits and shook my head, trying to use up the last few seconds before sick Big Jim found me. I had to keep the phone, it was my only hope, a chance to help Big Jim. Furious footsteps shook the ground. *Think, S.T. Think.*

Snatching the phone in my beak, I launched into the air and flew to the bedroom window. Shut. I slammed into it, bashing my wing and the phone, slick in my beak, feeling it slip and plummet to the carpet. Focus. Window. Still shut. I dove for the phone and suddenly Big Jim was in the doorway, more alive and not alive than I'd seen him in a long, long time. His neck was outstretched, craned unnaturally forward in that starving-vulture way. I flashed back to the Walgreens MoFos and gagged. Big Jim's eye was glowing red, wide, and lasered on my beak. A thick bone crack sounded out and his lower jaw released, flapping down and hanging by a thin strip of gum, freeing a river of red. He shook his head, his jaw flapping loose, white-pearl sliver of bone exposed. Blood streaked the walls. I clasped the phone tight as I could and flapped in the air, wing throbbing as I held my space. Big Jim let out a guttural roar and charged, the twisted fingers of his remaining hand extended like hawkbill knives. He pounded toward me, baring his yellowed teeth, cavernous jaw like an unspeakable red cave. Inches away from my feathers, so close my head spun from the wormy stench that was Big Jim as I ducked under his armpit and blasted through the bedroom door, diving down the stairs and toward the laundry room. Dennis stood his ground in the living room, hackles bristling like blades, barking sharp and fast. I yelled a muffled "DENNIS! SIT!" as loud as I could, praying I'd done the work to save his life. Big Jim's pounding footsteps stirred the air near my tail feathers; I felt him right behind me, on me, felt his breath and his snarls, seconds from yanking me from the air, shoving me into that terrible, terrible sanguine cavity. I tore through the laundry room, dropping the phone like a sunbaked stone. I shot bullet-fast from the tiny exit window, scraping my head on the window frame. Big Jim unleashed a raptor's scream into the yard through the tiny window and bashed his head against its frame. I swung back around, reentering the house by shooting through the kitchen window. I careened past Dennis, who barked frantically from a solid sit. Then I rocketed like a speeding black torpedo into the door with everything I had.

The door slammed shut.

Everything fell silent. No sounds came from the laundry room with the phone and what was left of Big Jim. Dennis panted silently, his legs aquiver. Nothing more was said. I couldn't go on pretending that nothing had happened and I couldn't lock the laundry room door, which meant we were no longer safe in our own home.

I just couldn't fix Big Jim alone.

With nothing but the whoosh of wing, I gingerly plucked Dennis's leash from the wall and, pinching the mechanism with my beak, affixed it to his collar. Grabbing the looped handle in my feet, I lifted into the air and flew forward, Dennis plodding beneath me. Dennis pushed through the rickety back door and our gate in silence, past the Japanese maple where I first learned to fly, and we made our way along the sidewalk and the cement, abandoning everything we'd ever known and loved.

We left slowly to the gentle song of lugubrious paw pads and the viscous beat of crestfallen wings, away from our home and our hearts.

It was time. Time to face the terrifying unknown. Time we had answers. And I knew who we needed to hunt down.

CHAPTER 6

So there we were. A rejected crow with an identity crisis partnering a bloodhound with the IQ of boiled pudding. We were perhaps the most pathetic excuse for an attempted murder on the face of the earth. Here we were launching ourselves into a world we'd never known, one that had new teeth and no edges and a recent and significant overhaul. I led Dennis along the sidewalk, passing dead traffic lights, Nargatha's fairytale house, and the yard with the now dusty swing set, releasing an involuntary cackle as I realized I was following cultural norms that may not apply anymore. With no cars in sight, we didn't need to look left or right while crossing the road, or halt at stop signs, but I did it anyway, because that's how I was raised and I had to hold on to something other than the leathery loop of Dennis's leash. The gutters choked on trash that blanketed the sidewalks. It had baked and cooled, leaving the air pregnant with saccharine decay. Obviously, the garbage-collecting MoFos had been at the NyQuil. When Big Jim took

NyQuil, he slept through all four of his alarms and I'd have to wake him by pelting beer bottle caps at his head. *Big Jim.* The trauma of nearly being eaten by my best friend was the single greatest pain I had ever known. It felt as though a sword had twisted itself through my papery skin. I now had learned the pain of betrayal, a pain that changes your very cells, writing itself into your DNA. All around us, the grass was tall, wicked weeds spiraling and impish, nature's barbed wire. If things were hiding in its chaos, they chose to remain invisible. Every few flaps, my feathers shivered with uncertainty.

Dennis seemed keen to be outside again, preoccupied with his nasal adventures, trailing his spongy black whiffer along the ground, pendulous wrinkles swinging from side to side. He had a lot to catch up on. Now and then, I tentatively dropped the leash and soared above to do recon, checking out what lay directly ahead of us. Looking for the dark outline of a predator. Looking for signs of twisted limbs, hungry vermillion eyes, and neck bones with no rules. Looking for the healthy MoFos I knew were out there. And most of all, listening.

I reluctantly tuned in to *Aura,* listening to the boastful hoarding stories of a magpie. A Townsend's warbler couple fretted about whether the eagle would return. Black-capped chickadees warned of a large troupe of Hollows clustered around a shop called Scarecrow Video. Hollows are what most fauna have long called MoFos, named for their dissociative state. In the natural world, MoFos are mistaken for milky-eyed machines intent on destruction, empty vessels that have lost their inner intelligence—the walking blind, dumb animals. What utter blasphemy! A pie in the face of the species that invented a magic box that can nuke a Hot Pocket in seconds! Pigeons bickered about personal space. A red-breasted nuthatch sang a song about digestive health, chuckling to himself between breaths. There was excited twitter about "The One Who Opens Doors." And then, through *Aura*, I heard the greatest news of the century. The description came as news of distant explosions fighting one another, bang against bang, described as a war of bombs, and then my veins flooded with adrenaline because I knew there was only one species who'd mastered the art of obliterating things, of puppeteering weapons to do their bidding, the bureaucratic art of war. MoFos! I knew it! Healthy ones that could drive a tank and release a nuke! Somewhere they were out there, fighting back, gaining ground, and reclaiming their territory, which meant that somewhere, someone in a lab coat was working on a cure. My heart soared. I listened more, puffed with happiness. I could hear crows calling to one another, sharing information about caches and spreading valuable intel about food stops. I listened for as long as I could handle, waiting for specifics about the heroic survivor MoFos, but the pressing topic never returned and it was exhausting getting bombarded with a constant butt-splosion of information.

I told Dennis to sit under the shade of a newly budding Japanese cherry tree, launching into the air for more recon. I perched on the moss-green roof of the university public library. Smoke rose in black coils from the horizon far in the distance, too far to be of immediate concern. I had a clear view of the library's surrounding area; eye to eye with the tree line, I peered down at parking lots and a patchwork of slate-gray rooftops. Not far away, the spire of the Blessed Sacrament Church caught the sun with its glacial green. I cleared my throat, stomach suddenly twisting into pretzel shapes. I spread my wings, opened my beak, and fluttered my gular—this sounds ruder than it is, it's actually just me flapping my neck muscles to stay cool. The burnt matchsticks that are my legs started to shake. Yup, I was a fella with stage fright. But, Dennis and I had plans, and I needed information desperately. So, I took in a deep breath, ruffled my plumage, and called out to a world I've never been a part of: the natural world.

"Can someone tell me how to find Onida? Please, I'm looking for Onida, *The One Searched For!*"

Silence. I waited a minute and then decided to try again, calling out louder with a sprinkle more bravado, a touch more bass in my tone.

The silence became eerie. The symphony of *Aura* ceased. A gust of wind blew through the tree crowns, rustling the branches of the cherry trees. The trees whispered the words of a sharp-edged warning, *beware, beware.* I wished they were more specific. I looked down to check on Dennis, who was lying under the tree, sniffing at the sky. Something did feel off. I felt like there were eyes on me. Not literally like when I cached Big Jim's eyeball, but like someone or something was watching me in the shadows. I tried one more time to get my post into *Aura*, donning a bit of an accent this time, a little soap opera flair to my delivery.

"Please! It is a matter of life and death! I must unearth Onida!"

There was no response. More breathless silence.

Just then, an Anna's hummingbird darted past me, a bullet in mother-of-pearl who shrieked, "Cheese cups, ass clubs, keep away!" Hummingbirds have a reputation for being curt and vague, but I began to wonder if this one had been at some fermented fruit. Turns out I didn't have to wait long to decipher her warning.

The big black doors at the top of the stone steps to the building of books swung open. Under the arches of the great white structure, under ivory pillars and large green letters bearing the library's name, loomed an enormous mass. It let out a deep huff, a low grumble that made the earth tremor. It squinted to orient itself in the bright sunlight.

Ruuuhuuuh.

Ruuuhuuuuufff.

A fucking grizzly.

My eyes locked in on the Japanese cherry tree, below it to Dennis, now standing on four paws, body posture tense and erect and facing the great tawny mass that had emerged from the library.

Cheese and shit niblets, Dennis, don't make a fucking sound. On cue, Dennis let out a burst of booming barks that seemed to say, "Fuck off, you douche flute!" which is exactly what a grizzly the size of a jumbo vending machine likes to hear after rousing from a nap. The bear spun toward Dennis. Even from this distance, I could see a ripple streak through the copper tips of its fur. It rose to its hind legs and started huffing, the silence clouded with guttural growls. Dennis responded by barking louder, faster, spinning on his axis. The bear moaned—a long, pointed accusation—huffed harder, stopped to sniff the air. Then it flattened its ears to its head and expelled a roar, a roar that tore through the bones of the building and ran up my spine. Long mustard-brown fangs were all I needed to see. The bear coughed out more woofs, panting frustration. It slapped the stone ground with its club-like paws, which was grizzly language I understood.

It was going to kill Dennis.

The bear reared back and charged at Dennis full tilt. I cried out to him. The mass of muscle and brown stopped just before reaching Dennis's front paws, lifting its head high into the air, lowering it to train its eyes on him. It lunged at him with open mouth and mammoth paws in flight; great black nose twitching. Dennis barked, darting from side to side to avoid the swipes, saliva frothing on his jowls. The bear began to circle Dennis, backing him up against the Japanese cherry tree. I didn't have much time.

Think, S.T. Think.

I dropped from the library roof, conserving my energy by hijacking a ride on a puff of air. Beak-first, I made a beeline for the grizzly's head. As I neared, I filled with smell—the smell of clover, wet grass, raw liver, putrid carcass—then right as I neared Dennis's tail, the bear threw its weight into a paw swipe. The blow smashed Dennis across his ribs, sending him rolling across the library lawn. He yelped, a string of tight squeals that I heard in my heart.

Dennis.

I slipped past the bear's right ear, maneuvered a tight mid-air flip turn, and drove my beak into the bear's backside. The bear lifted its teeth skyward and bellowed at the sun. Pivoting on hind legs, it lunged at me fang-first, missing my wing by an inch. I rose above the bear, snatching its ear in my foot and yanking hard. The bear whipped its paw up, driving a force of air that thrust me sideways. I recovered, lifting to safety. Still on hind legs, the grizzly woofed and huffed at me, rage igniting amber in its eyes. I stole a glance at Dennis. He was back on all paws, shaking off the hit, steadying, and no doubt preparing to put himself back into the jaws of an adult bear.

I was too focused on Dennis. The bear smashed me mid-air, giant club of a paw punching me through space and time and into the trunk of the Japanese cherry tree. I hit the tree with a *thwack* and toppled to the dirt, completely winded. A sharp pain streaked up my beak. Fluttering my gular, I righted myself at the tree base to see the bear lumbering toward Dennis. My eyes darted.

Come on, S.T. Do something!

Snapping up a huge silvery rock the size of a whole German boob in my feet, I soared high, high up into the air, wings burning from the sun and sting, and I released that fucking boob rock like a World War II B-24 dropping its load. The rock

struck the grizzly's skull with a dull clonk. I might as well have
kicked it in the nuts. The bear got very, very angry. It lunged
at me from below, roaring from its pancreas, arms swinging,
mustard fangs snapping at my back. I fluttered above it for a
few seconds, air-dodging the blows, my wing burning with a
staggering ache. I counted one, two, three, then whisked over
the bear's head and shot right over Dennis.

"ZzzzZZZt! Dennis! Here, boy!" I screeched.

I heard Dennis's frantic panting under my tail feathers as
I dove over the library lawn, my shadow a phantom below.
Crow chased by bloodhound chased by grizzly bear across
the university public library entrance lawn and across the
street and then tearing across the stretch of green that's
the university playground. Never in my life have I ever been
happy to see a Honda Civic, but today was a day of firsts, and
I dove beneath its undercarriage, below its royal-blue body,
whistling for Dennis. Dennis skidded into the Civic's passenger
door, then stuffed his wrinkled mass under the car with me,
where we waited for an enraged apex predator to exact its
revenge.

In an instant, the air was filled with calls. Screams, threats,
warnings, made a deafeningly horrid symphony. I peeked out
from behind a rear tire to see the sky inky with bodies, all of
them hovering above the air, flapping and cawing and pelting
rocks and bottle caps and shoes and Gatorade and condoms
at the stunned bear. The bear snarled and swiped, but quickly
realized it was outnumbered as the crows intensified their
attack, caws getting louder and louder. Suddenly the bear
lowered its head, shook its fur, and cantered back toward the
black library doors, a sky full of black demons driving it on.

"Enough!" screamed someone with the voice of God, or
James Earl Jones.

And the crows stopped. Quiet trapped us in its net. You

could've heard a mouse fart. They retreated, disappearing into the trees. I looked over at Dennis, who was licking his side vigorously. A flap of skin hung down from his ribs where the grizzly had clobbered him.

I inched out from under the Honda and lifted myself high enough into the air to see the grizzly back at the library doors. Flashbacks from the Discovery Channel haunted me, stirring up the Latin name for the grizzly bear, *Ursus arctos horribilis*. *Horribilis* indeed. As the bear paced and then started to lumber away from the library, three brown blobs emerged from the doors to shadow her. Cubs. Great, she reproduced— there are more of those fuzzy death-potatoes out in society, helping themselves to public facilities that are funded by our hard-earned tax dollars. Pffft. My mind belatedly translated the hummingbird's cry of "Cheese cups, ass clubs, keep away!" to the more plausible "She's up, has cubs, keep away!" I'll admit I had been a bit quick to judge her sobriety.

I lowered to *terra firma* and watched Dennis licking and whining at the angry gash in his side. Puttering along the curb where the Honda was parked, I located a brightly colored flyer for the "High Times U.S. Cannabis Cup in Seattle, Washington." Snatching it in my beak, I hopped back to the Civic and whistled, summoning Dennis to inch himself from the car's comatose body. I plodded toward him and gingerly pressed the High Times flyer to his side. He snapped instinctually, and I sprang backward.

"Easy, Dennis. Easy, boy," I said, mimicking Big Jim every time he loaded Dennis into the bathtub as I hopped onto the sink to avoid a tidal wave of water. Big Jim was always too busy wrestling the hound and camouflaging the bathroom in soapsuds to listen to me explain Dennis's predicament. It wasn't the bath Dennis was afraid of—it was the plughole. He was afraid he would get sucked down into the dark and we wouldn't find him. Dennis was onto something; I once cached the house key down there and it was never seen again.

Dennis let out a tight growl.

"Good boy, Dennis. It's okay. I gotcha," I whispered, shuffling toward him. Pain was licking up my wing in electric streaks, and my injury wasn't half as bad as Dennis's. Other than a sharp whine, he didn't protest anymore, seeming to trust me, to accept my medical assistance. The prismatic Cannabis Cup flyer stuck fast to his wet wound.

"Brother Blackwing," came the imposing voice. I grimaced. Both titles bothered me. I don't fully identify as a crow, finding the label to be overly simplistic. And I was *not* his brother. A constellation of shining black eyes tracked me from the bigleaf maples above. College crows. Dennis seemed too distracted by his pain to care. The maples themselves watched silently, gently breathing in some of the tension. Trees are known peace-keepers, though not very good with secrets.

I kept quiet, unsure of what to say or whether I wanted to say anything at all. Dennis and I were outnumbered, weak, and exposed. I waited, resisting the temptation to gular flutter so as not to give away my emotional state.

"Blackwing," the voice continued, this time like the chiming of cathedral bells, as a large black corvid dropped from the sun and onto a low maple arm. I cocked my head at him, hopping onto one foot. He craned forward, the brilliant blue of his sheen lulling me into a false sense of comfort. You might think we all look alike, but again, it just takes a bit of focus, attention, consciousness. MoFos tend to be too locked in the beautiful basements of their minds to notice certain subtleties. Sorry, I said I'd be honest. No, this wasn't your run-of-the-mill trash-raider. This was a bold and charismatic presence with a perfectly polished charcoal beak. I saw his game—this sneakster was out to disarm me with charm.

"Are you alright, Brother Blackwing?"

"We are fine and I'm not your brother," I answered.

The beautiful crow bobbed his head, a submissive offering. "We see that you have command over the dog." *Ahhhh, there it is,* I thought. *An angle.* Big Jim says there's always an agenda, that's why you've got to batten down the hatches, fight for what's yours, and look out for numero uno. That's why you don't let anyone in. Big Jim's philosophy, sound and clear as Windex-ed glass: everyone wants to steal your Cheetos®. I refused to answer the crow, keeping burning questions about what had happened to the MoFos in my plumage. I would seek answers from a trustworthy source.

"He's hurt," said the annoyingly flawless fancy of feathers, whose wings looked like something out of da Vinci's sketchbook. "Here." Another crow—smaller, with a burn-patch on the underside of her right wing and singed contour feathers—dropped from above. She released a petite bushel of herbs at my feet. The boss crow gestured. "Yarrow. For the dog. It will help with healing."

Dennis didn't like me approaching the Cannabis Cup flyer, his hide erupting in a shudder of flinches, but he allowed me to peel it from the wet red and press the yarrow against his wound with my feet as the crow crowd looked on in awe. A sense of importance warmed my throat like Woodinville Whiskey.

The Prince Of Perfect started up again, "You need to be careful out here—"

"We don't need your help," I spat, surprised by my venom.

"You are the one who called for help on *Aura*," said the crow, his legions gently chirruping in agreement. "We didn't know you knew about *Aura* or the ways of the Blackwings. We've watched you for some time now."

"Yeah, watched, harassed, threatened. Nice job, guys," I said, adding more of the stalks and miniature white flowers of the yarrow to Dennis's red, red hole. "Listen, I thank you for chasing off the grizzly, truly, but Dennis and I are doing just fine by ourselves."

Main Crow fluttered his wings, his head darting from side to side, displaying his displeasure to the black bodies around him. "I will apologize for any misgivings. I am sorry to hear of them. Perhaps I can help you—"

"I need to find Onida."

"Onida." Suddenly the crows were statues as the wind exhaled through the maple tree, its leaves dancing like a 1920s flapper.

Onida, it whispered, *The One Searched For.*

The crows waited, monuments of reverence, for the secrets to take the wings of the wind.

"Onida. How do you know of Onida?" asked the crow chief, his nictitating membrane licking his eye.

"Onida!" came a crow's voice from a collage of emerald leaves. "The one who moves between worlds!"

"The one of many names! The one of the stars!" cried another.

"The sayer of truths!"

"The master of escape!"

"Onida! The one of many minds!"

"How do you know of Onida?" the beautiful crow asked again. "Onida can only be found if Onida wants to be. Onida is everywhere and nowhere, and knows tomorrow's sun. If Onida calls, you are summoned like tides by the moon."

I would never tell them that I might have accidentally tuned in to their unavoidably noisy ass *Aura* a couple of times in the past, where I might have heard about The One Searched For, this so-called prophet, by mistake. I would never tell them that I was so desperate and in need of answers that I'd do anything, even follow the directive whisperings of *Aura,* to help my Big Jim. "Respectfully, that's not your business. And I definitely wouldn't tell those ass trumpets." I bobbed my head at Bonnie and Clyde, my two regular harassers. He gave them both a dark stare.

"I see. Well, if you'd be willing—"

"I don't think they'd be willing to associate with a hybrid like me."

"But you are a hybrid, aren't you? A hybrid Blackwing. Enslaved by the MoFos, caged and clipped—"

"Clipped?! My wings work perfectly! Probably better than yours!"

"We aren't judging you, Blackwing. We say how it is. My name is Kraai." (This is my best attempt to phonetically translate his name for you.)

"Look, Kraai, don't call me hybrid, or Blackwing; my name is Shit Turd and I am what I am. Just tell me where I can find Onida, please. And we'll be on our way."

"Since you are a hybrid Blackwing, you walk the way of The Hollows, you live trapped in a—"

"Enough!" I squawked, mimicking his earlier cry. "You don't know who I am! None of you fuckers do!"

This caused a frenzy among the crows, a bluster of throaty keening. I reeled, backing up and bracing myself. Dennis sprang to his feet, racing to the trunk of the tree and unleashing his warnings at the maple full of life. I'd only ever seen the dreaded UPS trucks inflame him in this manner. I beamed, my breast feathers puffing to inflate me. I had my own protector, my own murder. Kraai silenced his brethren with one slash of his beak cutting through the air.

He took his time with a slow nod. And then he gave me directions. I'm afraid I'm not able to precisely translate these for you. I don't mean to sound patronizing, but if you haven't been airborne, you have no context and the translation is complicated. I will try to simplify it for you. Basically, the sky is a bird's nature, home, an extension of the soul. They know it and remember it better than earthly destinations. Feathered ones, except penguins and turkeys because they're fucking morons, have wonderful memories—not sure why elephants get all the damn credit. They travel by tips heard through *Aura* (sort of like GPS) and by their relationship to the sun and stars who engage them in a sensory conversation. All this forms what we call a *mind map*. Conversations with no words are understandably very difficult to explain to MoFos, but they are happening all the time, all around. The hardest part to explain is the earth's magnetic field, which can always be heard, much like *Aura*. Think of it as the strings of a McPherson Camrielle 4.0 acoustic guitar in your heart, the strumming of which gives you insight and instruction. All flora and fauna listen to the earth's magnetism. It is how the sand, soil, clay, and dust communicate, how every element of our Infinite Universe and shared home talks to us, sometimes guiding us through our journey. I guess the closest MoFo comparison is how your gods speak to some of you, or the emergency broadcast system. We perceive ultraviolet light and wavelengths of color that allow us to see sexual dichromatism, which is how I could tell, aside from looking up her skirt, that the petite crow with the burn patch under her right wing was a girl. UV light paints a kaleidoscope of patterns and signals that MoFos appear to be blind to, a literal blindness, different from the commonplace numbed blindness of closing off the mind. I think it would just be fucking rude of me to harp on about what beauty and insight you're missing out on there. So, mind maps. I guess I could tap into all this majestic shit more often, but I'll be honest, I use landmarks like Starbucks, the Space Needle, and McDonald's. Way more practical and iconic.

Kraai and the college Blackwings watched us leave. A pair of cabbage-white butterflies danced around me, pirouetting in the sunshine. Butterflies live short lives because they have mastered the art of living. They serve to pass it on with luminous bursts of joy, bright flickers from the other side. I listened to their bell-like beckoning. "Onida calls you! Onida calls you!" they uttered, breathless with excitement. The paper-winged ones are truth-tellers, postage-stamp sized messengers who paint the air into a watercolor of magic and taste with their feet. We are best advised not to blast them with Roundup.

Knowing I had a fairly decent audience at this point, I decided to ham up my exit by sitting on Dennis's back while holding his leash in my foot, riding him like a stallion into the Wild West. I could hear chirps and incredulous murmurs all around. It was pretty freaking awesome. Well, it would have been had I not been more scared than a KFC-bound chicken. There was a corn nut of truth in what Kraai said. I was, after all, "clipped"—a crow who'd never really left his own nest. And Onida was far from home. And the West was wilder than I could have possibly imagined.

CHAPTER 7

BYEONSANBANDO NATIONAL PARK, JUST NORTH
OF HANBIT NUCLEAR POWER PLANT, SOUTH KOREA
(AS DICTATED BY A YOUNG FAIRY PITTA)

We are airborne. *Quick, quick, quick.* Dart through the branches, call out, "Run, run!" No time to dillydally. Below the tree crowns, a thousand feet drum, *tiki tiki tiki tiki.* Marten, weasel, badger, they run in black and white and brown. Hare leaps, *go go go*, legs hope to fly. Snake and salamander run, squiggly limbs and slippery belly. Moth and butterfly knew first; they are ahead. They felt it coming before it knew itself. They knew it in the wise of them. The air is busy with duck and goose and Baikal teal and tiger shrike. Flying squirrel glides like quick leaves. We woke to a new smell in the air, sharp as hawk's beak. Now we *run.*

The message came from *Echo* on the waves that preen sand near where the heat is rising. The rising hot comes from big buildings that look like a line of eggs. They are from the nests of Hollows. We must fly as fast as we can before the eggs crack...

I dart between trees; my family is a whirl of color through

the tips of branches. *Quick, quick, quick.* Below us, cats with rangy legs skitter-skatter. Mice run alongside them, a bigger danger on their earthworm tails.

I flit past crested ibis, beaky blur of white and pink, who says, "Faster! It's coming!"

We know it's coming. We feel it. It's a prickle on the beak, a soon sneeze. We hear it. We run for high ground.

The trees hum and sing to one another, breathing love and story. They cannot run.

Thin screams come. Fox shrieks below.

Quick, quick, quick!

Before the eggs crack. Before the waves swell with anger. Before the orange hot licks up the land.

Quick, quick, quick! I feel it now! The rumbling starts...

CHAPTER 8

Dennis seemed to have perked up after the yarrow application. I admitted to myself that it was a better remedy than my weed-competition flyer and had to eat a little crow, if you'll pardon the expression. Hey, in my defense, everything I learned about veterinary care was from Animal Planet and they didn't tend to get overly technical on *Breed All About It*.

We headed south, following Kraai's directions. I used the snaking gray river of I-5 as my guide, soaring above to check our immediate vicinity. Dennis had no qualms about me riding him now and then, as long as he got to catch up on his pee-mail and work toward his unwavering goal of watering every grass blade in the Pacific Northwest.

I-5 South was a ghost of itself, missing its pulse—the touch and droning hum of wheels. Cars were strewn around it, silent and sleeping. Some had crashed into one another, bodies black and crumpled with dents. I rapped my beak on the rear windshield of a mud-splattered minivan, tapping on the superheroes decal. Dad superhero, mom superhero and three little superheroes, even a superhero dog, all with capes and smiles and arms punching the air in victory. Other than a Pokémon toy, there was no trace of them in the van, but I had a good feeling about them because superheroes can survive anything—I saw Superman stop a bullet with his iris one time.

I dropped earthbound to check for survivors intermittently, finding evidence of horror-movie endings in the form of sparkling shards or in a MoFo's lonely bones and the tenacious blue and green skin that clung to them. And everywhere, that greedy reek of rotting meat haunting the air like a ghoul that grabs at your tongue. Many MoFos had perished there, in their vehicles, their destinations waiting forever. I thought of their families and felt a pang of gratitude that Big Jim was still mostly alive. My recon safety checks were frequent but cursory since I didn't like to leave Dennis for long. From the sky, I could recognize clusters of sick MoFos, their humped backs and snapping-turtle necks, scraping with their fingers, smashing their heads against medians and trucks and fallen motorbikes. We took detours where there were sick MoFos. My keen eyes hunted for uprightness—the miraculously vertical, straight-backed glory and the steady gait that exemplify a healthy MoFo. I knew they were out there. Hope flickered like a tiny pilot light inside me, keeping dark thoughts at bay. I thought of the frolicking in the Cymbalta commercial, and knew we had to keep moving.

A freeway sign caught my eye. It had been brightened with lightly faded graffiti, an intricate scene that had the runny, bubbled words BORN TO BE WILD over a realistic picture of a lion licking an ice cream cone. Instead of a ball of ice cream, the cone held a grenade. Anarchy or art—those MoFos certainly were creative. The doomed African king was surrounded by rudimentary scribbles. One said "rATheR NoT bE HuMan," another "Kurt Cobain 4Eva." Another scrawl said "the four horsEmEn are hErE. thEy camE on the wings of a breezE." Ridiculous. Horses are way too heavy for that shit.

With every step Dennis and I took, there was palpable agitation, airborne collywobbles clouding the air. Even the sun peeked through the clouds cautiously, unsure and perhaps afraid of what she might illuminate in the broken city below.

A swift flight to the west allowed me to hover over Gas Works Park on the north shore of Lake Union. From my bird's-eye view, the park was almost unrecognizable. Big Jim says that most things can be fixed with duck tape, but staring at the changed park, I was dubious. At some point, a Boeing 747 had tumbled from the clouds and collided with the red skeleton of the old gasification plant, birthing a mangled mess of aluminum and demolition and bloody rust. Bobbing gently in Lake Union, yards away, the tail and blades of a King 5 helicopter peeked out from above the waterline. The park's beautiful sundial—centrally located on a grassy hill, which allows a flightless MoFo to enjoy Seattle's skyline—was charred and burnt, its face forever scarred. Black bruises kissed the park where small fires had erupted. A couple of skeletons, big and small, cowered under a picnic table. Then a flurry caught my eye: a ghoulish gaggle of vulture-necked MoFos were huddled in a mass by the park's concrete arches—the gray ghosts of old train trestles. MoFos crawled over one another, a living tumor of blood and tissue. I couldn't see what they were scrambling for, what was at the epicenter of this pileup of doom, but knew better than to get close. No, the healthy MoFos weren't in Gas Works Park. They'd found shelter elsewhere. Sadness tugged at my tail feathers. Although whatever had taken over Big Jim had obviously hit my neighborhood the worst, it had spread farther than I thought, desecrating my home city and its gorgeously iconic bits.

In Lake Union, boats bobbed aimlessly, sails lying flat against the water like soaked surrender flags. The sky was painfully silent without the brassy blare of brightly colored seaplanes overhead. Everything felt too quiet, like held breath. This was no longer the fastest growing city in America. This was a battleground. A war zone. And yet, on the far side of the park, I saw deer grazing on the dense, jungly grass that grew everywhere, stretching their necks to reach the vines and creepers that hung down from tree crowns.

I told Dennis we should get a move on and we made our way farther down the phantom of I-5, stopping to fill ourselves with blackberries and salmonberries from the brambles that threatened to swallow part of the freeway alive. A section of the road was flooded, forcing Dennis to paddle through an algae-lake as I hopped alongside him across the tops of vehicles, acting as his neurotic swim coach. Once across, I stared back at the freeway lake, marveling at the soupy devastation, while Dennis shook himself dry, releasing a halo of wet. I pillaged a small blanket from an abandoned SUV with punched-out windows, gingerly dabbing at Dennis's wound to dry it. I hopped in place, anxious to move on. I was stress-stuffed, a Hot Pocket of angst. Who knows what might have been lurking under that quiet film of green scum?

A red-tailed hawk, talons tightly clutching at old habits, looped above the freeway, searching for roadkill—an extinct species. She started to follow us, but Dennis, full of piss and blackberries, told her where she could stick her razor-edged bill in strangled bugle-howls. Dennis was really getting into this murder thing.

Several streetlamps later, we approached a gruesome scene. Seven colossal rib cages adorned with nubs of rotten meat sat on the freeway like a horrifying art installation. The road was stained deep red with blood and the slimy residue of entrails.

Bovines. These were the foundations of what used to be some sort of cattle, picked almost clean by something. A bright rainbow suddenly streaked above us, almost too fast to register, a flock of colorful birds I couldn't identify or understand. So I was distracted, looking skyward, when a goat—skin stretched tight over bones, eyeballs bulging with the stress-shits—shot past, startling us. We both noticed the purple wound where his tail used to be. He didn't make a sound, skittering into the trees, gone before we could get answers. Very un-goatlike. He had survived something unspeakable, hooves propelled by survival instinct. Dennis sniffed at the bone sculptures and raised his head toward the bold frontline of evergreen trees. He didn't need to convince me further. We picked up the pace from there, knowing that Seattle had seen a change of Mount Rainier proportions and that whatever it was, it was big and destructive and largely hidden from us. It was also safe to say, at this point, that I-5 South was officially the freeway of death. In all fairness, I've heard it described this way many times on the radio before, so not much change in that respect.

Dennis and I followed the slippery eel of I-5 and listened to the trees: the moan of a madrone, the counsel of a Douglas fir, the shimmer of a cherry tree, the whine of a whitebark pine, paper birches, dogwoods, and oaks and maples and sweet gums and cedars and elms. Some shared memories of things that had occurred many, many years before on the land around their trunks, slow stories of fights between lovers, the massacre during the lumber industry boom, the Great Seattle Fire, and the Klondike gold rush. Trees are super nostalgic. Others recited soothing poems in *sotto voce*—oral balms learned as seedlings. Some spoke of when the bison and the wolf roamed this land; they talked of change and whispered about a pre-destined event, repeating the word "renaissance" in harmony.

I had no clue what all this had to do with Michelangelo, but you don't argue with a tree.

One thing was certain, they were full of beans, on fire with chitter-chatter. But—and I will swear on a Cheeto® here—the Douglas firs were talking to me directly. This is as much a surprise to me as it is to you. This had never, ever happened before, least of all to me, a weirdo hybrid crow. Trees are normally very general and all-inclusive with their wisdom pearls. When a tree decides to talk to you, it's a very, very big deal, as if the world stops, as if you are scooped up and held in a snow globe, weightless and womb-like. I felt their vibrations in my feathers, in the flutter of my little black heart. The Douglas firs were all pointing. Each had one solitary branch outstretched, urging me toward my destination, down I-5 and to whatever lay ahead. *To Onida.* As is polite and customary when spoken to by a tree, I answered back, calling out my thanks from above their towering tops. I followed humbly, pilot light rekindled, floppy skin-bag bloodhound in tow.

Intermittent MoFo clusters, lone cobra-necked MoFos, and Dennis not being a greyhound all added time to our journey south. To avoid MoFos, we hid behind medians, construction sand bags, an ice cream truck with rancid lactose sludge smearing its insides, and an empty Lamborghini with the Seahawks logo blazoned all over it, but most MoFos seemed to be exhibiting the same sort of repetitive behavior that Big Jim had. I couldn't figure them out. They were at once distracted and dangerous. Disturbed. Stuck and broken and yet somehow waiting for something. They smelled like hot garbage (not the delicious kind).

When we finally neared our destination, I shot above to take in Seattle's Pike Place Market, a touristic mecca that includes the original Starbucks, a wall encrusted with chewed gum, and men who lob fish at one another. Pike Place Market, its iconic

red sign unlit, was teeming with MoFos and my heart beat its
wings in delight. Hallelujah! Praise IHOP! They'd all come
here! They'd all travelled down I-5 South and taken refuge
in the market, among the beautiful flower displays, waterfront
views, and specialty teas that cost the same as a kidney! I
lowered, preparing to let out a caw of jubilation, and then my
stomach fizzed into boiling acid. The MoFos were shoulder to
shoulder, loping in a writhing mass, spewing from the underground of the market and through its souvenir-lined corridors,
bumping into one another, trailing their fingers, and bobbing
their snapping-turtle necks. Every single one of them had
what Big Jim had. I can only technically count to nine, but it
seemed like millions. No growling cars, just the remnants of
long-rotten fruit, rotten fish, rotten MoFos, and onesies with
the Space Needle painted on them. I gagged. How could this
have happened? How could *so* many MoFos be sick?

I was getting woozy from hunger pangs and wing-wrenching
dismay. A stand that called itself the Daily Dozen Doughnut
Company caught my eye. I perched on top of one of the stand's
last remaining shelves. The stand had taken a beating, its CASH
ONLY sign dangling like a severed limb. Stools lay on their
sides, legless and splintered. Glass sparkled from the market
floor. A body lay near a silver stand mixer that was fossilized
by its own icing. It hadn't been dead long; the perpetrator
would still be close. The eyes were frozen in terror, glazed with
torture. Someone had ripped its white body into two parts,
a bisection. Teeth marked its entrails. Ruby-red blood stained
paper-white feathers. Wonderful—some of them were eating
glaucous-winged gulls.

I watched the pulsing mass of MoFos as they swayed and
lumbered. Some were stationary and dragging their fingers
like Big Jim; some stared into the middle distance as if reading something on the horizon. Others crept around face-first,

bloodred eyes bobbing like a pigeon's neck, in search of something. One MoFo stood next to a pile of doughnuts that had been knocked off a three-tiered silver platter and lay next to a jar that said "God Knows When You Don't Tip." The MoFo directly between me and a pile of delectable doughnuts was wallpapered with nautical tattoos. A slouchy beanie sat on his head, his beard mimicking a comatose beaver. The suspenders and bowtie weren't fooling me though; I knew this MoFo's game. His left hand was pressed to his ear and you bet your ass I'd taken stock of that shock of bright red that dribbled down his plaid shirt.

The glaucous-winged gull eater.

On TV, I've learned that crows, by nature, can be pretty persistent. If you've ever pissed one off, you'll know this. I think it's coded, cocooned deep in the fluff of our down feathers to hold on to things—ideas, grudges, your engagement ring. There was no exception here. By the fumes of NASCAR, I was going to get a damned doughnut! A stealth swoop fueled by a growling stomach shot me past the glaucous-winged gull eater. He let out a high-pitched scream, a spleen-quivering skirl that caused the surrounding MoFos to snap their necks toward him.

Glaucous-Winged Gull Eater bit at me as I careened past him, just missing sinking his gull-stained choppers into my back. The mass of MoFos let out a series of low-pitched moans, some sort of horrible summoning, then rushed the glaucous-winged gull eater. They ran forward, toward us, crushing the Daily Dozen Doughnut Company sign, the counter, the silver fryer, industrial cooking machinery, the trash can, everything in the herd's way. They charged forth, blood and saliva flying; tubs of sugar hissed through the air, a blizzard of flour blew down hard. They brayed with jaws wide, emitting a sick song. A woman with black braids and a large dripping hole in her midsection raced forward. A man with a broken guitar hanging from his back and plucked-out eyes roared as he ran, pushed forward by a sea of MoFos led by an old lady with a knitted cat sweater and a face that looked like it had been sculpted from mashed potatoes. Two small, identical MoFos crawled on all fours, backs arched like quick cats, rippling with twitches and convulsions as they sprung forward, scampering up the other MoFos, a breakneck clamber to get ahead. I dove from above, inches from their outstretched claws, snatching a doughnut in my beak and a bag of coffee beans with my feet. I shot myself airborne as the crowd smashed into Glaucous-Winged Gull Eater, trampling him, a mass of sickness and moans and devastation.

Time to go. I flapped hard, soaring over Pike Place until the MoFos were a formicary of moshing ants. A teeming swarm, soldiers trampling soldiers. I lifted high, high, high above the implosion and dropped a sizable bomb of my own, as I emptied my bowels upon the wild beasts below.

I had left Dennis at Waterfront Park near Pier 59, tucked behind Waterfront Fountain, a cubical structure that looks like interlocking bronze keys. The area was familiar to me, as Big Jim and I had come here once to install an underground electrical conduit. The fountain water no longer flowed; instead, the still water was cloaked by a green algae veil. The fountain looked deeply sad without a purpose. Seattle now felt like this, as if it was choking under a thickening green skin. The partially demolished Alaskan Way Viaduct had none of its usual elevated roar and rumble. Now it was suffocating under an emerald-green curtain of English ivy and Parney cotoneaster.

A ferocious growl ran up my spine. I pivoted to find Dennis hovering over a mass on Alaskan Way. I leapt into the air and to his side. Dennis rumbled with anger, saliva dripped from his jowls, eye-whites shining. The object of his aggression was a large, shiny lump. A ballooning buildup of tissue and blood. Slimy bubbles popped from its surface. The blob rose up and down methodically. As if it had a pulse. It jiggled like the filling of an uncooked pie, each wobble sending Dennis into madness. He puffed his cheeks, pursed his rubbery lips, and released growls that swelled into bold, trumpeting bellows.

"Rooowwwwwooooooooooooh! Rooowwwwwooooooooooooh!"

"I don't know, buddy. I don't like it either," I told him.

Dennis's loose skin flinched. His barrel chest heaved with the exertion of every howl.

Starting to worry about his blood pressure, I lured Dennis with the doughnut, away from the unknown thing that smelled like death and decay and molten iron.

Weird lump out of sight, I had a little sample of the dough-nut, which had aged nicely to the consistency of a truck tire. Delicious, a thousand times better than the fried blobs Big Jim liked to get from 7-Eleven. He'd really been holding out on me. Probably because the Pike Place ones were too expensive. Big Jim hated that, like that time he ordered a latte from Caffe Ladro ("FIVE DOLLARS?!") and asked the barista when he should expect his accompanying testicle massage. A MoFo wearing a "manager" badge and a monkfish face disinvited us from their establishment for eternity. Some MoFos can be very obtuse.

After I'd plucked off the mold and had a good sample of doughnut, I dropped it for Dennis, who chowed down happily. I'd say it was a testament to the quality and endurance of Daily Dozen Doughnuts, but here I must remind you that Dennis's favorite snack is a dehydrated bull penis. The bag of Vashon Dark Side of the Moon coffee beans burst open easily, cloaking me in comfort with an ambrosial cloud of roasted nose-joy. Oh, those delightfully nutty little rabbit turds were a welcome sight. Finally, something familiar, something that made sense. I nibbled on the beans while Dennis cocked a leg and relieved himself in the fountain. We would soon lose light and it was time to find who we'd come looking for.

I rattled—a sound like I'd swallowed maracas—for Dennis to follow me to the doors, or what was left of them. The belly of the building was dark, a briny, ominous smell leaking from its bowels. A quick breeze ruffled my feathers, crow-bumps forming on my skin. Dennis stopped once we reached the white framing that used to hold glass entrance doors. He started to pace, swinging his pendulous head wrinkles from side to side. His paw touched some of the green water that bled from inside the building and he whined. It was clear that I'd be flying solo here.

"Don't be a nervous Nellie, Dennis. I'll be alright," I told him; obviously he actually *had* been listening to my lectures back home on not being a hero. I probably should have toned those down a little, as I can be very persuasive. Dennis let out a yodel of protest, sniffing vigorously at the air. He paced, prodded, and whimpered next to a plant making a tenacious evacuation from its pot under a broken metallic sign that now read, "Seat e Aquar m."

I told him to wait by the fountain again and flapped my wings erratically. He lifted his panicked, sad-sap eyes to me and barked, a stentorian alarm. The message, low and laced with desperation, needed no translation. *Don't go in there.* The nerves were making my legs quiver—probably should have had about forty fewer coffee beans than what I'd just enjoyed.

Swooping through the building's entrance frame, I was plunged into a damp darkness. The little light there streamed from gaping windows, the broken teeth of the building. A fetid stench, briny and billowing like an old wet animal, punched me in the dick (technically crows don't have dicks, but that doesn't make me less of a dude). I perched on top of the entrance counter below three burnt flat screens. Water, dark and murky as ink, submerged the aquarium's floor.

A scan of the lobby revealed a cinema screen–sized aquarium with its glass completely smashed out, water all around. Water dripped rhythmically from wood beams above. I lifted up and glided over the gift shop, a flooded mess of soggy, moldy stuffed dolphins and orcas and penguins—honestly, who the fuck wants an effigy of those fat assholes in their home?—floating postcards, shell pillows, otter and Puget Sound–themed T-shirts. Display stands lay submerged on their sides. I found Nemo, waterlogged, with his face ripped off and stuffing erupting from his stomach. He had been lodged between the soggy paperbacks of a book display this whole time.

As I dove farther into the building, Dennis's barks became strangled, disembodied, the warnings of a fading ghost. I passed over some sort of stony structure, a highly accurate re-creation of a rock pool. I hopped down to inspect closer, and found several starfish, tangerine and cherry colored, alive and living a quiet, thoughtful existence in the dark. Dead stingrays floated in the pools, a couple with chunks missing from their slate bodies. Anemones also lay dead in the water, tentacles stiff and unfeeling.

A giant, glass half-moon arch, now smashed through its middle, had spilled its watery contents, adding to the murky flooding below. A clear body, impaled on the edge of the arch's broken middle, told me it used to contain jellyfish. What had happened here?

I swooped into a walkway hidden in a cave tunnel that used to house a row of aquariums. The caves were flooded, every single aquarium face smashed out. Emerging from the tunnel, I flew over a decimated stand-alone Hawaiian fish aquarium and straight into the teeth of a great white shark. I squawked and shot back, startled by the MoFo-made shark model suspended up high from the wood beams; his ghoulish grimace suggested he was laughing at the aquarium's destruction. I circled back near the rock pools and hopped on top of another glass structure. This one was two tanks connected by a glass tube tunnel. The water inside was green and viscous, greedy algae slime licking all surfaces. This aquarium was remarkably intact, though closer inspection revealed several nuts and bolts at the bottom of the tank. The top of the aquarium had been removed. Something had found its way out.

The flood below me rippled, frenzied splashes flicking up spray. Fish. A school of fish were fleeing. A glance at the rock pool revealed hysteria among the remaining sea stars (sea star panic is very subtle, but I was onto that shit). My feathers ruffled.

"Hello?" *You idiot. Stop calling out to predators. How much of a douche canoe can you be?*

A sound. The sound of a MoFo hand wiping squeakily across glass. I hopped on one foot atop the tank, readying to take flight.

A voice, strange and modulated, cut through the silence like a hot knife. "I've been waiting for you."

CHAPTER 9

I said I'd tell you everything, so I have to be totally honest here and tell you that I shit myself. I was full of beans—literally— and I crapped myself right there on the weird-ass tank. It was the first time since the eyeball incident that I was relieved Big Jim wasn't around. That would have been mortifying.

But I had more pressing things to worry about. I couldn't find the body that went with the eerie voice. I hopped nervously, trying not to jump in my own excrement.

"Who are you?" I asked, and then followed up with the more pressing, "Where are you?"

Dark water near the rock pool started to stir—the sea stars were screaming at this point—and an arm, long and rust-red, lifted from its depths and into the air. The elongated arm suctioned itself to a rock and was followed by several more lissome limbs, which danced together to lift an enormous bulbous head from the depths.

The octopus's skin suddenly changed color and texture,

muting the autumnal red to a blur of shimmering silver shadows that looked like scudding clouds. My chest thumped hard, wings of my heart aflutter, as I watched the giant cephalopod emphatically maneuver itself onto the rock pool structure, reaching out one arm to suck up a terrorized sea star into the folds of its underside. I caught a flash of massive paper-white suckers at the thick base of its arms. The sea star gave a gallant cry. "It is my time! Our freedom is finally here, let us be gone from this terrible place!" The repressed sea star legions cried out in delight. "You are all next, Stars Of The Sea! The view up here is—" After some tense and awkward minutes while the sea star was ingested, the regularly red predator and I looked at one another. Dark, shiny crow eye to horizontal pupil shaped like a black smile.

"So, here you are." The rippling, puckered skin across its colossal melon was captivatingly bumpy, glistening. And as I watched it, the texture changed again—an effortless magic trick—suddenly it was smooth and glossy.

"I think you're mistaken; you think I'm somebody else," I said to the leviathan in front of me. Giant Pacific octopuses live up to their name. This one was the size of Big Jim's meat freezer. I watched a suctioned arm stretch out a good fifteen feet into the air.

The black smiles studied me. "You've come for answers."

"Well, yes, but, it's not like that's particularly specific to me; I'm pretty sure all of us have questions about—"

"You straddle two worlds and you have lost your reason for being, your way."

"Yes, but again, that could be said of the sea star you just snarfed—"

"You are a crow who believes he is human, one who has befriended a taciturn bloodhound. You have lost your connection to the world of man and you have come all the way from the

Ravenna neighborhood where you've been hiding in a small craftsman home to ask me what happened to mankind."

"Right," I said. "That seems more specific."

The octopus thrust a limber arm into the pool and fished out a small rock, which he rubbed rhythmically against stone. The scraping sound was at once sharp, repellant, and oddly hypnotic.

Questions flew from my heart. "How do you know any of that? How can you possibly know anything living in this—this place? Living in this tube tank?" I asked, tapping my leg on the top of the glass. "You *must* know *Aura*? Are you Onida?"

The octopus held time in its sucker-smothered arms, speaking in an orotund voice. "I am Onida. And I've known about you for a long, long time. Your world is small, Crow—"

"Shit Turd—"

"Excuse you?"

"My name is Shit Turd. S.T. for short."

A frown furrowed the wrinkled skin above the hooded black smiles. "It's time to expand what you know, Crow. I do know *Aura*. But there is not just *Aura* in the world. Your crow kind absorbs through *Aura*. My kind—those beneath the breathing line, those of scale and shell—we listen to *Echo*—the ocean's breath, the song of whales, the hum of a mollusk, the swish and sway of kelp. It is connected to *Aura* as all things are connected. I listen closely to the messages of water, air and The Other World, and beyond that which we can see." Onida slithered closer, still on the rock, a colossal, peristaltic mass of muscle.

"What sickness do the MoFos have?"

"I don't understand your question."

"The—humankind—what has happened to humankind in Seattle?"

Onida suddenly flashed a luminous pale gold, the ridges of

his skin smoothing and rippling pink at the edges. "Human-kind is changed. They have denied the Law Of Life by taking too much and are facing their consequences. *The One Who Hollows as well must return.*"

"What can we do to help them?"

Onida searched the beamed ceiling with those horizontal pupils. "I must tell you that it is not just Seattle, Crow. It is across The Whole. Mankind missed the essential calling to evolve. You are watching their extinction."

"NO!" I squawked, scaring myself. Then I gagged and vomited up a river of coffee sludge. My gular fluttered in panic. How could this be? No. No, no, no, no, no. "You are wrong, Octopus! No, I know you are wrong! I heard them fighting, I heard bombs in the distance! They are out there!"

"What you heard were the fires and explosions, the final words of the things they made. Here and there, all over The Whole, there have been and will be the last explosions and fires. Destructive things that make destructive ends."

The room swam. I stumbled, toppling down to the murky depths below, catching myself last minute with frantic flaps and returning to the top of the tank.

And here's what I thought of: hot dog–eating competitions. One of Big Jim's favorite things in the whole wide world. Every Fourth of July before beer, fireworks, and Jägermeister, we'd tune in to ESPN to watch the Nathan's Hot Dog Eating Contest at Coney Island emceed by the irrepressible George Shea. And I tell you, it was impressive. These magical MoFos of all sizes and backgrounds—like eleven-time champion Joey Chestnut or Megatoad or "The Leader of the Four Horsemen of the Esophagus" Sonya Thomas—would get announced by George in inventive ways. He'd introduce a contestant as "The David Blaine of the bowel, the Evel Knievel of the alimentary canal, the Houdini of Cuisini…Crazy Legs Conti!" We watched him present "the Salvador Dalí of the deli," "the David Bowie of the bagel," "the Liberace of the lunch line." Some of these master eaters were a quarter of the size of Big Jim and we'd watch them lube up slimy Nathan's natural casing wieners in water and when the buzzer went off and the crowd was in a frenzy, they'd slip those suckers down their gullets at lightning speed. These incredible athletes would put a pelican to shame. It was a thing of great fucking beauty.

You are watching their extinction.

There would be no more hot dog–eating contests or NASCAR or picnics in the park or Cheetos® or *America's Funniest Home Videos* or revving truck engines or books or children laughing or fetch with a stick or iPhone updates or shopping or electrical jobs or songs or genius inventions or drunken dancing or Fireball whiskey or snow globes or wedding vows or ugly ties or Christmas hugs or...families. Family. And there would be no more Big Jim. I felt the aquarium tighten, the water level rise. I was collapsing...The octopus erupted into electric-blue spots and I focused on those, not on the terrible, terrible thing I had heard.

One thing was certain. I wasn't going to tell Dennis about this. It would kill him and I'd made it my mission to keep him alive.

"I'm sorry," I told Onida. "I don't usually have this little control over my bodily functions. I feel..." I thought of Dennis and his dark depression.

"Where I come from we call what you're feeling The Black Tide. It will pass. Tides, by their nature, come and go." As the octopus spoke, I felt my blood flow slowing. He gingerly ran his suckers across the rock as if to taste it.

I said, "What if there is something that can change them back?"

"It is not known."

"Or, or what happens if they just stay in that state of sickness?

Just wander around really gross but still alive?" I bargained with The One Searched For.

"The part that made them human has flown away, Crow. What is left is a broken shell. Uninhabitable. A crab must always find a new home. Mankind will now destroy itself until there is nothing left. They exterminated the most real part of themselves first and now their complete physical disappearance is prolonged and inevitable." I flashed on the fleshy, pulsing lump Dennis and I had seen. *My god.* It was a sick MoFo, in its last stage on earth. Facing the last stand before extinction. "It is balance. It is how life gets back what was taken. The humans are dying, Crow, which means a part of you must die too."

"STOP CALLING ME CROW!"

Onida erupted into a light show, electric blues and neon flares swam across his skin, his arms rippling with emotion, a gorgeous and deeply disturbing dance. Something about this display slowed my pulse.

"You must reconcile with yourself, Crow. Your life depends on it."

"What the hell does that even mean?" I scraped at the tank with my foot. "I'm sorry. I don't mean to be rude, it's just…a lot. You don't know how hard it's been since Big Jim got sick…inside," I told the giant Pacific octopus, a creature I never imagined to see in three dimensions (unless Big Jim won the lottery and bought an IMAX theater like he'd always planned).

Onida lifted an arm, balancing on his two suctioned legs and five other arms. His movement was mesmerizingly fluid, otherworldly. The raised arm was severed three-quarters of the way down, tinged with blue blood. "Never presume to know the journey of another, friend," he said. I bowed to him, a sign of respect in crow I'd never, ever performed before. I have no idea where that shit came from.

"But how did this happen? How did the sickness start? There must be—"

"It doesn't matter, does it? This is what is. This is a New World, self-regulation in play. It is not my answer to give to you. What matters is that you have a choice, Crow. Your kind need your help."

"You said I can't help them—"

"The domestics. They are the others who straddle both worlds, other birds, dogs, turtles, cows, goats, sheep, snakes, rabbits—and yes, even cats. The domestics are the last of your kind, and they will be the very last of mankind's legacy. Buildings are crumbling, paper is disintegrating, mold and bacteria are quiet conquerors, and the soil is claiming back what is hers. The forces of The Whole have been contained and controlled for too long, and when those who break free from their cages do so they will not do it quietly. Humankind's stories in paint and ink and machine and structures that reach for the sun, they will all go. What is left is you. Millions of domestics have died, but there are still many, many more, stuck and abandoned and looking for a savior. Growth and evolution depend on our changing relationship to the beings around us. If you want to help mankind, this is what you must do. It is your choice, Crow."

"Domestics?" I puzzled over the idea while simultaneously noticing how enjoyable it was to converse with someone who didn't have the brain of a chicken nugget. I was finally—perhaps for the first time in my life—being heard. I let myself ponder the concept before saying, "You know so much, Onida."

"I have nine brains—which never stop growing—three hearts, and I can regenerate my arms; but mostly, it's because I'm female." Female. Well, shit. Admittedly, I had limited knowledge of them, but they had always seemed omniscient and formidable to me.

An erect blade cut through the water below, fast and determined. It was the color of a sky pregnant with a deadly storm. A fin. Onida's arms and legs twisted and coiled on themselves, one squeezing tightly as if to crush a quarter in its clutch. A tight shiver rippled through her muscular mass.

"What are you going to do now?" I asked Onida, beak pointed at the water.

"I'm going to eat and then I'm going to leave. You should get going, Crow. You have choices to make."

I kept a beady eye on the fin as it circled around the tank on which I was perched, Shark Week flashbacks blinding me. "And after that? What's next for you, Onida?" I asked in a flat tone, weary and stunned from all I'd heard. I had other questions but they wouldn't form, stuck and gluey in my head.

"I'm going to return to the ocean, mate, and die," she said, pride swimming through her words. I stared at the wonder of her, this fluid miracle, free from the burden of bones. Her arms undulated with excitement, dipping into the molasses-dark water. A mystic about to prey on the most feared aquatic predator, ocean's sharp-toothed bullet.

"That sounds fucking terrible!" I squawked, imagining a many-limbed snuff film.

"Everyone has a journey, Crow. More than just the one." And I think she winked at me with a black smile.

CHAPTER 10

‹❦›

S.T.

OUTSIDE SEATTLE AQUARIUM, SEATTLE,
WASHINGTON, USA

Since it was relatively quiet around this section of Alaskan Way and darkness was spreading its velvety wings, unimpeded by a single streetlamp or headlight, I rode Dennis under the Alaskan Way Viaduct and found a spot that looked like it had been a camp for a homeless MoFo. Big Jim and I knew a lot of homeless MoFos from our various adventures together and we gave them dirty dollar bills and Fireball whiskey. Big Jim said they served their fucking country and in return got told they were trash, and they must have believed it because they were always ferreting through the dumpsters. It wasn't a perfect shelter, but with the vines and English ivy hanging down in limp sheets from the enormous concrete structure, it would do us for a night. Dennis even used his unparalleled snuffer to track down a bag of Fritos ingeniously stashed in a removable concrete block, which he pawed loose. We shared them in the blackness, though I confiscated the accompanying small bag of heroin—Dennis still wasn't tremendously stable. Minutes later, Dennis was doing his ritualistic series of pirouettes and coiling himself into a tidy ball on a pile of wool blankets. I watched him closely from my perch as he snored gently, his fawn body rising up and down, wondering how he could get to sleep so well without the rumble of a TV. His wound looked a hell of a lot better—scabbing had started—but he certainly wouldn't be winning Best in Show anytime soon.

I suddenly thought of the only other non-MoFo I was able to stomach being around. Ghubari was an African gray, a bird who could count and do perfect impressions and articulate a dictionary of MoFo words. A creature whose crackling genius so closely aligned with his MoFo owner's, he filled me with envy. I ruffled my feathers, shaking off the thought of Rohan, Ghubari's kind MoFo who had taught Big Jim how to take care of me when I was a leaf-skinned nestling with cornflower-blue eyes and a sugar-pink mouth. Back when I believed tiny MoFos lived in traffic lights and clouds were flying cotton. I didn't dare imagine what had happened to the African gray and his owner after Ghubari had sent me the *Aura* message to stay inside my house. I just couldn't swallow any more sad thoughts.

Dennis started to dream through snorts and thin whistles and a kick that whipped off his starchy blanket. I dropped down and gingerly covered him. I studied Dennis's breath and its vibrant clouds in hopes that he dreamt of better days. Perhaps of when we'd play chase around the Green Mountain sugar maple in the yard, a rambunctious game of tag where I'd pull his tail and he'd lope after me with a goofy smile, wrinkles lagging behind him. Big Jim watched over our frolicking, calling us a couple of "goobers" and even the Green Mountain sugar maple and the Crocosmias would shake with laughter. I missed the Green Mountain and its sweet voice, and how it erupted into the colors of a Caribbean cocktail come fall. I missed *our* tree in *our* home, how it would bleed sap when it recalled memories too painful to share because it knew that holding things in is toxic. I hoped Dennis was dreaming of those days. I lulled myself by reliving those moments, feeling the kiss of dandelion cotton on my wings as I tagged Dennis— *you're it!*—and falling asleep to the sugary tones of the Green Mountain saying, "Renaissance...renaissance."

I woke before Dennis, breathlessly watching the sun rise and baptize the skyline in buttery tones. What an act of beauty, of unwavering faith, something to look forward to each and every day. Big Jim always said that nothing worth a shit pile happens before nine a.m., but still, I wish I could have shown him this. As beautiful as the sunrise was, my heart was a boulder in my chest that would make it hard to fly. All the winged, even fungus gnats, know that you cannot fly if you're carrying too much weight with you. It's a well-known adage, actually: "The light of heart is free to fly." Woodpeckers inscribe it into a lot of trees, those vandalizing assholes.

I missed the sounds of Seattle, the percussive rhythm of people. The clicking of heels, the throttle of an engine, the throb of a subwoofer, the siren song of an ice cream truck, the babble of caffeinated conversation, how I had to cock my head to digest a different accent, and boy did I miss the invigorating *chuck-a-chuck-a-chuck-a* of a chopper tracking down a sneaky MoFo. Lawnmower and motorbike and Beyoncé, oh my. I missed tidy, fresh-cut grass. All this long, tangled turf and greedy green devouring buildings made me nervous and also made an excellent case for the Homeowners Association's strident rules. Moss, especially the Spanish kind, is a deadly conquistador, dampening the sounds and edges of the city right before my eyes. MoFos kept a tight order to things, the world cupped in their hand, squeezing when necessary. I thought of the Green Mountain again, about how Big Jim had to trim it yearly to stop it from taking over the yard and so one day it didn't "fucking fall over and crush our house like a can of Coors Light." Our house belonged to Green Mountain now. Maybe that wasn't so bad. Maybe Green Mountain deserved it the most.

Though Seattle had lost its beat, it had gained song. A charm of finches called out on *Aura*, speaking of a pending meeting at a swimming pool in Bellevue for communal bathing and where "The One Who Spits" was, with a warning to avoid him. A white-crowned sparrow squatted on the viaduct ledge brazenly close to me, a bossy little so-and-so, you know the type. He belted out a lively ditty about believing in one's self—which he obviously had zero issues with—the air cool enough to see the notes dancing from his songbird throat. That monumental showoff. Psssh, singers, am I right? Satisfied he'd shown me up, he darted off, and then a creature I couldn't identify bellowed and it sounded like *how how how how* and *Aura* fell silent. I used the time to do some anting (a sort of manscaping I perform by rubbing pulverized ants all over my feathers to make them shiny and, ironically, keep insects off me).

As I waited for Rip Van Wrinkles to awake, I thought about the other Dennises out there. How many more of him were there, creatures who'd been loyal and good to the MoFos? Creatures who depended on them for water and love and Milk-Bones? Creatures who, like me, hadn't been born in the wild and didn't know the Law Of Life? Creatures with scales or bristles or down, slobbering tongues, good hearts, gentle souls, and soft mouths. Creatures who knew the magic of MoFos, what they give us in protection and affection, what it means to love them with all of your heart and nose and beak. The feeling of those funny bald fingers that can open books and cans of refried beans gently sliding down your back. MoFo is family. Onida was brilliant, the oracle of the ocean, but I couldn't believe everything she said. I couldn't believe in my heart that there were no MoFos out there, that some hadn't hunkered down somewhere and kept their necks straight. I had hope, and feathereds know that hope is the very thing that allows one to fly. I thought of the dirty minivan on I-5 South with the superhero family decal on it; that's what it was all about, being together and saving the world. When MoFos and the furred and feathered worked together it was beautiful and unstoppable. It is what nature intended.

I was thrilled when Dennis woke up; turns out it's very dangerous to be left alone with your mind. And without Seattle's beatbox, I was really hearing mine. Dennis was less thrilled. He leapt to his feet, hairs bristling up the ridge of his back. He sniffed at the sun and back down to the ground, pivoting and shifting his weight. A rumble released from his throat.

Something was wrong.

I didn't have time to ask him what. Before I could shake off the remaining ant carcasses, I saw the cause of his anguish. They emerged from a multi-layered parking structure, trotting toward the viaduct—toward us. I launched high to get a better look. I counted eight of them, which is lucky, since I can only count to nine. I didn't like how all their weight was forward, tails and ears standing to attention, as they cautiously neared us. To them, Dennis was guilty until proven innocent.

The pack encroached, blatantly disrespecting the boundaries of territory and personal space. Bringing up the rear: some sort of mutt, rangy as a setter with oil-slick fur and a long-legged white mongrel, mud caked and mischievous. A black and white dog with border collie and battery acid in him slunk in front of them, his nose intermittently tightening into a snarl. A terrier and a brown-white pointer padded in front of them, tailing identical brindle dogs and one very large, sinister fleabag that resembled an African social weaver's nest. In front, a German shepherd mix skulked forward; a gray scar swam angrily down his muzzle, and next to him, the muscle: a rust-colored chow, blue tongue hanging like a dead lizard. Oh shit, I think that might be ten or thirteen; I told you my counting sucks.

I started to panic—I could tell because I was bouncing in place, perched high on the viaduct. Dennis stood his ground, guarding his only possessions in this New World—the mass of smelly blankets and an empty packet of Fritos. I launched into the air, scanning my eye view. Escape. I had to find an escape route in case this interaction went south. The MoFos at Pike Place weren't far off, and I couldn't risk luring Dennis toward them, so I had to figure out something better. A bevy of black-tailed deer caught my eye, grazing on a thicket of brambles below. To the gentle grazing, that's where we'd head. I lowered and got the shock of a lifetime.

"This isn't your territory." Wait, what? The German shepherd was so articulate, so eloquent.

"That's mine," the chow gestured to the urine-soaked blanket.

I stared, slack-beaked, at Dennis. Nothing. So, I did a quick check all around me, almost blown out of the sky by the cosmic skullduggery I was experiencing. Of all the dogs in all of this supposedly round ball the size of, like, a thousand Seattles, I got stuck with the only one who speaks almost entirely through body language? The Tarzan of the canine world? You've got to be fucking kidding me. This, and we were about to initiate World War III over the planet's shittiest blanket? Dennis's lack of response and general staring in a bowlegged provocative stance incited a symphony of growls. Not good. Not good at all.

The chow and shepherd inched forward.

"Hey there, fellas," I said to the encroaching canines. "Let's be civil about this, alright? Let's talk about this man to man."

"He has my blanket," said the shepherd, flashing milk-white fangs.

"I'm confused," I said. "Is this your malodorous blanket? Or the chow's?" The shepherd's bark could cut through skulls. He snarled a final warning.

"Alright, alright," I said. "How about we give you the blanket and get on our way here. No harm done, right?"

Dennis showed no indication of moving away from the blanket. Have I mentioned that hounds are stubborn?

"Give. Me. The blanket," came a rumble from the chow.

"Dennis, you heard him. Step aside," I said with a shake in my voice. Dennis didn't budge. He just stood there like a witless wonder, but I knew he knew exactly what was going on, and he just wasn't about to relinquish a rag that was so plentifully bestrewn with mildew and smelled like French cheese.

"Listen, you guys, how about we talk about what's been happening in the world? We can work together; imagine how strong we'd be! How long have you been out here as a pack? Did you guys have owners? You there, Shaggy, I see you have a collar. What's your story?" I was stalling.

"You are weak, dog," said the chow to Dennis. "Remove yourself from the idiot bird's command."

"Idiot?" I asked. "Seriously? Are we—never mind. If you all could just back up a little and give Dennis some space, then I'm sure he'll gladly give you—"

"You are doomed," spat the chow with a flash of tongue, dark purple in the shadow of fangs. "You are nothing without a pack. You will die because of this black bird."

The pack inched forward. Muzzles lowered. Dennis released a string of drool. I had to do something before they ripped him to shreds. The collie's nose wrinkled. A blue tongue retreated behind white canines and that was enough for me. I plummeted beakfirst like a Supermarine Spitfire. I mobbed those fuckers. I dove at the chow first, snatching a beakful of his fluff and spitting it out midair as I shot at the shepherd. The muzzle with its gray scar swiped my side as I snatched his tail and pulled hard. The dogs lunged, the pack circling me. I shot upward to safety, with loud cries of "Liberty or death!" I careened back down toward the giant shaggy nest-monster and body checked him, coming in feetfirst and bouncing off the collie, who was a hurricane of black and white—fang and fur and fury. I was Bruce Lee of the fucking sky, wings and feet and lightning, but the pack wised up fast. The collie, setter, white mongrel, and the brindles all snapped at me, lunging in the air. The terrier was feisty but too short to catch the black bolt of badassery darting above. But now my pokes and jabs and fur-snatching were no longer keeping the real threats— the chow, the shepherd, the pointer, and the shaggy a-hole— from slinking toward Dennis.

I had to lure him away. I was just opening up my throat, preparing to call Dennis, when he bolted. Dennis shot down the underside of the viaduct, dodging cars and shopping carts, dead rats, blood stains, and the twisted fingers of brambles, racing past the Highway 99 Blues Club and Seattle Antiques Market, with me flapping hard to keep up with the pack hot on his heels. He burst from the viaduct and onto Alaskan Way, nails clicking as he ran, ears like wings in a blizzard, passing Ivar's Acres of Clams and the Seattle Fire Station 5, veering into the open-air parking lot of the Seattle Ferry Terminal. He weaved in and out of Chryslers and Lexuses and Corollas—all of it too fast for me to stop him.

The dogs all skidded to a halt. I treaded the air, flapping my anxiety. What was happening?

Next to the gargantuan wheels of a semitruck whose head was buried deep inside the tollbooth it had smashed into, was a white dog with beige patches. An American pit bull terrier. She cowered next to the wheel, pink nose lowered, her hind leg quivering, which made the pink collar around her neck tinkle out a haunted jingle. Her tail was hidden, tightly tucked between the pink skin of her jittery legs. And though she was entirely not my flavor or species, she was a very nice-looking specimen who happened to be in the throes of heat. The pack dropped their beef with Dennis and started that well-rehearsed skulk toward the delicate white canine who licked her lips on loop, eyes flicking back and forth. Terror filled her soft hazel eyes before those trembling legs shot her away from the truck and down the empty freeway, disappearing farther into a precarious future. The pack thundered after her. Sinister barks echoed.

Exhausted, I slumped onto the top of a butterfly bush that erupted from the cracked pavement, peering down at Dennis. He flopped onto an exposed slab of warm tarmac, panting. I hopped down next to him to inspect his condition.

He seemed fine, that resilient fucker. I felt relief that we both were still sucking in air. This half-mute murder would see another sunrise. And then came the anger. A jolting, acerbic anger that made blood rise to my head, pumping a furious baseline. That feral pack of dogs were probably at one point beloved companions. Well-fed friends. And here they were, reduced to thuggery, no better than a gaze of ruffian raccoons. Common thieves, bullies, scoundrels. Is this how we pay homage to our MoFos? To the ones who taught us how to be in the world? How to live our best lives and be as comfortable as possible at all times? I felt for the poor, pretty little American pit bull terrier, who had a name and had probably been waiting all this time for her MoFo to find her. And now, we all knew what would happen to her—I'd seen it go down in a few of Big Jim's more populated pornos. I felt a powerful pang of relief that I wasn't female. It seemed that being female meant to be prey, even among your own species.

All of it made me think of Dennis's testicles. Whoa, jeez, not like that. You see, when Dennis was young and basically an ottoman of folds, Big Jim went to the vet, complaining about the amount of action his right leg was getting. The vet advised Big Jim to have Dennis neutered. Big Jim kicked up a calamitous fuss about this, declaring it an assault on all manhood. He punched a feline leukemia pamphlet display onto the vet's shiny floor and stormed out. A week later, leg swaddled in vulcanized rubber fishing pants, he returned and ordered Dennis's huevos be ranchero-ed. All this time, I had thought it a bit barbaric and felt vindicated in not having dangly bits. But here we were, breathing, murder intact because of this decision. Clever, forward-thinking MoFos. Because he's modified and civilized, Dennis wouldn't desert me to chase some tail.

Enough was enough. Onida was right. I wasn't going to sit here and do nothing while the domestics rotted away or turned into a bunch of brutish buttholes. MoFos made laws against this sort of behavior for a reason. I was going to step up and do the MoFo thing. Take responsibility and bring peace to a world that was falling apart without them. We were losing what makes us human, losing the very best part of us. Even if what Onida said was right, that the part that makes the MoFos human has flown away, well then, what made me human was here to roost. I would not watch the spirit of a species wither and die. I was going to take back the world and restore it to its glistening glory and take a stand against the bears and the sick MoFos and the wild dog packs. I was going to find my allies—the domestics—and give them back the world they knew.

But first, lunch. Dennis and I raided the Subway at the ferry terminal, the building gauzed in the castles of spiders who cherished its cool shade. We found the windows busted, the cockroaches celebrating, and the bread to be suspiciously well preserved for its age. Dennis carried two loaves for us to enjoy, dragging them over to the water's edge. I dunked my portion in the water for an easy swallow and a touch of seasoning. We took in the view. A yellow crane lay still like a fallen giraffe, its neck broken and shattered. We admired Bainbridge Island across the water, a bouquet of trees guarded by the icing-caps of the Olympic Mountains. We turned our heads right to see the Seattle Great Wheel, our city's Ferris wheel, alive with MoFos, their twisted heads and spidery hands bent wrong at the joints, shimmying and swinging. The wheel used to be white. Now it was tainted by crawling cadaverous bodies and their red slime, their violent endings. Safe at this distance, we tuned them out to enjoy the quiet view of Elliott Bay.

There we were, a bear-mauled bloodhound and a crow covered in ant carcasses—not my best look—alive against all odds. We chowed down on Subway while watching a ferry, a creature of the utmost breathtaking beauty, her bold body a testament to the magic of MoFos. The ferry, a powerful and indefatigable swimmer, was winter white with rims of forest green. She was called MV *Wenatchee* and she was a beauty, even as the water roiled and bubbled around her, sucking her down, down, down. Even as she groaned under the pressure and beautiful parts of her snapped and cracked. I bowed to Lady Wenatchee, silently thanking her for her service. MoFos with sanguinary eyes and vacuous glares were clubbing their heads on her inside windows as her whole body, noble nose taking its last inhale, was swallowed by Elliott Bay.

I said goodbye, digesting bread and big plans, my heart throbbing with purpose.

CHAPTER 11

❧

THE ARCTIC CIRCLE, GREENLAND
(MEDITATIONS OF A POLAR BEAR)

The ice is shrinking. My body follows its suggestion. These are not the bergs of my cub season. The Ice Kingdom is a mere shadow of what it once was. Now there is eerie silence and the drip, drip, dripping of ice as it sheds its tears.

With every breath, I call your name. *Tornassuk. Tornassuk.* I have scoured miles of the great white plains to find you, wondering if I am the last of The Ice Bears. It happened so fast. I called you to watch me hunt. My eyes were on the seal, glinting skin slick and thick. I could feel its oils, warm and rich in the stomach, a break from desperate pickings—rodent and berry and garbage. And then you were gone. Perhaps the waves took you, their appetite evolving from sea ice. We are all starving.

And now I swim, days-long stretches between sheets of ice and I call for you. I swim until my bones drip, drip, drip. I am Seal's Dread, The Huntress Of The Floe, The Last Of The Ice Bears. What is a mother without her cub? I will paint the snow with my paws and tear apart glaciers to find you. There is no earthly law that can stop me.

CHAPTER 12

Guided by my instincts, Dennis and I started to trek south, and all the while I called out, waiting for a response. I wasn't getting a strong enough signal. *Aura* was silent. Where was the sprightly song of bird and tree, the voices that keep *Aura* alive? What had hushed the network? Instinct spoke to me through electric tingles that scurried across my skin. *A predator can silence Aura.* I didn't allow myself to dwell on what kind. We plodded on, eyes in the sky and a nose on the ground, hunting for movement, attempting to keep one step ahead of the danger we knew would come. Our goal? Keep moving until we made contact on *Aura.* Using my sharp MoFo reasoning, I'd devised a plan, but only *Aura* could help me carry it out.

We followed the Alaskan Way Viaduct south, shaded by the corpse of the 99—a dead freeway (not to be confused with I-5 South, The Freeway Of Death). We heard odd sounds, that savage, supersonic call again—*how how how how*—bouncing off the concrete jungle. The area had a cold, industrial feel. There were pockets of construction, now abandoned, with bright orange warning signs standing guard like ghostly relics: "BE PREPARED TO STOP." "DETOUR." "MEN WORKING." The forsaken district was full of corners and buildings for things to hide in, and dammit, I was on edge in this steely labyrinth of heebie-jeebies. When we reached King Street, I tried again, calling out to *Aura*. A question burned in my chest. And someone on *Aura* had the answer.

"Hello? Can anyone hear me?" The Lego-maze of steel and brick and metal stared down silently. I could tell we weren't welcome here, didn't belong. Why were there no birds around? London planes are tough, urban trees that tell their stories over the drone of streaking cars and sound like they've been smoking their whole lives. Because they have. Dennis lifted up his black truffle of a nose at grizzled trunks. Their camouflage colors rose to a sulking sky. His droopy eyes scanned their mysterious, shaggy crowns. A nervous whine escaped him. I gasped. The London planes were pointing with their branches. Pointing north. Three of the trees made a "husssshhh" noise.

"Go back!" one of them urged.

"Holy doughnuts! Why?" I asked, but didn't get an answer. "Are you really talking to us? Me and Dennis?" Trees are taciturn; you can't force them to do or say anything. Their idea of time is different from that of other beings; their philosophy is to exist in a steady and deliberate manner, slow as sap, as the spreading of roots. They don't rush anything, unfortunately for me.

"But we've just been there!" I told them. "I can't go back! I'm sorry! We have to find the birds to connect to all of *Aura* and they aren't back that way, for fuck's sake!" They didn't respond, just hushed and continued to point.

Dennis stuck his nose in a mound of garbage, found half a

tennis ball—a chunk of our old life—and lit up like a Christ-mas tree, bounding around and shaking it with his slobbering melon.

"Ssssshhhhhh!" I hissed at him. "Simmer down, Dennis!" His exuberant joy felt dangerous here, blatant as the Bat-Signal. But Dennis was on cloud nine, might as well have found Cheetos® headquarters or the MoFo cure. Convinced I was going to have an embolism, I confiscated the slimy half-ball. Dennis whined, but then conceded.

"Dennis, we're living in a different world now; this whole situation is a total soup-sandwich, and I'm not willing to die over half a tennis ball!" I said in a hushed tone. As usual, Dennis took the disappointment pretty well—he's sort of af-fable that way. I still expected he'd give it one last try, attempt to engage in a game of keep-away, chasing me down for what was left of that shitty ball in that ridiculous seizure-inducing yellow, but then his nose caught on to a new scent.

Dennis stood erect, staring with his nose so finely tuned I imagine he was smelling in pictures. *Oh no, not again.* His snuffer was doggedly fixed, pointing ahead. I followed its aim, down the stretch of King Street's smoky asphalt to a clock tower. The giant clock hands, stagnant and lifeless, appeared to have given up without the MoFos' souls. I understood. As we pressed on, Dennis's body posture changed again, his trundle morph-ing into a careful trot. We were nearing whatever he smelled. The trees we passed were pointing back the way we came.

"The other way!" they hissed.

Dennis suddenly startled at a cluster of eyes that material-ized next to him. I squawked in shock. MoFos, heads swaying, stretching out their rotting limbs, were inside what looked to have once been an oyster house. The glass windows were, of course, shattered and gaping, but metal bars had been erected to keep the MoFos in. Or something out. Dennis quickened his pace to pass them, maintaining his focus on the unconscious clock tower ahead. I looked at the writhing mass of MoFos—trapped birds in a cage—trying to make sense of the senseless. The sidewalk in front of the abandoned eatery was marked with green spray paint in hasty handwriting: "Never Enter, Never Release Them." A severed arm, slim and fish-white, lay near the locked gold entrance doors and a dusty happy hour sign. Its bluish wrist held a bracelet of bright emeralds captive. The fingernails, polished purple, clasped a napkin with a crude, hysterically written message scrawled across it: "Tell Peter John Stein I love him. Tell him but DO NOT USE YOUR PHONE." I looked at the bar's sign and lowered my head. There would be no more happy hours.

There was nothing on the stretch of King Street to the clock tower but deserted bikes, cars, buses, smashed storefronts, and an uneasiness that made my beak chatter. The concrete fought with flora that burst from its body, green vines taking their sweet time with the conquest. I didn't like the silence one bit. *Aura* was still off, no signal. A dead zone.

We approached the clock tower with reverence and quaking legs. The only movement was a sign below the clockface, hanging by its last corner and swinging gently. It said, "Amtrak." And then I remembered, yes, King Street Station, where Big Jim had picked up Tiffany S. from Tinder and she'd said, "Wow, you're a lot fatter than in your pictures." Dennis started pacing again. He was making it pretty clear that we should leave, his zigs and zags painting an ominous tableau. We had found his smell.

Then the real crux of the problem reared its molting head again: the part of me that is crow. I *had* to look inside, had to know what had happened in the station where MoFos had built an incredible machine that moved like a bullet and cut through the countryside like a flaming arrow. A train that went to Edmonds by the water—a place with salted caramel ice cream and art made with hands and a bookstore that smells like woodland mushrooms—and to Canada, a place where Big Jim said we should never go because their bacon is overhyped bullshit.

Dennis whined—a high-pitched plea to stop me from barging ahead in typical, valiant, S.T. fashion. I gave him a sharp nod of reassurance, hopped up to one of the doors, and flapped through the missing glass. I perched on an ornate brass light fixture. King Street Station had retained much of the beauty in its bones: its carved, coffered ceiling, the shine of marble walls, the wood benches for MoFos to sit on and wait for the train's shriek. But there were some notable differences since I was last here, meeting Tiffany S. from Tinder. For starters, there was what was left of a MoFo—a torso in a fluorescent yellow and orange jacket—squirming on the ground next to the Tickets and Information counter like a halved worm. The smell of recent death and fear pheromones dangled in the air, heavy as ripe fruit, and I quickly realized that the place was speckled with bones. A femur. A mandible. A smaller other leg bone—admittedly, my anatomy identification could use some work. A sticky meat-log with legs lay near a discarded back-pack. I gasped at the grisly scene. It had been some sort of small animal, perhaps a dog, dachshund maybe, now denuded of its fur and skin. A fresh blood trail smeared itself across the length of the enormous lobby, defiling its large mosaic compass. The crow part of me just couldn't resist, couldn't let it go, couldn't heed Dennis's warning, and I fluttered from one light fixture to another to get a closer look at whose bright, freshly freed blood it was. I could make out a black body on its side. The smearing blood trail stopped underneath it. I dropped down to a bench next to the black body in order to get a closer look.

The gorilla lay like a cheese curl, and I could see that most of its back was missing. A deep gurgle released from it, making me jump, and I saw its chest rise—a Herculean effort. I hopped closer, mesmerized by the deeply lined skin of its face, a gentle map, a bright round moon with pleasing features and lips that could form words and convey a library of expressions. Its bulging brow held history, lessons learned, pockets of sorrow. Its wrinkles told me stories; the white chin whiskers conjured a memory of the spiced, woodsy scent of shaving cream. A fire roared inside me—the urge to preen its sparsely fine fur. I fell deeply in love with its twitching hands, so beautiful and complex, with the wondrous joints and smooth spongy skin of a MoFo, briefly coiling as if to catch a thought, an idea, or to grip the whole world. The heartbreaking wonder of fingers. Then the gorilla opened its eyes, eyes that knew a lot of things I wanted to, eyes the limpid color of Fireball whiskey. Those eyes registered me, reflecting back the clear image of an inky bird, a plucky, twig-legged investigator I didn't recognize, didn't connect with. The bird looked at me, darting and dauntless with shrewd swagger. So fingerless and feathered. I felt the sudden suffocation of shame.

The gorilla sighed and I watched the vital spark in its eyes take flight. It entered me, I felt it take up residence in my heart. The gorilla—a female, I was sure of it—exhaled for the last time, her bluish, rubbery hand relaxed, body unclenching to send her soul airborne. An upward adventure.

I caught my breath and came back to earth. Wake up, S.T. Something had mauled the gorilla, and another glance around the station made one thing clear: this was that something's den. It wasn't far away and it wouldn't be gone for long. A trail of prints, perfectly captured in bright red blood on shiny marble, led away from the gorilla's fetal form and across the lobby floor. Big, bad prints that spoke to me in a particularly emphatic way, mainly saying, "Fuck off."

I rose into the air and dove through the station, slipping through a glassless window and arrowing down to Dennis, whose tail erupted into air-lashings as soon as he saw me. We bolted away from the station. Dennis's paws pounded the pavement, my wings set the wind free, and I cawed out to *Aura* for help, calling a name I'd heard before in *Aura*'s song and sigh, while scanning for biting things below. Sadness tugged at my tail feathers. I would have liked to have talked to the gorilla, learned its secrets and stories and how it ended up in a train station in downtown Seattle missing the flesh around its spine. I hoped my presence had at least provided a little comfort, because it had done absolutely fuck all to dispel our stereotype as the harbingers of death.

Minutes later, we found ourselves at the mecca of Seattle sports fandom, a fishbowl of Emerald City hope: CenturyLink Field. Strange sounds echoed from its deep chasm. I called out. No birds responded, so I told Dennis to lie down under another London plane tree, three of her branches vehemently pointing north. "Go back!" she rumbled.

"We can't! *Aura* is this way, I can *feel* it in my feathers!"

The London plane was near a blue trash can with the Seahawks emblem blazoned on the side. I was comforted by its familiar Pacific Northwest Coast tribal design, said to be inspired by a Kwakwaka'wakw mask. Kwakwaka'wakw is my favorite word because it is easy for me to pronounce. A damn sight easier than "rural brewery." A nap under the London planes would give Dennis a chance to rest and recover, but leaving him to do recon was getting harder and harder. Any time he was out of my sight, I felt my blood quicken, and I had developed the nervous, derpy head-bob of a damned pigeon. It was just me and Dennis in this spiky New World, a tiny but impactful murder, and murders are not something you ever, ever turn your back on. Every time he disappeared into the tall, unruly grass to do his business, I'd hold my breath, unable to inhale until his stupid, hangdog countenance emerged and he did that weird moonwalk-grass-kicking ritual. This got pretty dangerous for me at times, considering how he peed in three-minute streams like a goddamned Clydesdale.

I shot up the side of CenturyLink Field and was hit by a dank, putrid smell as I hovered over its center, settling onto a metal edge of the stadium's roof. The scene was shocking. The sky frowned in dark clouds. Pigeons had painted the stadium's partial roof in corrosive white, which had mixed with the rains to form a hole-burning acid, but their empty nests lay soaked and abandoned. I wondered who or what had sent them flapping. The stadium had flooded, filled with a swampy, green soup. A chorus of frogs harmonized in pulsing bursts like Dennis's squeaker toys. Vines and creepers hung from the stadium's sides, greedily smothering the bleachers, where I saw rogue bones and lost limbs, an upturned cooler, a muddy sneaker, part of a ball cap. Weeds and muck and fungus and creaky-legged insects had invaded, and the smell of bat shit stung my beak. Rust was conquering the stadium's metallic structure, the suites collapsed and spilling brick guts onto the bleachers below. A decaying stench rose from the swampy soup, where MoFos in algae-slick numbered jerseys bobbed rhythmically in the watery depths. Two helmeted MoFos drifted close, then smashed their helmets together as if gripped by the cuckoo-for-Cocoa-Puffs hormones of rutting season. Another MoFo, mossy, muscled, and missing both a helmet and a head to protect, smacked its arms against the deep, wet murkiness. One with the number 31 on his back clawed up the bleachers, red eyes hunting. Number 16 sprung like a flea to climb the face of the field scoreboard. Jersey-ed bodies floated facedown. I squinted from a high distance, distinguishing the rutting players as "Wilson 3" and "Sherman 25." These were Seahawks fans. I bet they'd known they were sick and cureless. They had come here in their jerseys to await their fate. Their final choice. Loyal until the end. As a home-grown Seattleite, this caused a throbbing ache to hammer on the chambers of my Space Needle–shaped heart.

A single sign prevailed: *Home of the Twelves.* The twelfth man, meaning the Seahawks football fans, the symbolic twelfth player on the field, cheering from the sidelines, loud as a jet plane. The twelfth man, proud peacocks who flashed their blues and greens, had roared like animals and broken sound records and caused false starts and earthquakes and believed their way to Super Bowl victory. Big Jim and I watched every Seahawks game, squawking at the screen, decked in spirited blue and green garb. Nargatha knitted me a nifty Seahawks scarf that I was very proud of, even if Big Jim called me "nerd bird" when I was wearing it. Nargatha, whose family lived on the East Coast and sometimes forgot her because of New York minutes, often got lonely. She would come over during half-time and bring us a chicken pot pie while reminding Big Jim he needed to eat healthier. I liked how she would prod him in his belly, perhaps the only one who had access to his soft spot. And sometimes we would win and Big Jim would set off fireworks in the yard and Dennis would wet himself and I'd tell the college crows to suck it as they dove for cover because I was a fucking phoenix. Big Jim would have given his right arm to have played here with the other twelves. I was glad he couldn't see what had become of our beautiful, glorious stadium. Our team's loyal fans. One could only hope that in days past they had smelled better.

I suddenly realized that the croaking had stopped. Something had silenced the frogs. Something or someone, I wasn't sure. Concentric circles rippled from an origin point in the green and I watched and waited, breath hitched. A sly sliver of dark broke above the water's surface. *Please be another MoFo*, I hoped, tapping my toes in terror. The circles stopped forming, larger ones dissipating and dying out. Wilson 3 and Sherman 25 continued struggling in the water, smashing their helmets together, oblivious of the new silence. The palpable threat.

An eruption burst from the flood's surface, algae raining down. An enormous mass—a barrel of gray and pink—lunged and fell on top of the two players, jaws clamping down on Wilson 3. The splash sent debris flying, drenching the bleachers in putrid green rain. I cawed out, but what could I do to stop it? As the giant mammal shook Wilson 3 from side to side, my eyes widened. I recognized the rounded ears, the wide-set marble eyes, the girth of a rubber-skinned beast that took up most of the TV screen when it showed up on National Geographic.

A goddamned hippopotamus. I couldn't believe it, couldn't believe that any of this was anything but horrible, hideous Ambien-induced psychosis. How had he left the confines of his zoo habitat? A gorilla and now a hippopotamus? African animals roaming the city of Seattle? The cogs in my mind began to spin, ideas forming like clusters of clouds. A white streak of movement above me caught my eye, and I looked up to see a solitary gull cruising past. I launched into the air calling after him, "Hey, hey, hey!"

The gull turned his head midflight to register me. "What's up?"

"I'm trying to make contact and I can't hear anything," I told him, breathlessly. "I need to follow up on something I heard...I need to know—"

"*Aura* or *Echo*?" he asked, tangerine beak slicing through the air.

"*Aura!*" I shot back.

"Follow me!" screeched the gull in that water-skimming pitch of theirs as he flapped casually. He was a cool customer, seemingly undisturbed by the thrashing water, the bloody carnage below, the violent demolition by an African predator in a distinctly Northwestern football stadium. I flapped hard to catch up and decided not to look down anymore. I tried to shake panicky thoughts about the hippo—an herbivore, I was sure of it—behaving like an insatiable carnivore. It must have been eliminating any suspected threat or competition. Either that or it had made an exception to its vegetarian diet, which was altogether possible. Big Jim went on several Tinder dates with females who were vehemently vegan "except for bacon."

The gull flew over WaMu Theater and Safeco, where the Seattle Mariners play, but I didn't look down, couldn't look down. From the sounds that echoed from below, I knew the scene would be similar to the stadium and I just couldn't. I didn't need to see to know. I caught up to the gull as a direct result of my crow-curiosity disorder. "You said *Echo* too; where would you be taking me if I wanted to get information from *Echo*?"

"Depends on what you want to know." Here his chest filled with air, puffed proud, and for some utterly inexplicable reason, I felt calm. "The bay, the ocean, the sound, wherever you need. I can do it all, crow friend. I can relay current events straight from *Echo* too. That's what we do. Us, the terns, sandpipers, kingfishers, and cormorants, we are the connection between *Echo* and *Aura*. Bridge of sea and sky. It's a beautiful thing. Life, my friend, life is a beautiful thing."

"Oh, thank you, thank you," I muttered, grateful for the help, as unexpected as it was. I would never again refer to them as "schlubby beach pigeons."

What he said next roughly translates as, "It's cool, man. Everything's totally cool. You just keep on doing what you're meant to be doing. You are flying the good flight." Glaucous-winged gulls. Turns out they're unflappable.

He flew east from there and I followed, enjoying the contrails of calm that came off him. It gave me a quiet, panic-free moment to think about the realization I'd put together from my encounter with the gorilla and hippopotamus in the urban jungle of Seattle. How I now had a plan for Dennis and myself. Despite my new sense of composure, I couldn't let my guard down. I was grateful to the gull, but I still didn't trust other feathereds easily. They can be tricksters and bullies, and according to CNN, they might just slap you with a spot of avian flu.

The gull touched down in a park with a spectacular view of downtown Seattle, freeways snaking around its periphery like a twisted noose. I stared at the city's skyline. Oh, how I longed to hear the blare of an impatient car horn, the malignant symptoms of road rage. How I longed for the wail of a siren, the roar of an airplane, the tinny voice at a pedestrian cross-ing, "*Walk sign is on at all crossings!*" I'm sure at one point the park was very well preened with tidy flower beds and John Deere tracks. Now it was choking on an army of sharp-toothed brambles that smothered the land with their spiny talons. I spotted one patch of exposed grass, not as tall as the rest, and walked on it for nostalgia's sake. An earthworm rose from the soil, dramatically postulating about "the great change" and how "She will show no mercy as She takes back what is Hers and that it is time for the Great Coming, the inevitable hostile takeover of Her relentless hands." I ate him.

I hopped on top of a sign that said, "Dr. Jose Rizal Park." The glaucous-winged gull perched on the roof of the park's barbecue shelter. I examined his perfectly ivory plumage and the shock of gray on his wings—the pale gray of a misty morning. His eyes, bright and yolky, had a calming effect. I had largely ignored the very occasional gull that flew over our house, aside from hurling an artful insult, "Begone, pubic badger!" or a Creed CD case at them. It had seemed so easy to dismiss them as floating French fry receptacles. I wanted to ask him about *Echo*, about what it's like to hear the songs of the sea, how it feels to fly great distances. What does it taste like when you are so free you can follow the sun until it dips down into the ocean? But it was best to keep these wonderings to myself. Best to keep up barbed-wire boundaries and focus on looking after numero uno.

"Hmm. The trees are talking to you, never seen that. That's cool." The gull nodded his head vigorously. "Go ahead, call from here. Everyone will hear. It's all perfect." He was so mellow that my nictitating membranes licked my eyes lazily.

I cleared my throat and called out to *Aura*, speaking a name that had excited me since I'd first heard it whispered through the limbs of trees. "Hello! Excuse me! I'm looking for those who know of 'The One Who Opens Doors!'"

Aura erupted in chatter, songbirds singing, charms of finches relaying my message, a murmuration of starlings taking flight to spread my query. And within some amount of time that I can't be sure of because I still didn't really understand time and none of the clocks worked anymore, I got an answer.

CHAPTER 13

S.T.
DR. JOSE RIZAL PARK, SEATTLE,
WASHINGTON, USA

W ord got back quickly. The ones with information about The One Who Opens Doors were on their way to me. I was warned it would take them some time, which was fine because I was absorbed by an unusual sight. Seattle spring has more moods than Tiffany S. from Tinder, and now the sun decided that it should shine brightly. Celebrating the sun, the murmuration of starlings were performing a synchronized dance, dazzling with a shape-shifting air show. The birds swooped and dove, carefree, oscillating, and shimmery, the afternoon sun bouncing off their wings. All together, they formed a black cloud that morphed into a circle, then cinched in precisely at all the right places to render a Pringles tube and then a twisty shape like a pretzel. They were one, a single entity. Expand, contract, breathe, dance, be. They were performing for an audience of one—a baby elephant. The young elephant, its skinny grass snake of a tail flicking high in excitement, limp trunk swinging to and fro, darted across Twelfth Avenue in front of me. He stomped excitedly with soft, flat feet that resembled young tree trunks. His fanned-out leather earflaps, undulating furless butt, and wide, shiny eyes were utterly delightful. The baby pachyderm, eager eyes to the sky, chased the wave of birds, buoyantly mimicking their dance, delighting in the way they painted the afternoon. Through the tree crowns, a cautionary trumpet sounded out in an unmistakably parental tone. Ma, or some other family member, was nearby and I was glad. The game of chase went on and on and part of me hoped it would never stop.

I enjoyed the pleasantness of the moment, surprised to find myself giddy, as if full of beer bubbles that fizzed their way to freedom. A healthy, happy elephant calf—turns out that's something that can fill up a heart. I'd read in the *Seattle Times* that the Woodland Park Zoo had phased out its elephant sanctuary, that zoos in general were doing so because of the difficulty in providing an enriching environment. Space was an issue too; it was hard to provide enough of it for the healthy interaction of a whole herd. Yet here was this little one, no longer facing the threat of having his tusks lopped off to make a letter opener or that his lasting legacy might be a photograph of a smiling MoFo standing, rifle in hand, on his lifeless trophy. I imagine he had come all the way from Point Defiance Zoo & Aquarium in Tacoma, from miles and miles away. Now he had all the space of a whole new earth to dance around in. Gorilla, hippo, and now elephant, stamping Seattle soil with their prints. How had this come to be? This was a strange new realm with new rules that were hard to keep up with. I wished the little elephant well. MoFos revered elephants, and even in this little pipsqueak, I could see why. They are large and charming, confident and curious, and apparently, they never forget…

DENNIS! DENNIS! I left Dennis!

I spluttered a hasty thank you and goodbye to the glaucous-winged gull and splayed my wings for liftoff—destination CenturyLink, where I'd left one half of my murder outside a stadium stuffed with carnivorous MoFos, as well as the animal responsible for the most fatalities in the whole of Africa. Just then, the ones I was waiting for arrived. The dark-eyed junco got there first, landing on a nearby hawthorn branch. It hopped, catching its breath. The glaucous-winged gull assuredly took to the air and gave me a quick glance that, I swear, seemed as if he knew a secret that he was having trouble keeping.

I quickly called out to *Aura* to get news of my bloodhound partner, explaining exactly where I'd left him. A ruby-crowned kinglet beamed himself down from a higher branch and offered to see to it himself. I agreed somewhat reluctantly, watching him dart and vanish. Why was everyone suddenly being so helpful to the ostracized hybrid crow?

A small eruption of soil burst from the grass as a creature like a tiny Komatsu bulldozer with a penile nose and a hamster butt emerged. It had MoFo-like hands in the thin pink hue of a newly hatched bird. A mole. Or as Big Jim categorized them, "Yard Demolishing Fuck Trolls." Shortly after, an opossum wobbled into view at the base of the hawthorn, eggshell-white, prehensile tail coiling behind him. I stared at a dark-eyed junco, a plump black-headed bird, waiting for an explanation. The junco was full of sassafras—I could just tell by the way he bounced around, twitchy and convulsive. He made a deliberate smacking *tick-tick-tick* sound, one I suspected he also used to warn predators away from his nest.

"Are you here to tell me about The One Who Opens Doors?" I asked the junco.

He cocked his head an infuriating number of times. "Yup, yup, yup."

"And why are they here?" I asked, gesturing to the blinking mole and the pasty-faced opossum.

"Same reason he's here," said the opossum, yawning to expose a row of crooked needle-teeth. "The One Searched For sent word about you. You're the half-and-half bird with a porpoise—"

"Purpose, you common conehead!" cheeped the junco.

The opossum ignored him. "You're The One Who Keeps. We're here to answer whatever you need answering. Help wherever we can."

A swell of pride rose in me. When had anyone ever seen a mole, an opossum, and a junco meet up, apart from in an unsavory joke? I was beginning to think that there was some sort of actual camaraderie between furred and feathered that I had overlooked before. A sort of basic respect, a communal backscratching. The idea excited me.

He added, "Also, some crows told us if we didn't come, they'd pluck out our eyes." I chose to ignore the additional intel.

The mole shuffled around the patch of grass, sifting the soil with those pink hands. I wished they were a little larger so they could be of use. "What are you half-and-half of?" he asked, dick-nose waving in the air. The mole was funny with his little MoFo fingers. I had an undeniable urge to put a top hat on him.

"I'm just who I am," I told him with some urgency. *Dennis.* "Tell me what you know."

The mole and the junco started at the same time, interrupting one another. "I'll go first!" said the junco, head darting.

"No, me!" said the mole, shuffling in place.

"One at a time," I said, looking up to the sky for signs of the ruby-crowned kinglet. "Opossum, you go first." The dark-eyed junco muttered rapid-fire expletives. I'd already picked my favorite of the three. I'm not sure why everyone hates opossums so much; they may look like someone shaved the buttocks of a poodle and taught it to talk through its asshole, but they are generally pretty likable critters.

"HSSSSSSSSS," came the hideous warning the opossum spat at the junco. It was pretty unlikable. "Okay, Half-And-Half Bird, I'll tell you what my cousin told me. He saw The One Who Opens Doors, alright. You see, my cousin got in through the cat opening and was shuffling around this house where they had sweet black-and-white rounds in plastic—"

"Oreos. We should discuss their exact whereabouts at a later date. Tell me what he saw."

"My cousin heard the door shake, then he saw the silver handle turning and he panicked and died."

The junco spit out more unintelligible insults in a disbelieving manner. "He died figuratively?" I tried to clarify.

"No, like how I die when there's danger, I can just drop dead like this." He passed away in front of us, tongue hanging out. I'd seen a buttload of death lately and this was very convincing.

"What did The One Who Opens Doors look like?" I pressed him.

The opossum resurrected himself. "He can't say for sure due to being dead and everything. But, he sounded like this..." He made a kind of indeterminate whooshing noise. "And he said he smelled like old smells, like old grass and leaves and things. Like hay kind of. And also old stuff."

"YOU IDIOTS!" yelled the junco. "He didn't even see him! What use are you, you damned sea anemone!"

Everyone gasped. Obviously the junco was a little unstable, but this was some serious line crossing. Calling someone a sea anemone was harsh; sea anemone are the mob bosses of the ocean, venom harpooning their enemies and striking sticky deals with shifty types when it suits. Also, their mouths happen to be their anuses.

The mole, the opossum, and I rose above the name-calling.

"What about you, mole? What do you know about The One Who Opens Doors?"

The mole sat up and rubbed his pink fingers together. A monocle. He definitely needed a monocle. He talked slowly, as if his words were stuck in soil. "I'll tell you alls I know. See, this was a while ago, see, 'cause we dark-soil moles have been doing our Great Migration, see? Anyways, I'd tunneled my way through the soil, had a few worms to keep my energy up, and 'cause my wife says I have to keep regular too, sometimes I get gas—"

"MAKE YOUR POINT, YOU HAGFISH!" screeched the junco.

The opossum bared its needles again and I actually saw the mole's eyeballs. This junco was really riling everyone up. You don't hurl a hagfish comparison around willy-nilly; no one wants to be associated with a blind, toothless tube that gets its jollies entering any orifice of a corpse to consume it inside out while producing up to seventeen pints of mucus.

"Hey! Calm down right now, Junco!" I made it clear I didn't have time to waste. I had a Dennis to return to and the longer I was away from him, the harder it was to breathe. "What did you see, Mole?"

"Well, my eyesight's a bit shit, but yeah, yeah, I saws that he was very, very tall. And he moved in sweepy sweeping motions, and my thinking was that if I didn't gets back to my wife, she'd start whacking me again, so I dove back into The Other World—"

The Other World. Onida had spoken of it. "What's 'The Other World'?" I asked, instantly receiving horrified looks from the unlikely trio.

"The Other World, you know, *Web*," said the Mole. "Under the soil. Yous can't go there, but you must have heard about it?" When I didn't respond, his nose twitched fiercely, his hands raking the soil around him. "It's sort of like lots and lots of talking and good information. My wife always says—"

"Shut up, YOU MUSHROOM TIP!" screamed the junco. This was an epic interspecies insult because not only is that MoFo slang for the head of a johnson, but also, the part of the mushroom above ground—the part sold at Albertsons and sitting on your pizza—is actually its sexual organ. The sexual escapades of fungi are a multifarious rabbit hole that, thankfully, I had too much on my plate to ponder. The junco then spoke again, with reverence in his tart voice for the first time.

"The Other World is the underground. Where the truths come from. The intricate snaking of magical message pathways, a labyrinth of fungal threads that share knowings, teach us the ways. It is the communication hotbed of the underlings. It's made up of the real part of the forest, the roots, magical mycelium, red and yellow mineral horizons…it's the foundation of the forest, the Very Beginning. That's where trees really talk, where they share their legacy through the elements, whispering through water, negotiating in nitrogen, prophesying in phosphorus"—I'm sort of filling in parts here; it's very hard to simplify and translate—"sage, mystic maple—their wise carbon council is available to those who listen to the stillness. The Truths of our world are sourced directly from The Other World. It is known as *Web*. And it's all run—well, mostly everything on earth that we depend on is run—by The Mother Trees. You know about them at least, right?"

I shook my head.

"Oh, flaming filberts! The Mother Trees are the matriarchs, the connectors of the forest, the leaders of The Other World. We feathereds honor them with seed offerings. *Web* is denser and richer than *Aura* and *Echo* put together. Surely you know some of this? This is hatchling stuff."

The mole suddenly seemed a bit euphoric. "Under the soil is

like . . . magical . . . and that's how the trees truly talk, none of the aboveground whisperings that take so much of their energy. It's not their real language, see? That's why, if they're talking to you, yous better be listening, because they are making a mighty fine effort." He rubbed those delicious fingers together.

I knew *Aura* and *Echo*, but *Web*? What other entire worlds within the planet I've inhabited don't I know anything about? My corvid brain was spinning. "What did it look like? The One Who Opens Doors?" I asked.

"Probably grayish-black in color, maybe with a hint of green. There might have been some moss on him. Maybe. I'm not sure. I could definitely swear that I maybe, possibly saw some moss," said the mole.

The wind-up toy of a junco had had it, spasming into some sort of meltdown on the branch of a hawthorn. "You fig-brained morons!"

"STOP!" I cawed. "While you are bickering, there are animals that don't belong in this city—gorilla, hippo, elephant—running amok. Someone let them out of their enclosures, someone who can open doors and I intend to find that some-one. So, tell me what you know NOW."

"Yup, yup, yup." The junco resumed its nervous hopping. "It came down this way and I followed it. It can crawl and climb and goes wherever it wants to."

"Feathered?"

"No."

"Fur?"

"Some."

"Scales?"

"Um, I think sort of. Kind of . . . like a coconut? Yup, yup, yup." It was clear that Mensa wouldn't be calling for these three anytime soon, MoFo extinction notwithstanding. The junco continued: "It had red hair and wore a wrap." What he actually said translates as "wrap around the torso," or in other words, "a shirt."

The world tilted.

"What did you just say?" I asked.

"Red hair. Shirt."

"You saw a MoFo?" My heart was a horse galloping across the plains. The junco didn't understand. "It walked on two legs...it was a Hollow?" Adrenaline burned a hole in my chest.

"Yes. The One Who Opens Doors is a Hollow. Last I saw, he was heading to the zoo." (Small fact for you here: the rough translation of "zoo" in bird twitter is "creature quilt" because that's what it looks like from above, a blanket made up of species-separated enclosures.) The junco continued: "You should have let me speak first, I already put out a call to *Aura* and I heard back from birds around the Phinney Ridge area, The One Who Opens Doors is there!"

Hope roared its luminous flames to life in my breast. With my brainy, MoFo reasoning, I'd figured The One Who Opens Doors was responsible for letting out the zoo animals in the Phinney Ridge neighborhood since I'd first heard his name there on *Aura*, and it made perfect sense that he was still in the area. But, oh, to hear that he was MoFo! I had never given up hope and it had paid off! There was one MoFo out there, which meant there were more MoFos, which meant that everything was going to be okay. It was time to get to the zoo and find a way to make him my ally. I was The One Who Keeps, a bewildering nickname, but a special nickname for me nonetheless.

I put out another call to *Aura*, projecting passionately over the hawthorns, the park's sprawling nest of bramble and knotweed, reaching across the Seattle skyline with my voice. I needed to know if anyone had heard from my bow-legged partner and the little ruby-crowned kinglet who'd gone after him.

How stupid of me to send such a tiny bird—what was a ruby-crowned kinglet going to do in the face of a hippo? I made my nictitating membranes shut out the world momentarily, but they couldn't shut out the vision of a flooded stadium teeming with sick MoFos. Twitter erupted as nuthatches and American goldfinches and even house wrens—who are known to stab other birds in the head for very minor infractions—called out, spreading the word. But I couldn't wait because my heart was now on fire, and I shot into the air like a BrahMos missile, higher and higher and higher, until the tree crowns were thumbtacks and the freeways were gray strings. I shouldn't have left Dennis alone. I should have been taking care of him. I scanned, looking for the fawn hue of a bloodhound, flapping like a lunatic toward CenturyLink Field, but I couldn't stop the horrible images that flooded my mind—Dennis sitting alone by the blue trash can with the Seahawks emblem. And then, enraged because a squirrel has raced up and flashed his junk, Dennis takes off after the little pervert, knocking over the trash can and disappearing, getting swallowed whole by the new wilderness we live in. A world where sharp things—brambles, teeth, and broken glass—rule supreme. I thought of the rotting crush of sick MoFos with snapping jaws and the size of the hippo—thousands of pounds of territorial killing machine, with tusk-weapons for teeth—and I just couldn't bear it. I knew I was about to have a heart attack and tumble from the sky.

Dots of movement stirring below. Deer. A flash streaked across an empty road—a cat, perhaps. Then a brown spot caught my eye. Yes, fawn, the tawny color of a Dennis. I started my descent, allowing gravity to guide me down, down, and as I neared, my throat closed up. The brown lump was on its side next to an oval pool of red. *No, no, no, no, no.* I dropped faster than ever before, until I could make out the dog shape, the damage done to canine legs, the torn skin, tufts of fur catching a ride on the wind. Then I was hovering above with stone insides, sucking in breath and saying, "I'm sorry, I'm sorry, I'm sorry," to the brown dog I didn't know. The brown dog that wasn't a Dennis. Relief flooded me. It felt like singing along to Bon Jovi with Big Jim, or when you think the Pringles are all gone but you stick your head inside the canister and THERE ARE MORE HIDING AT THE BOTTOM! *Not Dennis! Not Dennis!* I flapped steadily, moving my head side to side to get a better look at the body. It was a Rhodesian ridgeback, a breed characterized by the stiff Mohawk that runs the opposite way down its back, and it had lost its last fight. And then I felt like screaming and cursing whatever had done this to such a magnificent dog. A dog carefully bred and selected and loved by MoFos. This is why I had to free the domestics, to rally them together, because we were losing our civilized fauna, the ones who knew about loyalty, purpose, and MoFo magnificence. I quickly lifted to a sweet gum tree to recover and to make sure I wasn't in reach of whatever had taken out a dog that was bred to hunt lions. If this formidable specimen hadn't made it, what chance did Dennis have? My inner pilot light started to snuff out. I needed my murder more than ever. Where was my Dennis? If he ended up like this shell of a Rhodesian ridgeback, there would be no one to blame but me.

A skittish cat—a white and marmalade firework—shot across the road, disappearing into the bushes.

And then from the shadow of a cluster of American hornbeam trees, Dennis appeared with a bird on his head. He lumbered forward with his loose skin and those silly, silly paws and his big, beating heart and I cried out in joy. That burl-nosed butt pumpkin was smiling at me! I couldn't remember the last time I felt so ecstatic, light as a damned flight feather! The ruby-crowned kinglet bobbed along on his head and as they neared, carefully avoiding the Rhodesian ridgeback, may he rest in peace, I realized what Dennis was carrying in his slobbering, flopping jowl-ed mouth. He had a goddamned bag of Cheetos®, that crazy hound. I called out to him in English, using the back of my throat and doing my very best Big Jim, "Good boy, Dennis! Fuck!" And when they got close enough, I pulled his tail and fluttered around him. He dropped the Cheetos® and play-bit at the air, lunging at me with his goofball smile. Good ol' Dennis. What a champ. I blabbed at him, telling him that a MoFo was alive and well and that we were going to find him and the world would make sense again. Heavens to the Real Housewives of Beverly Hills, it felt good to be alive!

I thanked the kinglet and told him that, though I appreciated his efforts, the position of riding Dennis had already been filled. He seemed to understand. He told me that Dennis had already almost found me at the park on his own—he figured he'd used his amazing nose—but had veered off on another scent trail, which turned out to be for the miraculous bag of Cheetos®. Together we trekked our way back to the park, where I doled out the Cheetos®, splitting them among Dennis, the mole, the opossum, the junco, and myself, which meant that everyone else got four while Dennis and I got twelve, because as I've said before, my counting is so terrible. So with light hearts and bellies full of Day-Glo orange magic, we set off on a quest to find a MoFo who looked like a coconut that could open doors.

CHAPTER 14

Dennis and I set off, leaving the opossum, the mole, and the junco to argue about which of them benefited most from the recent resurgence of the honeybee population. The opossum licked his lips while describing the thrill of tucking into a freshly broken-open hive, while the junco screamed about the sanctity of pollination and how the bees bring luck to the ones they choose. The mole yelled mostly unintelligible things. Blinded by their egotistic squabble, they managed to miss the very thing they had in common—mutual reverence for the bees of this world.

So it was back to me and Dennis again, our little murder, just how it should have been. We headed north, the trees shivering their leaves in approval, breathing relief into the wind. Their desperate pointing had stopped. A couple of blue-assed flies flitted around Dennis's scab. I called them "opportunistic troglodytes" and then called them lunch. Flying low with contented flaps in the shade of Dennis's shadow, I thought about the other worlds I'd learned of. Worlds that had always been here, but that I'd never seen or even heard about from the confines of our little house in Ravenna. Maybe it was because the MoFo world was so much louder. It drowned everything out with its clamor and fluorescent lights and bubbly pizzazz. And yet I felt a tickling cognizance, dewdrops beading in my mind. Perhaps I'd always known, always been aware that there is more to be seen than what is in front of me. Perhaps I'd deliberately chosen not to acknowledge the story a flower tells or the particular vibration of rocks. When the mole spoke of The Mother Trees, I didn't question him because somewhere deep down, below feather and skin and bleached bone, I *knew*. As we made our plodding way toward Seattle's central zoo, I thought about the life I'd lived between four walls and wondered how different I was from the animals in the enclosures.

I tuned in to *Aura*, listening to the back-and-forth of birds. There was much chatter over the missing eggs of a willow flycatcher, a band-tailed pigeon pined for its mate, and there were concerned murmurs over the unknown whereabouts of "The One Who Spits." We filled our bellies and bladders so that my partner could douse what was left of our fine city in urine, and then we set off again. I rode Dennis, reluctantly leaving the loose, slippy, dark fur of his back only to do recon. The area directly north of Dr. Jose Rizal Park was quiet. Quiet in that dangerous, pernicious way that invites you to relax and lose your vigilance.

Midair, I spotted a gaggle of MoFos flocking on top of an RV. Growling and braying, they obsessively drove their nails into the RV's rooftop. Many more of them—some burnt, one faceless, one wearing a flagpole in her neck—thronged the RV, rocking it from side to side, a vehicle so full that parts of MoFos stuck out of its windows. Returning to Dennis and *terra firma*, I called for him to follow me with a whistle and a

"Come 'ere, boy!" and we carefully avoided them by passing through a neighborhood. The first house we approached had an Etch A Sketch doodle of tire tracks across its lawn. A leggy Japanese maple lay on its side, the casualty of the car's hasty retreat, its leaves curled at the edges as if it had been grasping at something just out of reach in its final moments. The driveway was littered with credit cards and crumpled cash notes. Big Jim used to tell me that "money talks," but this stash was mighty silent. I suspect this is one of those MoFo expressions meant to confuse, like when I wasted an entire afternoon searching the yard for an ax and a body because Big Jim said he'd buried the hatchet with his friend Mike. I picked up the shiniest quarter, then dropped it upon realizing how pointless caching it would be given our new nomadic life. Old habits die hard. The neighboring home had a moss-shrouded roof and a MoFo that caught us off guard. Dennis shot across the street and hid behind an abandoned table shielded by a sign that said, "Lemonade $1" in chubby chalk writing. I rose above, scanning for more craned necks. Finding none in the immediate vicinity, I lowered enough to get a better look.

The MoFo's neck was bent unnaturally at an inquisitive ninety-degree angle, and he had four gashes deep in his forehead. He wore a once-white Cougars shirt, now covered in bright paint splashes and filth, the red predator cat emblem barely visible. The MoFo had worn a ring of mud into the overgrown front lawn. Who knows how many times he had trudged this constricted circle, the leash—attached to an enormous dog collar around his dislocated neck—taut and tethered to a wooden stake in the ground. Several feet away, someone had erected a small white cross festooned with photographs of a young, athletic MoFo. Candles and letters acned with purple hearts crowded the stem of the cross. Another sign, Sharpie on plywood, sat near the tethered MoFo. It read, "LEAVE MY

SON ALONE." *Family.* I was at once haunted by the image of the minivan on the freeway of death, the decal stickers on its back windshield showing its MoFo occupants in superhero garb, alongside another white outline with a smile and a floppy tongue—the family dog. A domestic. I fluttered over the MoFo and landed on the windowsill. Poking my head through the glassless window frame, I was walloped with an olfactory offense. It was worse than the rotting, neglected garbage that now speckled Seattle, worse than Nagartha's homemade patchouli oil deodorant or Big Jim's post-camping boxers. The dog, a Boston terrier, lay quietly in the living room, a bone-shaped chew toy by his side. Under his paws was a small collection of T-shirts that probably held the smell of his MoFos. The terrier had been partially eaten, possibly by the ones who raised him, bitten by the mouths that taught him to sit and how to be in the world. I was angry, fueled with rage that some wild monster with no regard for the laws of life got to thrive and build a lair in King Street Station and this family member, no doubt a loyal and loving companion, was here. Feeding maggots.

I shot back to Dennis as if filled with diesel and sriracha; I was fucking going to do anything I had to do to get The One Who Opens Doors on my side. Before we moved on, I checked the next couple of houses for signs of MoFos and domestic life. If there were pets in any of the homes, I couldn't see them. I was met with closed windows—glass intact, which threw me— and doors I couldn't open.

We passed a house that had at some point caught fire and was now charred, black and white as an old photo. The only sign of remaining life was the crispy pages feebly attempting flight from books, their spines black and broken. Down the street, perhaps inspired by the blaze, someone had made a bonfire and stacked it high with logs and deceased cattle. Closer in-spection revealed that only one body was a cow. The rest were

MoFos. Parts and pieces, still twitching and writhing in spite of everything. These were the things that were hardest on the eyes, even tougher to digest than apple seeds. I guess when the spirit of a species leaves us, it doesn't go easily. I ushered us past and didn't comment on the horror all around, concerned for Dennis's mental well-being. I reminded him that we were on our way to meet The One Who Opens Doors, a MoFo like our Big Jim with a clever brain and kind fingers. I had to keep Dennis afloat—to stave off what Onida had called The Black Tide—so I told him jokes about promiscuous blondes and even one I'd made up, which I was exceedingly proud of.

"Hey, Dennis. What did the koalas say when their keepers shaved them?"

Dennis awaited my response with baited dog breath.

"Eucalyptus. Get it? You-Calipped-us!"

I'm pretty sure he snorted in delight. I reminded him that it was a Shit Turd original.

Dennis and I passed more housing, even one that was covered in crudely tacked sheet metal, with no visible windows or doors. Covering your crib in sheet metal is a pretty intense "back off." But amidst the darkness of that zoo-bound march, there were undeniable sun spells. Close to that metal house, in a stand of magnolias that had erupted into a confection of pink and white, came a chittering. Three golden lion tamarins shot across the arms of the magnolia trees on a medley of cheeps, their funny little gray "what's going on?" faces and flat-ironed noses framed by a mane of flame-orange hair. They hopped and scurried along the branches, sending pink and white blossoms snowing onto Dennis, who came to life barking at them, padded paws slapping against the tree trunk. His droopy eyes lit into a warm amber, and his bulky body gained a little more bounce.

I watched them torment my partner playfully, enjoying it

all—tree, dog, and monkey, all taunting one another in a way we were now desperately craving. Vibrancy. Zest. Life. The high-pitched cheeping suddenly stopped and the tamarins— perhaps experiencing life at a different pace from us—took off, tangerine tails trailing behind them. The third tamarin stopped midbranch, turned, and nailed me squarely with Milk Dud eyes. Nothing was said, just a silent exchange that didn't need translation. We recognized the great change that had occurred and I knew we were both unsure of what it would bring. We saw one another. The tamarin turned to catch up with the others and exposed two tiny orange nuggets fused to her back. New life. It gave me a jolt, a Red Bull rush to the heart. It was so refreshing, I was only mildly offended that it was the tamarins who had put the pep back in Dennis's step.

We ushered each other along and I reminded Dennis about the big thing Big Jim did, the thing we can never forget. He listened wordlessly and then stopped in his tracks. With a whimper, he stared at an enormous structure covered in blue tarp that hadn't looked like much from the sky. The tarp billowed and rippled where something underneath moved. A forklift sat nearby. I fluttered to the top of the forklift and contemplated whether it was worth going near the breathing tarp. Oh yeah, wait, *crow*. A fly around the blue tarp mountain revealed that it was as tall as a magnolia. I selected a piece of the tarp that wasn't moving. It felt rough, crinkling in my beak. The plastic, blue material was heavy and I flapped and flapped, yanking hard until I felt the tarp beneath me start to give way. I opened my beak and rose above. The heavy tarp fell on itself, causing a great section of it to slip off the mountain and reveal what had been sequestered underneath. Dog crates. A mountain of dog crates. And stuffed inside each one was a MoFo. A MoFo in a designer suit, one in yoga attire, another swaddled in some sort of homemade armor. MoFos of all types and colors and degrees of degradation. The tarp's movement animated them and they responded in snarls and hisses. Attached to one of the crates was a sign. I swooped closer to read, "DO NOT REMOVE TARP. TRANSPORT TO AREA 7."

At this point, I was wholly absorbed in reading the black letters—and fixated focus, in this New World, spells certain doom. I slipped up. I lost my vigilance. Fingers, dexterous and long, snatched my left wing, curling around it. I shrieked, a panicking flurry of midnight feathers. Dennis burst into a barking frenzy, his booms getting louder as he neared. The fingers pulled me in, crate bars getting closer and closer. I was heading into a noxious smell, into yellow teeth with lumps of rotting tissue between them. No! I contorted my body with a sharp twist and shot backward, freeing myself of the dirty digits. The MoFo who owned the hand stared at me from its crate, a caged prisoner who was feral and free from the bars of sanity. It was a female MoFo, and at once I knew her because I don't forget faces, even ones that look like they've exfoliated in the garbage disposal. She was a local news anchor who had brought us stories of heroes and horrors. She still had her TV red dress on. Big Jim would be falling over backward if he were here. He loved this local news anchor and I approved. She had kind eyes and seemed to be able to afford more clothing than a lot of Big Jim's TV crushes.

Dennis stopped barking, but trotted nervously at the base of the crates, licking his lips. He didn't like any of this, not the threat on his partner or the unstable MoFos. He'd also never been great with crates. I thought it best to keep moving—it's harder to catch a thing in motion.

The sun played hide-and-seek behind clouds, bathing us in light when it saw fit, mimicking our unsettled mood. Our journey north became more and more pressing with every pawprint. Dread sat undigested in our bellies like day-old ramen. We stuck to open roads, walking toward a horizon of hope. Hope that balanced on the mysterious, faceless frame of The One Who Opens Doors.

From the air, I made out a mass of MoFos ahead—hundreds and hundreds of bent bodies. These ones were also swarming, an army of craned necks and shedding skin, all looking up. It was horrible to see them from the sky, a frenzied horde with bloodred eyes staring up at you. But it turns out they weren't staring at me. I descended to find them teeming around a lamppost, stretching their rotting limbs, and coughing out their intention in thick, mucusy bellows. Their leathery fingers slipped off the post, and those who lunged up the pole smacked it hard with their bodies, sliding back down to be swallowed by the crushing rabble below. I flapped closer to the post to find it was slick with some sort of grease. And at the top of the lamppost, dangling from a wire fastidiously twisted around the lamp head, was a cell phone. I flashed back to Big Jim, after his eyeball fell out, how he'd chased me down like a possessed fiend when I had his cell phone. I flashed on the napkin scrawled on by the MoFo lady trapped in the oyster house: *Tell Peter John Stein I love him. Tell him but DO NOT USE YOUR PHONE.* The MoFos—searching red eyes and stooped skeletons—were hunting for phones. This was bait. A trap set as a way to lure them in or away from something.

I whistled for Dennis, and we snuck around an abandoned apartment building to avoid the hysterical mass. We made it to Fremont, where I insisted on a short detour, zipping through the smashed glass doors of a place called the Flying Apron. Dennis and I, being from a family of devoutly religious eaters, committed not only to socially designated meals, but also less traditional mealtimes like, "it's *already* Taco Tuesday in Sweden," "tater tots are mood-enhancing potato pillows," and "cheese is the cure for boredom." The thing about family traditions is that they are sacred and should be upheld at all costs. The Flying Apron—singing its gluten-free, vegan status in swirly writing—turned out to be a quaint little bakery, or it probably was before its tables and chairs had all been smashed to splinters. Wall hangings lay in shards on the ground. Its exposed kitchen was blanketed in winter white, doused in some sort of flour. It was empty of mobile occupants, but for one apron-clad MoFo who was too busy smashing what was left of its cranium onto what was left of a hanging mirror to notice us.

I carefully selected a treat from the counter of surprisingly intact goodies with pink identifying labels. I got to work on a vegan chocolate chip cookie made with garbanzo flour, plucking out the chips with concerted effort. It had aged nicely and had the complex consistency of compacted sand. Dennis helped himself to three apricot thumbnails, a blueberry–oat scone, a rock-hard portobello mushroom sandwich, half a cardamom chai cake, three green tea macarons, a cinnamon roll, and a pumpkin ginger muffin. Dennis is effectively waste management on legs. I'd always had a glorious daydream of signing him up for Nathan's Hot Dog Eating Contest on Coney Island. I'd show up as his manager, you see, decked out in a pinstriped suit and hat, and George Shea would pat me on the back and come up with some witty name for Dennis. "The Rapacious Rapscallion of Ravenna!" "The Peckish Puppy with Peristaltic Pancreas Power!" Then I'd carefully go about placing some serious cash with the bookies.

My strategy was not to hang around anywhere for too long, so once we'd ransacked the Flying Apron's baked-goods counter, we fired up our jets, made like geese, and got the flock out of there. Before we knew it, with our hearts in our throats and sustainable, gluten-dairy-egg-soy-corn-free, alternatively sweetened treats in our stomachs, we'd made it to the Woodland Park Zoo. The sun was settling into the horizon and the sky suddenly darkened with the black bodies of crows. College crows were flying northeast, heading to their stupid night roost to snuggle up together like a bunch of poop terrorists. They chatted about plans for the evening, some calling out to me. I ignored them. They were not my business.

As I sat atop my trusty hound, preparing to cross the abandoned west parking lot of the zoo, we spotted a red GMC Yukon that sat unnaturally upright—trunk on the ground, hood in the air—against the bole of the European white birch it had collided with. Two titan trunks had done battle. It was the birch that had survived. But it had suffered, parts of its bark peeling like sunburned skin, and I bowed my head in respect, thinking of The Mother Trees. "I'm sorry this happened to you," I told the tree, feeling a prick of self-consciousness. Everywhere I looked was more vibrant, more alive—like I was seeing it in 4-D—in the new knowledge I'd acquired. Life is not the same once you've learned just how deeply a tree can feel.

The parking lot meters had their glass screens smashed out. One lay in trampled pieces, dried blood smearing the mashed metallic keypad. Preparing to follow the ramp that led down to the entrance of the Woodland Park Zoo, a sharp breeze ruffled my feathers.

"Alliiiiveee…" I heard the word, a thin whistle that whipped through the air on the limpid wings of a dragonfly. Dennis stopped. I recalled the words of a mole with icing-pink hands: *Under the soil is like… magical… and that's how the trees truly talk, none of the aboveground whisperings that take so much of their energy. It's not their real language, see? That's why, if they're talking to you, yous better be listening, because they are making a mighty fine effort.* I had heard the effort. Dennis and I both turned to face the house that summoned us. It peered from behind an enormous Douglas fir, timid and tiny with a teal and white paint job. An exposed brick chimney rose like a surrender flag. And then I

noticed one of the fir's colossal branches was pointed toward
the teal house's front door. A shiver scurried up Dennis's back,
jumping species to scamper up my legs and under my down.

"Alllivveee..." The silvery voice sounded out again.

"Yup, I got it!" I squawked to no one in particular, suddenly
feeling like a blue-footed booby. I was really living outside my
comfort zone these days. Then a thought struck me. *Alive.*
Could it be? Could there be a healthy MoFo inside this
home? My whole body began to shake with excitement, my
beak chattering uncontrollably. Dennis ambled up the short
driveway and stone steps to a teal front door. The Douglas fir
loomed above, a silent guardian. The door remained closed,
an impenetrable obstacle, essentially Fort Knox to me, Dennis,
and the Douglas fir—The Ones Without Opposable Thumbs.
I pecked fruitlessly at the door handle.

"Hello?" I asked in English, appealing to the MoFo within.
"Hello?" Hopping onto a doormat that seemed to be a liar
with its message of Welcome, I scratched desperately against
the green wood with my feet and beak. A bated silence. Then
an outbreak of barking filled the air. I shot up, flapping like
a loon to the nearest window. My face smacked into the glass,
pain shooting up my beak, embarrassment burning my veins.
I shook my head, thinking I should be immediately vindicated
for this classic bird faux pas, because THERE HADN'T BEEN
GLASS ANYWHERE ELSE IN THIS DAMN CITY! Dennis let
out one deep and sonorous woof. A greeting. The yapping
coming from inside became panicked and frenzied. The
window was painted with a film of dust and the dotted imprint
of my snooter, but I could see in alright. I could see the quaint
living room with the family portrait and the sooty fireplace,
how the powdery hardwood was littered with empty wrappers.
I saw dust motes dancing through the light beams coming
through various windows, all intact. And the source of the

yapping became clear. In among the King's Hawaiian bread bags, hollow dog-chow sacks, punctured peanut butter jars, shredded cake-mix boxes, a graveyard of graham crackers, Chips Ahoy, Lucky Charms, quinoa, and a landmine of raw pasta lumps and turds, was a Pomeranian. Signs told me there had been no healthy MoFo here for a long time, but still, there was a survivor.

She yipped at the window, a chaotic SOS song in the key of fear. Her button eyes were brimming and shiny. I marveled. This was a creature who deserved life. She had managed to avoid getting attacked by her changed MoFos, she'd avoided getting mauled by wild creatures despite practically living at the zoo. She had been imprisoned for who knows how long and she'd lived on the American diet and persevered. I felt a sense of awe for this Pomeranian, historically a lapdog for German royal MoFos, desperately loved and respected by her own MoFos, as evidenced by the custom-framed eleven-by-sixteen portrait of her in a Christmas sweater and her tartan, monogrammed bed. Her name was Cinnamon and I was going to break her out of there. The MoFos wouldn't have stood for her imprisonment and suffering; they'd have called the ASPCA or NASA or AARP and they'd smash the teal door in and save her life like the heroes they were born to be. She was someone's Dennis and I was going to give her one more chance at survival.

"Cinnamon! Sit!" I told her through the glass. She cocked her head, seized by palpable jubilance at words she knew and utter bewilderment at getting dragooned by a bird. My heart soared as she parked her tiny furry butt next to a fossilized Fig Newton. It worked! In that moment, I felt more powerful than Scarface and his little friend. I rapped my beak on the glass one more time, cursing its impenetrable force field of a surface—the bane of all birds. I might not have been able to open windows, but I was lucky because Big Jim taught me about the dangers of them back when I was just a nestling, a tiny toothpick-boned goblin. The first time I bumped my beak into the glass, he scooped me up in his sausage fingers, told me not to be embarrassed, and showed me YouTube evidence of MoFos slamming into glass doors.

"It's the reflection of trees and plants that's confusing, S.T.," Big Jim said. "One time, I plowed into a Walmart door and spilled hot coffee all over my balls." Then—just for me— he marked each window of our house with a hastily bought, gas-station bumper sticker, like "baby on board," "well behaved women rarely make history," and "I love my Belgian Malinois."

I gave Cinnamon a nod through the glass. I dropped from the window ledge, shuffled back over to the front door, gave it a mighty kick, and let out a lengthy "Caaaaaaaaaaaaaaw!" to cover up the self-inflicted foot pain. Dennis rolled his eyes and whined. Nope, we weren't getting in.

"We're coming back for you. I promise," I told her in croaky clicks.

As we reluctantly turned to leave, she began to whine, paws padding away inside her prison. The last glimpse I stole was heartbreaking. She was a tornado of fluff, spinning round and round. The tiny survivor didn't want us to leave. But I didn't know how long it was possible to stay alive—even as a real tough fluff survivor type—in a sealed cemetery of empty wrappers and excrement. We had to hurry.

I went airborne and Dennis thundered across Phinney Avenue, lit with purpose. We would find The One Who Opens Doors and this little teal and white house would be our very first stop. Our first freeing. And we would do the MoFo thing and free the others. We'd find all the surviving Dennises and give them a chance at living.

We crossed the street and stood under the bold white letters that said WOODLAND PARK ZOO. You can imagine how elated I was to discover that they'd placed cutouts of frolicking penguins all over their sign. Fucking newspaper-colored, ice-balled dick goblins, yeah, that's who you want as your brand ambassador. It was a deeply ominous portent, right in front of the entrance. I could only hope that there would be some balance, that inside, we'd find The One Who Opens Doors and they'd be in sync with our vision, our plan to set the domestics free. To give them a chance to thrive and keep the legacy of the MoFos alive. The problem was, I didn't know what was on the other side of the zoo's turnstile gate.

Dennis barfed, and I wasn't sure whether it was a comment on our nerve-wracking predicament or the portobello mushroom sandwich staging its final protest.

CHAPTER 15

JUST ABOVE THE ROOT STRUCTURE OF A
200-YEAR-OLD SPRUCE TREE
(TRANSLATION BY A STELLER'S JAY)

What if I were to offer you an extraordinary gift? What if it were to change the way your eyes took in the world? Would you accept? Would you keep it or toss it aside?

You see, I know you. I've been watching you your whole exquisite life.

I am Mother Tree. Part of something greater than my one. We, of ancient forest and all of us, are connected through swirling root. Here and there, so tightly we interweave that when one of us dies, the other must die too. Our stand is one, braving licks of lightning and the sticky scarlet appetites of insects. We warn neighboring crowns of drought and danger with our scent song and send quick, silvery messages through *Web*, fungal lattice. Like you, we sweat. We scream when thirsty, we bleed when sliced. And we remember.

Listen.

Our words, through crackling roots and the echoing pulse of a mushroom's gossamer threads, are not bound by time.

And a secret for you: if one of us is felled and left as a bloody stump, we will send it our healing, quietly cheating death for a hundred years. You don't know about these things because until the gift, you haven't been listening.

Your magnificent eyes have been down.

Do you know how many years I am? Do you know that if you press your shell-like ear to my bark, you can join in my drinking? Did you know there are more lives in a palmful of soil than of your kind on this big beautiful blue?

Perhaps you still cannot see that I am fighting the greatest battle of my years. A bark beetle army has declared war on my body. It started like many beginnings, with a singular soldier who chose change. He burrowed into my skin. He summoned a militia and I hammered back, unleashing gluey syrup onto the glossy armor of an infantry. And now a complexity in the art of war—the army has brought reserve soldiers, this time with a fungus on their backs. Now the fungus will aid them, burrowing under my bark to sever my defense.

Listen; life is worth a fight. Expectation must be shed like winter leaves. Even in death, there is wondrous beauty. And death is not The End.

I have given you a gift. Now you see me. You see the stippled scarring on my trunk where a woodpecker drilled into me for blood. You see moss, my emerald cushiony companion— watch her survive, she was the very first of us on this big beautiful blue. You see my children who stand at my feet. One day, I will crumble and shatter to the forest floor where my bones will feed a thousand hungry mouths and my children will stretch for the sun.

The One Who Hollows as well must return.

Life is as beautiful as it is deadly. Fungi might be friend or foe. Breathe. Listen. Look.

The forest is where all secrets are kept under lock and key, deep in soils dark and rich. The woods are where the truth lives, etched into the veins of leaves and the prismatic skin of a dewdrop.

If you are alive—whether of blood or bark—you will be struck by pain, love, longing, fear, anger, and the particular ache of sadness. There will be joys that quiver your leaves and betrayals that will sever your roots, poisoning the water you pull. These are the varying notes in the music of living. Look up, to close your eyes is to stagnate. To rot and stop the song.

My gift to you is to know that we are here, all around you, talking to one another and dreaming of your success. Sorcery is everywhere, in the silver stroll of a slug and lighting up the very veins of you. Open those beautiful eyes to a world who is a mosaic of magic. She is just waiting for you to notice.

CHAPTER 16

❧

S.T.
WOODLAND PARK ZOO, SEATTLE,
WASHINGTON, USA

We were losing light and I didn't like it. I instructed Dennis to wait by the turnstile gate. It was safer for me to be airborne and my heebie-jeebies were telling me to do recon of the zoo solo. Besides, Big Jim never brought Dennis to the zoo, even though he snuck me in once. My suspicion is that Big Jim had been shielding him from an alpaca exhibit. Inexplicably, Dennis is deathly afraid of alpacas. But leaving him on the ground at the mouth of the Woodland Park Zoo, vulnerable, a survival green-horn, felt like nothing I'd ever experienced. Caches—especially ones I'd stuffed with special, sought-after treasures like golf balls, antique MoFo collectibles, Rolls-Royce hood ornaments, or Tinder Tiffany's diaphragm—were always very hard to leave. After the electric thrill of meticulously concealing my treasure, I'd always embark on the Oscar-worthy theatrical production of nonchalance, pretending the new cache didn't exist and that I wasn't thinking about it twenty-four-seven. This was so much worse. Leaving Dennis was to feel a chronic, hollow ache, untreatable until I saw his ridiculously saggy skin again.

I fluffed myself up and fluttered over the gate, finding stacks of rock formations. In full investigation mode, I lowered to perch atop one of the large, beige rocks. Speckling of the very worst kind of white shit told me what I needed to know—this was where the penguins lived. I gagged, barely holding in partially digested garbanzo-flour chocolate chip cookie. The thought of those bollock Jedis living here, shitting their lives away on MoFo property, was difficult. And now, where were they? The glass that looked to have held a large pool of water for the wang-bags to swim in was now in shining shards. A world where penguins roamed free. God help us all.

I thought about how Big Jim hated penguins, and how we had laughed at them the time he took me to the zoo. They were weird, fake-ass birds that couldn't fly, strange and useless. "What in the hell is the point of a bird that can't fly?" he had said in between bites of a chili dog. He said they were a waste of space, much like people who believe in ludicrous things like environmental protection and tofu.

A comet shot across the sky. Then I saw something else—streak, jet black—careen above the tree line. Two crows were performing aerial gymnastics, soaring high above only to descend into a pirouette of corkscrew dives. They were fucking playing. My blood boiled. I snorted my contempt and got back to attending urgent matters and exhibiting productive behavior in a world that was falling apart.

Across from the penguin enclosure was a large roof I recognized as the zoo store. Dipping down, I saw the store had been ransacked, floor-to-ceiling windows smashed, counters and tables shattered, wooden display walls crushed into fine powder. T-shirts lay mud-smeared and trampled. Something had made quick work of a snack display, then gone on to decapitate and de-stuff a mound of plush animals. Hats, bags, coffee canteens, and African drums lay abandoned and wrecked. In an unambiguous statement, a mountainous pastiche of dung sat under a busted doorframe.

The disrespect for MoFo property and the eerie silence bothered me. But the image of a tiny, dejected Pomeranian, all alone with her ginger head in her paws as The Black Tide came in to swallow her, tugged at my heart and kept me focused. I lifted, more determined than ever to find The One Who Opens Doors—a MoFo, blood pumping through his veins, his head populated with red strands and innovative thoughts. I knew he was here.

Woodland Park Zoo had changed its spots. There had been monumental upheaval here. From above, I could see how the foliage had declared war, bursting forth from the soil, electric-green and surging with life. Tropical vines and stranglers were performing a creeping asphyxiation of the zoo. They were forming their own vertical superhighways as weeping willows surveyed them from above. Carnivorous pitcher plants with their baited jugs of acid had spread, readying for carnage. Bromeliads and Japanese quince and Tatarian honeysuckle, magnolias, red elderberry, English laurel, and bishop's hat were active commanders in this battle, all wild and hungry and glossy green. I thought it a diverse and unnatural tussle. In some areas of the zoo, walkways were smothered in plant life, the sides of buildings held hostage by a weedy ambush. What I saw was silent war. This was a hostile takeover, the foliage committing mass destruction, swallowing up concrete one millimeter at a time. The MoFo who'd been freeing the animals hadn't been maintaining the flora. I could see how it would just be too big a job, how garden greens can fight back and swallow a city whole. And I imagined he'd been busy doing what we'd been doing—surviving.

A flash of movement caught my eye, so I gingerly perched half-way up a towering Sitka spruce and traced the motion. Ambling below was a hulking mass of muscle with the prickly skin of a durian. It took its time, veined and prehistoric, dragging its legs and shadowed claws along a walkway of weeds. Locked in terrifying jaws that leaked frothy strings of spittle was the limp body of a meerkat. The Komodo stopped, lifting his blocky head to register me. Our eyes met and my knees buckled. The dragon let the meerkat's lifeless form drop like a winter stole. A daggerlike tongue in salmon pink stabbed the air, tasting me, licking information about The One Who Keeps. I felt my throat close, an anger I could barely contain surging through me. This creature was godlike, mesmerizing me with his armored form, genes that stretched back millions of years through time; I would never be a match for him. We both knew this. And here he moved with the slow sovereignty of the vines and the ivy. He was silent and insidious in his takeover, assuming dominance over his new domain with no respect for the lives that we were losing, no understanding that this wasn't his world to conquer.

"This is the world of the MoFos!" I yelled at the dragon. They had sculpted and designed and trimmed and cut down and bettered everything. And here was Komodo, cool and commanding, an indomitable takeover. Like Nature—the predator that shows no mercy. He was lumbering, puissant proof that MoFos were losing a battle against the earth.

"You disgust me, you scaly fuck-bucket!" I screamed at him. Then I took flight before I did something utterly stupid.

My eyes darted, wings cutting through the air with frantic flaps that sounded like the flicking of cotton sheets. I scoured for movement, for red hair, for the soldier who'd help me win this war. I lowered into an area called Banyan Wilds, a re-creation of tropical Asia, rife with thick vines and bamboo. I hovered over an enclosure that said it contained sloth bears, but found its star occupants missing, the glass wall along the front of the enclosure in shards. Perching on a large rock,

I studied the terrain, searching for signs of life. A burning sensation in the back of my head told me I was being watched. I hopped and spun to find three sets of shining eyes watching me with heads cocked. I felt the feathers on the back of my neck hike up. Crows. They sat on a thick log that balanced on the sloth bear's sunbathing rock and conferred with one another in a series of clicks and rattles. I blocked them out.

I flapped to a neighboring enclosure, finding it to be the densely jungled home of the Malayan tigers. Again, the enclosure was empty, glass front gone. My heart started to race. To avoid the nuclear meltdown that was building steadily inside me, I lifted again, looking for my MoFo, flying above an enclosure that had a covered viewing area, which had information and signs about its inhabitants. The safety glass, to prevent visiting MoFos from coming face-to-face with eight 350-pound western lowland gorillas, lay shattered all over the hay and concrete. Acid rose in my throat. I swallowed and hurriedly took flight. My MoFo was here and I knew it. Discovering fragmented glass at the front of the jaguar exhibit made flying difficult, as a tremor took hold of my wings.

Where are you, MoFo?

I beat my wings, trying to stay airborne, trying to breathe as I fluttered over a building in the rainforest loop. It had a glass roof and when I found it to be intact, my pinions stabilized, normal flight possible again. Intact glass, a crystalline beacon of hope. I ducked into the building and was transported to the tropics by thick vines and the bulbous, gnarly rooted buttresses of exotic trees. Animal exhibits sat side by side: goliath pinktoe tarantula, yellow anaconda, false water cobra, poison dart frog, emerald tree boa, tiger rat snake. The animals were all gone, a tiling of debris and glass glittering on the ground. I started to hyperventilate, as if the anaconda had its muscly middle squeezing tightly around my throat. I shot by the enclosures, searching for life and signs of a MoFo's intent—a glass-shattering ax, a life hammer, an emergency window-breaker escape tool—when I felt eyes upon me.

Squatting on a log in the rainforest building, surrounded by thick foliage and signs of a mass evacuation, sat a shiny body. He stared at me with a smug expression, a pseudo smirk.

"Where are the healthy MoFos?" I asked him, my breath hitched. "The ones who walk on two legs?"

"Pass the moonstone river." His skin was lime green, as polished as an airport shoe. His funny little nostrils twitched and his face made it hard to believe he wasn't making fun of me, which was adding to my agitation.

"What? That's not what I asked you. Where are the MoFos?" I asked, reading the sign behind his shattered terrarium that identified him as a waxy monkey tree frog.

"Pass the moonstone river." He repeated himself and I shot out of there, the fury inside me billowing like hot gas. I didn't have a second longer to spend in the company of a bewildered frog and his stupid, waxy rictus. It seemed beneath me to eat a tropical frog out of spite, so I bottled my rage and took off.

I scoured the Tropical Rainforest building, huffing in tight-chested breaths, a reedy whistle emanating from deep inside me. I searched tropical bird aviaries—bananaquits, red-crested finches, blue-gray tanagers, spangled cotingas—they were all gone. An ocelot and a bushmaster—which, according to the unflattering sign by its empty enclosure, is a venomous serpent with delightful heat-detector pits on both sides of its head that hides in the soil, waiting to assassinate passing mammals—were nowhere to be seen. Even the home of my acquaintances, the golden lion tamarin enclosure, lay empty. And the glass, everywhere, sprinkled like fallen icicles, every shard breaking my heart.

And then I found the toucan exhibit.

There was no visible toucan, no lollipop-beaked bird who lorded over your childhood cereal bowl. The exhibit was pitlike, with an open, grated roof and intact wire-mesh fencing on its periphery. Stuffed like Spam were all the MoFos who had fallen in through the grating, filling every inch of the enclosure. The mass pulsated like a breathing tumor. The MoFos were rotting and moaning, eyeballs pressed through the mesh fence, greenish skin torn and ripped. They looked and smelled like Dennis's canned dinner. Animals free, MoFos caged. My heart trailing along by my feet, I searched in the mass of meat for red hair, one eye open for the am-bushmaster that The One had, at some point, freed. It was impossible to identify every MoFo in that palpitating tumor, but I felt a glimmer of hope spark. I couldn't see red hair. Feathereds, furs, MoFos, the scaled, we all share the gift of a special sense, intuition—our otherworldly knowing. Mine told me that he wasn't in the pit. But that I would find him.

Thwack. Something struck me in the back of the head. I squawked, shooting off the toucan habitat's viewing ledge. Five crows with dusty feathers and mischief alight in their eyes peered at me from branches inside the golden lion tamarin's busted enclosure. These were not college crows. These were a different murder, a spiteful, careless bunch of clowns who belonged behind the bars of an aviary. One had pelted something at me, a seed, a piece of fruit, I didn't know and didn't care what it was. I hated these inky fools, these lentil-brained ass noodles.

"Get away from me!" I screeched, flapping alongside the mass of disfigured MoFos. Had they no compassion? No understanding of what was happening to the wonderful world around them? The devastating mass of sick MoFos caged beside them really meant nothing at all to them? One of them cackled and launched another rapid-fire round of seeds at me. I ducked. I'd fucking had it. I charged, screaming my anguish, flapping my ferocity. I dove into the golden lion tamarin habitat, flushing out their black bodies and chasing them through the enclosed tunnel of exhibits. They squawked excitable panic and nervous laughter—gas on the flames of my fury. We burst from the tunnel and the crows shot skyward, scattering into the evening, cackling and chattering.

It was a game to them. I'd lost my whole life, everything that made sense to me, and they thought it was funny. I hated crows. Hated everything about their horrible, shadowy chicanery and ignorance. They were a limited species, bird-brained and primitive. I fluttered my gular, hating the part of me that they recognized, desperately wanting to pluck off my wings and walk on two legs and have a limitless imagination. I was sick of being a patchwork of puzzle pieces, parts of this and bits of that. I was one color but not one thing. I wanted to be perceived, to look and sound and act, like I felt inside. Like a MoFo.

In a state, I puffed and huffed as I flew southward over the zoo, ravaged by adrenaline and fear and the pain of hope. Hair-raising omens popped up in the forms of a limp raccoon that hung over a branch like a Christmas ornament, and dazzling white bones that littered the Family Farm petting zoo, informing my decision to steer clear of the nearby Temperate Forest area. The African Savanna seemed a wiser choice, so I settled onto a black locust tree, squawked as I impaled a foot on one of its hideous thorns, and quickly abandoned ship for a Russian olive instead. I worked on trying to calm my nerves, using Lamaze techniques I'd learned from MTV. The pressure was strangling me, pressure of time, of leaving Dennis, of losing light, of finding The One Who Opens Doors, of rescuing a desperate little Pomeranian, of hating what I was born as. Of wanting change in every single iota of my life. I Lamaze-d methodically, listening for guidance from inside, from trees, from anywhere. Nothing came. My pulse started to stabilize.

From my high branch, I had an unobstructed vantage point of a series of Kikuyu huts, a quaint rendering of an East African village. I wondered whether the real East African MoFos still had their thatched homes, painting their faces in bold white and red pastes, fashioning their jewelry from bead and cowrie shell. Whether lions were still a threat to them. My bones were tired from my panicked tour of the world through a zoo.

I realized I wasn't alone. A grating honking trumpeted into the air. The horrible sound tightened into staccato shrieks, immediately recognizable as a call of distress. In the middle of the African village, a flamingo dragged itself along the ground, singing its anguish in sharp and flat notes. Her sugar-pink wing hung at an odd angle, dangling near fuchsia, chopstick legs that thrashed, kicking up sand. I had a bad feeling about this, thinking of the brawny King Of Reptiles and his casually chilling swagger. And the bushmaster, the largest of all pit vipers, lurking somewhere in the burgeoning shadows. The flamingo's cries echoed among the Kikuyu huts, the smell of fear tight and sharp in the darkening air. I grappled with whether to drop down to help the flamingo. If she wasn't a domestic but was still cared for by MoFos, did I get involved?

A silvery shadow encroached, making the decision for me. The leopard was the color of a winter sky, sprinkled with a snowing of perfect black circles. She was at once soft and formidable, rounded with gentle curves and pillowy paws—sheathes for her retractable weapons. A study in contrasts. A voluptuous tail trawled behind her. Her movements were methodical, each paw placement deliberate, the pellucid green eyes that lit her round face trained on the injured pink bird.

"RUN!" I screeched at the flamingo. "Get out of there!"

I didn't want to watch but I couldn't help myself. Ten

pawprints in the sand were all the flamingo had left, and then its neck was in the jaws of the snow leopard. A sharp shake. A snap. She fell silent. The leopard suddenly dropped the flamingo's limp salmon neck, her rapt attention on one of the Kikuyu huts. Her body changed, the ripple that shuddered under that plush winter coat almost invisible. She had known he was coming before she saw him, before either of us saw the brooding body that strode from the hut. We hadn't seen him waiting, watching, his camouflage blending into shadows. He is seen only when he wants to be. Now the flamingo had been dispatched and he was here to claim it. A guttural growl rumbled the roots of the Russian olive tree. From ground and branch, the snow leopard and I shared terror of brilliant orange and black stripes that stood in the center of the African village.

The tiger let the growl rev and crescendo into a roar, exposing long, yellowed fangs, eyes and nose wrinkling. The snow leopard tensed, placed two plush paws in front of her pink prize. Here was another war. The tiger rushed her, stopping short of her face, thrashing enormous claws. Snow leopard swiped back, her silvery paw colliding with the side of his head. Roars erupted from the throat of the tiger. The cats—one of jungle, one of snow—lifted onto their hind legs in a horrific embrace, clawing and thrashing for dominance. A lightning round of powerful, reflexive attacks. Jab. Claw. Swipe. Lunge. Charge. Agile jerks and pivots, fur was airborne, so fast, fast as flames. The leopard let four paws hit the sand first. The tiger paced, huffed. He inched forward, met by a flurry of swipes and strained, high-pitched yowls from the leopard. Teeth and claw and fury flew. My feet strangled the branch. Tiger's face twisted with a snarl. He bit at her head with three-inch scythes. Leopard snatched the scruff of tiger's throat. She slammed him onto his side.

And then it stopped.

The leopard shot back, eyes on the tiger as she retreated, exposing the flamingo. The tiger shook his massive head and postured over the bird that lay like a broken lawn ornament. Snow leopard backed up slowly, farther, relinquishing her coveted kill. I didn't understand. Hadn't she been winning? And then her reason became clear. A sinister veil of orange and black skulked from the huts. The stripes of two more tigers, shoulder blades undulating in a liquid rise and fall, entered the African village. There were three brothers who met one another. Two tigers sniffed the victor, and with a minor squabble over the blushing bird, they tore apart her corpse.

I was losing my mind. This is what Seattle had become, a battleground, a gladiator's pit of savages? And then, a delicious acorn of a thought dropped: If I was a lone healthy redheaded MoFo, surrounded by a brotherhood of tigers and a bushmaster and a snow leopard and an acid-mouthed Komodo dragon, I wouldn't make myself easy to find either. I'd be hiding somewhere sneaky and difficult to locate. Just like how after the big thing went down with Tiffany S., Big Jim battened down the hatches, taking up residency in the basement with World of Warcraft, Jägermeister, and Papa John's on speed dial. He'd gone to ground. I'd been searching out in the open, but that's not where a MoFo in his predicament would be. Alone, he would find himself prey in these surroundings. Suddenly, I was deafened by a hideous chorus of raucous screeching. It was that murder again; the trees around me were alive with their opened beaks, their insistent screams. They were taunting me.

"Get away! Get away!" they squawked and I hated them so very, very much, even more than the smell of Abercrombie & Fitch, those crumble-cheese turd burgers. Crows shot out of the trees. A storm of them charged forth, beaks careening toward me.

"HEY!" I squawked as one of the crows body checked me

square in the chest. Instantly winded, I tumbled from the tree. Plummeting toward the earth, I quickly righted myself at the last inch, turning just in time to see an orange paw swiping down at me. I shot sideways, evading the tiger's hair-trigger killer instinct, escaping into the air. The brother jumped, hurling his striped bulk at me from below, excited by the thrill of a chase. I flapped hard, consumed by hatred for the pistachio-brained birds who'd almost gotten me killed.

"What's the matter with you assholes!" I squawked rhetorically. But none of them were looking at me. They continued to scream, "Get away, get away!" but I realized it was directed at a monster who was inching its way along the Russian olive, its trowel head tasting me where I had sat seconds before. The crows had pushed me away from the strike of a twenty-foot snake whose glossy body shone with the diamond pattern of a Persian carpet, even in the growing darkness.

I was stunned. In shock from the savagery and the unexpected source of help, I bolted. I had to get away from the craziness. I couldn't process anything that was happening and I couldn't leave Dennis a second longer. If I stayed here, it was only a matter of time before I became as delusional as that waxy monkey tree frog.

I was having a lot of trouble with my breathing, which I chalked up to nearly getting quesadilla-ed between tiger paws and becoming a Hot Pocket for a snake the size of a sewer pipe. But I didn't have time to rest. My search from the sky continued as I passed over the rest of the zoo's African Savanna, once crisp and dry, now gaining green and looking like it had been ravaged by a storm. I flew north to an area thick with firs, cedars, hemlocks, and plants native to my Washington home. None of this helped diminish the sharp pain in my chest, which ceased only when I spotted a cluster of moving bodies below. I made out the top of a ball cap, dark hair, a bald spot,

long brown hair and, in the middle of this group of MoFos—
a redhead. I crowed my triumph to the clouds.

"He's here! He's here!"

I dipped down, carefully checking the branches of a black
spruce before perching. The bird's-eye view and lack of light
wouldn't let me see the MoFo's face, just his bright ginger
hair as he and the small group of straight-backed MoFos he
was with made their way along a path on the Northern Trail
toward a cave. They were seeking shelter! I shook my head,
incredulous. There was hope! There was life, a living MoFo! A
chance at saving the world.

I ducked down to follow them into the cave. It turned out
to be a ground-level viewing station for zoo visitors to watch
the brown bears and the otters. Unbelievably, the glass to both
enclosures was still intact. They'd come here to seek refuge, to
use their heads. They were here to devise a plan for survival
and to contain the escaped animals. The MoFos gathered
together in front of the glass of the brown bear exhibit,
ripples from the wading water catching the last traces of light
and making them dance around the cave. From the ground,
I watched my redheaded MoFo as he approached the glass,
pressing an intact hand against its surface. He drew his head
backward, as if in mesmeric reverence, expressing gratitude to
a power high above. There was a moment of silence. Then he
bashed his head against the glass with a hollow crack. *No.* He
shot his head back and launched it at the glass again with a
thwack. *No.* The romp of otters in the neighboring enclosure
swarmed in a cloud of panic. The MoFos around the redhead
joined him in bashing their skulls with superlative power. *No.*
In front of them, separated by a small wading pool and some
glass, two famished brown bears paced on the water's edge. *No.*
The smacking became more frantic. CLACK. CLACK. CLACK.
No. The first crack in the glass was born, shooting like a tiny

lightning streak and allowing for the breath of chaos. CLACK. CLACK. CLACK. The MoFos kept using their heads. *No.* The crack grew branches, which ripped through the glass. *No.* The bears' impatient dance intensified, one of them excitedly lifting on his hind legs. He was standing, a mirror of the MoFos. They waited, stomachs and throats releasing low growls of anticipation for what was coming to them.

From the air I heard the horrific sounds of gushing water and a bear breaking fast, a sound I will forever hear on clammy nights when sleep is elusive. I'd been given false information. A scheme. I had blindly trusted the information from *Aura* and it had been wrong, a lie, no better than an e-mail scam. It was exactly like the real Internet, filled with festering weirdos and keyboard clowns. I should have known, should have remembered how Big Jim felt when he'd fallen hard for Oksana, a duck-billed Russian beauty with whom he'd been messaging for months. After swapping intimate details, addresses, deep secrets, and a series of Anthony Weiner–inspired photos, Big Jim sent Oksana $4,000 (to cover her airline ticket to Seattle, her rent, and liquid courage in a bottle of Stolichnaya Elit so she could leave her abusive husband). Oksana turned out to be a cyber-fabrication. Big Jim had been spilling the contents of his heart and scrotum to an online troll. Now I'd fallen for it too, fallen for the lies of three asshats who'd concocted a story about a redhead. They had sold me the same thing that Oksana had sold to Big Jim—false hope. Because what I realized watching the redheaded MoFo in the bear and otter viewing area was that all of the glass in the city had been smashed by the sick MoFos. I remembered the cell-phone bait, dangling from the lamppost, where MoFos teemed below, hurling themselves to reach it. I thought about the message at the oyster house: *Tell Peter John Stein I love him. Tell him but DO NOT USE YOUR PHONE*, and I thought about Big Jim when

I pulled out his cell phone, how he'd gone from swiping the basement walls mindlessly with his finger to being a savage hunter. A desperate monster. There had been no vigilante redhead setting the zoo animals free out of the goodness of his heart. The sick MoFos no longer had hearts. I'd known they were looking for phones, but I hadn't put it all together in my blindness. They were attracted to all the glass because they'd mistaken it for what they were really looking for: screens.

I flew above the zoo's twisted green mass, the stabbing pain in my chest back again. It was hard to stay airborne, maybe because of the weight in my heart, because you can't fly when it's heavy; the adage is so true. Maybe, I thought, something is deeply wrong, and suddenly I found I could no longer flap my wings and I plummeted, crashing into rolling tumbles. Head, wing, side, foot, repeat, hitting the ground. I came to a stop, wings akimbo. The landing of a challenged fledgling. I righted myself, shaking off the dirt, and staring at the sign in front of me. It depicted a scene. In its center was a picture of a green stroller. Next to the stroller was a picture of a sandwich bag full of Goldfish crackers. A sinister silhouette had taken the sandwich bag hostage, holding it above the stroller, taunting, malicious. "Stow Your Snacks!" said the sign. The silhouette was a crow.

I couldn't take it anymore. I launched into the air using every ounce of what I had left, heart on fire, and flapped as fast as I could, away from the crows and the savagery and the lies, streaming above a world that had too many thorns for me. I had to get back to Dennis, to the last remnant of sanity I had. Darkness had spread its onyx blanket and that might have been why I committed the most classic and fatal of avian bloopers, particularly ironic given the lack of intact glass to be found. I smashed full speed into a glass window. Stunned on impact, my legs stiffened as I plunged to the earth, vision turning to black.

CHAPTER 17

Air is hot. Full of things to come. Have to get home, scurry there, be safe again. Air is getting dark and angry. I hurry my way through the jungle that has grown. Green vines cover everywhere I go now. Bush and flower and shrub. Fields that were once of grass and the bones of cow and sheep now belong to the vines. Kudzu vines are from another place far away, but now they have made my home theirs. They are hungry to cover and smother everything they can and now we live in green.

CRACK!

The air is angry. It roars and gathers its black clouds for a reckoning. Hurry home, Elwood, hurry to the home. Scurry over flat kudzu leaves, look up and see them crawling all over buckeye, pawpaw, devil's walkingstick, hornbeam, holly, and hickory. A great green battle.

When the kudzu came to our home, it brought its bugs, little creatures with red eyes and mean spirits. They eat other greens and the kudzu grows and grows here, King Of The

South. They bring secrets from a faraway place, stories of molting cherry trees and snow monkeys that bathe in hot spring water. We cannot tell if they are truthful. They don't share everything they know and we don't welcome them because they are not like us.

CRACK!

Hurry home, Elwood. The sky flashes hot white. I am almost there, almost home. Groundhogs and skunks are heading to their dens to hide from the hot, angry air. I am home. I get ready to dip down into my tunnels, but another great white flash splits the air. The white streak strikes, cobra quick. It has declared war on the kudzu! The kudzu is now hot, bright orange, and burning. Smoke rises, mean gray curls. "I'm here," says the smoke. "The sky is mine." The burning spreads, killing up the kudzu. I smell its smoky green death. Hurry home, Elwood! I dip into my tunnels and wait. This is *my* home. I'll just wait here to see who wins.

CHAPTER 18

My nictitating membranes slid open like rain-slick patio doors. A nose the size of Saturn took up my entire field of vision. As it gave a weather vane–spinning sniff, its gravitational pull sucked up my feathers. The nose then retreated, allowing me to take in more of its owner's face. Flapping fawn folds of skin, drooping, near-melted eyes that gave an air of constant hopelessness. Dangling dangerously close to my eye was a bizarre turkey wattle reminiscent of an elephant's testicles. Never in my wildest night terrors did I think I'd be so happy to see Dennis's slimy jowls, the bubbles of saliva poised to spill over their sides. Dennis snorted his happiness at my consciousness, excitedly sniffing me from tail to beak, licking my feathers, and nudging me with that spongy, omniscient schnoz.

I righted myself and shook, freeing a shower of sticky droplets from my feathers. The scorching stabs in my chest had gone, and then I remembered my collision and lowered my head in embarrassment. I couldn't believe that I'd beak-planted in a mostly glassless, Windex-free world. As I lifted my wings, a tightness and vague numb sensation constricted my movement, but I was lucky. I'd gotten away mostly unscathed. Dennis must have found me in a crumpled heap at the zoo. And then he must have carried me, held my limp body in his soft mouth, and waited with me here. Hoping I would get up again. This may be a projection, but I'd like to think he felt lost without me.

"Where did you bring us, Dennis?"

A glance upward revealed a towering pyramid of needled branches. The Douglas fir. We were sitting on the stone steps of the teal and white house. The air was the blistering cold of freezer-burnt venison. Above, peeking between spiny fir limbs, blanketing blue laced with orange and raspberry sherbet told me it was very early in the morning. Not really a time either of us were yet accustomed to. I could tell Dennis hadn't slept by the wiry energy coming off him, like he'd been plugged in and blown a fuse.

Dennis plodded to the front door and whined. He looked back at me with a face that could sink a thousand ships, then dragged his catcher-mitt paws down the length of the door. I hopped to where the window was and lifted to get a look inside. I launched my body into the air but it immediately pitched to the side. I flapped harder, a frantic rooster's flight, and clawed on to the window ledge to peer in.

Cinnamon was by the front door that separated her and Dennis, looking like a flattened hand muff. One thing was clear: The Black Tide had come in, its dark spume lapping at her little ginger body. She was giving up. I launched from the steps, flapping with all my might. One of my wings felt tethered as I descended to the ground in a hideous corkscrew shape like a duck penis. The other thing that was now clear was that I couldn't fly. Something had happened to my wing where the numbness lingered like a winter chill. Dennis was watching me with amber eyes. I didn't want to alarm him. We certainly couldn't have two dogs in the throes of depression—these were Cymbalta-less times, for shit sakes. But the implications of being a near-flightless bird in this brutal world were horrifying. I felt the weight of doom, as if I should be preparing my will, perhaps penning some pithy quips for my own eulogy. My defense had always been to take to the air. Now what would I do? I was a sitting duck.

Perhaps a penguin, who already can't fly because they were born utterly useless, would give up in the face of a setback like this. But this wasn't an option for me. I'd been raised as a MoFo, and I knew that of all the things MoFos are, they are not quitters. MoFos never gave up on the belief that they could land on the moon, and by thunder, they did it! (After sensibly sending up a few test subjects including cats, tortoises, mice, mealworms, a rabbit, chimpanzees, rhesus macaques, squirrel monkeys, cynomolguses and pig-tailed monkeys, a boatload of dogs, and some fruit flies.) Winston Churchill, an English MoFo who liked cigars and his curtains to be made from iron, famously said, "Never, never, never give up!" Steve Jobs, the MoFo who invented the iPod and the black turtle-neck, said, "Be punctual, never give up, achieve your goals, even when everything goes bad." He was pretty amazing; he may have been a wizard. And when Jackie Chan or Chuck Norris was surrounded by hordes of inexplicably sweaty bad guys, did they give up? Never! They fought back, avoiding a hailstorm of bullets with their mid-air body-torpedo spins, "who farted?" expressions, and long, feathery mullets. How's that for optimism and an indelible spirit? MoFos didn't need wings to soar! Maybe being grounded would make me more MoFo than ever.

So, I got to doing what MoFos do best: I got to thinking. I

thought about not having hands or working wings and then I decided—much like a penguin tuning out the massive amount of danger it constantly faces—not to focus on what I couldn't do, but rather on what I could do. And when I thought of the things I was capable of, well, then and only then did a plan start to form. It was risky, wild, and far-fetched, but it was all my own. And it started with a treasure hunt.

I fluttered haphazardly onto Dennis's back and gave a sharp whistle. It had become clear on this second attempt at going airborne that I now had the aviation skills of an obese chicken. Again, I tried to focus on the positive and not the comparison to a bird who likes to sing while ovulating and has the worst retirement plan of all time (pot pie). Dennis understood that I had a plan, and both of us could feel electricity in the morning air.

After Dennis urinated on the Douglas fir and I bobbed up and down, bowing out my apologies like the arm of a *maneki-neko* cat, we set off along Phinney Avenue. Maneuvering Dennis wasn't as straightforward as one might hope. I could have really used some reins, but we didn't have time for these sorts of luxuries. Instead, I relied upon the training I'd done with him, ordering him to "Stay!" or "Let's go!" The trickiest part was not having a system for telling him to go left or right, but I eventually found that he got the gist if I leaned in the desired direction from my perch on his thick back. Unless he smelled something that piqued his interest; then we were screwed, and I resigned myself to fulfilling his quest to water a fire hydrant or investigate a pile of rotting trash. As usual, we were at the mercy of his honker. But for the most part, our mission was full steam ahead.

Aura's stupid song had started up but I blocked it out by humming tunes I'd once heard on the radio, including one about memories by a songbird of a MoFo named Barbra Drysand. The sun was drizzling the rows of buildings on

Phinney Avenue with the liquid gold of a pale ale. The first area we investigated was an apartment building. The windows were all smashed, which allowed us to hop over the base of the white doorframe and into its ransacked lobby. A fake kentia palm lay on its side, terra-cotta pot smashed, soil spilled on the lobby tiles like leaking blood. A wall of metal mailboxes were dented and warped. A broken door beckoned.

"Hello?" I said, hoping to flush out any sick MoFos or anything else hiding near the lobby. Dennis and I waited. Silence. You could have heard a dust mite queef in there. Satisfied that we were alone for now, I hopped off Dennis and began searching. I had explained to him what we were looking for, but didn't feel he'd fully grasped the concept. A door was hanging by one hinge, half-blocking a room that called itself the "rental office." Something quite gruesome had gone down in the rental office, as evidenced by the MoFo leg that was sticking out the top of a mangled filing cabinet. It appeared to have been there for quite some time, certainly long enough for a collacine of maggots to take up residence in the calf's skin, buzzing about how grateful they were, how wonderful life had become. The youthful arthropods were in full celebration, excitedly commemorating their sacred Feast Of Meats, which precedes The Phenomenal Transformation wherein they blossom into shit-seeking houseflies. It was a sobering reminder that everything is a matter of perspective. All of them sounded drunk with happiness, fat with food and future, and disturbingly like Stevie Nicks.

Blood spattered the office walls. One of those insidious inspirational posters that said LEADERSHIP was barely hanging on to its place on the wall. It had a bald eagle on it. Irksome. What the hell do bald eagles know about leadership? The EXCELLENCE one had shattered on the ground, flimsy poster naked and exposed. It also had a bald eagle. I stepped on it,

ripping the eagle's white head with my foot. It felt great. Some
sort of tornado appeared to have ravaged the place. Rental
agreements, keys, and packages littered the cramped office.

"Find it, Dennis!" I cawed. Dennis got to sniffing around,
but I couldn't be sure he wasn't just looking for a rogue
sausage. I poked my beak into the keyholes of the filing
cabinet. They wouldn't open. The drawers of the desk were of
particular interest to me. I pecked at the wooden fortresses,
but couldn't persuade them to open-sesame. By this point,
Dennis was lying down with his paws over one of the packages.
He got to work slapping it with his black toenails and tearing
apart the cardboard with his teeth. I watched, impressed by
his determination. Bright colors emerged from the brown
box. Teals, pinks, chick-yellow polka dots. Dennis had hit the
mother lode—artisanal chocolates and a package of elite hand-
made marshmallows. I hobbled over to him and immediately
confiscated the chocolate, having seen how, after pillaging
Hershey's bars, he could lacquer a living room. We shared the
marshmallows and then got back to the hunt at hand.

I hopped up the apartment building's stairs to the first floor.
The corridor was right out of *The Shining*, dark but for the
sliver of morning light that snuck in through a sad porthole.
Various items lay strewn on the corridor's maroon carpet. A
hairbrush. Hair ties and pins. A bottle of Aqua Net. An empty
protein shake bottle. I had an idea. I sidled up to Apartment
100 and wondered if it was possible. I snatched up one of the
bobby pins and used my beak to straighten out the wire. Then
I called Dennis to the door and hopped up on his back, lining
myself up with the lock. I inserted my pin into the lock and
jostled. And jostled. And jostled. The jostling went on for quite
some time, until my beak was sore, and Dennis kept sighing
because he was bored shitless. I abandoned that idea, cursing
MacGyver and his perfectly preened mullet. It had been a long

shot, and even if I'd picked the lock, we still had the matter of the handle to deal with. The rest of the doors were all shut to us, save one: apartment 107.

107 had a door, but it had gone several rounds with the machete that lay on its doormat. I approached with caution, Dennis plodding behind me. I could hear the MoFo before I could see him. Bubbling gurgles echoed, bouncing off the once-white walls of the apartment. I allowed tiny sparks of hope to rise inside me. Perhaps, just perhaps, we'd find one injured but not yet touched by sickness. The apartment was fancier than my home, with properly framed paintings that weren't just thrift store art like our kitchen masterpiece, "Skeletor and Jesus Fly-Fishing." Signs of a struggle announced themselves as upturned ottomans and pieces of porcelain on the floor. The musky smell of rotting algae filled the air. I found an aquarium filled with fish that had long since perished, floating like milk skin on a film of green. The gurgling persisted. Dennis got busy chewing a high heel with a red sole—old habits die hard. I hadn't seen him this enthralled with a shoe since he was a puppy, so apparently not all footwear is created equal. I can't fault him; as Dennis has shown me, dogs eat shoes so their MoFos don't leave the house. I left him happily squeaking leather on his canines and went to investigate the gurgling.

The MoFo was in a soaking tub, marinating in his own secretions. He was wrapped in rope that was knotted around both the curtain railing and the faucet. He wore a hairdryer and its cord as a necklace. Since his head was above the brown sludge, you could clearly see the burn on his face in the perfect outline of an iron. The red of it really set off the color of his eyes. There are bad days and then there are days when you've been bitch-slapped with an iron. There was a pink letter opener sticking out of his neck, and a KitchenAid mixer bobbed in the water with him, still plugged in to the wall socket. Perfumes and shampoo bottles and lotions lay all around the bathroom with their liquids now congealed on the floor, leading Detective S.T. to deduce that they'd been used as projectiles. When I put them together, the signs hinted at a potential domestic disagreement. Bloody prints—the dainty size of Big Jim's Tinder dates' feet—led away from the bathroom and out the front door of the apartment. There had been a woman here, which meant...

I summoned Dennis, excitedly insisting he join me in the excavation. After thoroughly ransacking the bathroom, I took my sleuthing skills to the bedroom, where clothes vomited from a dresser—someone had been in a hurry to leave. I scoured the closet, disturbing dust clouds and pecking at mountains of clothes. No dice. Where did Tiffany S. used to leave hers? The kitchen smelled of rotting gases, of geriatric chicken eggs. But on the counter, next to a blood-slick hammer, a chair leg, and a spilled prescription of something called Klonopin, was a purse. I plunged my beak into the soft pink leather that was called Kate Spade and rifled through. A bottle of bear repellent, a wine opener, a ream of condoms, Alka-Seltzer, a mini bottle of Tabasco, a spring-assisted rainbow-blade tactical hunting knife, and a sizable packet of Midol took up most of the space. Sign of a ladies' night out? I couldn't be sure. A note that had a list of names like *Downtown Emergency Services Center. Dr. Hsu's Acupuncture and Herbs. Seattle Medical Center. CDC* and a list of corresponding phone numbers was crumpled at the bottom. Another note, this one in hurried handwriting, said *Cash, canned food, flashlights, water. ~~Find H.~~ Find Sarah. Find a way to Whidbey.* Were the healthy MoFos hiding out on Whidbey Island? Could it be? I swallowed my hope. In the side pocket of the pink bag called Kate Spade was what I was looking for. I chirped, opening the rectangular black case to find...a compact mirror. *Dammit.* The expectant black bird peering back at me was not at all what I was looking for. I hopped up onto the perfume-stained couch, digging my beak into its crevices, a known treasure cache. Stuffed down the side of a cushion, a hidden velvet pouch had been sequestered, containing a packet of birth control pills, a receipt for Lovers—birthplace of Big Jim's blow-up dolls—and a bracelet. Evidence of an affair.

Dennis abandoned his shoe and disappeared into the closet. Moments later, he emerged with a look of jubilation, excited to show me what was dangling from his mouth. An argyle sock.

"No, Dennis. That's not what I asked for."

His rudder of a tail swung left to right. Upon seeing my disapproval, he dropped the sock and retreated to the closet. I had decided we should leave apartment 107 when he re-appeared. This time, he had an iPhone in his mouth. Open beaked, I stared at the bloodhound I'd grossly underestimated his entire slobber-slimed life. Dennis returned to the high heel, flopping on the ground to resume masticating.

"Good boy, Dennis!" My dear Dennis had cracked the case.

I encouraged Dennis—in shoe ecstasy, now having removed the heel and punctured through the scarlet sole—to say a small prayer as I pushed my beak on the power button. I held my breath. Dennis stopped chewing, staring at me with a giant saliva leash attached to the collapsed ex-shoe. He emitted a thin whine. I hopped from side to side, waiting.

Come on.

The phone's screen lit up and in an instant it was Christmas, July Fourth, the Seahawks winning the Super Bowl, and a 7-Eleven–wide sale on Cheetos®! I hopped up and down, un-able to contain my glee. That cool electric beam was the same majestic luminance that came from the enchanted interior of a refrigerator and Dennis and I stared, enjoying its instantly cloaking comfort, realizing how much we'd missed it, how long we'd been in the dark.

I powered off the iPhone and we got the hell out of that hideous apartment complex, making our way along Phinney Avenue in search of the second part of my plan. There may or may not have been a very quick detour into A la Mode Pies, where Dennis snarfed down what looked to be an ancient cobbler. I helped myself to something that had once called itself a bourbon butterscotch pie, but only a little—I had to reel that shit in. Jesus, at this rate, if the predators didn't get us, the diabetes would. Still, a little sugar rush might not be the worst thing for what I was planning.

I clutched the smartphone in my beak, feeling a growing sense of terror. The cell phone represented power, a lusted-after treasure. All the sick MoFos were wearing out their limbs and eyes searching for its luminous glory. And in a world with no electricity, we had as long as the battery would last. We set down Phinney Avenue back the way we came, under a bright overcast sky the color of silver silk. This time, I was the one who was hunting. On the road ahead, between the Ride the Ducks vehicle that lay on its side and a pile of empty beer crates, a willowy MoFo wandered alone in front of us. He was naked as a mole-rat apart from the neon body paint splashed across his hairless torso that said "Live in full color" and his unicorn hat. He staggered toward a corrugated metal sheet that had been torn from a storefront. He placed his twisted face up close to the metal and started to trace his eyes and head left and right, left and right, as if tracking something written in its grooves. On his back, the rainbow of paint spelled out "Proceed with love and you will live forever." He was missing a butt cheek. We walked right past him. We knew he was lost in his sickness.

I found my prey in the middle of the avenue, standing on letters where someone had poured out a message in gas and lit it on fire. TURN IT ALL OFF, the blackened message cried. She was staring at the sky, still and white as a birch. Her pants and vest were of shiny black leather, her hair a long, silver rope. Tattoos spidered up her doughy arms—a naked pinup woman straddling a torpedo, a laughing skull wearing a beanie, a motorbike that was on fire—art prophetically imitating life, seeing as how a Harley lay charred on the sidewalk nearby. She was corpulent, surprisingly intact, and with a wattle like Dennis's. She was absolutely perfect for my purposes.

I croaked at Dennis, preparing him for what was to happen next. With his fur grasped in my feet, I could feel his stiffening reluctance to go near the biker MoFo. But time had been brought back to our world in the form of a battery whose limited life drained away by the minute. We needed to act fast. We passed the biker MoFo to give ourselves an advantage. I ruffled my feathers to calm my nerves, quietly telling myself that this was what I was good at. S.T., A+ honors student of luring, had become the teacher. Gingerly, I placed the cell phone onto Dennis's thick back. It was time.

I used my beak to long-press the power button, remembering Big Jim's delight the first time I'd gotten it right, the Cheeto® reward, that cheddar-y flavor of success. "Good boy, Shit Turd." The phone lit up underneath me, an electric bright screen and an apple silhouette. I looked up. The biker Mofo's neck snapped toward me, red eyes widening. A horrible shrill whine streaked through the midmorning silence. The Unicorn MoFo swiveled. Horn and penis swinging, he locked us in his sights.

"Let's go!" I screeched at Dennis, driving my claws into his back. The MoFos broke into a run. Dennis kicked into high gear, thundering across Phinney Avenue. Ducking and clenching so hard my feet shook, I pressed against the wind that threatened to topple me from Dennis. A peek behind me revealed two MoFos, necks craned forward, bouncing unblinking red eyes, their legs pounding the road at an unnatural speed. They were gaining on us. Dennis was fast, but he was no greyhound, and whatever the sickness was, it gave the MoFos strength and speed they'd never had before. Another quick glance—the MoFos had halved the distance between us. I could smell them, the hot scent of decay. I heard their tendons and bones creaking under the impact. They were galloping.

"Faster, Dennis! Faster!" I told him with my feet and the panic seeping from my plumage. The biker let out a deafening shriek. The unicorn coughed back. They were gaining on us. We shot past more apartment buildings, the day care center, and then I could see the Douglas fir pointing from the sky and I said a small prayer that I made up on the spot, as best as an agnostic crow can do. Then Dennis was hurling us up the stone steps of the teal and white house and I jumped off his back using everything I had. I fluttered up to the window ledge, grasping its splintery wooden edge with my feet. I turned. The biker MoFo was in the lead, silver rope swinging behind her, glistening leather and rolls of doughy white skin surging forth, pounding the stone steps, naked unicorn right on her heels. I had seconds to get it right. As her foot touched the Welcome doormat, I whipped my head sideways, sending the iPhone airborne. Throwing myself from the ledge, I scattered out of the way.

I heard the glass shattering before I had the chance to turn and witness the glory. The biker MoFo burst through into the living room, rolling onto the ground and releasing the room's hot breath of fetid air. The unicorn scampered in after her. I fluttered back up the ledge to see both of them diving for the hardwood where the iPhone had settled. They huddled, necks craned unnaturally, worshipping the screen's bright glow. They extended their arthritic pointer fingers, tracing them listlessly against the iPhone's screen. Silence. It worried me. My eyes darted around the glass carpet, around the empty wrappers and dusty furniture. Where was Cinnamon? I bobbed my head in preparation, then, in my best Big Jim, I said, "ZzzzZZZt! Come!"

Several painful moments of stillness slogged by. Just decay and dog shit and broken MoFos feeding their mysterious addiction. Had she run? Panicked and hurt herself? Had she curled up in a corner and...I couldn't bring myself to think of it. And then two tiny button eyes framed by a mane of flaming ginger appeared from under an armchair.

"ZzzzZZZt! Come! Quickly!" I repeated. Cinnamon gave the MoFos a skittish wide berth as she scuttled to the window. With one agile leap, she cleared the ledge and was met by Dennis, who had emerged from his hiding spot. He was especially goofy in his rapture, all dangling ears and flopping wattle and four left paws. He huffed in open mouthed delight. The pair inspected one another's buttholes, upholding perhaps the very worst tradition from our old life, and Dennis offered the little redhead a play bow. Cinnamon didn't seem ready to play yet. She panted heavily, overexerted, high on freedom and fear. The whites of her eyes showed. I nipped that play shit in the bud, jumping on Dennis's back and rallying the troops forward. Cinnamon scurried to catch up, eager to escape the place she'd done hard time in.

"You alright?" I asked her.

"Yes," came her response, as fragile as the first tinkling notes of a hummingbird hatchling. Perhaps it would take time for Cinnamon to be herself again. I would give her space to come around. Our little murder had grown, and the three of us had the rest of a purpose to carry out. We'd lost our bait to a biker and a unicorn, but I had another plan. And for the first time in an age, the clock was ticking.

CHAPTER 19

❦

S.T.
GOD KNOWS WHERE ALONG PHINNEY AVENUE,
SEATTLE, WASHINGTON, USA

We had set off, the three of us, determined to find the others. The other Dennises and Cinnamons and S.T.s. The survivors. Telephone poles lay collapsed on their sides in the middle of Phinney Avenue, their wires twisted like discarded dental floss. An electronics repair shop had been ransacked and gutted, hit at one point by a hurricane of searching MoFos. I told Dennis and Cinnamon to wait by the front of the shop as I hopped through its graveyard of smashed plastic, motherboards, televisions with busted faces, and snaking wires. Shelves had been ripped from the walls, now rife with beckoning black holes. A strange, hauntingly high-pitched song provided an eerie soundtrack. I set out to find where the music came from.

A teeming mischief of rats and a clutter of spiders with hairy, beaver-brown bodies had divided the shop into their respective territories. The spiders watched me near their precious nest, rearing onto their hind legs and hissing obscenities at me. The female one was particularly vicious, vowing that if I took one more step closer, she would bind, gag, and torture my entire family with her infrangible silks. The rats were quick to assess that I wasn't a threat, continuing with their avid grooming—they're massively anal about personal hygiene—while some convened for a meeting about plans to create a network of tunnels they were calling "The Real Seattle Underground." The eerie song turned out to be the symphony of rats filing down their ever-growing choppers on a hollow lead pipe, a wailing, sinister siren song that seemed perfect for the times we lived in. There were no cell phones. Cinnamon, Dennis, and I set back off down Phinney Avenue. We came across a King 5 helicopter that had crashed on top of a silver Tesla, bisecting it. Its once-sleek lines were now severed, jutting and sharp. Oily tire tracks—signs of panicked escape—zigzagged across Phinney Avenue, now a phantom of its former self.

Then we found a row of houses. The first was a towering brick Tudor home, its front yard choking on weeds, its arched entryway leading to a covered porch. I indulged in a fantasy—I just couldn't help myself—of rapping my beak on the door. The door opens and there stands a MoFo with a straight back and clear eyes. "Are you alright?" they ask me. And then I tell them everything and, nodding their head, they stroke the length of my feathers with a smooth finger while offering me a condolence Cheeto®. The MoFo with clear, bright eyes tells us everything is going to be okay, that there's a cure. That everything will go back to the way it was, goodness I'm devastatingly handsome, and would I like a croissant?

I was still warm, glowing from the daydream, when I hopped up the steps and under the arched entryway. I thrust myself onto a porch bench—the wooden swinging kind—to peer in through the intact bay windows. The home looked unsullied—floor-to-ceiling library of undisturbed books, orca-black grand piano, a marble bust of an old white MoFo. A wall-sized painting of two African female MoFos laughing together, heads swathed in bright blue, red, and green wraps, their long necks dripping with gold, faced the front door. I hoped, a deep hope from the part of me that answers when I'm very still, that they were still out there, laughing together under an African sun. That they weren't just a gold-framed painting in a broken city. And then my eyes tracked along a Persian carpet, at the edge of which was a large beige lump. My heart plummeted. I could tell from the stillness of the scene, from the chest's lack of rise and fall that the English mastiff's heart no longer beat. This would be the picture in a lot of homes, I imagined, where the domestics couldn't get out, didn't have anyone to answer their desperate pleas. Dennises with no S.T.s. I started to move away from the front door, ready to find the next home, a small stone lodged in my throat.

I hadn't noticed Dennis and Cinnamon come up the steps. They were side by side at the front door. Dennis dragged his pancake paws down the wood, Cinnamon pacing in tight circles by his side.

"Look again," she was telling me. I hopped back onto the swinging bench and surveyed the scene again. This time I caught the shining sets of eyes staring at me from underneath the grand piano. There were two other living beings in the Tudor house. Ignited with purpose, I fluttered back to Dennis and jumped onto his back.

"Dennis, let's go!" I told him. We had to act quickly. I couldn't tell what shape the cowering dogs were in, but the deceased English mastiff told a story of starvation. I tried to think—where else would we find a phone? It had been such a trial to find the last one, only to have it pillaged by the sick MoFo equivalent of the Village People. There were more houses to our left, but how were we to get inside to find a phone if a phone was the very thing we needed to get inside? It felt like that whole chicken-and-egg conundrum that MoFos are always squabbling about. Phones were now our highest currency, and it would take me time and MoFo-like imagination to find one.

"Let's go, Dennis! Cinnamon!" I said, and with little scampering Cinnamon bringing up the caboose, we took off back up Phinney Avenue, stopping before we reached the electronics repair shop. I jumped from Dennis and sidled up to the mangled mass of twisted metal that was left of the King 5 helicopter and the silver Tesla. I gingerly stepped between lumps of scorched metal, shredded bits of airbag, and masses of splintered glass. The Tesla's steering wheel was embedded in one of the chopper's seats, now lying in the middle of the road like a terrifying art installation on vehicle safety. Eventually, I found what I was looking for. I picked up a sheet of glass, approximately the size of a tablet screen, and gingerly waddled back to Dennis.

The glass felt like Big Jim's framed photo of Tiffany S. that I once tried to jettison from the upstairs window, heavy and awkward to hold on to. It took the last of the aged bourbon butterscotch treat in me to flap back onto Dennis, glass sheet balanced in my beak. I laid the glass flat onto Dennis's back but as soon as he started to walk, his lumbering sway made it slip. I barely caught it in my beak, settling for holding it, as uncomfortable as it was, partially propped up on Dennis's back. Dennis sat down abruptly, causing me and the glass sheet to slide down the length of him. I was pushed onto my back and pinned against the tarmac by the glass.

"Caaaaw! Help…I can't…ugh…stuck…heavy…fuuuuuck," I squawked, trying to wriggle out from the hefty sheet. "Gah! Nfff! Raa!" It wouldn't budge. *This is it,* I thought, *this is where our beloved hero gets flower-pressed beneath glass for eternity like some sort of priceless sports collectible.* "Dennis!"

Dennis's enormous nose lingered above me, his breath

clouding the glass with moisture. He stared at me blankly for a few moments. There was a subtle spark in his saggy eyes— a look of amusement.

"Dennis! For the love of Tostitos! A little help?"

He yawned.

"Dennis! GET THIS OFF ME!" I squawked, feeling like an unsold Barbie.

A weight literally lifted from my chest. I struggled to my feet to see that Dennis had the glass between his jowls and was patiently waiting for me to hop back onto his back. He'd enjoyed the crap out of the whole scenario, that Skittle-brained scoundrel.

We walked back along Phinney Avenue in a tender shuffle. Cinnamon scurried along next to us. She was a skittish little thing, tongue lapping the air like a tiny plumeria petal. Her scars did not line her body, but nevertheless showed in her darting eye movements, the flinches that rippled under her fur. She was at all times ready to break into a run. Like Dennis, she wasn't much of a talker, and I didn't know how much of that had to do with what she'd been through.

As we shuffled up to the overgrown primrose, lilac, and Black Beauty elderberry bushes that once framed and now were proliferating around the Tudor house, we encountered our next problem: where to find a MoFo. The unicorn and the biker had been too fast once riled and were now too far away, no sense to backtrack. This section of Phinney Avenue was quiet and deserted. Fluttering to the ground with a body full of adrenaline and an injured wing was tricky. Much to my surprise, I was beginning to feel a microscopic fleck of empathy for penguins, finally understanding what it's like to essentially be a winged Mr. Magoo. But I wasn't going to let it get me down, no sir. MoFos didn't have wings and they were the greatest creatures on earth. After almost impaling myself on a crystalline

edge, I helped Dennis gently lay the sheet down onto the tarmac and looked around. No sign of MoFos. We would have to
wander in search of them, but that meant carrying the awkward
slice of glass with us, which slowed us down, made us incredibly
vulnerable, and put us farther away from where we wanted to
be—the Tudor house. I fluttered back onto Dennis's back and
then noticed something. Cinnamon was trembling. A full body
shake had her in its talons. She stared ahead, across the street.
Dennis, seeming to sense my intentions, plodded forward to
where she was staring. Cinnamon did not follow. She stood on
the tarmac, fear squeezing her throat.

"What is it, Cinnamon?" I asked with a head cock.

"There. They're right there." Her ginger fur was puffed.

Across the street was another house, a Seattle foursquare
home festooned with sleeping Christmas lights. In the front
yard, surrounded by an ambush of brambles, an inflatable
Santa and his compressed reindeer team rippled at the mercy
of the afternoon wind. The wind blew to a crescendo, tousling
my feathers. I looked up at pregnant, darkening clouds that
converged overhead. A syrupy smell of anticipation filled
the air; the grass was anxiously awaiting the rain, its thirst
palpable. Dennis's careful lumber slowed, his head hung low,
ears and facial folds flapping against the glass sheet, as he
inhaled clues to a world most of us will never know. He was
taking us to the source of Cinnamon's tremors. He stopped
as we neared the rusted green mailbox of the house, before
we'd reached the trunk of a voluptuous pin oak tree. Slow as
a snail's silver, he raised his nose and the glass sheet in line
with the oak. My face now numb from clenching my beak, I
fluttered from his back, and helped him gently prop the glass
against the curb. A sharp blast of wind lifted me off my feet. I
flapped hard to lower back to the tarmac, a jolt of pain streaking up my wing. The ringing quiet of it all bothered me. It

wasn't good that I couldn't even hear the boil-brained twits of *Aura* squabbling and gloating about their sexual capabilities. A few steps took me underneath the gigantic pin oak that draped me in shadow with its plethoric dressing of leaves. Not being able to see the sky summoned winter to my veins. Then I saw what made Cinnamon tremble.

Above me, six legs dangled from separate branches. One owner of two legs was a geisha; the white paint of her face had mingled with blood, streaking her olive-green kimono in sickly pink. Her once-impeccable ebony chignon and its decorative *kanzashi* now hung limp, strands like greasy eels. She had no eyes, just red-crusted, empty holes. On the thick collar of the branch was another MoFo dressed in frilly Victorian garb, rib cage suffocated by a corset, billowing bloody fabric cascading from the branch. The third MoFo wore a traditional Korean *hanbok*, once resplendent in crayon orange and pink, now speckled with moss and gelatinous lumps of MoFo tissue. One of her arms hung by a few defiant strands of skin. Around her grimy neck hung a lanyard, an access card for Seattle Historical Costuming. Between the three MoFos was a gaping tree hollow. The MoFos were silent as midnight tombstones. They used their humped backs and unnatural elongated necks to stretch out and touch their skulls to a black object. Stuffed into the tree's cavernous hollow was one of those headsets you put on your eyes to transport you to another world. The three costumed MoFos repeatedly leaned in, pressing their foreheads to the shiny black plastic. I stifled a cry of horror.

Many months ago, I had sat in my cozy craftsman home as Big Jim lay gently marinating in Fireball whiskey and Ben & Jerry's, snoring like a DeWalt power saw. My heart soared; I loved this part of the day. I fluttered over to him, commandeering the remote and channel surfing for hours, absorbing the rich and nuanced history of MoFos. I learned about the Maasai tribe of Africa with their elongated earlobes and ability to speak Maa, English, *and* Swahili! I learned of the Alaska Inuit, the Aikenhead clan, and the Kwakwaka'wakw tribe, how the young Brazilian Sataré-Mawé MoFos dip their hands into a woven basket of fire ants for eleven hours to show their bravery. I watched the porcelain politesse of a Japanese tea ceremony, the Icelandic celebration of Sjómannadagur for the seafaring MoFos, the Monkey Buffet Festival of Thailand, and how young Greek MoFos' teeth are thrown onto rooftops with an expectant wish. These were all ways to paint a life, customs to celebrate the phenomenal gift of living. I'd been so mesmerized, my heart as light as the barbs of a semiplume, thinking of how a MoFo was capable of carving out the world to be anything they wished. And here sat three representatives of MoFos' rich history, rotting in the boughs of an oak. I was witnessing the slow extermination of MoFo history and culture. And it was absolutely devastating.

But no damn time to wallow; I had to appreciate the opportunity presented, no matter how gory and tragic, how much a cesspool of heinous fuckery. This wasn't going to be easy. I shuffled back to Dennis and the glass, emitting a series of clicks to let Dennis know it was time. Grasping the crystalline sheet in my beak, I thrust myself onto Dennis's back, propping the sheet upright. Dennis made several careful paw placements to inch us forward until we were almost underneath the pin oak and the three sinister swaying dresses. I tilted the sheet to allow it to catch any light and, most importantly, attention. My heart thundered. Another cold snap puffed our fur and feathers. The MoFos persisted with their disturbed undulating above our heads, focused on the headset. A nervous whistle freed itself from Dennis's nose. Readjusting my grip and the angle of the glass sheet, I projected a tiny light ray onto the oak tree. Lowering the glass, I navigated the little white ray, forcing it to dance up the tree and onto the soiled fabric of the kimono. *Steady.* The ray fluttered up the olive-green fabric, up its desecrated embroidered chrysanthemums, and onto the glaucous skin of the MoFo's face. It lit up the vandalized holes of her eyes. Dennis flinched. She didn't move. I carefully flew the ray across the oak's branch and onto the face of the Victorian MoFo. My breath hitched as the ray lit up her crimson eye. Dennis braced. I fluttered my wings, driving my claws into his back, holding on tight. And then nothing. The MoFos didn't move; they weren't swayed by the light or the sheen of glass. Frustration billowed in my chest. Why weren't they interested in the glass, the movement? Why were the MoFos all exhibiting such unpredictable behavior?

Remembering that I promised myself not to focus on limitations, I set to thinking. An idea struck me, though I wasn't sure I could pull it off. But then I heard Big Jim's booming voice echoing through time. Big Jim would often channel the advice of superstar quarterback of his beloved Seattle Seahawks, Russell Wilson (long before he probably became hippo food): "Always persevere, always have a great perspective, and always have a great purpose in your life." He would often follow this with another Russell-ism: "Why not me?" Buoyed by the good memories and positive words, I swallowed and silently repeated the mantra: *Why not me?* I could do this. Flooding my mind with the memory of a sound, I opened my beak wide, and from deep down in my throat, I let out the noise. Against all odds, having never recreated it before, I did the world's most flawless rendition of an iPhone text message alert.

"Ding ding."

The MoFos snapped their necks down toward us in unison. Four eyes and two red holes lasered in on us. Time evaporated. Suddenly MoFos were scampering across the oak branches, a heinous low whine piercing the air.

"Let's go, Dennis!" I screeched, but Dennis had already taken off, dropping from the curb and onto the tarmac to cross Phinney Avenue. Ahead, Cinnamon darted into an elderberry bush. The MoFos were on all fours in a breakneck arachnid run, gaining on us by the second. They were faster, more agile than the other MoFos, dresses ripping as they thundered across Phinney Avenue. Dennis was in a panic, running for our lives, bouncing me up and down on his back. The glass started to slip and I couldn't hold on with the jostling and bumping, but we were nearing the windows of the Tudor house and I had to. My beak aching, Dennis shot up the stairs to the porch, the glass sheet slipping off his back. I held on tight, the weight of glass pulling me from Dennis. And suddenly, Dennis was running alongside the swinging porch and I leapt into the air with the glass in my beak. The MoFos jumped, hurling themselves into the air with me, horrible yellow and brown fingernails reaching out for me, for what I was carrying. They burst through the bay windows, launching me into a meteor shower of glass. I hit the wooden floors, rolling into a series of tumbles. I lifted my wing to shield myself from the raining shards. Raising my beak, I found myself face-to-face with the mastiff's carcass, skin in deep valleys between its mountainous bones, its tongue spilled out onto the floor. A fate I didn't want to share.

One sonorous bark from Dennis didn't need interpretation. He was telling me to get the hell out of there. I hobbled back toward the bay windows, fluttering over a sea of sparkling glass. Just then, two brown bodies hurtled past me, leaping to freedom through the gaping windows. Behind me, the three MoFos were on all fours, their faces close to the ground. Horrible wheezy snuffing sounds choked the silence as they hunted, sniffing as if truffle hogs. The MoFo in the *hanbok* had clambered to the lustrous piano and was smashing her face against its black lines. The Victorian MoFo rose onto two legs, her head twisting 360 degrees in search of a screen. I didn't have long. Flapping hurt, but I was able to launch onto the windowsill and then tumble from the ledge onto the familiar fawn fur of Dennis's back. Cinnamon was practically Velcro-ed to his side. We took off, running as fast as we could from the ravaged Tudor house. And as we ran, passing neighboring shops, we saw the brown-and-white bodies of two dogs—German shorthaired pointers, a strong legged, agile hunting breed with a fighting chance at life—disappearing into the distance. They were alive and animated, running under a swirling gunmetal-gray sky. Their paws kissed the tarmac as they ran. Sweat shimmered across the rippling muscles that would give them every chance at a future in their new territory. And suddenly, I was surrounded by life and vibrant color, in the tickling laughter of the leaves, the viridescent hope of glistening grass blades and an ashen sky that was ready to give birth. We weren't even pissed that they didn't stop to thank us.

CHAPTER 20

S.T.
IN FRONT OF SOME SHADY-ASS TOWN HOUSES,
SEATTLE, WASHINGTON, USA

It was Cinnamon who stopped in front of the cluster of town houses. She seemed to have embraced our mission, a light in those Hershey's Kiss eyes. I no longer saw their whites, the sparking fear. Finding life and those who needed our help, I learned, was her great strength. Cinnamon had an innate sense for what was behind a locked door and a fortress of brick, seeming to know whenever someone was in need of rescue. Her vibrancy had returned, perhaps sparked by a sense of purpose, and Dennis and I got to see her in her full glory, a little dog who resembled a cute soufflé but was fueled by a fiery passion.

"Here! In here!" she said, darting around the ground-floor window to a town house where a flower box hung, full of long-deceased petunias and pansies. Her quick, saucy steps and the sheen in her eyes told me we had work to do.

"Do you think there's—" I let my question and the hope it held trail away. To feel hope for a healthy MoFo meant to feel the heartache of disappointment. I had to stop doing it to myself. There was a small crack in the window ledge. I fluttered onto the window box, inhaling the ripe bouquet of rotting flowers, to peer into the window. Inside was a humble home with country-style furnishings—cushions with embroidery about grandma being a badass, chicken decor, plaid for days, and a buttload of mason jars. I saw a rocking chair but no sign of MoFos. The beige carpet, however, was mottled with what looked like little black-and-white slugs, some shiny, wet, and slippery, some long–dried-up. I knew what it meant and I searched for the culprit among the gingham, farm-inspired effluvia and hanging wooden signs that said "Trust me, you can dance—Vodka" and "No bitchin' in ma kitchin'."

"Come out! Come out!" barked Cinnamon.

An agitated little puff of white, brown, and black burst into view, flittering around the periphery of the town house, its cage. I lodged my beak into the gap in the window, pushing hard, leveraging against the glass. Wood and beak fought against each other. I pushed harder. With a groan of protest, the gap in the window widened. The house sparrow—a saucy bird known for its mischief, undeniable ingenuity (they were the first of the feathered to start adorning their nests with cigarette butts to ward off insects), and synanthropic shadowing of MoFos—shot out through the gap in the window. Cinnamon, energized by the victory, spun in circles.

"You're free, little bird! Free to fly again!" she chimed, speaking from experience. She let out a tight yip, darting toward Dennis and engaging in the first play bow we'd seen. Dennis bowed back and the pair chased one another across the tall grass in front of the town houses, goofy faces stretched by smiles. Their spongy paw pads flashed into view as they pounded through the dandelions. The sparrow hovered, wings a beating blur as it addressed me.

"Thank you, thank you, thank you," cheeped the sparrow.

"Is there anyone else inside? Anyone living?" I asked, the hope of a live MoFo tasting sour and decadent, like a stolen tart.

"Just me, me and the insects I've been living on. I will never forget this, Blackwing. I'm indebted to you." He was twitchy, something inside him wound so tight it was ready to snap. I wondered how long he'd been trapped. Sparrows travel in vast quarrels, dependent on one another to stay out of the digestive systems of predators (who doesn't find a sparrow to be a delicious hors d'oeuvre? They're like airborne pizza rolls). But sparrows don't do well alone.

"We're trying to rescue the domestics, the survivors that are trapped in homes," I told him.

The sparrow, treading air, darted its head to get a view of the bloodhound and the little ginger dog cavorting below.

"You'll want to go next door."

"What's next door?" But the sparrow, a bird with a thug reputation for the acts of violence they often commit against other feathereds, had vanished into the gray pall. I hopped to the neighboring town house's window. Cinnamon appeared by my side.

"He's right! You must look in here! This is the place!" she yipped.

This one had no window box for me to perch on. Dennis ambled underneath the ledge and I gratefully scrambled onto his back to get a look. A gap in black curtains allowed me to see inside. The scene was bleak. In callous contrast to the country abode next door, this town house held dark secrets. Shredded newspaper, rusty hypodermic needles, and hoarders' squalor littered the floors. The walls bore holes and graffiti in dripping red ink that said, "We brought this on ourselves." Empty cereal boxes, broken plates, rogue bicycle wheels, weird white tubes, smeared brown shit, and spoons and chaos. And hanging by a dirty rope necklace from the staircase railing, with a needle stuck in his arm, was a decomposing MoFo. I gasped, instantly taken back to the day Big Jim and I went to his friend Pete's house for an intervention. Pete had succumbed to the needle, and Big Jim burst into his home like a hurricane, showing tough love with his angry words and eventually his fist. It hadn't worked. Pete chose the needles and the pills over friendship and eventually his heartbeat. Big Jim had swallowed back his tears at Pete's funeral, but I could see them brimming in his eyes, could hear the pain crystalizing in his barreled chest. Pills, needles, headsets that take you to other worlds, perhaps it was something I would never understand about the MoFos. If I had the good fortune to be born a MoFo, I would spend every second of it wisely, enjoying my many talents and gifts. Why run away from perfection? From such immeasurable opportunity?

A stockpile of food, cans of beans, peas, pumpkin, soup, cranberry sauce, and water—some punctured by tooth marks— were sequestered in a corner with a makeshift bed, a sort of paranoid cardboard fortress. On the wall, someone with great skill—the skill only a MoFo could have—had made a black ink drawing of a bird rising above an evergreen. In its beak, the bird held an eight-pointed star. Next to the bird was a perfect MoFo handprint. My skin rippled with bumps.

The bird was a crow.

And below that eerie drawing, writhing on a soiled shower curtain, was a litter of puppies. There were five of them (thank goodness there weren't many more because of my shit counting skills), four black and white, one brown and white, sluggishly worming across the grimy plastic with newly opened eyes, some crusted over. Their mother, a skinny husky, stared through the walls to her coveted freedom with ice-blue eyes. We had to get them out of there. The window was sealed shut.

This would take another round of luring, another carefully executed liberation. Our murder would have to launch into action again, hot on the heels of the sparrow liberation success. I turned to find myself alone and whistled for my partners with a sharp "ZzzzZZZt!" Dennis trotted across the grass, his sunken sad-sap eyes watching me before lifting to the slate sky. Dennis knew a change in the weather was coming. Cinnamon had a delightful case of what Big Jim called "going nuclear" and was tearing around the stretch of tangled grass in wide circles, ginger hair streaming behind her, her tongue—a postage stamp in pink—tasting joy and an air thick with moisture.

"Freeeeeeeeeeeeeeeee!" she hollered. My bloodhound partner had already picked up the scent of the puppies and was at the front door, learning about the town house and its occupants through his olfactory bulb. I was contemplating our return to the chopper crash site to select another tablet-sized sheet of glass, already feeling fatigue in my bird bones, when Cinnamon let out a succession of alarm barks. Her panic, high-pitched hysteria was the soprano yip to Dennis's bass.

"Get back! Back, back, back, away!" Cinnamon was crouching as she coughed out her barks, ginger fur standing on end. Dennis sniffed at the air, turning from the door to face Cinnamon. I followed Cinnamon's anguished gaze to several feet away from her, where a long-legged creature stood, dwarfing her. It was still but for a slight wobble, a small intermittent tremble that caused it to sway like a listing ship. Its eyes, wild and shiny with a forest fire behind them, were fixed on little Cinnamon. A wild dog that's supposed to roam the plains of sub-Saharan Africa, the African painted dog looked out of place in Phinney Ridge, with its satellite dish ears and its exotic coat, a patchwork quilt of mottled pigments. My intuition drummed SOS messages in Morse code. Aside from not belonging in our fine city, there was something else that was very, very wrong with this scenario. African painted dogs are pack animals, strictly social, and this one was utterly alone.

My hunch was confirmed as we watched the wild dog open its mouth. As if possessed, puppeteered by some invisible force, the dog's head was seized by convulsions. It twitched and shuddered for a few horrifying moments, releasing strings of frothy saliva from its gums. And then I knew exactly why this pack animal was alone. *Shit.*

I launched into the air, ready to soar above and mob the wild dog from the air. Three feet into my ascension, a streak of pain shot through my wing, sending me careening, a bumbling mass of black feathers, back to the front step of the filthy town house. I had forgotten my limitation, and I lay crumpled on the cement. But it was going to be alright; there were three of us and one of it and it was sick and faulty, quivering in defectiveness.

Think fast, S.T., think fast.

What we needed was fire, or something sharp—a needle or a spear. I spun to face the trees around us, looking to their trunk bases for fallen branches, something I could wield in front of that wild dog to drive it away from Cinnamon. I hopped forward, announcing myself to the African painted dog and letting Cinnamon know we were there for her, because murders are forever, and what happens to one happens to all. I got five hops forward, vitriolic caws igniting in the air, when I felt a great force envelop my body. I flapped with everything I had, but I couldn't get away. Seconds were ticking by, seconds where Cinnamon needed us, and it took more seconds for me to connect the dots and realize what was happening. Dennis had clamped his jaw down on my good wing. I struggled to free myself, yelling at him—that scrotum-jowled buffoon—that we had to leap into action!

"Dennis! GET OFF!"

Dennis, his mouth soft but firm, held on with a pressure that might as well have been an ocean current. I was an injured minnow, helpless against a great tide. The earth stopped spinning as the African painted dog bared its long teeth, and in the middle of a fit of spasms, I swear it looked right into my eyes, right deep into the part of me that has never changed. And then I knew exactly who I was looking at. I had met The One Who Spits. And The One Who Spits was completely alone, pack-less, and without its murder. It was alone because it had rabies.

We had run out of time. The One Who Spits released a surge of bubbling white foam, the spume of an insidious sickness, and then broke into a run, a twitchy, mechanical charge, hitched by ticks and those intermittent seizures.

"Cinnamon, come! ZzzzZZZt!" I heard myself yell, channeling Big Jim in crisis mode, desperate Big Jim with rocks in his throat as Dennis flew out of our Ravenna yard—*the gate, oh god, Nargatha left the gate open*—and Dennis galloped into the road, Big Jim bellowing at the minivan that was going too fast, and we all screeched—MoFo, crow, brakes, tires—and the van stopped right in front of Dennis's wrinkly face. Big Jim yelled at Dennis again, "DENNIS! COME!" in a stormy voice, nostrils flaring on his bar-fight face, but when Dennis waddled back through the gate sheepishly, Big Jim held our bloodhound in his magnificent arms for a very long time.

"CINNAMON! COME!" I yelled with Big Jim's thunder.

Cinnamon held her ground, brave and defiant with her sharp yips, baring flashes of paper-white teeth. Just before the African painted dog reached her, Cinnamon shot me a look like a deep, knowing smile. She took off in a spirited lunge that catapulted her from the weeds. The One Who Spits tore after her, fueled by a possession it couldn't name. Cinnamon made it halfway across the patch of grass before The One Who

Spits caught up to her, bringing its frothing jaws down on her tiny body. I couldn't move, couldn't get out from Dennis's grip, couldn't look away. The One Who Spits held Cinnamon by her neck and shook her, three sharp snaps sideways, and then she was still. The One Who Spits dropped her ginger body onto the tangled grass, a monstrous seizure assuming control of its head. It bit at nothing in the air and then fell onto its side next to our little fiery friend. The shaking was winning, a hideous tremor, an internal earthquake that would finally conquer its host.

Dennis, with me still in his mouth, his slimy, soft jowls blanketing my body, left the town house and our partner and The One Who Spits by taking off down Phinney Avenue. The sky, perhaps also in mourning for our little friend, released its promised rain, thick sheets of cloudburst that felt like heartbreak. We were drenched by the downpour. Dennis was walking now, a slow, plodding amble, until we were a good distance from the town house. I couldn't tell you how long the walk was or what we passed. "The One Who Keeps" had been broken with pain and frustration, drowning in disappointment. Our mission felt fruitless, too big to accomplish. After everything we'd done, we'd only saved two pointers and a thuggish common house sparrow. A wild bird. And now the puppies would die because I was inept. I was weak and disabled, unsuitable to take on such a big task. I hadn't saved our beautiful friend. It felt like a cosmic joke. Dennis eventually sat us under a stand of western red cedars, dropping me gently onto a pile of damp moss. The cedars were silent and I wanted to scream at them. Hadn't they led us here? Hadn't the trees all made me believe this was the right path? And now, when it actually mattered, when I needed guidance, they were audaciously unspeaking, drinking in the rains, and taking care of only themselves. I could barely breathe, anger and frustration and pain squeezing my arteries, choking me from the inside out. The world was too difficult, too painful. Without the MoFos to keep it in check, rabies would be spreading through the natural world, foaming at the mouth and spilling into their systems through a bite, reducing animals to violence and seizures—to utter madness. The One Who Spits couldn't be just that African wild dog. It had to be the name those idiot birds of *Aura* had given to the collective, to all the animals caged in the grips of the disease. I shuddered to think of how many there might be.

Dennis lay on the ground with his head on his paws. Rain soaked him to the skin despite the shade from the red cedar. Dennis had known it was over before I had. Perhaps, with his Umwelt, the incredible stories his nose tells him, he saw some of this coming. He had saved me from my own stupidity. My plucky, idiot self. His breathing was heavy, The Black Tide crashing in around him, but there was nothing I could do. And for the first time, I knew exactly what he was feeling. I missed Cinnamon, the guilt of not being able to save her like a plastic bag on my face. The end had been fast and she hadn't suffered and become The One Who Spits, but there was little comfort in that. And then, a tidal wave crashed into me without warning: how much I missed Big Jim. I had been waggish and upbeat and I'd believed the best in everything and it had gotten me nowhere. I missed how Big Jim took care of me and knew my favorite treasures and how he'd tell me all the things that were on his beautiful mind. I missed how proud of me he was when he took me to the local bars or Wings of the World where everyone else had parrots and cockatiels but he had a mother-fucking crow who'd do anything for him and that got him a lot of respect. I missed how when he'd almost reached the end of a bottle, he'd tell me how much I meant to him, how special I was, how Dennis and I were the only ones he could talk to. I missed Big Jim and I missed feeling the wind in my wings.

The Black Tide swallowed me up, drenching me in sadness, its undertow dragging me down, further than I'd ever been.

Things couldn't get any worse. But then I realized that was a particularly idiotic thing to suggest, because they suddenly did get worse, as I raised my drenched head and realized that Dennis and I were surrounded.

CHAPTER 21

ANGUS, HIGHLAND COW
STRATHPEFFER, SCOTLAND

Where the hell is my human? I huvnae seen her in weeks. At first I thought it was a wee joke. A wee prank on auld Angus, but sure as I shit grass, it's been absolutely ages.

I've been standing alone in this bastard field for days. Who is going to bring me my alfalfa cubes? My welly-wearing human, that's who. Soon as she bloody remembers. Poor old Angus out here in the countryside, waiting and waiting like some sort of ginger-haired poultice.

Awright. I suppose I'm not totally alone. I'm stuck here on these boring rolling green hills with Nubbins the donkey. The weather is absolute shite. I'm bored out of my mind. I'm so bored I've taken to making up wee songs and poems. Here's a cracker:

Again, again, again with the rain,
I hate the rain.
Pitter patter, shitty shatter,
Where are my alfalfa cubes, you walloping twonk.

Nubbins cannae do poetry or songs. Nubbins is too busy rolling around in his own shite. I'm a prized Highland cow. Nubbins is a rescue donkey with a mind like melted haggis. Surely destined to be a wee glue pot.

Och, I shouldnae be so rude. He's a wee bit traumatized, our Nubbins. Yesterday he said he'd seen Farmer Stuart in his jammies chasing a sheep that was wearing a biometric collar. Jings, I told him to stop eating thistles, it's frazzling what's left of his wee pea brain.

I stuck my head under the fence to ask Hamish about this whole Farmer Stuart gossip. Hamish is a Hebridean sheep, a black wee jobby. Hamish says that he heard Gregor the goose telling Esme—a Scots Dumpy hen who sticks her beak in everyone's business—that he saw Farmer Stuart staggering around the dog kennels the other day. Said he was blootered—his eyes were bright red. Who knows what the truth is? You cannae trust a black sheep.

So Nubbins, that numpty, is going bonkers and I'm bored of the green hillside and the rain and the rabbits are absolutely out of control. They bonk day and night and now there are thousands of the wee bastards. I try to send the foxes after them, but you know foxes, what like are they? Bunch of absolute arseholes. Cannae be trusted. Have you heard them at night?! Bloody banshees!

I told Nubbins to have a wee word with Margaret, a Highland heifer I've had my beady eye on. I plan to approach her myself when I've figured out what to say. Margaret is an absolute ginger goddess. Udder like a bloody bagpipe filled with custard! Och, I mustnae get too excited. So, Nubbins goes up to the electric fence, right up to Margaret in the next field, and he's there for ages and I'm giving him the eye, like, "Come ON, Nubbins you giant pillock!" and eventually he comes back with this stupid story about how Margaret's wee pal Shelly the

Shetland pony told Margaret, the super sexy Highland cow, that all the human farmers have been crawling on top of the barn in town, smashing their noggins on the roof to get inside where all the agricultural robots are. What a load of gossip for the gullible. If humans wanted inside the barn, they could just open the door, for Christ's sakes. Nubbins is a nutjob. He still believes in the Loch Ness monster! It's all those sweetie wrappers he's been eating.

My human will be here soon to trim my toes. Sure of it. Angus the ginger cow is an Overall Champion at the Royal Highland Show and he's got glamour standards to uphold for God's sakes! She's probably down at the pub. Or at a horse show. Do you think she's gone away on holiday without me? Aye. Maybe Blackpool. Och no, she's probably stuck in the queue at Marks & Spencer. Ah, it's absolutely mobbed this time of year.

She'd better hurry up before Nubbins chokes on a discarded can of Irn-Bru, that scabby wee fart lozenge.

"Eh? What's that, Nubbins?"

Och, he's mumbling again, that silly wee boot. He's saying the electric fence is off and we're free to go for a wee wander. What a load of tosh. Full of absolute fantasy, that Nubbins.

CHAPTER 22

❧

S.T.

UP SHIT CREEK, SEATTLE, WASHINGTON, USA

The rain pummeled down, spitting and weeping in cool sheets. An ass-load of fuliginous, unblinking eyes watched us from the branches of red cedars. We were besieged, winged beings outnumbering us. I looked up at their glares, the anticipatory judgment that rained down on me from above. My heart started to race. A fluttering from a high branch caught my eye. A beautiful bird, resplendent with an opalescent sheen, glided down from a red cedar, dropping to the earth near my patch of moss. His contour and facial feathers were elevated, a sign of his breezy dominance. It was Kraai, the head cheese of the UW Bothell murder.

"You are injured," he said, spreading his magnificent pinions, waterdrops releasing like tiny crystals.

"No shit."

"Times have been tough for you," he said.

"What the...what is this? You're going to fly down from your high branch and just start stating the obvious? Thanks, dick-wad. You can take your blatant observations and your annoyingly flawless feathers and functioning wings some-where else."

A smattering of crows cawed out. They weren't happy with how I was speaking to their beloved brother.

The beautiful crow raised his head up to the sky, raindrops running down the length of his onyx beak. "You are rescuing the domestics. That's why you were searching for The One Who Opens Doors."

This guy was just all about wounds and salt. And he was really ruffling my feathers. "Not that it's any of your damn business, but I got bad intel from the farce that is *Aura* and your stupid kind harassed me at the zoo so I nearly got snarfed by a tiger."

"They are our kind, but the zoo crows are not a part of our murder. You shouldn't just lump us all together like that. We are all individuals, even our murders have their own charac-teristics. I'm sure there were humans that you didn't like."

"No one comes to mind," I lied. "Why don't you just leave us alone?"

"Because we look after our kind. That is part of what it means to be a crow. The code of murder."

We both looked at Dennis, now a wet rolled rug under the trees. Dennis was my murder. A memory surging like a jolt of electricity hit me. It had been the first thing Kraai had inquired about when I met him by the university library. He had wanted to know about my control over the dog. It was Dennis he was interested in. And I swore right then on the whole of my cache collection that he would never have him. "I'm not your kind; I want nothing to do with you and your sky-squatting, bitch-beaked ways. I am not a crow, I'm a MoFo!" As my words bounced off the rusty trunks of the old cedars, the corvid lungs in the trees gasped.

"But you are a crow. It is known." Kraai cocked his head. *No. He would not take away the last good thing Big Jim ever said to me, "Shit Turd, you're one crazy MoFo." Those were my words, my last piece of Big Jim to keep forever.*

"Stop telling me who I am and invading my space! Get the hell away from us!" I shrieked, feeling something inside me rising, boiling like stew.

"The humans are dying out because they upset the natural order of balance. You must accept this. You must return to your roots."

"It isn't true and I don't have to accept a fucking cracker of what you say. You're a bunch of idiots who think you know everything and you're wrong! I know they are still out there! You can't claim to know for sure—"

"We know through *Aura*—"

"*Aura* is nothing but spam, a network of totally unreliable fabrications, no better than the *National Enquirer*. The MoFos will survive this."

"Blackwing, the humans were a plague on the earth. They were not able to control their numbers or their consumption of the land, and so Nature did it for them. She is not kind, she is balanced. *The One Who Hollows as well must return*. It is known. For every species there is a calling to evolve, an opportunity for change to ensure survival. If a species misses the calling to evolve, they are destined for extinction. This is the law of the earth. I know that deep down you believe this. We have lived side by side happily with humans as their aerial allies and now we must thrive without them. Surely you do not miss those treacherous—"

"MoFos are treacherous? What about Nature? What about the orca who catapults a seal forty feet into the air just for the hell of it, or when an assassin bug wears the corpse of its victim for camouflage? Or when a baboon eats its young!

That's savagery! MoFos are kind and resourceful and clever and unparalleled in their ingenuity. Masters of creativity! You don't know what you're talking about! I AM A MOFO!" A cacophony of complaint came from the branches, the brassy song of angered crows.

Kraai held on to his patience like a top-tier canopy branch. "Perhaps the truth is that the part of you that's smart and resourceful is the crow part. We're smarter than you give us credit for."

"You are birdbrained and simple compared to the MoFos," I spat.

"How many of us can recognize a human face? Even with a mask on or when they try to disguise themselves?"

"We all can, we all can!" came unanimous squawking from the trees.

He continued. "Our children's children know to heed the warnings of an enemy. And how many humans can recognize an individual crow?" His eyes were hypnotic and shiny. I thought of how once, after I'd gone to stretch my wings around the neighborhood, I returned to catch Big Jim squawking at a college crow with a white streak on her wing, agitatedly beckoning her from our Green Mountain sugar maple. He called her Shit Turd, yelling for her to hurry up and sit on his shoulder because he was late for beer pong. She was molting, half my size, and had a sebaceous cyst the size of a jawbreaker sticking out of her breast. It had been a serious blow to the old self-esteem.

Kraai continued. "How many of us do you see crumpled roadside like the squirrels and raccoons?"

"None! None!" cried the avian audience.

"We are soaring shadows, adapting on the wing. We are everywhere on this big beautiful blue and that is the privilege of being a crow, Blackwing. We are not caged, never confined to bars and walls. We build tools and communities and use our mind maps to navigate the world, so much easier now without the electro-smog blurring our flight paths. And we are survivors. We thrived in the hollowing time of trash and plastic, and we will thrive in the New World, as Nature settles her debts. It's time to take what is ours." The crows cawed in agreement.

"I am not. Like. You." The steaming bubbles inside me were rising.

"You can't run from who you are, Blackwing. If you try, you will always suffer."

"KISS MY CLOACA!"

"You are a crow. It is your privilege."

"GET AWAY FROM ME!" Counterintuitively, I hopped toward him, rain streaming down my face.

"You may have been close to a MoFo, and I can understand that, but they did not heed the warnings and are suffering the consequences. Your human is gone and now you must move on. It is time."

He'd gone too far. He could smack talk about me and his idiotic theories, but he couldn't make a single squawk about Big Jim. I wouldn't let him.

"You're right. It is time," I seethed through my beak. Time for me to knock him off his high branch. I snapped. Lunging into the air, a strangled caw released with some of the heat inside me. My feet came down onto Kraai's chest, pinning him to the earth. The cedars broke out into ferocious alarm calls, crows screaming into the rain. Kraai cried out, flapping with great strength to push me off him, but my assault had just begun and I struck at him with my beak. He blocked it with his, lifting into the air. I jumped up, body checking him, sending him mud-bound, hurtling into tumbles. Then I pounced on him and we were a mass of wings and beaks and feet, strained screaming and darting, jabbing movements. Kraai gave one

fierce whip of his wings, shoving me off him with a thrusting
kick. He lifted again, striving to get away, but I wouldn't allow
it. I snatched at him, clawed at him, strange sounds flying
from me. My feet found his, locking them tightly in my grip.
He lifted me into the air with him. We spun, airborne, bound
and battling, a hurricane of black feather and burning heart.
We lifted higher, our screeching tearing up the sky, wings
shredding the air. Dennis's thunderous barks rose to us as he
bayed up to where I squabbled with a crow stronger, fitter, and
faster than me. Better than me. Some dark urge from deep
inside me had taken control, driving my beak forward toward
the crow's eye, aiming to plunge it right into his brain. Kraai
blocked me with his beak. He might have been better than
me, but I had passion on my side, a fury that gave me the
strength to wallop him with a sharp kick. And then I tumbled
from the sky. I plunged down the length of the cedars, a fall
I knew would kill me. My nictitating membrane shut out the
world, cocooning it into milky blue and I held a memory that
would be my last: Dennis and Big Jim and me, dancing around
our Green Mountain sugar maple, laughing as dandelion fluff
snowed around us. I fell down, down, down.

I must have been a branch's stretch away from the soil
when the sharpness dug into my skin. My fall slowed and for
a moment, I was weightless. I opened my eyes, finding myself
slumped in a mud puddle, my legs sticking up in the air. Above
me, four college crows hovered. I felt the breeze from their
wings, the rain sliding off their shiny bodies. Satisfied they had
broken my fall, the crows shot to the sky. I caught a glimpse of
Kraai, cresting the canopy of the cedars, a magnificent inkblot
on a paper of gray sky. He vanished. A swarm of oscillating black
specks, like a great gust of ground pepper, followed. As they
departed, Dennis held his nose to the sky and whimpered.

I righted myself. I was soaked. Drenched from the rain and

the puddle, but mostly in hot humiliation. I had lost the fight and had to be rescued. The rain stopped abruptly, just in time for a wave of shame to crash into me. Never had I felt so small or stupid, so utterly defective. And the worst part of it? I had started it. I had launched myself at him, feral, desperately wild, and savage. An *animal*.

Dennis was still sniffing the sky. The residue of rain dripped off branches and hardy leaves. A carpet of moss and mud stretched out around me, lime green and glowing with satiety. Gray, shaggy parasol mushrooms sat with proud postures, slick and shiny. A few leopard slugs inched their way across the earth, leaving a silvery train, evidence of a great journey and adventurous living in their wake. Pastel-pink earthworms writhed joyously, having waited for the rains to commence travel. They breathed through their moistened skin. We were still in the city, but somewhere under a grove of cedars where the forest was teeming and ready to reign. There was a break in the clouds, audacious sunrays glowing through the gaps in lime-green leaves. Electric-green ferns and spongy moss hugged copper-brown bark and soil. A hermit thrush, freckles decorating his breast, raised and lowered his tail. He let out a powerful flutelike trilling. It was a chirruping aria about strength and resilience, something he had learned from his father and practiced immeasurably, a song that had been passed down his long line of avian ancestors until it was utter perfection in pitch and resonance. It was hauntingly beautiful, tight notes piping up to the sun, shattering the ultraviolet light into a prism of dancing rainbows. I realized, wet and defeated in a puddle of mud, that I was surrounded by devastatingly beautiful things. None of it called attention to itself, no preening and crowing here. Everything just was what it was, intricately complex and simply stunning. This was what was happening to the world; this bewitching woodsy scene that sighed creaks, croaks, and willowy whistles was a preview of oncoming attractions.

Peering down at the mud puddle, I saw the waggish, saucy countenance of a crow reflected back at me. A bird with quizzical espresso eyes and twitchy head bobs that, much like the leopard slugs and the earthworms, had been on a great adventure. A bird who had survived a mass extinction, a grizzly bear attack, a python's muscular strike, the jaws of a tiger. A bird who had a heart that had been broken again and again, but that had refused to stop beating. A crow who was seeking. In seeking for life and meaning and a return to balance, perhaps I had been blind to the truth about who stares back at me from the ripples of a murky puddle. It was a crow. In wanting to be like a MoFo, why did I have to deny the part of me that was crow? Perhaps Kraai was right. Perhaps Nature *was* balancing. And if you cannot evolve, you cannot survive— that is Nature's way. I had to be honest with *myself* and admit that, dammit, I'd always known this. As well as I knew when a storm was coming or the speed of an oncoming car or when Big Jim was going to shit the bed because he'd had too much sriracha. It was madness to think that I could take on saving the domestics alone. Just me and Dennis and our poor little Cinnamon. It was a suicide mission. Hadn't I always been the one to harp on the importance of murder? Of family?

The cedars are not just one thing, they are many things— food, homes, protection, life-givers, communicators. Maybe it was time to get real and realize I could never sprout ten fingers and be just like a MoFo. Perhaps it was time to stop turning my back on my roots. I had been wrong. And lying in a gross puddle with the heart-stopping beauty of our world all around me was like an alarm clock's call, the brassy crowing of a rooster at dawn. I had to change and evolve or I would become extinct. Even Dennis knew it. I could see it in him as he sniffed at the sky, wishing the crows had stayed. Hadn't I admired Kraai? So what if he wanted to learn about how I could create a relationship with a dog? He wanted to share that knowledge with his family, for their survival. He saw evolution, intelligence, and ingenuity—perhaps my MoFo influence, or perhaps entirely the crow in me.

Rejecting a part of myself had been rejecting all of myself in a world where you needed to believe in yourself to survive. If I could open my eyes and see the beauty in every sapling and shimmery dewdrop around me, and I could see the beauty in Kraai, perhaps I could also see the beauty in the spunky, twitchy scrutiny that postured back at me from the surface of a puddle. Maybe what really mattered was what was on the inside, as was the case with Big Jim's refrigerator. Change had overtaken our entire world. And now it was my turn. It was time to be a crow.

The only thing that I'd hurt during the fight with Kraai was my pride, so I shook off the mud and resentment and waddled over to Dennis. I hopped onto his back and apologized. I told him I was going to be more open, less judgmental; because for Twinkie's sakes, Dennis and I deserved not only to survive, but to blossom and flourish. Big Jim would have wanted it, would have been cheerleading for his boys from the sidelines.

Dennis, in classic Dennis style, had already forgiven me. He shook off a waterfall of damp and slobber, ears like maxi pads in a hurricane, and put his nose to the business of tracking down a murder of crows who would hopefully do the same.

CHAPTER 23

Dennis and I plodded westward along the streets at the whim of his nose. Intermittently, I put out a call to *Aura*, gulping down my pride and asking for the whereabouts of the college crows. Northern flickers, barn swallows, and cedar waxwings darted past, absorbed by duty. Sharp chirruped responses told me that I'd been heard. A great blue heron cruised the sky like a giant Airbus. Dennis seemed particularly absorbed, lost to trailing the crows. He had abandoned his immediate surroundings and even his sense of sight—bumping into a signpost and then stumbling over a cooler filled with long-rotten organs—consumed by what the smells said and on pinpointing one particular odor thread among billions. Never had I seen him so utterly spellbound, so I made us into one entity to protect him. He was our legs and GPS; I was our eyes and ears, in charge of immediate vigilance. We passed store-fronts, homes, a gas station whose bones were blackened and burnt. We came upon a sick MoFo whose fingers were missing from clawing at the road. It appeared that she had been trying to escape, to flee her vehicle, but the long, teal scarf around her neck had gotten caught in the wheel of her red Prius, snapping her neck and tethering her to its body indefinitely. Forever on a leash. Nearby, perhaps newly dislodged and with a story it could never tell, a MoFo's lonely green head rolled down the street like a volleyball in a sandstorm. No amount of duck tape could put that back where it belonged.

The crows had mostly flown over residential areas, home after home, each painful to bypass. But what could we do, just the two of us? I kept alert for signs of life, MoFo or domestic or animal shuddering with disease, but my heart focused on the task at hand. Dennis lifted his head only once, droopy eyes focusing on three protracted necks that stretched up to the top of Starbucks' iconic mermaid sign. For once, long necks didn't fill us with quick terror, and we fleetingly enjoyed the sight of the towering, long-lashed giraffes, their bodies a brown mosaic. With their tongues flickering out like blue lizards, they munched on the ivy leaves that were slowly consuming the building, draping over the Starbucks sign in a deadly hug. We pressed on. Soon after, a chestnut mare trotted past us, a cluster of weeds churning between her velvety lips. Her unshod hooves clapped against the dying cement. We locked eyes.

"So, there you are, Crow," she said, incredulous.

"Excuse me?" I asked.

"I thought you were a fairy tale." She let out a laughing whinny. There wasn't much point in trying to engage with her—she was clearly a Happy Meal without any nuggets. Her coat shone and her portly belly was distended with her fill of abundant grass and perhaps even a foal. She was still saddled with her bridle and the ever-twitching, severed legs of a rider that didn't seem to bother her or impede her sweeping freedom.

Several blocks of a neighborhood were flooded and we

chose to swim through them. Dennis paddled through the murky, frigid waters with his nose suspended in the air, still soaking up the scent of the college crows. I kept a lookout for ripples in the water, for the shine of eyes above the breathing line, for anything that might have made this its home. There was just no telling. Opportunity and danger were everywhere. We emerged, soaked but unscathed, and continued the trek, finding ourselves crossing the spacious grounds of Ballard High School, a sprawling brick edifice framed by a crescent-shaped driveway. Its walls and windows had been barricaded crudely with nails and wood. Spray-painted signs with ghostly, ephemeral messages said, "RUN!," "Survivors Gather Here," and "POWER OFF!"

Survivors gather here. My heart started to race. *Steady, S.T., steady.* But maybe there was just one, hiding out, living here. I tried to tuck my excitement under my wings and kept alert. Intermittent pools of blood, mounds of weathered books, and a rogue pair of red-smattered sneakers told a story of panic and mayhem. I fixated on a lone backpack. Near the pink backpack were lumps of muscle and tissue, breathing and bubbling in that nightmarish way I'd seen before. I studied the army of lined candles and a chalkboard set up to pin photos and "missing" flyers. Tethered to its staff, the American flag fluttered gently in the breeze, a survivor. I bowed as we passed underneath it.

In hindsight, it was probably my fault. I had dropped my vigilance again, distracted by the bus riddled with bullet holes, what sort of bomb had blasted such a gargantuan hole in the road, and wondering what had happened to the young MoFo whose haunting sign read "whAT wE plANTed haS COme bACk to STRAngle uS." What I should have been thinking about were the pools of blood and the smell of fear that pinched the air. Dennis didn't have a chance of seeing it coming; he was possessed, too engrossed in the flight path of black birds. They had seen us already though, had long-smelled us lumbering toward them. That is their way. And it was because of me, my particular condition, that had switched their genes on. Lit them up inside.

The one time I had snuck into the Woodland Park Zoo, Big Jim and I had strolled around, me on his shoulder. It had been a quiet day, as the weather was weepy and most of the children were back in school. After what had happened with Tiffany S. from Tinder, Big Jim needed a distraction and this had been his solution. He didn't want to be around other MoFos, and the calming beauty of our city's fine zoo was nourishing to his battered heart. We had been watching the Malayan tigers lounging in their newly restored habitat—a mecca brought to life by a monolithic banyan, sinewy ficus trees and bamboo, with a keeper's "up close" section to allow the zookeeper MoFos to touch and interact with the cats safely, offering them squirts of milk from a spray bottle.

When we arrived, the tigers were luxuriating, sprawled out, one tracing his ebony stripes with a barbed tongue. Their fiery fur was tinged with the moisture of recent rain. A small crowd of MoFos had assembled to admire their serene dominion. One young MoFo started to roar at the tigers and Big Jim told him to shut his fucking face up. The mother, fear glistening in her eyes, scuttled the little MoFo away sideways like a crab. Then a curious thing happened. A MoFo with glasses and an oxygen tank on his back, life-sustaining wires snaking across his face and up into his nose, was wheeled into the tiger viewing area. It happened at a speed too fast to comprehend; The Terrible Three shot toward him like bullets. Pounding paws on mesh, their ocher eyes fixated, trained on the wheel-chair MoFo with sheer and utter tunnel vision. They had been *switched on*. Tigers are triggered, summoned, awakened by weakness. They react to it instinctually, a knowing in the stripes of their souls.

Here again were those Terrible Three. And now, I was that weakness. They had smelled the damage in my wing, perhaps from miles away, and here we had walked right into them. The larger of the three brothers, with eyes like burning embers, took two steady steps toward us, massive paws pressing into the earth. Tall, unruly grass framed a feline face, a coconspirator in his stalking. Dennis bayed, formidable deep-chested, long, low howls that reverberated through me.

OOooooooooo, Ooooooooooooo, OOooooooooooo!

Brothers two and three stepped forward, forming a triangle of teeth and stripe. The largest brother's lips curled, whiskers hiking upward into a snarl that could stop a heart.

A V of geese flew overhead with harried honks. In desperation I called out to them, "Help us! Help, please!" In a flash they were gone, honks echoing behind them. The biggest tiger wrinkled its broad nose, narrowing its burning eyes, baring its canines, porcelain smooth and yellow. Meat-tearers. The gravelly growl released in a slow, shuddering stream that rumbled the earth. The fur along the three tigers' backs stiffened. Dennis bayed and bayed.

Oooooooooooooo! Oooooooooooooo! Ooooooooooooooooo!

He paced on the spot, stamping his paws, and I dug my feet deep into his back, holding on for life, preparing for the wrath of *Panthera tigris.* The shoulder blades of all three cats rolled like slow waves as they slunk toward us. They froze. The largest tiger lowered, distributed his weight onto his back legs and haunches, readying to pounce. My beak was open, panting clouds of distress into the air. Three brother tigers would now share the bird that got away.

Ting. The sharp chime startled us, tigers flinching. The tiger brothers scanned for the source of the sound. *Ting.* Another ringing clatter that spun our heads to the left. Something had struck a row of glass vigil candles, shattering one of them. Dennis whined. I looked up. The sky was dark, filled with the bodies of hovering birds that emerged from over the tops of red maple trees. More and more crows, black beauties, clouding the airways above us, claiming the sky with their magnificence. Their wings filled our ears with ceaseless whooshing as they flapped with intention. *Ting. Ting.* More tinkling, the shatter of glass, a New World soundtrack. *Ting. Ting. Ting.* The crows were releasing objects from their clutched feet: rocks, pebbles, quarters, wristwatches, batteries. *Ting. Ting. Ting. Ting.* The tigers lowered their heads, pacing to avoid the raining projectiles. New masses of crows appeared, pelting down their treasures. Missiles from beak and feet. *Ting. Ting. Ting. Ting.* Nails, bolts, light bulbs, screwdrivers, crab claws, the mandible of a mouse, scrap metal. *Ting, ting, ting, ting, ting.* Forks, coasters, salt shakers, Alcoholics Anonymous recovery medallions, dentures, figurines. Dennis seized the distraction by its lapels, running for cover. I crouched, splaying my wings to stay on his back and we tucked under the broad branches of a nearby Norway maple.

We watched the tigers spin and snarl at the avian onslaught, swiping and lunging at the air. The pounding was relentless, bits and bobs, knicks and knacks, tokens of MoFo creativity raining down on them like a tropical monsoon. The tigers flattened their ears, roared their contempt, and bounded away, tails whipping behind them. A swarm of black trailed them from above to make sure the job was done. I fluttered my gular, utterly amazed at the ingenuity of the college crows, how they worked together as a single entity. A damned smart one at that. The objects had been valuable ones, honestly good enough for a sneaky cache. And they'd all been sacrificed for me and Dennis.

The whooshing of wings signaled the landing of many crows onto the thick grass surrounding the Norway maple. Some perched in the branches above us. More breathtaking than the image of the Greek mythological angel Ichabod who flew too close to the sun, a glossy sheen of feathers drifted down to the ground in front of me. Kraai. Silence floated in the air between us. I didn't know how to start, how to pull myself together and stop fluttering my gular. Dennis slumped into the mud at the tree's base, utterly exhausted.

"I...I'm sorry. I was wrong. Wrong about everything. We came to find you—" I started.

Kraai cut me off with one curt bob of his head. Such a simple and powerful gesture. He was absolving me of everything. Like Dennis, he was quick to forgive. He shook the feathers of his neck, the living embodiment of grace. Dropping down from the sky was a tiny, feathered puff I instantly recognized. The house sparrow jutted along the branch, head darting to and fro, performing a jerky little series of jumps.

"I told the crows about you, I told the crows how you saved my life," cheeped the sparrow. "Thank you, thank you, thank you."

"The sparrow tells me that you pulled him from a Hollow home," said Kraai, his voice as steady as the tide.

"Yes," I answered. "We are trying to free the domestics that are trapped in homes. I want to preserve the last living legacy of the MoFos."

Kraai nodded slowly, his eyes shiny. "All of them?"

I felt a sharp pain inside. Overwhelmed. The dread of defeat. "We are doing the best we can."

"You and your dog?"

"Yes, Dennis and I. And Cinnamon, but...but we lost her to The One Who Spits."

Kraai nodded; he'd seen it before. "We can help one another. It is time. Show us how it is done."

"How what's done?"

He leaned his magnificent beak toward me. "Teach us to touch through the glass." Crows cawed in rampant excitement from the surrounding branches.

There was an angle to this; I felt it. "Why do you want to know how to break the windows, Kraai?"

Weighted silence. A multitude of dark eyes looked down from the forks of branches. What would breaking glass allow Kraai to accomplish? A muffled slurping sounded out. All eyes landed on my bloodhound partner. Dennis had picked yet another stellar moment to polish his peeper. The little sparrow looked on in revulsion. I cocked my head sheepishly.

Kraai delivered his answer in a grave tone: "We don't have a lot of time. Listen to me. Danger is everywhere and something bigger is right now on its way to us. There is a war coming, Blackwing. And you have very little time to decide whose side you are on. The Hollows are dying. The Unbroken— bear and wolf, cougar and coyote—are coming down from the mountains, growing stronger, feeding and birthing young, increasing in their numbers. Creatures have escaped the zoos and parks and the homes of Hollows. With the top predator changed and gone, Those Who Hunt are looking to claim the land with tooth and claw. This is a fight for territory. The War Of Land is coming, and every single species has begun to slaughter for the biggest piece of it. Every predator is vying for space. Look around you, Blackwing. Look at the ravenous green—the trees, the weeds, the grass. There is an explosion in all directions, life colliding with life. Nature is looking for her balance with unbridled brutality. There are no longer barriers to hold anything back. And someone will become the victor, someone will swoop in. *We* were The Hollows' black shadows, living by their sides. The land in our flight path is crow territory. It is known. We are strong in numbers and

I intend to claim what's ours. My murder wants access to the Hollow homes, to make them our own and claim the inside treasures. We have an opportunity here, a chance. We *must* help one another. We are more powerful when we work together because we look out for one another by being one. That is the code of murder."

"War…"

"Yes. War is coming. And I tell you now, while we still have time, that it won't be like anything we've ever seen."

I lose myself for a few moments to thoughts of World Wars I and II, the American Revolution, the Battle of Hastings, the Gulf War, Tibet, Kosovo, Cyprus, some of the many, many times when MoFos fought over land and resources. Territory is the source of almost every battle ever fought. Every inch of what Kraai called the big beautiful blue had been fought over many times. I hadn't thought about this—that without the number one predator on earth, there would be savage bloodshed to conquer the spoils.

"So, will you help us rescue the domestics?" I asked.

"And we will provide you with—" he paused, eyes taking in the desecrated high school, the pools of blood, the scars of a bomb, the recent memory of The Terrible Three— "protection. For both of you."

An alliance. Dennis had fallen asleep under the Norway maple, wiped out from the trekking and baying and the general keeping alive in a sharp-toothed world. Gentle snores and whistles fluttered from his jowls and that magical nose, our secret weapon in the new beautiful blue.

"Yes," I told Kraai. "We will show you how to shatter glass."

Kraai nodded. He released a shuddering rattle from deep in his throat. Then he stretched his wings to the ends of the earth and let out a hoarse caw, a curious utterance I didn't know.

Clarion crow calls lifted into the sky. I had no idea what or whom they were addressing with their strange song, but they were doing so with an urgency I'd never heard before. *Aura* strummed, crooned, and trilled with intensity. Dennis rolled his cherry eyes to register I was okay and then resumed his slumber, tired to his bones.

"Come. It is time. We must fly." Kraai was calm, stoicism in the feather. He stood under the stretched limbs of the Norway maple with the command of a King, the wisdom of the wind. His brethren poured sound into the sky, expelled their lungs around him, a never-ending summoning.

"But Kraai, I can't fly. Something's happened to my wing, I'm as useless as a fucking penguin—"

Kraai turned away from me, his glossy tail feathers stroking the grass. He raised his head and waited. Within seconds, a shape burst through the clouds, a dark V that rode the air.

"Who…what's—?" I started, but succumbed to staring up at the approaching entity. Kraai kept his focus on the V. As it dropped down in looping circles, a flash of white gave its identity away. It was a bald eagle. This didn't seem like a wonderful development; eagles and crows are known nemeses, crow hatchlings taught to detest the birds of prey for their egg thievery and predator power. Crows mob eagles every chance they get. I waited for the murder to activate, to commence a Herculean mobbing of the taloned one. But Kraai didn't move. Something about the way he watched so purposefully, or perhaps just because I had developed a respect for this crow king, made me trust his choice to silently watch an archenemy draw near his family.

The crows fell silent as the eagle dropped down with a piping chatter of high-pitched notes. I have to be honest here and tell you that I'd always resented eagles and their undeserved status as our national emblem. But having never personally mobbed a bald eagle, I'd never been in this sort of proximity to one before. This bird—with her buttercup-yellow eyes and perfectly alabaster head plumage, her voluptuous shuttlecock tail, and the rich chocolate of her body—rendered me a statue. She was flawless in feather, strong and savvy. She looked at me—right fucking at me!—with that iconic regal expression, daffodil-yellow eye absorbing and adjudicating with a sharpness rivaled only by her talons. Bald eagles are majestic as fuck. If we were going to dive headfirst into a war, I couldn't think of a more emboldening mascot.

Kraai strode toward her. The eagle chittered. She spread her magnificent wingspan and lowered her formidable beak.

"Hurry," Kraai said, turning to me. "It is time."

CHAPTER 24

I refused to leave Dennis, setting aside the utterly absurd prospect of mounting a bird of prey. But Kraai had a way with normalizing insanity—for example, by calmly convincing you to abandon your best friend and cavort with a deadly raptor. He assigned an intimidating mass of crows to station themselves silently among the limbs of the Norway maple, their sole job to keep one eye out for danger and the other eye on my bloodhound. Tippi Hedren would have peed herself. It was utter madness, but I did it. I clambered my way onto the back of a fucking bald eagle, or rather hobbled up there, as awkward as an elevator fart. With a tight chitter, she spread her powerful wings and lifted us into the air. The Norway maple below us rustled and shimmied as hundreds of crows shot from its branches. The crows' strange summoning song rose with us, softening and fading.

The bald eagle's mighty flaps rose us higher, shrinking the grass, the Norway maple, and Ballard High School. I dug my feet into her back, feeling the muscle under her carpet of smooth down, the composed power of our flight. Her feathers felt silky and strong, their wispy plumes lifting to dance where the wind kissed them. This was her destiny, to ride the wind. She was air*borne*. Pride fizzed inside me. To be feathered, I thought—as the eagle owned the sky, gravity tipping its cap—is to eschew captivity, to taste the pulpy fruit of freedom. Oh, how I had missed it. Gliding smoothed out the ride; she flapped half as much as the crows, slicing through the air as if it were whipped frosting. Her fleece-white head jerked mechanically in front of me as she used those keen yellow eyes to navigate, monitoring the Lego pieces of Seattle below. I didn't say anything to her because I felt awkward as hell. I mean, what would you say? "Have you done this before? Am I your first crow?" No, if Big Jim had taught me anything about talking to females, it was that sometimes you can save yourself by shutting your Cheeto® hole. The fluff-puff sparrow sped along beside us among the Blackwings with rapid wing flaps, a bullet of a songbird. My body buzzed with exhilaration, with being the badass crow on the back of a bald eagle. With just being.

Trees were broccoli. Roofs were playing cards. Roads were ribbons and hills were mole mounds. A muddled cluster of army trucks and tanks looked like the olive-green G.I. Joe toys of young MoFos. The world seemed more manageable again, as I'd known it to be when I could fly. Flanking us were hundreds of crows, now silent but for the whooshing of onyx wings. Then, curiously, I realized that it wasn't just crows around us. Clenching my feet tighter, I stole a glance behind me, almost losing my grip in shock. My eyes were met with an avian horde that was on our tail: an immense flock of crows, but also the white-and-black bands of Canada geese. There were song sparrows and house finches, frantically flapping mallards, and great blue herons, the sky's RVs. The bright yellow blips were American goldfinches, shouldered by dark-eyed juncos, pine siskins, bushtits, robins, wrens, and nuthatches. Flickers and jays and swallows and towhees. Parakeets and starlings, flycatchers and vireos. A cast of red-tailed hawks hovered above, dangerously near their prey, but everyone focused on flight alone as if we were one airborne entity. That's when the nerves got me, snatching my legs with pulsing shakes. Here we were, all flying side by side, elbowing out the clouds, all led by me and the bald eagle I was riding. I was the ringmaster. No one made a sound, not a single cheep or chirrup. My insides quivered like microwaved pudding.

"Shit Turd!"

I startled at hearing my full name, ducking before darting my head in search mode.

"You're alive!" came the voice. I took in the gunmetal-gray body, the determined flapping that brought it alongside the eagle. I shook my head in disbelief upon seeing those pale custard-yellow eyes, still playful and lit with wisdom, and a tail as flaming red as a cayenne pepper. It was Ghubari.

"Is it—is it really you?" I asked the volitant parrot, scared to face another disappointment, another taunting ghost from my old life. A heart can only take so many dangling carrots.

"'Tis I!" he squawked. "Didn't think you made it out alive! You appear to have hijacked an eagle too; bit of a change from Big Jim's shoulder but very intrepid. Good for you!" *Big Jim!* What a burst of joy to hear his name spoken, stoking the glowing embers of his memory. I tried to remember the last time I'd seen Ghubari and his MoFo, Rohan. It must have been at Wings of the World, the exotic bird store in Bothell, because that was always where we saw one another, but the times all blended together. Big Jim and Rohan always exchanged tiny talk, finding an infrequent oasis of common ground amidst a sea of differed opinions. I would jabber with Ghubari, one of the only birds I would associate with because of his sharp intellect and deep insight into the world of the MoFos. The African gray could speak English, so many more words than I could. He could do impressions and count and be funny and entertain a crowd with his clever tricks. He was a brilliant being, a straddler of worlds.

"Why *are* you piggybacking on a bald eagle?" he asked, as one might.

"I think I wanted to be a MoFo so much that I wished away my wing."

"I see. You're grounded?"

"Yes."

"Permanent?" he asked.

"Who knows?" And that's all we said about that. Creatures of the animal kingdom don't dwell on disability, they accept and carry on. "Tell me, Ghubari. Where's Rohan?" I asked, frightened of an answer.

Ghubari, his flight like glitter dropping from an envelope, lowered his custard eyes to a mass of sick MoFos scurrying below like ants around spilled Kool-Aid. He clicked his tongue and whistled. I listened in rapture to this Old World bird who held cities in his mind, whole history books deep in his belly. "Hold on to your heart as I tell you this, S.T. Neera got sick. Rohan told her to stay at home because her symptoms seemed odd. She rained with sweat and her hands were swollen, fingerprints distorted, twice the size they normally were. But our matriarch insisted she was fine. Of course, the time-old lesson; she should have hung back, abandoned her fighting impulse. But Neera had fought her whole life and knew nothing else. It got worse while she was teaching that day and red-and-blue flashing lights took her to the hospital. Rohan and I raced there to be at her side. It was chaos. Armed guards seized the sick and were quarantining them in plastic bubbles and holding cells. There were needles and Tasers. People screamed about conspiracies and the reckoning. Some had grayish skin, one was cannibalizing his own foot right there in the hospital lobby, I tell you. Priests in penguin colors were called in, but most ran away screaming. There was a young child, a brown-eyed girl whose skin was sloughing off; her tears couldn't stop it. I saw a man whose head had swollen, features bulbous and shiny, his jaw twice the size of a normal man.

"Then two armed men in yellow suits and masks snatched Neera. She started to scream, a sort of primal keening. It didn't sound like our Neera. Neera had always sounded like the May rains, spring's lullaby. Rohan ran to her. A guard brought his club down on Rohan's temple." Here Ghubari paused to pluck Rohan's voice from the sky. He mimicked him perfectly, yelling, "Leave her alone! I beg you!" He transported me back in time to the horrors of a hospital lobby, watching Rohan plead with a soldier. Begging, desperate, as raw as a fresh wound.

"I pecked and scratched at the guard's face, pinning him into a corner, holding him as best I could with my claws. The other tried to tranquilize Neera. She ripped his arm clean out of its socket. I no longer knew her. Neera, custodian of Rohan's heart, our brilliant professor of gender studies, our gentile, soft-spoken sage. Then—and I tell you, Shit Turd, I've seen some things in my day—but Rohan and I could do nothing, as if we were stripped of our minds, feathers, and fingers as we watched Neera…change."

"Change?" I asked, thinking of Big Jim, his rogue eyeball and endlessly swiping digits.

"Neera started secreting something from her skin, different from the sweat. Something…sticky. And S.T., right then and there she climbed up the hospital's insides, scaling drywall. She just hung there silent, stuck in the middle of the lobby wall, watching us. For a few moments, she didn't move, but

I knew that would change. I could feel something coming, something so dark it couldn't be named. I screeched and panicked because I could feel that she had gone, S.T., but Rohan's love was so big. He couldn't leave her. His heart was fused to the wall with her. I shot up and perched on an air vent and watched the descent in horror."

"The descent?"

"There was a...degradation. They all...changed. Or they were devoured by The Changed Ones. I saw a newly hatched human, fresh from the egg, and I tell you it had ridges on its skin and thin, jutting limbs and it was scuttling around the hospital like a bleeding spider. Not yet a day in the world, and—it was hunting. Rohan was taken as he tried to rip Neera from the wall. The human with the monstrous jaw brought his teeth down onto Rohan's neck. There was nothing I could do. Nothing but to fly away before what Neera had turned into made it up the wall to where I was perched. I took Rohan's *kanthi mala* from around his neck when The Changed Ones were distracted. I flew back to our home to bury the necklace to pay respects to their memory."

"I'm sorry. I'm so sorry," was the only thing I could think to say. Ghubari must have carried the same weight I did, hard on the wings.

He asked me about Big Jim. I nodded and swallowed because that's all I could manage. "But Dennis is alive!" I told him.

"Dennis! Well, well, well. The Golden Nose. That is cheery news. A bit of sparkle from the Old World."

My heart thumped like the hind legs of a rabbit. Ghubari was a therapy bird, permitted to go everywhere as a celebrated member of MoFo society. He was a treasure trove of knowledge, an idol of my past, and now my much-altered present. And he was here for me to ask the questions I could of no one else.

"Ghubari, what happened to them?" I pointed my beak at the

humpbacked broken MoFos that dotted the land between tree crowns and the hats of buildings streaming beneath us. Ghostly shadows of the wondrous creators they had once been.

Ghubari's tone remained as steady and stoic as the Cascade mountains. "It was a virus."

"Like an infection? A disease. Like the dreaded bird flu?" I asked, hesitating to bring up such a skin-sore for our kind.

"No. Not like AIDS or Zika or Ebola. This was man's creation. This came from the Internet, through the screens, S.T. This came from the connectivity."

"I don't understand."

"I don't have all the answers. And in any case, they are not mine to give. But I know it started with the addiction. Technology was an intangible seductress, a siren calling for ships to meet her jagged rocks. It was a virus that spread through the systems, through the network, chips, watches, phones, tablets. Through eyes, skin, and synapses. Rohan had seen it coming. He burned everything connected long before the first warnings were sent out—the wireless emergency alerts. We lived for a time in the dark. Choppers doused the city in their lights and blasted taped instructions. Trucks passed outside with loudspeakers and panic and, later, when the planes fell from the sky and the cars collided, a few men with farmland and big hearts yelled their warnings from horseback. Women with swollen bellies headed for safety underground, burrowing like rabbits. But the World Wide Web had the humans tangled in its threads. Seattle became a mecca of explosions and screaming and a hunger that could never be satisfied. Then the change, that virus, caused them to have physical morphing. Now, it seems that it has made them voracious; they are constantly hunting for—"

"The Internet. Electricity. Power. Screens," I answered, staring down at MoFos teeming over a billboard, clambering to cover every inch of it with their twisted bodies. Through gaps in their flailing limbs, I could make out its message. It said, "Will The <u>Last Person</u> Leaving SEATTLE <u>Turn Out The Lights</u>."

It made more sense to me now. After what happened with Tiffany S., The Black Tide began to drown Big Jim. He hid at home with his bloodhound and his crow as the world fell apart. He had no more fight left inside to fight what was outside. I'd been in denial about all of it, about the condition of Big Jim's heart, about the terrible things happening in the world around us.

"There is something more to it, S.T., though I can't yet say what it is. Something greater is at play here. In time, it will reveal itself." I shuddered.

"We have lost the very best part of our world," I told Ghubari.

Ghubari laughed, a laugh to split open a star. "Change is inevitable, dear crow. We must adapt. You cannot stop the tide, S.T. You must be more like the log that bobs along its surface."

"My life is not—"

"Everything is a tide, in and out, in and out. Even your humans. We have every advantage to us in this New World, harnessing the power and knowledge of the old one. A fresh start is sometimes just the ticket. We must recognize that our greatest gifts sometimes come in the ugliest of shells." He sounded like Rohan with his butterscotch cadence, his buoyant wisdom.

"But it will never be the same! It will never be as good; we are losing the MoFo touch. We will lose the most magical essence of them...creativity! To create is the greatest gift of a MoFo!"

Below, the brambles writhed like a great black dragon, a breathing creature of thorn and spine. We flew over a seaplane that had plummeted from the sky and collided with an apartment building, severing its neck. Even in utter devastation, wounded brick, and shattered glass, the ingenious development and dreams of the MoFos were scintillatingly beautiful.

Ghubari laughed again, the frothy laughter of a bird who has lived many lifetimes, a bird who weathered worldly change like a seasonal malt.

"Take a good look around you. In a teaspoon of soil there are more organisms than there were people on this planet. Creativity swims freely all around us, and beauty is everywhere. Look!" He gestured below to a herd of dogs, a gargantuan canine patchwork quilt billowing through the streets in a splendid blur of browns, silvers, ebony, and snow, big and small, running as one against the change. Cattle dogs, collies, shepherds, pointers, dogs with survival in their sinew. They were painting the earth with their success. Parading their freedom in a way only the once-enslaved can.

"Don't shackle yourself to an ideal. Always go with the tide; listen for guidance. Creativity is not a uniquely human trait. Creativity is everywhere, in the barb of every feather and each audacious sapling. To err is what's human."

"To what?"

"To err. Humans marked their distinction with their mistakes. A creature can be heartbreakingly powerful and loving while also being a destroyer of worlds. You are mistaken in thinking they are the only rational animals. What you are looking at is just a chapter in their story, one they narrated. Perhaps—" he paused as we soared over the silent bodies of two apartment complexes that had collapsed onto one another, their guts glistening and gray. "Perhaps there is still a whole book for us, many chapters ahead. You must evolve. Float with the tide. Trust that She knows what She is doing. We must listen to Her through *Aura, Echo,* and *Web*. Onida has spoken."

"If you think so much of *Aura,* how come you never spoke of it before?"

"Shit Turd, the last time I saw you, you wouldn't associate with other birds or be called a crow. Things change every second. Embrace it and know that it is always for the best," he said with a wink. "For now, we must listen to what's been on the voice of the wind and follow the lessons of who we have been summoned to see. Let us see what The One Who Keeps has to say."

"Ghubari," I told him, as vulnerable as when my home was a rounded sweep of eggshell, "I am The One Who Keeps."

Ghubari's lemony eyes filled with mirth as he let out a full-belly laugh. His wings flapped harder in delight. "Onida's full of surprises. And a killer sense of humor." Before I had a chance to digest the terror and uncertainty that pooled in my belly, the eagle started toward earth.

She signaled her descent with a down-turned head, lowering in a smooth figure of eight. Still in miniature, a Caterpillar bulldozer and construction trailers slept on the sand mounds below. Tarp, brick, the skeletons of scaffolding, and orange cones that looked like candy corn from above all lay scattered. It was some sort of sports facility that the MoFos had been working on, a half-finished track and baseball fields exposing their guts, the snaking veins of electrical pipes spying from the sand's surface. The crows must have chosen this spot, since construction sites are known meeting grounds for our kind. The crows appeared to have a lot of clout, and I liked it. We touched down onto the sand of the abandoned construction site with a careful landing, as if onto the top of a soufflé. I wobbled off the magnificent raptor's back amid the deafening whooshing of wings as hundreds of birds descended, some perching on sleeping tractors and trucks, others dipping the webbing of their feet into the sand. The crows stood in the center, holding court, strutting proudly as only crows can with their casual, sauntering swagger.

We were utterly surrounded. Plovers, kingfishers, ospreys, sapsuckers, larks, nightjars, shrikes, and buntings. I got starstruck at the site of a snowy owl, because, I mean, *Harry Potter*. I had never seen these birds except for in pixel form, and here they were, shiny eyed and ruffling their magnificence. Golden eagles and Steller's sea eagles filled a crown with bodies, bodies so beautiful and majestic it was hard to look away from them. They kept their raptor glares on two MoFos who were hunched and staggering along the side of the town house, their heads stooped and fixated on their empty palms. In their current state of absorption they were harmless, but the giant birds kept watch, using eyes eight times as powerful as a MoFo's. So very little can escape an eagle eye. Birds of the shore—the airborne voices of *Echo*—birds of the forest, even birds of the tropics like the tanagers and a marmalade-beaked toucan (presumably zoo renegades). There were migrators and nesters. Pillagers, thieves, nurturers, and sages. Bone-splintering talons, bright bursts of color, and camouflage quills. Urban birds and forest dwellers. Sun-loving birds and those who zigzagged the sky in the dead of night. Most had nothing in common, their only connection through *Aura*. They were all here for me? The One Who Keeps? What did that even mean? How did I get myself into this mess? I had none of Ghubari's certainty as I realized— a sobering realization that felt like a belly full of ants—that they had made a mistake. Just as The One Who Opens Doors hadn't been a savior, I was not who everyone thought I was. It just wasn't possible. I was a silly bird with an identity crisis and a moderate-to-severe Cheeto® addiction, and it was all going to be exposed right here under the unblinking eyes of a thousand feathereds. I swallowed hard so as not to projectile yarf—that's only acceptable for vultures. A single crow rattled. Otherwise, there was just uncanny silence.

Kraai, his chest shimmering black and purple, addressed the crowd. "Sentinels Of The Sky, we here—all of us—are the overseers. The eyes in the clouds. We have talked of this gathering for some time. We know that The Unbroken are coming, baring their teeth with an unparalleled hunger. We know they are encroaching and claiming our territory, snatching our bodies in their mouths, and swallowing our eggs. But this is our land and so a Great War has begun. We must remember the words of Onida, passed on to us by the groan of a great oak: "When the grass fights the concrete, She shall usher in a new era." The domestics are dying. We have been called upon to help them, and in turn they will rise against The Unbroken, driving them back to the mountains. We will claim the territories for ourselves. Access will be granted to the food in the Hollow homes, the shelters, the materials to build strong nests and fortify our own. Since The Hollows are vanishing, what was theirs is now ours. Onida said that The One Who Keeps will lead the way, and now finally, Sky Sentinels, The One Who Keeps is among us and our time has come. I know it in the part of me the butterflies speak to, the part that is tugged by the stars. We must act quickly because every minute they draw nearer. It is known. This," he stepped aside way too dramatically, thrusting his damned perfect beak toward my noggin, "is The One Who Keeps."

Hundreds of bird eyes, keen eyes that can spot a baby field mouse from the clouds and read the diaphanous dance of ultraviolet light, burned into me.

"He is going to teach us how to touch through the glass so that we may claim the homes of The Hollows and defend ourselves against The Unbroken. Onida has spoken."

A chicken lost its composure and clucked. They all waited for my sage counsel. My heart raced, the pressure unbearable. I opened my beak and nothing came out. I tried to say something and a sort of "heeeee" came out that sounded like a dying blow-up doll. Luckily, someone's question filled the air before I passed out.

"Um, excuse me, but, wait. Uh...uh...are all domestics our allies?" came a frail voice from a bushtit whose name roughly translates as Gary.

"During this War, they are all our allies. We will work together," said Kraai.

"Not cats though, right?" asked a yellow-breasted western meadowlark.

Kraai gave his measured answer: "Not every cat is bad."

Mutters of disbelief rose like bubbles. Gary the bushtit, shifting his balance, lifted up his sad twig of a leg stump as a silent rebuttal.

"You're right, Gary. Cats can't be trusted. But everything else."

"But—" Here came the stentorian cries of a northern goshawk, urgent beeps of an alarm: "We don't stand a chance against The One Who Spits and The One Who Conquers. I have watched their devastation."

There was a collective gasp, several shrieks at the mere mention of those names. Great, I thought. The One Who Conquers, another predator I'd yet to meet.

"We will spread word through *Aura* and all will know of our War," said Kraai. "Crows live by the code of murder. What has worked for the few will work for the many. We are stronger in great numbers and that will be our advantage, our only way to win. When we band together, we will be victorious."

"Birds of a feather!" I squawked. All eyes shot my way, regarding me as if I was something that a gull regurgitated. Apparently, no one had heard this expression so I was left standing there like a blue-footed booby, utterly lost in translation. I briefly contemplated sticking my head in the sand in solidarity for the ostriches not represented here. But no, I'd come this far. This was a chance for the domestics who deserved a shot at life in the New World, a chance for Dennis and me to do something good.

"Kraai is right, we must free the domestics," I said, a shake in my throat as I addressed a million feathereds, a club I'd never felt welcomed to. "They deserve a chance at life in this New World, as much as we do, and we can help one another." But I didn't really have to tell them about the value of every life. Those who burst from shell know the gladiator's fight for survival. A bird recognizes that every life that surpasses a first breath is a miracle.

"So, what are we waiting for? If we're in such a hurry, tell us!" chirped a snow bunting, bobbing its head up and down.

"Well, it's…I should start by…the first thing you'll need to do is, assuming there is no way to jimmy the window…" I was struggling, floundering. How to explain all the variables of breaking glass? The glass breaking I'd done so far had been a cobbled blend of on-the-spot deductions and a few Hail Marys. How to translate the actions of a MoFo, the cool reasoning, to all these feathereds?

A cockatoo, naked as the German Big Boobs Calendar's October MoFo, chimed in. "Show us! Show us how you did it! I escaped through an air vent. Show us how you break the glass!" The cockatoo's bumpy, gray skin told a story of stress and anguish. She had overplucked, her body suffering the same fate as Tiffany S.'s eyebrows. And yet, here she was, exposed to the elements, as vulnerable as it gets. Here she was, speaking up without armor or protection. It bolstered me.

"Show us! Show us!" birds began to sing, screech, trill, and warble. I turned to Kraai and he nodded. A great stirring of the air signaled the bald eagle's landing by my side. She trilled that lovely scattering of elevated notes and lowered her back for me. I hopped on as a Monster Truck Show's worth of birds watched in fascination. She lifted those archangel wings and suddenly we were taking flight to the rhythm of a thousand pinions whipping the air. The evening tasted green and clean. I leaned forward and whispered where we needed to go, the place that hadn't left my mind since we'd first been there and probably never would. The tiny sparrow darted through a sky of birds and was suddenly hurtling alongside the eagle and me.

"Don't worry," he said in a jittery whisper. "I believe in you." They were tiny words from a tiny bird, but perhaps sometimes all you need is a speck of encouragement, an acorn of belief.

The sparrow perched in a stunning Sitka spruce that sat on familiar territory. The tree limbs filled up with black birds and the bald eagle gently touched down on the grass with a brisk flapping of her wondrous wings. The air suffered a storm born of feathers, by the flogging wings of thousands of landing birds. I hopped to the grass, cool and damp on my feet. Darting my head, I searched for Cinnamon, the tiny ginger form I hadn't wanted to leave behind. But there was nothing left; something had taken all of her. Perhaps the same something had ravaged the body of the African painted dog that lay nearby, its tissues stretched over the gleaming rib cage. And you couldn't hate it. You had nothing or no one to be angry at. Everyone had been a victim. Turkey vultures huddled around the carcass, admiring the pearlescent beauty of it.

Kraai dropped down in front of me, his head cocked. Black eyes peered at me from everywhere with a weighted expectancy. The pressure bore down on my plumage. I looked up at the townhomes, and a spark of hope zapped my insides. Eyes in yellows, blacks, browns, oranges, burned into me. If I fucked this up, then what? Dennis and I wouldn't be long for this world. They'd catch up to us. We'd be tracked down and taken by a trio of brotherly stripes.

I hopped over to the sparrow's former prison, vaulting to the planter box of decaying plants and demonstrating how I had wedged my beak into the crack in the window and pushed it open farther. The sparrow hopped up and down, ecstatic in his bones, reliving his moment of release. But a cold murmuring bounced among the crows. Cackles ripped through the leaves. They were unimpressed.

"The window was already open!" came a rattling heckle.

I looked at Kraai. His head was still cocked. He did not address the heckler, which pecked at my panic. What if I couldn't find the things I needed? They were doubting me. Worse still, I was doubting myself.

"How do you touch through the glass with no opening?" came a jeering voice from the leaves. I sidled up to Kraai.

"I'm going to need a couple of things," I told him. He nodded and I whispered them to him. With Kraai's throaty rattle, four crows fluttered down to join him on the grass. Once they'd received instruction, they took flight, disappearing into the distance. The next minutes were tense. I could feel that I wasn't yet fully accepted by this murder, wasn't even accepted as a crow yet. What would they do to me if I didn't deliver?

A black-headed grosbeak, sensing the tension, broke into a warble. The song was his father's father's father's song, unrepeatable by any other living being. It was a song about kindness, a unique and casual caroling. It was soothing and leisurely and all his to share with the hundreds of beings around him. Nearby, a female grosbeak cocked her head in rapt attention and I wondered if this was the beginning of a new chapter for them, whether on another page further along in the book, an egg would hatch with this very song in the lining of its shell. It made me wonder if Ghubari was right, if maybe the most beautiful things were still all around us.

The crows returned. Fluttering a foot from the ground, they released the items in their clutches. A black eye shadow palette. A TV remote sans batteries. A lump of metal. A severed tailpipe. As my stomach sank, my heart rose into my throat.

"I can't...these aren't the right things...I can't break through glass with these objects, they're not what I asked for." As I expressed this, I realized how much it sounded like I was bowing out. Like a TV evangelist whose paralyzed parishioner is refusing to walk again.

"This crow is a phony!" honked a tundra swan. "He sounds strange because he is an imposter! He is not The One Who Keeps!"

A Steller's jay puffed his chest and hopped toward me. I felt the bodies closing in, the sky falling down. Kraai placed himself between me and the encroaching mass of birds, some of whom had talons designed for dismemberment. Suddenly, cool, booming laughter rained from above, lifting the heads of the masses. A gray silhouette was framed by clouds. An African gray opened its feet and released a cell phone that dropped onto the grass. He touched down gently. Ghubari looked at me, his face bright and cheerful, full of a hope I thought had been long extinct in our world. He had saved me.

"Watch what I do closely," I told hundreds of eyes. "This will all happen very fast." My pulse was quicker than the sparrow's as I hopped with the cell phone toward the town house window. It took an uncoordinated leap to hoist myself to the window's ledge. I took in a deep breath, making a small prayer to the Gods of Samsung, as I pushed my twiggy black foot onto the power button. One second, two seconds, three. This was do-or-die. Everything riding on the hopes of a charge, that at some point, a MoFo had plugged in—

The Samsung cell phone screen surged into an electric glow. Two MoFos, listless and lumbering at the side of the town house, cracked their necks toward me, eyes radiating focus. Two jaws dropped, expelling a bloodcurdling, rage-powered roar. They broke into that twisted horror-show run. Birds screamed from the crowns of trees—screeches, caws, shrieks, squeals. I had seconds to get it right. I grasped the cell phone in my jittering feet and lifted it, perched next to the window, on the splintery sill. The MoFos clambered, running on all fours, heads elongated—too long to be MoFo, an animal's run—and then they were leaping into the air, careening toward me. I released the phone, barely missing the dislocated jaw of a sick MoFo, as they shattered the glass window, breaking through. The impact shot me sideways, thrusting me onto the ground beside the window with a series of painful rolls. Breakthrough. Relieved, I finally inhaled.

Alarm barks sounded from the bowels of the town house.

"Help me!" I cried, belatedly realizing that in opening the gates to the town house, I'd unleashed terror onto a mother dog who would now do everything she could to protect her dying babies. Five red-tailed hawks swooped in through the jagged frame of the broken window with tight screams, fearlessly mobbing the MoFos. They screeched at The Changed Ones, who screeched back, more feral, wild-eyed like desperate underground things. As the MoFo holding the cell phone swiped at a mobbing hawk, another bird snatched the phone from its thick, yellowed fingernails, darting back through the window, Team Hawk in tow. The MoFos galloped after like broken hyenas, howling at the sky. The cell phone started to sing a song, a stark contrast to the melodic ditty of a black-headed grosbeak. Its tinny call, the sound of violence, haunted us as it dissipated in the shadows of the town house of horrors.

It was done. The glass had been touched through. I shook crystal shards from my feathers and sidled up to the window, waiting for signs of life within the building. Then I felt a presence behind me and spun round to my very worst waking nightmare. A waddle of Humboldt penguins—the zoo penguins—those shit-beaked Spam-gremlins were inches from me. I braced myself, trying to snatch one of a million insults that swirled in my head. And then, right there, in front of everyone, they bowed to me. One of them, with a sugary pink spill around its almond eye, doubled over and yarfed up a fishy mound of mostly-digested paste. Minuscule bones and the odor of a SeaWorld dumpster confirmed they were once sardines. It was an honor the likes of which I had never experienced. Like well-dressed butlers, they sidled away, beacons of manners and respect. Everything I'd thought about them, everything Big Jim had told me, had been utterly wrong. Penguins, it turns out, are pretty fucking delightful.

Sensing movement, I spun toward the town house. A sliver of a dog slunk from the shadows. Surely once a bushy husky, she was now all hollow hip bones and hunger and the first stanza of decay. A tiny, sickly puppy with crusted eyes dangled from her jaw. Hundreds of birds watched in stunned silence as the husky stood on her shuddering hind legs, unable to make the jump to her freedom because she no longer had the strength.

And here it was, my ultimate limitation mocking me cruelly. I couldn't help her because I couldn't open the door. None of us, from hummingbird to barn owl, could turn the handles that we needed to help the domestics, and for this shortcoming, this lofty genetic hurdle, they would die. I had accomplished the goal I'd set out to achieve, to pass through glass, and I had delivered the information to a mass of powerful feathereds. And still, here it was, the metallic taste of failure. We were so close. And being this close, we would now all watch her die.

The sky erupted into an explosion of piccolo notes. The calling was urgent, high enough to touch where airplanes once soared, and we looked up to see more bald eagles descend, flapping their wings with an excitement that lit the air. My eagle, the one who'd carried me all this way, was last to touch her talons down onto the branch of a western hemlock. The eagles fixed their buttercup eyes onto five figures that had

appeared below them, figures they had guided here. I stared at
the largest of them, a beautiful hulk of flesh and bone, whose
breaths were deep and healthy. His face was a map of time,
moon-shaped and as soft as the finest leather. His hands had
their heartbreakingly beautiful digits coiled around a lump of
grass. He looked on at us, wearing a supercilious smirk and
a wild knowing. Red hair hung like a shower of straw around
his hominid body. A piece of burlap was draped across one of
his shoulders like part of a shirt. And right then I knew that
it had all been true. *Aura* was real. There was magic still left
in the world, quiet magic that wasn't as showy as the tricks of
a cell phone or one of those headsets that you put on your
eyes to transport you to another world. The eagles chittered
with spine-tingling excitement as the hulking male pressed
his beautiful knuckles into the grass, his bulky legs propelling
him toward us. He walked with slow stoicism as if he owned
the earth. I caught a glimpse of a tabby cat watching him
from behind a tree stump, glowing green eyes fixed on him
in reverence. Ladybugs and grasshoppers paused their buzzy
lives to admire the straw-haired giant. He passed me and my
skin broke into bumps as I took in his smell, a smell that was
just as the opossum had described. *Like old smells, like old grass
and leaves and things. Like hay, kind of.* His feet—with toes and
wrinkles and dexterous digits—flattened against the concrete
steps as he approached the door and lifted an anthropoid
limb and its draping red hair up to the doorknob. His four
red-haired family members watched silently, running fingers
through the grass and time. His bewitching digits closed
around the doorknob, and as hundreds of birds caged the air
in their chests, he twisted.

The door didn't move. My legs buckled. It was locked.

No, no, no. It can't be over.

He swept his hand along the ground and effortlessly picked

up a pale rock. Drawing back his magnificent arm, he aimed the rock at the closest window and released it, shattering the glass. I watched with open beak as he plunged first his gray fingers and then his whole arm into the window. A sudden pop, then a metallic *clack*—the sound of freedom. The door was open. He'd unlocked it from the inside. The skeletal husky slunk from inside her prison, the puppy in her jaw sucking in its first fresh air and the herbaceous bouquet of grass. A thousand bird eyes looked on in reverence and utter awe. The husky's liberator had a triumphant look. He knew what his powers meant.

Here was the answer to freeing the domestics, the secrets to touching through the glass. Here was The One Who Opens Doors, an orangutan, a powerful ally who could turn the knobs to a future.

When the grass fights the concrete, She shall usher in a new era. It was known.

Here was how we would win the War Of Land.

We pondered the implications in utter silence, except for the rhythmic masturbation of a nearby squirrel.

CHAPTER 25

WINNIE THE POODLE[*]
A RESIDENCE IN BELLEVUE, WASHINGTON, USA

Winnie the Poodle drew her last beautiful breaths. In her life, she had been an exceptionally dazzling specimen of poodle, and she took comfort knowing that this would continue even when she was no longer a breathing Winnie. Her tummy was hurting and hollow, her delightful pink tongue was dry like kitty litter and she no longer had the energy to lift her flawless head. She only had energy for a final growl at the cat's escape that wouldn't open anymore in a final conspiracy against Winnie. Lunch skittered past her and then ran all over her, because lunch had reproduced prolifically and was now defiling Winnie's house with horrible little pellet turds. Lunch had developed a very cavalier attitude toward her, she thought.

Winnie just didn't have any more wait.

She closed her perfectly breed-standard almond eyes and

---

[*] who continues to talk about herself in the third poodle

said goodbye to Spark Pug, and Walker, and Veuve Clicquot, and she let the guilt saturate her like a urine-soaked pee-pee pad.

"Poodle doodle doo," she murmured in a pitch-perfect tone, and that was the end of Winnie the Poodle.

Except that suddenly a violent shattering of glass window alerted Winnie to an intruder! She jumped up with what little strength she had left, chased away nearby lunch, and raced toward the window. A Walker fell in through the window, with red eyes and horrendous seasonal allergies and insides that were leaking onto the marble entryway. Winnie the Poodle was very brave, but also realistic, so she hid under the Restoration Hardware sectional. And suddenly, there was very high-pitched squeaking! And you might not believe Winnie the Poodle, but you should because she is exceedingly truthful and gets all her facts straight. There was a group of little monkeys with faces like lions! (Winnie was later told they were golden lion tamarins, but she liked her description better.) The little smelly wizards had come in through the window after the Walker and they used their little hands to open the great front door for Winnie! Then little magical monkeys with faces like enchanted lions ushered her out and she breathed in the green of the grass and she bounced up and down! And there were the other little neighbor dogs that had been freed, Fitbit and Tofu, Chanel and Macaroni Fleas, and they all danced and danced and sniffed each other's anuses and then they took off together with tongues in the air because they were free! And the great big potty world was theirs for the sniffing.

CHAPTER 26

❧

DUBAI, UNITED ARAB EMIRATES
دبيّ، الإمارات العربية المتحدة
(AS DICTATED BY A YOUNG CAMEL NAMED
DAWUD)

Here sand swallows my city. It gathers in my eyelashes; they
are long like spiders. Sand scratches on the windows of buildings. It wants to get in. So much wants to get out. If you know
the nature of sand, like me, then you know it will not kneel for
anyone. There is no fighting it. Sand is a silent lesson on the
impermanence of things. They called us Ships Of The Desert.
We're made of sand, bold hump to rubbery lip. If the shape-
shifting dunes call us—"ندعوكم ان تسلكوا هذا الطريق!"[1]—we follow
with a blustering *haboob* inside our humps, feasting on thorny
shrubs The Sand Sea offers, sidewinders at our feet.

No more days of being ridden or milked. No more robots
on our backs and racing on a track where masters chase alongside us above wheels to control the hard little robots stuck to
our colorful saddles. Grandfather spoke of times before him

---

1 "We invite you to take this path!"

when it was young masters, not robots, that rode us, fused to our saddles with Velcro. No more neon glow or echoing golden songs of Mosque.

Look! The Sand Sea is taking over. Look how it covers the streets and signs. It likes to sit on buildings and cars like orangey mist. Some masters will be missed. Others will be nothing but scars.

We are under palm trees. I rub my flank against a palm's rough bark, its ridges rise and fall like small sand dunes. I smell sweet dates that cluster and cling high above me. My family has wandered near the villa homes of masters, great shelters that block out the sand. For now. The masters' little lake is filled with sand, lion statue dusty. Sand covers the master's car, but I still see its red and gold peeking out. And انظر! [2] We watch hoopoes appear above the villa from the sun, fluttering their black-and-white wings, their crown of striking burnt-orange head feathers wobbling in excitement. The hoopoes chatter to one another and drop onto the roof of the villa.

They start to call, "Hoo hoo hoo! Hoo hoo hoo!" dipping their needle beaks low and high. A peregrine falcon arrives! انظر! He has something shiny in his talons, a master's watch that sings a song. Over here! Two masters, their dishdashas spilled with red, reach their arms upward, snarling. They are hunting the falcon. The falcon drops low, nearing the full window of the big villa.

Dogs are barking. Dogs inside! My family moves, leaving to follow the sand's beckon as they sense the danger, but I hold on to the last moment; I must see. The master pushes through a hedge and smashes through the window. انظر! The falcon drops the watch and screams. He is calling for the dogs, but

---

2 "Look!"

they won't come! He swoops in and out of the window, the hoopoes calling, "Hoo hoo hoo! Hoo hoo hoo!" My family calls for me to follow them. They do not joke.

"أسرع! يجب أن نذهب!"³

I pretend and show that I'm pressing my hooves into the sand, but I keep watch while I can. Cockatoos! Cockatoos flutter over the top of the villa, calling out to the hoopoes and the falcon. They cluster around the villa's wooden arched doors, squawking and hopping on the ground. They use a small black stick, I see it, and they are poking it into a small hole in the door.

"أسرع يا إبني!"⁴

I don't listen to my family now; I'm watching, waiting, and their impatience collects in my eyelashes with sand. The cockatoos shriek; now one is sitting on the big door handles and more of them are sitting on the door handles, and انظر! The door is open! The dogs, red and black and a spotted one, are running out past the master's lake and sprinting ahead of my family!

The master with the red dishdasha comes out of the door too with the singing watch. I think he looks right at me with eyes as red as sunset.

"أنا قادم!"⁵ I tell my family, and I trot quickly to catch up with them as we head for the dunes.

---

3   "Hurry up! We have to go!"
4   "Hurry up, my son!"
5   "I'm coming!"

CHAPTER 27

BANGKOK, THAILAND
กรุงเทพประเทศไทยกรุงเทพประเทศไทย
(THE LOW RUMBLINGS OF AN URBAN ELEPHANT HERD)

walk with us
our numbers grow and we gather
family woven together like nest of a cave swiftlet
both wispy fragile and Life's One Keeper
we move together through time
and the *tuk-tuk* streets of once-buzzy Bangkok
through grave site of bus and motorbike and carbon cough
where we once begged
under neon lights
while a noose caressed our necks
we are great gray clouds who remind you how to unfold
now that the air has remembered herself
our trunks sway in honor of Ocean's pulse
like the shaggy rain tree who shivers under our footprint
and knows that you are as fresh as orchid's first bloom.
we will push aside car and continent to free you
lighten the burden you must learn to shed

like skin of snake and winter leaf
we use our bodies to splinter glass and street stalls and wood
denting metal and stripping wire of its power
violent acts of devotion
to free those who dream of water's promise
and the smell of lotus flower
dog and cat and horse and mouse
fly from their cages
and we
we swallow miles, our ears velvet instruments
we carry your chain-link burdens
trampling the noose that caressed your neck
holding your beautiful story in our bones

คนที่เป็นผู้รับ ย่อมมีหน้าที่ต้องเป็นผู้ให้เช่นกัน[*]

---

[*]   The One Who Hollows as well must return

CHAPTER 28

❧

GENGHIS CAT
EVERYWHERE LIKE AN OMNIPOTENT NINJA,
WASHINGTON, USA

I am still utterly amazing. I have honed my sock-stealing skills and added to my mosque collection. The collections have now expanded to include all bras and bus stops.

THEY ARE MINE DON'T TOUCH THEM.

Something else has changed. It changed after that bewhiskered, unsanitary Orange with sausage fingers and a face like a large platter of beef jerky waltzed into my mosque. After I showed him my fierce—chased him and swiped at his truck-tire face with my murderous claws—I decided to spy on him. I followed him like the magnificent ninja I am, always out of sight, which is a shame because I am very, very good-looking. I stalked him through leaves, sewer holes, from halfway up a telephone pole and the inside of a Pringles tube.

Then something happened. I began to find him captivating, that galumphing eggplant that smells like microwaved Tender Beef & Chicken Fancy Feast. He became more entertaining to me than handicapping lizards or squatting in boxes or even eating grass so I can barf it back up again. His shitty excuse for fur hangs in long cords and trails like the fake snakes my Mediocre Servants used to dangle for me, and I chase his cords when it suits me. Bottle caps and sticks and pens get stuck in those cords and when I hear them jingle, I know they must be swatted into submission. Orange's face, round as a great dark toilet bowl, is exceedingly stupid and yet pleasing to me. Clearly, he is a giant animated ball of yarn who was conjured entirely for my pleasure. I have decided that I own him and have made this clear to every being on earth by urinating on him intermittently in my potent signature. Orange has his own smaller Oranges. I allow them. I am just and wondrous. I am Genghis, Owner Of Orange.

Others try to take my Orange from me. A cougar in a sand-colored coat and hungry mood thought she could sneak up on him, but I pounced on her head and chased her into an upturned porta-potty. A brown bear the size of my bus stops stumbled into the Oranges. The Oranges panicked, bared their long teeth, and swung their arms in an embarrassingly feeble manner. The brown bear roared from her bones, her litter of littles close behind her back claws. Naturally, I threw myself at her eyes, sharpened my claws on her pillowy body, and drove her back into the tree line.

Orange needs my protection. He is very, very fat. I summon my feline kin to join me in his protection. Striped ones with laser-pointer moves, jumpers, long-haired assassins, night kings, mousers, shadow stalkers, tree scalers, and one strange naked one that looks like an uncooked chicken. We are killers, warriors, hunters.

Orange likes to hold my kittens in his gentle, leather-couch hands. Not all of them, as my unparalleled fertility has made this impossible. We share sleep space and this suits me because Orange is as warm as silver lap box and sometimes runs his fingers on me when I let him. Other times, I smack him to remind him who is in charge of all The Everything.

WHAT IS THAT IS THAT A LIGHT BEAM RUNNING UP THAT TREE?

Orange—my smelly trinket—can read the rainbow light just as I can, though doubtfully as well. What I know is that he is being called to go somewhere he believes is important in his fat Orange heart. What I know is that death is coming. I see it in the rainbow light that dances across the lips of roses and paints white walls with prismatic pirouettes. I feel it in the wind that tickles my whiskers. Cats know death as well as a storm before it's born. It will not touch my falafel-shaped toy. I will protect him, even as he continues to mercilessly torture himself by ingesting fruit. There is nothing I can do about that shit.

Orange takes me to interesting places. I am ready.

Prepare to watch me take on anything and everything that gets in my way.

Just don't touch my fucking Orange.

CHAPTER 29

S.T.
UNIVERSITY OF WASHINGTON, BOTHELL CAMPUS,
BOTHELL, WASHINGTON, USA

For a period of time, things were pretty copacetic. I don't want to call it bliss, because it didn't involve neck scritching and lazy football Sundays with melty queso dip and all-you-can-eat Cheetos®, but there were things about it that were pretty damn special. Each day, we took to the wing—me on the back of Migisi, Kraai's bald eagle friend, who silently shredded the sky—for a dawn-till-dusk day of touching through glass and freeing any domestic we could. This all proved to be a hell of a lot of cardio for poor old Dennis as he thundered below us past abandoned houses. You see, as fast as the luminous streak of a shooting star, Dennis had wiggled his way into the hearts of the college crows, who brought him small gifts like buttons, dish sponges, and an abandoned NuvaRing. Even a dung beetle would have eschewed some of these things, but Dennis would graciously wag his tail and smile. Everyone fell for the droopy ears of a loving oaf. The college crows lovingly scratched his belly and back with their feet. Everyone's hearts were lighter around Dennis.

One crow, a gentle character whose name means the particular feeling you get when you find something you'd lost and long forgotten but it had held a place in the back of your thoughts, brought Dennis sprigs of mint, laying them by his paw pads as he slept.

"Dennis is the purest soul I know," said the crow, thick love spread all over him like cream cheese frosting.

"Hmm. He'd shank you for a French fry," I told him, matter-of-factly. I just wasn't that willing to share all of Dennis.

Even though I've always been pretty plucky and motivated by my various passions, I'd never done anything like the Freedom Flies. Nothing that kept me so excited that my heart trilled like the songbirds that bolstered us on lunch breaks. They serenaded us with stories about bravery and long-lost loves as we drilled into cans of finely aged SpaghettiOs and syrupy peaches with our beaks. The work was dangerous and made us so tired our bones hurt like old memories, but our hearts were overflowing as we dreamt about the dogs, goats, and all the other domestics we had offered life. I cannot recommend this to you enough: find something that you believe in, right down deep in the depths of your silvery plumage, and then throw your heart at it, blood and valves and veins and all. Because I did this, the world, though brambled and frothing at the mouth, looked more vibrant; blues were bluer, and even the fetid puddles that collected under rusting cars tasted as sweet as summer wine. Disclaimer: I've never actually had summer wine, but once I had the remnants of a fuzzy navel wine cooler that Nargatha had only half finished then pitched into her trash with her Poligrip. So, I'm not as uncultured as all that.

At night, the college crows invited Dennis and me to roost at the University of Washington's Bothell campus wetlands. That's right, yours truly officially became an academic corvid. The UW Bothell campus was empty and had been heavily

barricaded during the height of the MoFo fray, which meant
Dennis had to burrow a Dennis-sized hole to get under
its barbed-wire fencing (and for me, the flightless wonder).
A crudely spray-painted sign said "*cordon sanitaire,*" which I
assumed was some sort of fancy French stuffed chicken dish
and didn't make a whale of a lot of sense to me. There were
no MoFos or MoFo body parts in the campus—we searched—
but we found evidence of science-y goings-ons; that is to say,
Petri dishes and microscopes and lab coats that had blood
on them. Tire tracks that zigzagged haphazardly across what
remained of the flower beds told us that at one time, there
had been a panic and an evacuation here. But now, UW
Bothell was silent and calm, becoming greener by the minute,
blood-and-tissue-lump–free.

During the nights, I took comfort in the black beings that
shrouded the wetland trees above me. I got used to the college crow dialect, different from other murders I'd heard in
passing, and learned more about crow culture. Roosting with
Kraai's murder, I found that crows are witty, enjoy practical
pranks, and find the humor in everything, which felt right to
me on a cellular level. Storytelling is part of the spine and lifeline of a murder. Even Kraai told comical tales of a time when
he pilfered a garbage man's wallet and, after rifling through
its contents, dropped it onto a school playground. Once, he
stole a pair of scissors from an unknowing MoFo family as
they set up their garden for a piñata party, watching the
ensuing Three Stooges hilarity from a weeping cedar. During
this time, I became a sponge, absorbing and trying on my
new crow suit. I held back my own stories because they were
mostly MoFo-centric.

They invited me to their nests and I was asked to help
feed the hatchlings, which was funny and delightful because
those black puffs are already so full of ideas and personality,

prebaked in a speckled egg. I was offered a desirable high spot in a western red cedar, but instead chose to sleep perched on top of Dennis's newly muscled physique, rising and lowering with his every breath, a gentle lullaby to which I fell asleep. The wound on his side had healed nicely and now looked like a cartoon smile. It made me happy to look at, so perfectly and ridiculously Dennis.

Before the roost's eyes closed for the night, a crow with singed contour feathers and an angry burn on the underside of her right wing would drop from above and administer a beak full of herbs to my injury. Her name translated as "Survivor," but she told me she didn't like it much. I asked her why and she said because she is a female and all females are survivors so it was massively redundant. I asked her what she would like to be called and she told me (again, my apologies, this is my attempt at a translation), "Pressa." I prided myself on my self-taught flora and fauna identification, but whatever plant she brought was usually an earthy mystery. The clean herbaceous smells made me think of MoFo stories of witches and magic spells.

She always approached me slowly, head lowered. She took cautious hops forward, light on her feet.

"Trust me," she'd say in a soft whisper, like a fizzy drink poured on ice.

It did take trust to allow her to get so close, to touch my traumatized wing. Trust, it turned out, was a very beautiful and fragile thing with a taste like wild raspberries and experienced only by the very brave.

"Will I fly again?" I asked her.

"Maybe you will. Maybe you won't," she said with a gentle rattle like beer bottles in a truck. "Both ways will be okay."

One night, I plucked up the courage to tell her I thought she had nice pinions, to which she rolled her head and scoffed. Listen, I'm a work in progress.

Then one day, Dennis, never a hound for histrionics, staged a protest. Although it was almost imperceptible to the untrained eye, to me it was as epic as when three million MoFos marched through Rome to protest the Iraq War, since Dennis hadn't outright declined so much as a flea bath in his entire life. The concrete miles had been hard on his paw pads, and I suspected he was mildly disgruntled that we all expected him to perform impromptu marathons like some sort of Alaskan husky–greyhound hybrid, when really, he was a purebred slob. That morning, after *Aura*'s dawn symphony and a breakfast of worms, the phalluses of mushrooms, and somewhat regrettably, a can of Amy's Organic Spicy Chili, I mounted Migisi's beautiful back. As we were about to take flight, Dennis slumped onto his side and moaned. It was a deep, exasperated moan, surprisingly MoFo in nature. He rolled his lugubrious eyes at me, lifting a bloody, cracked paw pad, and I was absolutely horrified. I made a big fuss, stomping my feet and thrusting my wings around like the resurrected evil twin of a soap opera. Between melodramatic caws, I declared that his days of watching the sky for signals to run and dragging a SpongeBob SquarePants pillowcase filled with canned goods were over.

I suggested to Kraai that Dennis and I take up "grounds guarding" instead, which meant that while most birds were still freeing domestics and a smattering of Sky Sentinel crows monitored UW Bothell from the air, Dennis and I patrolled from *terra firma*, walking the perimeter of the university like a couple of cowboys. During our border patrols we ran into the increasing domestic population—packs of dogs and the occasional cat that Dennis lumbered after, with me screaming MoFo cries of "Here, kitty, kitty!" from Dennis's thick back. We met a western rattlesnake who was terrified of us—the two-headed monster that we were—and slithered away at supersonic speed. We later told a slightly embellished death-defying

tale of reptile ambush to the roost during the evening blue
hour. We talked to rabbits and moles, snacked on earthworms
and plump berries until one day, we came across something
very strange.

Dennis and I were plodding along near old-town Bothell,
with its once-quaint little storefronts and restaurants, whose
glass had been busted in by birds and were now the homes and
sacred roosting spots of said birds. We came to the intersection
where a coffee shop, a convenience store, and a nearby post
office faced one another. The post office was separated from
the pack by an enormous puddle, a stain of recent flooding.
Outside The Den Coffee Shop, we came across a migration. A
large army of ants were streaming across the pavement, crossing a carless road in single file. I suppressed my natural urge
to pulverize and rub them all over my body and instead tried
to understand the reason for their fleeing. Once they'd spotted us, ant voices yelled panicked orders and strategic evasion
techniques. I assured them we weren't there to eat them, step
on them, or rub them all over us for aesthetic purposes. There
was a ringleader who I honestly couldn't tell from the other
ants except that she carried her tiny frame like a gladiator
who'd seen cities crumble.

"Where are you going in such a hurry?" I asked.

"We're getting away from them," said the ant's leader, whose
voice could shepherd planets. She waved her antennae like
wands, communicating in chemical signals. Her pheromones
danced in the air. The other ants absorbed these, listening in
turn with their antennae.

"From whom?" I asked.

"The Weavers," said the ant leader as if the words nipped
at her mandibles. A collective panic spread through the ant
line, hysterical mutterings elbowing one another, chaotically
unintelligible. The ant leader yelled a command, antennae

waving, and the ants filtered into perfect formation, silent and civil once again.

Weavers brought to mind my tropical avian friends, tiny yellow-nest craftsmen. It seemed odd that a bird native to Asia and Africa would be the source of a Seattle ant's terror, but an uncaged zoo had certainly changed the dynamics of things. "Do you mean birds?" I asked. The ant army didn't answer, so I pressed them. "I don't understand, who or what are The Weavers?"

The mention of the name sent the ants into rippling panic again. The ant leader hollered another directive and the ants poured themselves into a glimmering formation, much like the dance of the starlings. They were commencing their retreat.

"Where are you going? I just want some answers!" They didn't have the time to answer me. The ant leader had given them an order that caused them to shuffle, reforming into one incredible shape right before our eyes. One hundred ants wrapped their (I'm guessing) six hundred legs tightly together, the larger ants, including the ant leader herself, huddled in the center. With a final shouted command and flailing antennae, the cluster of interconnected ants launched itself into an enormous puddle. I let out a caw of horror. A mass suicide! The ants were so traumatized, they'd drunk the Kool-Aid and resigned to drowning themselves!

"Whoa, whoa, whoa!" I squawked, hopping back and forth, scanning for a nearby leaf to throw out to them since this seemed unnatural, barbaric, and a perfectly good waste of an anting sacrifice for the benefit of my plumage. Wet ants are no use to anyone! Dennis stepped closer to the large puddle, his pendulous ears swinging, head cocked to one side. He was studying the ants. As I approached with a crispy maple leaf grasped in my beak, I suddenly realized that I'd misinterpreted the scene. The larger ants in the center of the cluster had formed pockets of air and were keeping the ant-made raft afloat. They drifted on the shiny surface of the water as one unit that had chosen to tackle a deadly element rather than face what they were running from. I couldn't believe it! As a self-proclaimed ant connoisseur, I'd only known fire ants to do this, and here, these thatching ants had adapted, mimicking their southern cousins. Dennis and I watched the ant raft float farther into the large puddle toward the post office. *The Weavers.* Something told me it wasn't a creative tropical bird that they were afraid of.

Dennis lifted The Golden Nose and sniffed at the wind, facing the direction the ants had come from. I hopped onto his back and we lumbered where The Golden Nose told us to, toward a MoFo physical therapy center and abandoned Bothell apartment complex. It really was only then that I noticed how quiet it was. Because of the crow patrol, many domestics had taken up residence in the Bothell area surrounding the UW campus. Chickens, goats, alpacas (who continued to instill terror in Dennis), pigs, horses, iguanas, dog packs, cats, even the odd ferret. But as Dennis and I trotted along the pavement, I realized that we were utterly alone. A pandemonium of parrots—Ghubari's new crew—had taken up residence in the Bothell area, their ear-piercing banter echoing for miles—and there wasn't a peep from them. Apart from the ants, we hadn't seen as much as an aphid. This was the sign of some sort of mass evacuation.

Dennis picked up the strange scent as soon as we approached The 104 Apartments. He sniffed more frantically than usual, dangling ears stirring the scent and sweeping it up into his magnificent snoot. His gangly, udon-noodle legs propelled him. The apartment complex was quiet and glassless, modern but now overgrown and lacquered green. A Douglas fir, savagely uprooted during a storm, had at one point slammed down onto one of the building's roofs, snatching a fistful of telephone wire with it. Since the building was relatively new, the Douglas fir had not won this fight; its bark was splintered, its trunk and spine severed midway. A brutal crime scene. I bowed my condolences.

Dennis started to whimper. He was agitated; I felt it in the muscles of his back. I hopped off him and went into detective mode. All around the broken body of the fallen Douglas fir were strange black-and-white lumps, each about the size of a packet of Doritos. As far as I could tell, the unusual blobs weren't living, and they had a strange, acidic smell that burned the beak a little. It must have been torture for Dennis, who erupted into sneezes, his ears flapping like ping-pong paddles. The air felt tight, as if it was holding its breath, but then a quick breeze sent me another scent: the saccharine smell of slow decay. Curiosity had pinched my pinions and I hopped around looking for the source of the putrid aroma. It wasn't in the intersection near the fallen fir. Not near the battered political MoFo signs tucked in the overgrown grass by the side of the road. It wasn't in the overturned trash can, its insides long ravaged, its plastic outsides scarred with impatient talons. It wasn't on or near the motorbike that had twisted itself around a stop sign. We found it tucked into a bored-out hollow in the fir tree's side. The carcass, covered in filmy slime, looked like it had been regurgitated. I couldn't make out what it was or had been, though it was about the size of a raccoon, a large bird, or a small dog. Its head had a bit of a shape, but the rest of it, seemed…digested. Dennis let out a long groan.

"I have no idea, buddy," I told him. The loose folds of his skin wobbled as he shook his head. He backed up at warp speed without looking where he was going like Nargatha on her Rascal 615 mobility scooter. Dennis didn't like this one bit, and given his nasal acuity and the state of the unidentifiable body squashed into the corpse of a tree—a sort of Russian doll of night terrors—I wasn't about to argue.

I had taught him well. Instead of facing whatever had partially consumed an unidentified being, he ran us away from it at top speed, the wind in our fur and feathers, self-preservation first and foremost on our minds. I had plans to enlighten the crows on watch duty with these new findings, but I didn't get a chance.

We found that as we approached the barricaded UW Bothell compound, the serenity had been severed. Adrenaline turned the air static, and *Aura* was humming in panic. The crows stationed to guard the compound had left their posts and were fluttering just outside the campus's barbed-wire perimeter, their alarm caws croaky and hoarse. Dennis slowed as we neared them, watching them dive from the air and swoop over several mounds. The bodies of six crows. Their bones were picked clean, gleaming white under a pewter sky. I felt my knees buckle, and I squeezed my feet to stay on Dennis's back. The crows' furious calls echoed hauntingly and were picked up by other birds who sang and spread word of the killings that had happened right at our doorstep. They called for the rest of the college crows to return to home base. I stared at the bones with sand in my throat. I had never seen a dead crow, had never been faced with a mirror of my foundations. Is this what went on underneath my skin? These brittle slivers of pearly white? The tiny skull with boned beak? Are these really the roots of us, just an insignificant collection of sprig-like connectors, a rib cage no bigger than a MoFo palm? Is this little nest, this smattering of splintery white twigs, what makes a crow? What makes me? I had always had trouble with self-identification, but perhaps never more so than now. Dennis's shoulders slumped with his heavy sigh.

"Who are they?" I asked the frantic crows.

"Sisika and Chogan, Croa, Tuk, and..." he couldn't finish, this crow I'd come to know, whose name translates as Lucky Peanut Balanced On The Highest Branch Of A Very Particular Cedar At The Wetlands, so I'll just call him Sam. "They were part of the guard group. I don't know when they ventured out of site. We should've..." He stopped himself. Crows are not known to dwell on should've-would've-could'ves. They are too busy living.

"What has done this to them? What could have ambushed a crow this way? Six of us at that?" I asked, nausea rising in guts I was very glad to have. I thought of three brothers with eyes like flames and bodies made of stripes.

"I don't know," said Sam, breathlessly. "But we will not stand for this. This is an execution. This is an act of war." The Blackwings are known to hold grudges for generations. A crime against one is a crime against all.

I heard them coming. The sky turned black as Kraai and the college crows returned from a Freedom Fly to the grim display outside our safe zone. Hundreds of crows filled the space all around the six skeletons, screaming out their caws of grief. Kraai landed on the grass among the bone bodies, touching down like a single feather, and he let out the sounds of sadness from deep inside him. None of the murder shied away from looking at the cluster of white cartilage, at the bodies of family members. Some crows stayed airborne, circling their pain from above, diving through branches with their chorus of grief. I realized that this was a crow funeral. Dennis seemed to know this. He lay down with his head on his paws and kept his breathing shallow out of respect, his amber eyes following the looping birds above. After some time, the caws lessened until there were no sounds but the rustle of leaves and the wind that ruffled feathers and whistled among the gleaming white remains. Then two crows I didn't yet know approached

the bones. One touched a slim wing bone several times as if
to gently kiss it with her beak. The other placed two twigs
on either side of the bodies. Many of the crows took turns
bowing from wherever they sat or perched. I didn't know the
six crows who had been taken, but I still felt the loss. I thought
it felt as if the python at the zoo had gotten ahold of me, as
if it had coiled its muscular middle around my chest and was
squeezing out my final breaths. It felt like how I missed Big
Jim and the life I'd known. But I also felt the love that sizzled
and frothed around us, a love that touched through life and
extended to the bones of six beings. Sometimes you can feel
two very different things at once—both searing pain and joy,
feelings as deep as the ocean.

And then it was all over. Kraai lifted to the sky and a black
cape of crows trailed behind him toward the roosting roof.
Dennis lifted to his paws and waited for me to catch my breath
and hop onto his back. Then we trailed the perimeter, found
the Dennis-sized hole, and snuck through it, meandering our
way through the campus to the area around the roosting roof.
The murder had mostly settled on the grass and benches—
lower ground, which I knew was to include me and Dennis.
Dennis lay down for a snooze and I listened intently as Kraai
gave us our marching orders. As the sun slept and night
swallowed the last of the light, *Aura* gave us the name we were
looking for, a name on which to lay our sizzling blame. The
Blackwings were going to take on a new enemy, our greatest
threat yet. This war was no longer just about territory and
resources; the killing of crows had made it personal. We were
fueled by revenge, seeking one eye for another, oblivious to
the unimaginable adversity that lay ahead. But we held each
other's hopes alive. We would sleep, dreaming of shrieks and
bones and when we woke, we would exact revenge on the crow
killer. We would hunt down The One Who Conquers.

CHAPTER 30

❧✿❧

S.T.

PLOTTING AT UW BOTHELL CAMPUS, BOTHELL,
WASHINGTON, USA

The plans were drawn up fast. Most of the college campus murder would fly to the last known lair of The One Who Conquers. When they revealed where that was, I felt the residual Amy's Organic Spicy Chili in my belly shoot off a bazooka and then set itself on fire. With their mind-mapping, they described somewhere Dennis and I had already been, somewhere we didn't want to revisit ever, ever again. King Street Station. The One Who Conquers must have killed the gorilla. I remembered the feel of her rubbery hand, the very last light in her limpid amber eyes. The slick smear of her red across the polished marble. My philosophy about not being a hero but maintaining a pulse had gotten us this far, so Dennis and I volunteered ourselves for the ground mission, far away from King Street Station and anyone's known lair. The Golden Nose would take us on another journey, this time following a sharp distress scent that haunted the air. The breeze told a story and Dennis was reading it cover to cover like Big Jim and his *Big Butts*™ issues. While the crows went to hunt down The One Who Conquers in its lair, Dennis and I would track down the creature whose panic pheromones filled the airwaves; we were the search and rescue team. I was dazzled by this genius discovery of Dennis's because it meant we'd be doing something blatantly heroic but also not cavorting with predators who eat gorillas. We started near the scene of the crime, where the crows had perished, Dennis inhaling in big sniffs. I could tell by the glazed look in his eye, flinches that ticked and rippled under his loose folds, that he was reliving what had happened, ingesting the plight of an animal in peril. Once he had the scent of the victim who needed help (I was hoping for something very tiny to rescue, like an infant muskrat or an underdeveloped dust mite), I hopped onto his back and we began a long journey.

We headed north, following a chemical cocktail—the smell of suffering. It took us through long-abandoned neighborhoods where neglected Halloween decorations sat in eerie tatters, hardly as grotesque as the hobbling MoFos who slithered past them. We, self-admitted nonheroes, hurtled past raccoons and rabbits being shaken to death by the rabies that swam in their blood, choking on their own froth. We passed a Brown Bear Car Wash that had collapsed on itself and had become a roost for pigeons who wished us well on our hunt. We passed makeshift graves and machine guns strewn across the sidewalk like the leaves of fall. It was all silent school buses and the charred scent of ruin. All around us another battle was taking place, making itself known through our nasal passages. The pungent assault of urine defiled fresh air as felines, raccoons, and creatures of the night fought for territory by graffitiing with their waste, a vicious pissing contest. We came upon turkey vultures pulling thin strings of meat off a Labrador. Dennis charged them, causing them to scatter, but I told him that it was in their nature to eat the dead. I apologized to the Carrion Kings. This was a time of feast for the vultures, cloak-winged birds who are at home with the grosser side of things and who whiz on their own legs when feeling too sweaty. But it was also a time when *Aura* and no doubt *Web* and *Echo* were alive with stories and hopes for a new future. I listened to the audacious melodies while maintaining a careful watch, serving as Dennis's eyes.

Wherever we went, our reputation preceded us. Songbirds would intermittently dart from the sky to praise us unctuously or attempt to buoy us with a small song or limerick. Initially, it was delightful, but after the eighth time I'd heard Dennis referred to as "Mother Nature's Gift, a mythical stallion of the canine world," and me as a "flightless half-breed," I was over it. Many of them couldn't believe their beady little eyes when they first saw me, because apparently word had incorrectly spread that I had no legs and was made of tumbleweeds. Birds and their imaginations, honestly. Dennis seemed to enjoy the bolstering, so I let them go on.

Herds of freed horses galloped ahead of us, their hooves clattering down on broken pavement. Deer, pigs, and goats grazed openly on the abundance of green, and speckled across the land were sick MoFos, stuck in a loop of swiping, bobbing, and searching, twisted and pulseless. But throughout the journey, I couldn't shake a familiar feeling, one that tingled up and down my spine. I was sure we were being watched. But as much as I scanned the skies and the ground all around us, I couldn't find the culprit.

We had walked for some time when Dennis needed to take a break. He squatted in the cover of some black nightshade and I hopped around, stabbing at the earth with my beak because that shit is always awkward. At least I didn't have to hover over him and collect his specimen with a plastic bag and then carry it around with me while swearing under my breath until

I found a trash can, like Big Jim would sometimes do. Sometimes. Mostly, he just whistled at the sky and left the unclaimed turd wherever it lay. When I'd stare at him, he'd roll his eyes and say, "It's fertilizing, giving back to the earth."

I found myself, once again, lamenting my lack of flight. I could tell we were near a body of water and it was a pile of absolute hippo shit that I couldn't check it out for myself. All I knew was that following the scent of The One Who Conquers had led us to what appeared to be a town center. Mill Creek had an elaborate sign for an apartment complex with a cutesy functioning water mill. Its town center had a Starbucks, the Central Market, which appeared to once have been some sort of upscale grocery store, a Cold Stone Creamery, sushi joints, tapas, and more. All of the glass was long smashed. Trash and debris fluttered like ghostly wings. And suddenly, as we plodded through the town center with the Starbucks clock tower and pretty double-story buildings, we realized that we were all alone. There were no sick MoFos here. Nothing in the grips of rabies. Not even the cloying smell of urine dared make itself known here. A quick breeze rustled up some empty Starbucks cups and levitated plastic bags like airborne jellyfish. But nothing here had blood running through it. And I still had that uneasy feeling that I was being watched. In strict accordance with my philosophy, I suggested to Dennis that we get the shit out of there. He didn't seem to take issue with this and began a hasty trot that took us past a tanning salon and a Thai restaurant. Nearby, the remains of a tent lay shredded and tattered, barely covering stacked mountains of canned goods and bottles of water. All that remained of the MoFo that once stood in front of those cans of beans and soup was a bloody puddle.

Dennis's sniffing suddenly intensified, his ears swinging back and forth in anticipation. The Golden Nose trailed along tarmac that missed the touch of a wheel, nosing aside plastic bags and cigarette butts. As he lifted his wrinkly jowls, he cocked his head at the silvery lump before him. Smoky fur lifted from the body, tickled by the breeze. Dennis and I marveled at the size of a carcass the approximate length of a pool noodle, wondering what had been able to stop its heart and remove all of its entrails, except for one sliver of intestine that lay pink and muculent like an unearthed worm.

"Is this who we came to rescue, Dennis?" I asked him, feeling a chill creep up my spine.

Dennis whined—*no*. He sniffed the air, breathing in more details. We then both saw—on the sidewalk ahead of us—a leg, large and lupine, pulled clean from its socket. Nearby lay a ravaged mass of fur and red and tissue, too grisly to investigate further. I assumed it was a torso that had been robbed of limbs and appendages. Farther out, a rogue ear, a swath of ashen-furred skin, a severed muzzle that had sniffed its last. These were parts of more than one wolf. Each paw we found was slick and crimson, several claws scattered like spent bullets. Blood scrawled its violent signature across the ground around the pieces of predators. The wolves had put up the fight of their lives. Dennis whimpered.

"I don't know," I told him.

Wolves. What was above them, these creatures so firmly at the top of the food chain? I thought back to the mama bear and her cubs. Could one bear have committed this much carnage?

What on earth had shredded a pack of wolves into pieces?

A sharp shriek caused Dennis and me to jump out of our respective skins. We looked up. Dennis's tail swung pendulously. He crouched, moving his rubbery lips as if to speak. There, on the awning of a restaurant, below large letters that spelled "Thai Rhapsody," were two inquisitive eyes peering down at us. We'd located the source of the smell—the distressed creature.

"Are you friendly?" asked a bird with head and chest a hypnotic blue as dizzying and mesmeric as the evening sky.

"Are you?" I snapped back. A little saucy, I know, but I was pretty on edge at this point.

"I'm friendly," he said, though his voice was strained, scratched thin by fear. "I've been hiding up on the roofs because it's safer up here." The peacock's mesmerizing tail, a tango of teal and turquoise, hung low behind him, draped like a vintage couture skirt. I saw it twitch. I imagined that in a different time, this bird would have been strutting, his incredible display fully fanned out and shaking with pride. Now, it was closed and trembling with terror.

"Why don't you come up here with me?" asked the peacock.

"No, I'm fine here," I told him. I might have learned that trust was a thing as beautiful as his tail feathers, but it could be just as easily ripped apart. "What has done this to the wolves?"

The peacock didn't respond for a moment, but I didn't miss that his legs suddenly shook with a pronounced violence. "Have you got somewhere to be?" he asked. It was a strange thing to say and I wondered what he meant exactly.

"My friend can smell stories, the past, everything. He knew you were in trouble. We came looking for you." I looked back at the carnage. "You have been hiding from a terrible predator…"

The peacock shuddered. "It seems the world is full of them now." And then, as if the peacock summoned them, a gaggle of Canada geese streamed across the sky and honked from above.

"RUN!" they blared. "RUN! RUN! RUUUUN!"

The alarm honks were deafening. I looked up at the peacock, whose body erupted into quivers. Dennis growled way down low. My eyes darted, scanning the center of Mill Creek, but there was nothing but gray street and sky. I saw nothing. Then up ahead, beyond the shattered storefronts and the silent street, clouding the air, came a dark mass. The mass was growing. Nearing. It blocked out the clouds. A swarm was headed our way. And then I could hear the airborne panic, and as their bodies drew nearer, I could make out the shapes of feathereds like fiery arrows splitting open the sky. What was happening?

"Is it The One Who Conquers?" I screeched upward. Nobody had time to answer. The swarm shot past. Suddenly, crows I recognized, college crows, were surrounding me, agitation expressed by rapid wing flaps.

"S.T.! RUN! NOW! Get to safety!" came the voice of a crow I'd shared a few meals with.

"Tell Dennis! Now!" shrieked Pressa, the svelte crow who rubbed herbs on my wing nightly. A brilliant flash, a ruptured Skittles bag of color filled the air above us. Greens, blues, yellows, turquoises, and teals. The parrots. The parrots were escaping from something too. What had come for us now?

Vibrations shook the ground. I felt them through Dennis, who lowered himself, sending his own growling vibrations toward the stretch of empty road in front of us, past Thai Rhapsody, past the real estate office and kitchen-trinket storefronts. The crows cawed at us from above.

"GO! NOW! THEY'RE HERE!"

But Dennis and I were frozen. Fear, curiosity, shock, whatever it was, it had us in its icy claws and we were fused to tarmac. The source of chaos appeared on the horizon, cresting over the edge of cement. And we saw them. Dennis whimpered, and the air was punched from my lungs. A strange sound bolted from my throat.

A herd of long legs thundered down the road toward us, mottled and wrinkled gray, ending in two enormous talons. The legs carried torsos the likes of which I'd never seen—fleshy chests barreled and puffed out, the skin of them puckered into goose bumps. They ran with their heads thrust forward, arms tucked by their sides, but it was their faces that made me reel where I clung. They had egg-shaped domes for heads, singed black cavities where, deep inside, their eyes hid, and in place of a mouth was a half-formed dark, boney bill—a beak. I didn't have time to make sense of what I'd seen. The herd was barreling toward us, something distinctly MoFo about the shape of their heads and the color of their chests, but they were too large to be MoFos, Jurassic in leg and mouth. One of the hideous creatures lifted its boned beak to the sky and let out a tooth-scraping shriek. And then I believe I shit myself, because the call was in a language I knew. It was the predatory call of a raptor. These creatures knew the language of a bird.

A wall of crows formed above us, driving toward the oncoming herd of monsters, and I snapped to attention. I looked up at the peacock who was cowering behind the Thai Rhapsody sign. I couldn't join him without flight and I couldn't leave Dennis anyway. *Think, S.T., think.* What would a crow do? I looked up at the wall of crows, realizing I couldn't do what they were doing, my self-confidence suddenly in tatters. What would a crow do? I racked my brain—*crow thoughts, crow thoughts, come on, S.T., be who you're meant to be!*—the herd coming closer, closer to meeting the wall of crows, and closer to crushing those ostrich legs down on Dennis and me.

"Help us, S.T.!" I heard the faint call from an unmistakably beautiful voice, a voice that was almost swallowed in the fray. Kraai. He was at the front of the wall of crows, readying to mob creatures fifty times his size. He was counting on me. My head swam, my thoughts too slippery to hold on to. All I could think about was what a failure I was because I couldn't fly, about how on earth I could call myself a crow if I couldn't act like one. And then I had run out of time. The clamor was deafening, sounds of angry crows and the twisted prey calls of creatures that jumped up at them from below, so close to where Dennis and I had frozen. And then Dennis thawed out.

Dennis leapt into a run, away from the battle, tearing down the center road of downtown Mill Creek. I clung to his back feeling faint, weak, and inept. I felt a great pull, gravity's punch, and suddenly we were airborne. Dennis leapt over a toppled trash can and I couldn't hold on. I tumbled from his back, rolling onto the road and smacking against the curbside under the Cold Stone Creamery storefront. Before I knew which way was up, what was ass and what was wing, Dennis had me in his soft, slimy jaw and just as quickly, he dropped me into a sequestered Cold Stone to-go tub. And ran away.

The Cold Stone to-go tub was hidden behind a planter pot. He'd hidden me and taken heed of my non–hero training. I poked my head out the top of the ice cream tub, covered in shame and rotten rocky-road sludge. I watched Dennis run away, ears, limbs, and skin folds flailing, as he tore down Mill Creek town center like a weapons-grade coward. His friends were fighting against a force we couldn't name and here he was, saving his own saggy skin. But instead of being glad, I was ashamed of what I'd done. Wasn't this my fault? Hadn't I taught him to self-preserve and look out for numero uno? I had shaped him into a perfect defector and gone against the code of murder. How would I ever look Kraai in the eye again? That is, if he didn't die because of my negligence. The One Who Keeps. What a joke. I was just a weird half-breed made up entirely of tumbleweeds.

A fluttering stirred the air around me. Gray and white and custard-lemon eyes engulfed my view. Ghubari.

"Shit Turd!" he said, pushing at the Cold Stone tub with his feet. "Come now! We must hurry!"

"I've failed everyone," I said, my voice trailing into the tub. He pushed harder, toppling the container. I rolled out back onto the road. "I am not worthy to be a crow."

"There's no time for that," he said. "We have to get out of here!" Both of us flinched at a scream that tore through our feathers. It was that same raptor's call of death. Ghubari helped me to my feet and I looked back at the horrible scene. Crows dove from the sky, mobbing at the great beasts below with their hideous skin and jet black holes where there must have been eyes. The creatures jumped up, colossal legs propelling them to great heights, and they snapped and shrieked with beaks the color of death. And then one of them launched itself after a crow. It unfurled and flapped its sides—veiny, pink appendages stubbled with the beginnings of feathers— and jumped up the side of a Greek cafe. And for a moment, it flew. The crow shot back, cawing and screaming for help, but the birdlike creature snatched it in its hideous malformed beak, snapped its neck and swallowed it whole. Cries of horror sounded out. The mobbing crows raised up into the sky, collectively taken aback by the slaying and new discovery. These monsters were almost airborne.

Ghubari and I heard him coming before we could register who it was. We spun our heads in the opposite direction of the horrible battle and made out a fawn-colored mass of wrinkles and flappy skin pounding the tarmac. Drool strings, trash, and gravel flew, scattered by the spongy paws of a dog on a mission. My heart seized. Dennis, against everything I taught that shining turd monster, was running full steam toward carnivorous cannibal quasi-birds. I opened my beak to stop him but nothing came out, my throat a desert. I jumped forward to somehow intervene, but Ghubari blocked me with his gray-and-white form.

"No," he said, gently.

And then the light caught something, a glassy glimmer bouncing off it. In his drooly, scrotum-sanitizing mouth, was an iPad. I couldn't breathe and I couldn't stop him and I

couldn't move as I watched him come to a sharp halt, taking in
the battle across the four-way stop before him. He dropped the
iPad with a clatter and let out a series of deep Dennis booms,
the sounds of a hound who means business. The screeching
stopped. Horrible beaks snapped toward him, their black eye
holes facing my friend. Dennis barked again. He pawed at the
iPad, slapping his cumbersome paws against its screen.

No, Dennis. No. SIT. STAY.

He picked up the iPad and the light caught its screen again
with a sharp glint. The screams that came from the creatures
were in the language of a raptor. They were sounding out
prey calls. And Dennis was the prey. The crows commenced
their mobbing from above, risking being digested for the sake
of our bloodhound. But the Hideous Ones were fixated on
the screen Dennis had presented them. Locked in. And they
started to run.

Dennis dipped his floppy head down to pick up the iPad but
struggled. The edges were difficult for him to get his rubbery
jowls around, too flat against the road. He pawed and gummed
at the iPad, painting it with drool. I was certain I was already
dead as a dodo from the stress of watching this, from being
stuck and completely unable to help my Dennis. He began to
look desperate, the whites of his eyes and teeth flashing as he
bit at the iPad. And then he caught the edge of the tablet
on his lower jaw and lifted it in his mouth. He turned and
sprinted, faster than I'd ever seen or felt him run. Dennis was
the wind. A whippet. A shooting star. He barreled back down
the way he'd come, iPad in his jowls, a herd of unspeakable
horror pounding the earth to get at him.

"We have to do something!" I squawked. Ghubari nodded
his head vigorously. And then, a sound as wonderful as the
rustling of a Cheetos® bag or the Taco Bell gong, I heard high-
pitched notes that freckled the air and raised my beak to a

sight that almost made me sing. Migisi lowered to the ground, offering her back to me, her butter-yellow eyes revealing that look of stern consternation where she inadvertently seems extra judgy. I hopped onto her back and we lifted, us three, into the sky, soaring above with hundreds of birds. Blackwings, songbirds, geese, raptors, we all filled the sky, following from above, every eye on the bloodhound with the bait and the birdlike monsters that chased after him.

"Throw whatever you can at them!" I screamed. The Sky Sentinels obeyed, dipping and diving to retrieve whatever they could. They pelted things at the racing beasts below. Rocks, trash, books, scrap metal, license plates, acorns, buckets, anything they could snatch up quickly. But it did nothing to stop the runaway train that had locked onto Dennis. I couldn't breathe watching our bloodhound from above, his body no bigger than a hamster's as he tore right through the town center and headed up a steep road, dodging crashed cars and toppled trees and store signs. His ears streamed behind him like the most beautiful wings I'd ever seen and then a sharp pain in my chest stabbed repeatedly because I knew he couldn't keep up this pace for long. Dennis didn't have the endurance for it. He wasn't a greyhound or an Alaskan husky. He was a professional slob. And as soon as he couldn't keep this up, those nightmarish beings would gain on him, and I'd just seen them swallow a crow whole and I couldn't let that happen. I couldn't. I scanned the area and racked my brain, what would a crow do? What would a crow do?

Dennis tore up the enormous hill, the herd of horror on his heels. And then, just like that, he disappeared under the crowns of maples where I couldn't see him anymore. I cried out for him—a wounded yell—as the Hideous Ones thundered after him, tearing at our skulls with their screams. Migisi and my stomach dropped, and we plummeted, rapidly losing altitude, plunging below the tree crowns to follow the fray. We had burst into a small park, whipping past a young MoFo climbing frame, barbecue pits, and picnic tables. And just up ahead, the herd charged forward, shredding grass and mud that flew at our eyes and engulfed us. Migisi dropped like a rock onto a picnic table, her talons scratching wood. The impact threw me from her. I toppled onto the table's gum-lacquered bench, horrified to have stopped our race after Dennis.

"No, Migisi! Keep…" I leapt into the air, all wings and prayers, thrashing my feathers, willing them to take me up, up, up. I had to fly! Sharp pain and gravity dropped me back to the bench. Then I froze, watching. Up ahead, a shoreline. A sliver of sandy beach. And a bobbing fawn body that swam furiously, disappearing into the body of a lake. The herd tore after the paddling bloodhound, a spray of water fanning into the air as those terrifying gray legs launched into the lake. Dennis swam on, head jerking side to side, rudder of a tail propelling him. The Hideous Ones screamed as they pursued him, jerky thrusts pushing them farther into the lake after my best friend. I called out to Dennis in Big Jim's voice.

"Come on, Dennis! Let's go!" I wanted to tell him to give up and let go of that stupid tablet and be done with it, but the damn shiny plastic thing was still in his mouth and that slobbering rapscallion was going to sea-otter this shit until his last breath. And then one of the blanched creatures, with its thawed Thanksgiving-turkey skin and its black holes for eyes, disappeared under the water. And then another. Another let out a territorial scream that was drowned by bubbles.

They. Couldn't. Swim.

And still they couldn't break the fixation, wouldn't let the tablet go; and so they thrust themselves out toward the middle of the lake, the deepest part, thrashing their ostrich legs under the water. Birds landed around us, calling out their cries of jubilance and threats toward the strange beings that couldn't swim and couldn't give up their prey. They were driving themselves extinct.

One by one they disappeared into ripples and the birds around me shrieked and squawked and bounced up and down in place. We called for Dennis in a thousand bird voices, summoning our hero. And Dennis, my very best friend, kept on swimming. Finally, I sucked in a breath and called for him in Big Jim's voice.

"ZzzzZZZt! Come here, Dennis!" And just like that, he turned around and showed us that magnificent spongy black nose and he started his long swim back to shore. Back to everyone who loved him and back to safety. When he emerged from the water, doggy wet, covered in lake, his avian audience lost their minds, dancing and diving and singing. He aimed those drooping eyeballs at me and gave me a look that was both sheepish and triumphant. Dennis was not a gloater or an "I told you so" type of dog. He was just a hero, plain and simple. The flocks mobbed him lovingly and swooped down around him. Needle-beaked plovers danced around his feet in the sand. Salt-winged gulls and finches alike opened their throats and let their joy take flight. And Dennis shook off the lake water and our blues and dropped the tablet in front of him with a snort that sounded a hell of a lot like laughter.

CHAPTER 31

Celebration sparked around Dennis like the fireflies of summer's gloaming. *Aura, Web,* and *Echo* lit up with an electricity the world had been deprived of, and I knew word of Dennis's cunning maneuver would spread far and wide. As we plodded away from the lake—me on the slobbering hero's thick, soggy back—birds dropped petals and tiny flowers from the sky, showering him with their gratitude. We made our way back through the small lakeside park, seeing it through calmer eyes than before, and stopped once we reached a road called 164th, where across the street a Walgreens sat, quietly harkening back to dark times that seemed as if from another life. In the distance, in the direction of the towering Olympic mountain range that leaned against the horizon in the West, the road's sick swaying suggested MoFos clustered there. The kind that were looking for screens and were wearing themselves down like pencil erasers. The kind that we were used to. The college crows, joined by another murder that called themselves the Marymoor crows, fluttered down from the sky like black playing cards. I filled with dread as I saw a familiar set of wings. Buffed black and blue feathers dropped down in front of me.

"S.T.," said Kraai. There I was again with my mixed feelings, relief to see his magnificent self, the eyes that made me think of a midnight lake, but utter shame and revulsion at my ineptness. I had proven to be a coward, no better than a prurient squirrel.

"I've let you down—" I started.

"We are grateful to you."

"What? I panicked, froze, and then hid in a bucket of ice cream."

"Dennis knew what to do because of what you taught him. You and Dennis are a partnership. You are murder. And we consider you family."

I didn't know how to digest this; it felt so right and so wrong. I had tried so hard to be a part of this murder, to prove myself a crow, and was certain I had failed. And here I was being validated, being told that I had been enough all along.

The birds flying above continued to shower us with petals and small twigs and what I believe was a radish, which landed directly on my head. And then a bird the color of a faded newspaper fluttered down next to Kraai and me. Ghubari. I hopped down from Dennis's back, and "Mother Nature's Gift, a mythical stallion of the canine world" wandered away from me. A clowder of cats congregated nearby, ever watchful. The Ones Who Open Doors had caught up to us. The youngest one, a juvenile male, used his lengthy arms to shimmy up to a branch midway up the maple and pout at us sullenly. His mother and sister settled on the grass, trailing their beautiful fingers across its blades and watching as their patriarch slowly approached Dennis. I hopped forward, worried about the interaction. The male orangutan with his carpet of coarse ginger hair lifted an arm and placed it on Dennis's back. Dennis didn't flinch. He sat, drooling for the Olympics, seeming to enjoy the contact, and I wondered if he was thinking the same as me: that it was like a pet from Big Jim. I was jealous that he could feel the touch of a hand again. Jealous, but so very happy for him. The One Who Opens Doors ambled away from Dennis to join his family and the feline congregation. Raccoons, opossums, and dragonflies joined in the collective worship of Dennis, and he lumbered along as they cheered around him as if he were a wrinkled and odiferous Snow White.

Kraai spoke to Ghubari and me: "What were they? Those...things?" He sought the answer in cement outlines of the endangered buildings around us. We knew that they were not The One Who Conquers, a known smell, a known enemy. Ghubari and I exchanged a look, and I realized he hadn't told me everything. There was more to the MoFo story. He scratched a foot along the tarmac before he spoke.

"They don't have a name because they are new," Ghubari said, his voice somber and steely.

I resisted the urge to stay quiet, the comfort of clinging to old thoughts, as if saying something would make it real and keeping it to myself would mean it wasn't really happening. But I had made a promise to myself on Migisi's back as I watched my bloodhound friend blaze a courageous trail with my heart in my beak. No more hiding from the truth.

"They are MoFos," I said, voice low. "They are Hollows. They are evolving. It is a last-ditch effort at survival."

Ghubari nodded his head methodically. "We were wrong. I thought that we were watching their total obliteration. But they are not leaving this world without a fight. This has never been seen before. I had not thought it possible, Shit Turd, so I haven't told you everything. I heard something else."

In that moment, Ghubari performed the greatest magic trick I have ever seen. He opened his beak, and the voices and sound effects that poured from his throat were not of feathered or furred. They were the voices I had been pining for, and hearing them snapped me in half.

"What is happening? Please, please don't dismiss me, sir. Please. I'm here because of my wife. Please, sir, I'm asking for one thing from you—the truth," said Ghubari, only it wasn't Ghubari. It was Ghubari's flawless rendition of Rohan. I could suddenly see him, his oil-slicked hair in chaotic tufts, his intelligent MoFo eyes sleepless and shiny. I could feel his thorny desperation.

"I don't have time or answers, excuse me," came the curt voice of someone new. Ghubari was using his stupendous skills—his voltaic memory and his gift of mimicry—to summon the past. To bring the MoFos back to life. Ghubari mimicked the creak of a door. They were moving. Clinical clicks and beeps. This was in the hospital.

"Sir, I beg of you. I have no one else to turn to and I know you have some idea. Please. The truth," Rohan pleaded, his heart sliced open, voice cracking like an ancient branch.

"I—look, come in here—" The MoFo With The Answers paused. A door opened and shut, and I imagined him ushering Rohan's panic into a janitor's closet at a hospital as frenzied as a zoo, his brow speckled with sweat, the bags under his eyes crow-black and heavy with the weight of the world. "I can't make this easier for you, Rohan. Your wife, my daughter, we're all stuck in this nightmare together." An alarm sounded out in the hospital, muffled to the two MoFos in the janitor's closet.

Rohan pleaded, his voice choking on grief. "Henry, please. Surely, the CDC—"

"The picture is the same everywhere, Rohan. At every hospital and research center. I've called everywhere—" He paused again, swallowing a large stone. "We are on our own. We can't expect help."

"Then tell me what you know."

"We have no cure for the virus. We know nothing about it. Technological bioweapon, disease, what? It doesn't even seem to have a name. You've seen what it does, it ravishes the human form. The news reports weren't sensational. We are undergoing a mass extinction; the virus, an increasingly toxic environment, all of it is a perfect storm and, Rohan, we have no shelter. The changes you've seen in Neera and these new-borns is some sort of unprecedented phenotypic plasticity, an immediate genetic response and survival mechanism."

"I don't underst—"

"Our genes are changing faster than we imagined possible. Much in the way cancerous tumors can adapt or acclimate to chemotherapy, humans are rapidly evolving to survive the virus. That's what you are seeing in these accelerated physical deformities. My daughter—" He inhaled sharply, as if filling up with air could keep him from crumbling. Shrieks sounded outside the closet. A nurse yelled for help. "My daughter's skin has changed, her whole tiny body is—" His voice cracked. He sniffed. "What I'm realizing, Rohan, is that there are parallels to cancer. Cancer is a newly evolved parasitic species, the uncontrollable growth of abnormal cells in the body that metastasize, spreading to invade nearby tissues. In order to survive this insidious virus, to survive total obliteration, I think the human species is becoming that cancer."

Rohan exhaled. "There must be a hope, there must be a cure, we cannot..." He couldn't finish his sentence.

"There is always hope. Always," The MoFo With The Answers offered up snake oil, tiger bone, and rhino horn. And he almost sold it.

Ghubari squawked, bringing us back to the present, to a

world without those clever, clever voices, those beautiful minds. I fluttered my gular, flapped my pinions. Oh, the pleasure of hearing those bewitching MoFo tones, to be reminded of their sharp intellect, the sparks of electricity running through their words. I braced against the skewering pain of remembering that it was just a memory, a haunting, a recording. I understood why Ghubari had held this inside him. Who would believe it? It was all too much.

"*The One Who Hollows as well must return*," came a low whisper from Kraai. He had taken the news stoically, but I felt something change about him. He must have felt the sharp shock I did, how suddenly the world felt even more unstable; the ground seemed to rumble under our feet. In an instant our future looked different. The MoFo remnants that slimed our cities weren't going to die out quietly with a bloody gurgle. Instead they were growing feathers and wings, a mockery to our very beings and a cancer on our world. It meant that our whole lives would be a war. Kraai gathered himself quickly. "And so we start with our immediate enemies. We will strengthen our numbers and track down The One Who Conquers. We will take on this new enemy without compromise. I will align us with our Marymoor crows, our U District crows, the Queen Anne crows, all Bellevue, Redmond, and Kirkland crows, and we will call on the Tacoma murder, the Renton IKEA crows, all the San Juan Island crows, the Portland murder, and all the others. We will put out the call through *Aura* for every crow on this big beautiful blue to unite. We will fight for a future."

Dennis was now across the street, in front of a building wearing a banner that advertised Thai food, songbirds frolicking around him, playfully pulling on his ears and twittering their gratitude. He looked small under the enormous shredded banner that hung from the side of the building by mere threads. Stubbornly hanging on, I thought; everything is stubbornly hanging on. And then I looked at Dennis in all his silly splendor with a bunch of sycophantic critters hovering around him and I felt very full. Full of love and gratitude and suddenly ready to take on whatever had to be taken on so that we could have a better future.

Dennis's head froze and his ears perked up, a slight movement. His head pushed forward, The Golden Nose training on something. A shiver danced under his coat. The birds around him lifted and gave him space, sensing he was focused. Ghubari, with his oboe solo cadence, was speaking quietly to me about projections, battle plans—the thoughtful ramblings of a brainy bird—but I wasn't listening to them. They were background noise. I was watching Dennis, whose lips pursed and freed a small, chesty growl. He broke into a trot with his ears swinging metronomically and his big paws striding ahead.

To gain a better vantage point, I hopped onto a mound of rubble and then up on top of a crooked sign for a housing development with a fake Italian name—Trivalli, Toscanitti, or Umbilica, something. The clouds parted to allow a billowing skirt of spring sunshine through. The light illuminated the destruction that defiled the Lynnwood street, its cracked buildings and severed telephone wires. Dennis broke his trot into a run down 164th Street. He ran west toward the Olympic mountain range that had stood its ground under all this change. I focused on the mountains momentarily, wondering in a split second what was happening to the creatures who lived under those snowy caps—*was it better over there?*—and then shifted my focus closer to us, on a cluster of sick MoFos up ahead, a herd of sluggish shadows that dragged their bodies around the middle of 164th. Dennis passed two freeway entries—north and south—old graffiti and bullet holes decorating the once-emerald signs. Birds tailed him from the sky as he thundered toward the mass of MoFos. *He has seen something,* I thought. A rabbit? A garish yellow tennis ball? And then I brought into focus a van and its sliding door.

Time slowed down and I saw everything as if it had been condensed into one of Nargatha's shitty little snow globes, as if watching the jostling scene from behind a glass bubble. I took in the MoFo that had trapped itself in the sliding door, its torso and the wisps of greasy hair that clung to the mottled skin of its head, hanging and thrashing its one free arm. A swath of skin from the side of its face hung like the flap of a leather satchel. In slippery seconds, I realized just how many MoFos were all around that truck, how they were huddled together like the ant army I'd encountered, as if one entity. I frantically scanned for rabbit or tennis ball or Cheetos® bag as Dennis careened toward the MoFo crowd. When I found the source of his intrigue, the ground shook and I am sure somewhere far beyond the clouds, beyond where a little crow caught in a sudden nightmare could see, a star burst and shattered across the galaxy.

The truck was brown and yellow. The MoFo's shirt was brown and yellow.

It was a UPS truck.

I screamed, but no sound came out. He was already too far away, and I watched as the ground split apart beneath my feet and Dennis raced into the crowd of MoFos to get to the UPS truck, the sworn enemy of every domesticated dog.

And somewhere out there, somewhere very far away, a precious egg tumbled from the heart of its nest, plummeting down, down, down…

Dennis barreled through the MoFo crowd, baying and barking at the truck ahead of him. The MoFos stirred and groaned, something snarled. And then a strained whimper. Dennis's friends and allies, birds of all sorts, mobbed the MoFos from above, who were starting to come to life, starting to swipe their palsied limbs and make noxious noises. The birds told Dennis to run, but I heard him yelp—a sharp sound that stopped my world on its axis—and then the MoFos were crowding in on him, deviant limbs reaching for his beautiful brown body.

I heard Dennis snarl and yowl and I was running, hobbling, and tripping over myself as I scurried along 164th to get to him. And then I didn't hear Dennis anymore.

And somewhere out there in the depths of an Arctic landscape of blue ice, a heart beat its last.

Birds filled the air with shrieks of sorrow and the woeful call that meant an end had come. Ghubari and Kraai dove down, down from a sky that had surely ripped in half, in front of my shaking body, blocking me from moving any closer to my very best friend who I didn't know how to be without. They spread their wings like great feathered shields, forcing me backward. I cawed and keened and wailed, I thrashed and pecked and scratched, but there was no way past their protection.

Somewhere out there, a thousand-year-old redwood snapped in two.

And then there were just the horrible sounds of sick MoFos and their destruction as they took the being I loved most in this world away from me. Everything was broken. Everything was a violent blur until I bowed my head to the ground and brought into focus a gossamer cluster of beautiful blues. It was a lone peacock feather. It lay there at my feet, too beautiful and fragile for this world.

And somewhere in the boundless Universe, a star's light went out.

CHAPTER 32

S.T.

164TH STREET, LYNNWOOD, WASHINGTON, USA

I didn't leave Dennis when the college crows went to roost in safety. Migisi and several crows chose to stay with me in solidarity. Migisi lifted us—herself and me—onto the top of a telephone wire where we were relatively safe from the MoFos and the potential danger that lurked around every corner. She didn't leave my side, and I took comfort in the rhythmic rise and fall of her chest, which reminded me of the ocean. The next time *Aura* started its song and the sun started its great climb over the horizon, drenching me in powdery pastels, the rest of the crows returned. Once the sick MoFos were lured and cleared by a flock of Mohawk-ed Steller's jays, we stood around Dennis. Someone, someone with empathy and a heavy heart, had draped a blanket over him. Now a piebald of red and brown, the blanket had once been cream colored. Its velvety canvas held rows and rows of cartoon cream sheep and just two black ones that I could count who were facing the wrong way. I thought they represented me and my Dennis.

I thought Dennis would have loved this blanket. The college crows fluttered to the ground in solidarity with deep sadness pooling in their inky eyes. They had been good to me and had flown on a quest to acquire provisions I'd asked for. Kraai stood near me and I took comfort in his presence. The world was topsy-turvy. My heart was fractured. We stood in reverential silence and I felt the solemn heartbeats of a hundred crows.

I felt Kraai nodding behind me, and I picked up what my crow brethren had scoured from the skies to find. I rolled the endangered bottles of Pabst Blue Ribbon up to Dennis's blanket. Two crows helped me place a shoe near him, a classic two-tone leather zoot-suit shoe I thought he would have loved the taste of. I placed the partially eaten hot dog down near him in honor of Nathan's Hot Dog Eating Contest on Coney Island—I'd always wished Dennis could have been a contestant. He would have been a champion. Then I waddled back to where the bag of Cheetos® lay. I punctured a hole in the Cheetos® bag and laid out the wondrous electric-orange puffs and I made a *D* for him because I knew how to. D for Dennis. D for dog. D for delightful dingbat I'd chase around the Green Mountain sugar maple, where I'd pull his tail and he'd lope after me with a goofy smile, wrinkles lagging behind him.

I heard a stirring behind me and turned to see an influx of wings. Feathereds were silently alighting to the ground, goose and swan, thrush and sparrow, hawk and owl. Birds of day and birds of night. Some touched down on the curbside, others landed on the tops of dusty vehicles. Not one of them made a sound. Even the whispering whoosh of their wings was barely audible.

It felt as if I were in a strange dream. I stared at the white sheep and the two black sheep, feeling nothing and everything all at once. The college crows, one by one, hopped forward toward my Dennis. Each laid an offering around the blanket. There were twigs and blossoms, unopened candy bars and bottle caps, pens and cuff links and paper clips and lighters and jewelry and shoelaces. Treasures abounded. It was hard to look away from the smiling sheep and the next time I did, I saw that it wasn't just feathereds of every persuasion that had gathered. Skunks had arrived. There were raccoons and Pacific chorus frogs, leopard slugs, a family of goats, caterpillars, mice, rabbits, and butterflies. Although I couldn't see them, I felt the silvery presence of spiders. I saw an opossum whose grinning face I remembered well. A flock of glaucous-winged gulls circled above, calm and cool. As they looped, they released empty mollusk shells from their beaks. The shells dropped around us, raining down a tinkling tune that sounded like a choir of tiny bells. Their leader—my friend—gave me a nod from the sky. There was a family of moles who looked friendly and familiar. And behind them, lying down with their paws crossed or standing with deft attention, was a beautiful melting pot of dogs. Poodles and puggles, mastiffs and mongrels, terriers and scent hounds, juvenile and senior. The breeds that had the MoFo-tailored instincts for a fighting chance in a new earth—vizslas, pointers, rottweilers—and those who had made it despite the odds stacked against them—Chihuahuas and papillons, French bulldogs and golden retrievers. And standing among them was someone I knew—a small white American pit bull terrier with beige patches and a pink nose and collar, whose belly was swollen with puppies. Vibrant snapshots of our adventures fluttered all around us. There were two German shorthaired pointers that I remembered watching run from a glass fortress to their freedom, fit and healthy now. There was a tiny white poodle with a sparkling collar and a whole lot of self-importance. And there was a mother husky with meat on her ribs and a litter of boisterous pups who had crust-free eyes and the chance to grow their bones. They were all here for my Dennis.

Ears stood to attention or hung like dish towels, drool drips silently puddled on the ground, panting clouded the air with moisture. Tails, long and sweeping or docked and stubby, were still. And the wriggling, balloon-bellied puppies tugged on ears, chased one another's tails with the occasional yip, or slept with tummies rising and falling, quietly dreaming of enormous adventures that lay ahead.

The One Who Opens Doors moved through the crowd like a king, pressing the cement with his magnificent knuckles, his hairy orange Herculean arms trailing like moss-matted vines. He looked at me, his face a great gray moon with eyes that held the world's secrets. In the seconds that we shared a glance, we felt like one being, no borders or edges dividing us. My breath hitched as I spotted an army of domestic cats of all sizes and pigments flanking the great ape. At the helm, the feline leader striding closest to The One Who Opens Doors was a ferocious-looking tabby. Squinting, I made out "Genghis Cat" on his collar. Genghis Cat sat down on the curb to oversee everything in the way only a cat can, commanding a wide berth and quiet respect. The thing about cats is that they're always where they want to be. Genghis Cat was here for Dennis. And everyone on earth knows that if you have the respect of a cat, it means your soul is one worth being around.

The female orangutan, a ravishing red beauty with cognac eyes, ushered her offspring forward with their wispy ginger fur and bright, innocent expressions. They were all limbs, gangly and buoyant in their youth. The morning light caught their fur and surrounded them in golden halos. Dogs and opossums, skunks, beavers, and river otters scuttled aside for The One Who Opens Doors. The great apes, with brown, yellow, blue, and green eyes upon them, ambled up to the sheep blanket. The male groaned as he sat his bulky body down, sweeping some of the offerings aside to make room. His family sat around him, the young orangutans fixated on the sheep blanket and the resting bump below it. Like an ancient wizard, The One Who Opens Doors placed his perfect palm onto Dennis's broken body and smoothed it gently. And we all sat— an unprecedented unity of fur and feather—breathing in and out like ocean waves, as Dennis was pet for the last time.

The One Who Opens Doors lifted himself with considerable effort to the whimsical jingle of a couple of bottle caps that freed themselves from his dense, knotty coat and moved away from Dennis with family and felines in tow. And then, every bird in its own time bowed its head long and low toward Dennis. I watched, mesmerized, turning slowly to see a gratitude that rose up out of hearts' darkness.

And here, I silently said goodbye to Dennis. And to my brave little friend Cinnamon. And finally to Big Jim.

I thought about Big Jim and how much I still missed him. I thought about the thing he did. He had met Tiffany S. on Tinder, where she described herself as a "Jolly Rauncher" and he a "Strict Vagetarian"; though I squawked my disapproval at his choice, it was marginally less self-defeating than his original "Sausage Titties." Tiffany S. from Tinder had never taken a liking to either Dennis or me. Dennis once mauled her purse, and she threw a beer mug at the wall, screaming that the purse was something expensive. I made her nervous, she said, because it was unnatural to share a space with a wild animal (also, I cached some of her hair extensions). Big Jim and Tiffany S. got into a screaming match and Tiffany S. said that Big Jim had to make a choice: her or Dennis and "that horrid black bird." Big Jim's face was red, his eyes were watery, and he begged her not to ask him to choose. But she insisted: a relationship ultimatum. And then he told Tiffany S. that he would never get rid of Dennis and me, that we were family. Big Jim was not a crow, but he knew about the loyalty of murder, which makes him as much crow as any I'd met. "Crows before hoes," said Big Jim, pretending he wasn't drowning as I sat on his shoulder and collected his tears.

Soon after Tiffany S. left, The Black Tide rushed in and he fell into a deep depression. Not long after, Tiffany S. was attacked by a man on the street and put in the hospital. Big Jim couldn't forgive himself for not being there to protect her. And that's when I think we really lost him. He energized himself with malt liquor and talked with his fists. His shooting-range friends banded together, planning to shoot their way out of the spreading sickness. They came to pick him up to start a revolution but decided he was too weak, too heartsick for a woman who was the wrong color. They ridiculed and abandoned him. No one in his life would accept his love for us. That's what killed Big Jim, ultimately. Before the virus got him, his life-sustaining organ was broken, because if you aren't allowed to love freely, a part of your heart breaks. Perhaps my Big Jim was just too tender for this new world.

This part of our story is sad but I always try to see the silver lining. One of the reasons that it is not such a tragedy that Big Jim is gone is because he would have died of a heart attack at seeing all the new weeds in the neighborhood any-way. The English ivy and Himalayan blackberry takeover alone would have killed him off. Also, there was no more lactose intolerance for him to suffer through. And also, I befriended penguins. He wouldn't have stood for that shit.

A murmuration of starlings took flight, creating an intricate kaleidoscope of shapes above our Dennis. And then, when I thought there were no miracles left to keep me on my feet, the dog packs shifted. They were moving out of the way to allow an animal through. Appearing from under one of the freeway signs was the baby elephant I'd seen on our travels. The dog packs watched as the young pachyderm lumbered purposefully toward Dennis with its head low, its trunk swinging to and fro. Crows hopped toward Dennis, forming a black shield until I nodded my head, assuring them it was safe to let the elephant through. The baby elephant stopped by the sheep blanket and hung his head low. His eyes took in the scene around, the quiet respect that was being absorbed by the earth through the trunks of nearby trees. Vibrations in the ground caused several dogs to whimper; some birds squawked. And emerging under the ravaged sign for I-5 North was the rest of the baby's family—the entire elephant herd.

The giants moved as one like a great gray cloud, shifting their weight from flat foot to flat foot that kissed the ground methodically. Elephants command attention. But their size is not what makes the heart skip a beat. It's how they walk with the world's weight on their shoulders, sensitive, noble, their hearts pulsing and as wide open as the great gray leaves that are their ears. MoFos used to say that an elephant never forgets and until this very moment, I hadn't understood what that really meant. An elephant's memories don't reside in organ or skin or bone. They live closer to tree time than we do, and their memories reside in the soul of their species, which dwarfs them in size, is untouchable, and lives on forever to honor every story. They carry stories from generations back, as far as when their ancestors wore fur coats. That is why, when you are close to an elephant, you feel so deeply. If they so choose, they have the ability to hold your sadness, so you may safely sit in the lonely seat of loss, still hopeful and full of love. Their great secret is that they know everything is a tide—not a black tide but the natural breath of life—in and out, in and out, and to be with them is to know this too. And here they were, suddenly lifting the weight of our sadness for us, carrying it in the curl of their trunks. We all sat together in our loss, not dwelling, but remembering. For an elephant never forgets.

The presence of the elephants jogged old words to the front of my mind, the words of an octopus named Onida. "Everyone has a journey, Crow. More than just the one." I felt a great deal of comfort in remembering her wisdom.

Addiction to an electronic world caused the downfall of the MoFos. They'd forgotten to connect with each other, to connect with the creatures who missed them and to Nature as She called for them to come home. The crow part of me knew not to dwell on what was, but the MoFo part of me would always carry my best friend in my heart. Because we never give up on anything, especially love, and that's the very, very best thing about being a MoFo.

The elephants smelled like churned soil and freedom as they passed me, blocking out the sky and the possibility of darkness. They slowed to a stop as they reached their baby elephant and the tiny lump under the sheep blanket. And there, they took their time, shuffling back and forth, swinging their pendulous trunks with lowered heads to the whispers of the wind. They formed a circle around our Dennis, facing outward. And the sun shone because that is her impassioned duty, to keep us from being swallowed by the dark. And I swear I felt the warmth lifting off nearby stones and an ancient song of sorrow that the evergreens shook from their leaves. The elephants swayed to this music, protecting him, honoring him. And we grieved like this in harmony, calling on the ocean with our breath.

CHAPTER 33

THE ARCTIC CIRCLE, GREENLAND
(MEDITATIONS OF A POLAR BEAR)

My bones. Like whale ribs in times of plenty, they press against my fur, dank and brittle. I have swum for days with a broken heart, hunting for a reason to swim and draw frosty air. I am the very Last Of The Ice Bears.

Tornassuk. Tornassuk.

The last of my hope rides on the wind. It is a metallic smell of blood and brine, the promise of a walrus ahead a few miles that spills red onto sparkling white powder. I follow with laden paws and vanishing body.

The walrus is fresh, tusks now stationary swords. Blood pools on the ice and then in my frozen veins as I see my once-little cub who was swallowed by the sea. It is you! You have grown, Tornassuk. You, and the others. We, Seal's Dread, The Hunters Of The Floe, The Ice Bears, have returned as the sea's fish have. You have made the ice your kingdom.

The sky bursts with opalescent strokes of color that dance across icicle shadows.

We eat.

And The Ice Bears live on.

CHAPTER 34

We were still gathered and grieving when our new kingdom threw its head back and roared once more. On the horizon, a pastel scarf whipped satin loops in the air, performing acrobatics. As it neared, the scarf revealed itself to be feathereds. Cedar waxwings, with their silky gradient of dusky sunset colors and rakish black masks, came to us, panicked and breathless.

"It's happening," they said, hearts trilling, "The One Who Conquers is in our territory."

I turned to Kraai and saw a fire light in him, a smolder that lifted his flight feathers.

"It is time," he called. "Send word to all the crows, rally our allies. We must fight for what's ours!"

The crows mobilized with a cacophony of caws, and other birds followed suit. The air was filled with frantic wings, black, green, white, brown, blue, and yellow. Migisi dropped down next to me, chittering with anticipation. Woodpeckers drilled into the wooden telephone poles, sending a sort of emergency

Morse code through *Aura*. News would travel on the wings of an Arctic tern, and circulate with the keen and cackle of *Echo*'s sea birds. Dogs barked and spun in circles. I hopped onto Migisi's back in a daze and suddenly the dogs were getting smaller and the wind was ruffling my feathers and the elephants looked like Stonehenge from above, standing guard of our Dennis. Leaving him this time felt no different than any other time, my heart lodged itself somewhere in my brain and my insides felt like chile con queso. Out of everything I'd been through, leaving Dennis was still by far the hardest thing I'd ever done, but I had no choice. Because I lived for the two of us now; I lived for Dennis and I lived for me, and apparently we both had an insatiable thirst for danger. And we had to save the one place where our crows and our domestics had a shot. This was the one thing we could control. When you have the power to stand up to oppression, you must. Time with the elephants had strengthened me and I'd remembered myself. The crow in me had loyalty and passion. The MoFo in me, hope. I was about to unleash a motherfucking hurricane.

Migisi flew high over 164th Street, high above the small park and the lake where Dennis had been a hero and the hideous creatures had drowned. Flanked by thousands of wings, we headed south, mind maps guiding us with precision by UV light and strumming vibrations that turned our hearts into tiny ukuleles, toward where the waxwings had seen The One Who Conquers infiltrate our territory. They had snuck up on us, invading while we were distracted by our grief and honoring our friend.

We flew over the dying concrete jungle below, over carnage and decay, bursting beauty and the optimism of seedlings alike. A sign for Bothell Landing identified a park with its rusting climbing frame, weeds slowly digesting picnic tables, and the Sammamish River, gorged and swollen, snaking through

hurriedly to other adventures. It didn't take me long to locate
The One Who Conquers, only to discover that once again, the
feathereds had let me down with their lack of a grip on plural
nouns. The One Who Conquers was a "they." More than one
predator had taken down the gorilla at King Street Station.
More than one had been terrorizing and conquering Seattle.
In keeping with the calling of their blood, they had formed a
pack. And now, below us, the pack was holding ground against
the birds that mobbed them from the sky, local crows, gulls,
geese, with some brave and foolhardy charging from the ducks
and cormorants calling for backup from the river.

　　Their power was immediately obvious. One wolf is a threat,
a fearless assassin, but this pack was enormous, too many for
me to count, and at the front of the legion of silver-tipped fur
and seasoned fangs were four snow-white wolves. I knew them
instantly, their rangy bodies and striking cool glow, white as
snow-buried bones. The sister wolves from the Woodland Park
Zoo. Big Jim and I had watched them from behind the safety
of their enclosure as they wandered its periphery in a territorial trot. And here they were, freed and fused to a prodigious
new pack that rallied behind them. I flashed back to the dead
wolves I saw in Mill Creek's town center, a smaller, weaker pack
that couldn't survive the new realm. Wild wolves who didn't
have the leadership and savvy of the white wolves familiar with
the ways of MoFos. This pack was different. Larger, stronger,
it had grown its numbers to survive. They had made lairs and
eaten gorillas and become formidable. The wolves held their
ground, backs of their stiff bodies arched, heads lowered in
toothy snarls. Tails were tucked, hackles stood up like newly
mowed grass. Birds dove at them, screeching a fight song,
and I watched in horror as several were swiped from the sky
and from this earth. Feathered mounds dotted the grass like
molehills.

Kraai shot past Migisi and me, shouting directions to the black mass that was ready to die by his command. The crows cawed and began their mobbing, pulling at tails and facing lines of glistening teeth. And then Ghubari was beside me, flapping in place, with Pressa by his side, the burns of her underwing exposed.

"There is another threat!" Ghubari wheezed, out of breath.

Pressa took over for him. "Others are taking our territory not far from here! Kraai has sent more crows and summoned for help through *Aura*, but he can't be in both places at once!"

"Show me!" I demanded, and we took off as if shot from Sigourney Weaver, Big Jim's Marlin Model 336 lever-action rifle. We were skimming over trees and my mind was whirling and then we were above a golf course and a cluster of western white pines. Migisi, Ghubari, and Pressa touched down onto a high branch and we stared down at our next problem.

Below us was another creature I had never encountered, and I was willing to bet that I wasn't alone in this regard. Dotted on the ground were strange black-and-white lumps that I'd seen before, each about the size of a packet of Doritos that gave off an acidic smell. And then I knew that these lumps were fecal matter. They were droppings, and what had made them was what had sent the formidable ant army running for their lives, daring even to take to water as a chance at survival. It dawned on me that the cocooned body Dennis and I had found in the tree trunk had been prey, woven tight and decomposing in silk. These were The Weavers. I stared openmouthed at the second hybrid monster I'd seen, something that was both MoFo and not, with its strange horizontal body, dark mottled skin. It had a head where a head shouldn't be on a MoFo body, surging directly from the center of its horizontal torso and it looked up with fuliginous holes where there should have been eyes. Homo sapien, but not. And where there should have been a mouth, there was a mandible with a sensory pedipalp, jaws that leaked silvery strings of fluid. Its sides sprouted arms, but they weren't arms, they were legs, and everything about them, from their sharp angles to their coating of spiky hair, suggested that they were arachnid. The gift of animal instinct is this—knowing a danger before it has shown you its teeth. My animal instinct told me I was looking at an unspeakable danger to our world.

"Look what they've done!" hissed Pressa, pointing her beak at the trees below.

The Weavers, chronic and cancerous in their destruction, had burrowed into the trees, leaving great holes, scratched sap-streaming scars across their beautiful trunks. The decaying bodies of birds, raccoons, and squirrels were suspended in the trees, silk wrapped and strangled. Cocooned corpses. I thought of Rohan's desperate conversation at the hospital. *Cancer is a newly evolved parasitic species. Humans are becoming that cancer.* The question begged, was the earth healthy enough to fight off this parasite? I held back nausea as we watched them, these five lion-sized monsters with no names, shift mechanically around the base of tree trunks, and then I lost the air from my lungs as I watched one of them rise up, lifting its horrible bristled limbs to the pine's bark and hoisting its enormous body. They could climb.

"We've been watching them move," said Pressa, her normally cool voice stricken with dismay. "They are heading in the direction of the campus. They're coming for us."

The domestic safe zone. Beaks and talons and the hollow bones of birds were no match for this type of predator. My first instincts were (in this order) to scream, run around in circles, shit myself, and perform a stiff-legged faint like those myotonic goats, but this wasn't a time to panic. It was a time for me to use my melon, every trick in my crow-MoFo mind.

"Migisi! Rise!" I yelled, and she did, Ghubari and Pressa joining us in the air, lifting from the pines. I addressed *Aura*, calling out to nature's network for help. I asked for specific information—a location. Now, I was the one who was hunting.

"Look!" cried Pressa, her feathers ruffling.

A butterfly whose wings were the most brilliant iridescent blue fluttered toward me. A species native to tropical rainforests, she was at once delicate and a joyful icon of survival, a symbol of the impossible. How could she have survived this climate? This world? She was so very far from home. She bolstered me. Her glowing cerulean wings held my attention as she showed me a mind map by using her wand-like antennae to paint a picture in ultraviolet light. She watched me leave and I felt that I was protected by her gaze. I knew then that I was being watched, cheered even, from worlds I couldn't see.

My love for Dennis fortified me as I followed the directions from the blue morpho butterfly. Ghubari and Pressa flew at top speed behind me, and I felt them on my tail feathers. We didn't have to go far. The ones I was hunting for were patrolling the large backyard of a mansion, their shoulder blades rising and falling as they skulked through the long grass. One of them was lying on a MoFo's deck, resting but always, always vigilant. His limpid eyes scanned for movement in the grass and the long-abandoned chicken coop. Another was busy marking his territory by squirting urine all over the place. Cats, I'm telling you. From above, their stripes looked like eels swimming in a blazing fire.

I was almost hyperventilating. My head darted from side to side as I instructed Migisi to swoop around the surrounding area, being careful to steer clear of the Brothers Burning Bright. A neighboring house, another McMansion with a front lawn covered in trash, seemed like it might have what I was looking for. Migisi touched down onto the grass and I got to work, sifting through the piles, tossing up tissues, wine bottles, yogurt cartons, condom packages, and old editions of the *Times*—New York and Seattle. Ghubari and Pressa perched on debris in the shadow of the enormous house. Pressa seemed unsure, sitting on the top of an empty Amazon box. Ghubari hopped toward me, as I spat various items from my beak and made disgruntled noises. Pressa hopped down from the Amazon box, eyed the clutter, then picked up something with her beak and plopped it in front of me.

"How about this turtle egg?" she asked.

"That's a golf ball," I said.

"Hmm. This dried up weasel turd?" she asked, gesturing with her foot.

"That's a cigar."

"How about this shiny chestnut?"

"That's a Ken doll hairpiece."

"Oh. Colorful worm?"

"A shoelace."

"These corn kernels?"

"False teeth."

"Well then, what about this? This looks like a *very* useful thing!" She was just so chipper and trying so very hard to be helpful. I didn't have the heart to tell her how off the mark she was, offering up a locket with its tiny amateur oil painting that was supposed to be Nicolas Cage but looked more like a Yukon Gold potato. I kept up my search, beginning to fear we'd never find what I needed. But when a young MoFo's foreclosed Barbie Malibu Dreamhouse came into view, my hope surged. I hopped over to a pile of scraps leftover from MoFo children—Legos, Star Wars figurines, coloring books— and finally selected an item I felt would work, even if it was a little disturbing. Then I got to work on searching for the second part I needed.

"Tell us what else you're looking for so we can help!" said Pressa.

I felt dubious. The enthusiasm was there, she just didn't know what MoFo things were. How could she?

"We need...a snake. A long, dead, brown snake," I said.

Pressa hopped determinedly behind an uprooted toilet and emerged victorious, dragging along a tatty old rope as long as our yard in her beak. It was perfect.

"Dead snake," she scoffed. "What do you take me for, a turkey?"

Ghubari let out Rohan's melodic laugh.

I thanked her and got to work plunging my beak into the side of the plush toy I'd found, ripping a hole in its side and spitting out fluff onto the lawn. Ghubari helped me to push the rope through the hole, and I punctured another hole in the other side of the toy's head, slipping the rope all the way through it. I gave Ghubari an inquiring look. He appeared satisfied with my toolmaking. Pressa seemed disturbed by my lobotomizing an Angry Bird. I did see the irony that the only plush toy happened to be a feathered. Next was convincing the largest and most powerful of us to help us carry out our plan.

"Migisi?"

The beautiful bald eagle was sitting on a small wooden chest she had broken open and was carefully studying the images of herself she recognized on seven denominations of U.S. currency. Seemingly flattered, she ruffled her feathers, then took lunging strides toward me—which continued to be, quite frankly, intimidating as fuck.

"I want to ask you for a favor," I told her. She listened to me carefully and then let out a sharp shriek. Pressa looked panicked and confused.

"S.T.! You cannot ask her to do that!" cried Pressa.

"Why not?" I said.

"Because she might die! Because you might die!"

"Trust me, this will work! I'm using MoFo knowledge here!"

"You trust *me*! S.T., things that are Hollow or MoFo or whatever are dangerous to the feathereds. I won't let us die for this!" Pressa spread her wings to fully showcase the burns underneath. I felt so sorry that she had been injured. That somehow MoFos had caused it. That we had such different experiences.

Ghubari intervened. "Well, there's certainly no use in us just standing around debating like a married couple trying to pick a restaurant. What say we settle it like our, as you call them, MoFos used to?"

"Fist fight!" I screeched.

"—By respecting the depth of each other's feelings but ultimately deferring to the only one whose decision really matters—"

"Mine!" Pressa and I chorused. Ghubari gave us a patronizing look. He's good at those.

"Fine," I said. "Migisi gets the final say! Do we all agree on that?"

Pressa and Ghubari nodded. The three of us turned to our eagle friend. Migisi had returned to the carpet of American dollar bills to study her ravishing likeness again, bored with all the arguing and the endless gibberish that flew from beaks. She had never been a bird for a lot of noise and language, but rather, she was an adventure eagle.

"Migisi?" asked Pressa, her voice choked with worry. "What is your final decision?" Migisi threw back her bright white head and let out a scream that needed no translation...

"WHAT THE FUCK ARE WE WAITING FOR?!"

And that settled the matter.

"Pressa, I know you're worried. That's a thing we no longer have time for; our friends are in danger and it's do-or-die. Or do-and-die, but at least one involves no regrets." I chuckled.

This didn't seem to alleviate her worry. I remembered that in the animal kingdom, trust is not given away. It is earned. I looked deep into Pressa's shining eyes, echoing words she'd said to me the first time she dabbed my wonky wing in special herbs. "Trust me?"

She nodded.

I hopped onto Migisi and she held the rope ends in her formidable talons. Ghubari positioned the Angry Bird plush toy so that it would hang low to the ground as we lifted the rope ends it was attached to. Migisi rose into the air and dragged the Angry Bird below her. The bait.

There wasn't any time for practice. We each gave each other a look. Ghubari—resigned commitment. Pressa—panic and fear. Me—here we fucking go. We took off, and I felt the change in Migisi's flight as she dragged the long rope, an Angry Bird bumping along the ground and another one riding a bald eagle, out to rescue his murder.

We flew over the fence of the mansion to where the big cats lurked. I felt fear that fizzed and bubbled inside me, tempered by a determination so strong I was dizzy with anticipation. The Angry Bird scraped against the top of the tall wooden fence, then dropped onto the grass and bounced through the weeds. It happened fast: the tigers acted on genetic instinct, something I was counting on. All three shot from their positions and lunged toward the bouncing bird.

"GO, MIGISI!" I cawed. And Migisi shot through the air, trailing the rope in her talons. Ghubari and Pressa shrieked and hollered as they flew with us. I kept my eye on the tigers as they scaled the wooden fence, their agile feline bodies trained on a stuffed bird with slug eyebrows. We tore across backyards, using any obstacle we could—a paddling pool, climbing frame, barbecue pits, and fire tables—to our advantage. Migisi lifted up higher to pull the bird above these objects, while the tigers had to navigate around or over them. But they were fast. Frighteningly fast. So fast that I felt quick rising nausea for fear that they'd gain on the bird and we'd lose our shot. Migisi yanked the bait over the last of the neighborhood fences and—terrifying an innocent herd of cattle who were congregated curbside and took off like their asses were on fire—trailed the rope down the length of a road. And this is where the tigers picked up speed and really showed their stripes. There were no obstacles to jump over, just a few vehicles to dodge. The smallest brother gained traction, and powerful back legs lunged him into an enormous leap, his body lengthening like a striking snake. He drove his claws into the body of the Angry Bird, and Migisi and I were yanked downward. She let go of the rope, and the tiger rolled with the impact of the attack, falling back to the ground with the Angry Bird. The three tigers circled the toy, shaking the earth with their growls, fighting over who got the kill.

"Fiddleshits!" I yelled. We were so close. "Migisi, the Angry Bird *has* to fly again! We have to get that rope back!" Migisi circled above the tigers and the filthy plush toy, both of us looking for an opportunity to swoop down and snatch that line. But the cats had the reflexes of, well, cats, and all it would take is a swipe from one of those massive claws and Migisi and I would be dead as door handles. Migisi chirped.

"Not yet, look; that one is watching us," I told her. And he was, with a ravenous look I'd given many a Cheeto®.

And just like that, in the manner of cats the earth over, they got bored. One of the brothers prodded at the Angry Bird half-heartedly. Another yawned and squished himself into a motorcycle sidecar that was too small for him. The third, the smallest and fastest, kept his eyes in the sky, at the bird on the bird that had been puppeteering the stuffed bird. It was becoming a tiramisu of complication.

"Get up, you prison-striped meat loaves!" I screeched. The tiger looking at me as though I should be slathered in basil aioli threw his head back to roar at us. The other two were no longer focused on the Angry Bird.

We had lost them.

"What do we do, Migisi?" I asked. "It's like herding cats!"

I heard a desperate yell. Pressa. "Come back! We'll figure something else out!"

A hollow feeling burned inside. Failure. The tiger spilling out of the sidecar stood up, slinking over to his brother, and the pair turned toward a tree line. The brother with the anger management issues took his eyes off me, turning to join them. They were leaving. It was all over.

And then Migisi's back muscles tightened. Suddenly, my stomach and eyeballs felt like they were suspended in the air above me. We were falling from the sky. Migisi dove, launching us toward the trio of tigers and yanking at a striped tail with her beak.

She was not a deliberator. She was an adventure eagle.

I called out, taunting them.

"ZzzzZZZt! Here, boy!"

The brothers turned and snarled, showing me the sheen on their fangs and a ferocity that chilled the air.

"NO! Don't! Come back! They'll kill you!" I heard Pressa squawk. Even Ghubari started screaming for us to stop. But Migisi screeched and dove again, stirring up our scent for the carnivores and narrowly missing a paw swipe. She swept past two of the brothers and their raw meat breath, snatching at the ear of the third with her talons. That was the straw that broke the camel's back.

The brothers chased us down the length of the road. It was on! Migisi flew fast, swift, and low, keeping us as bait to engage them in the hunt. And then we were approaching a cluster of familiar western white pines and a horrible acrid smell filled our noses. The outstretched fingers of pine limbs loomed before us. Migisi dove to avoid them. My skull rattled, filled with a thunderous roar. A tiger had caught up. Migisi tilted hard to avoid the tiger who thrust himself into the air as she'd lowered. I felt his claw swipe and barely miss us, a cold gust on my feathers. I was thrown from Migisi, smacking down onto overgrown grass. I jumped to my feet, orienting myself. Migisi hovered close by, above the tigers, all three of them now stalking her, inching forward, teeth and wrinkled noses and rumbling fury. Her great wings beat the air like twin cloaks. Her legs thrust forward, deadly black talons clenched and extended like two grappling hooks. Glassy eagle screams rose to the pine crowns. She couldn't see the western white pine right behind her.

"Migisi! Behind you!" I yelled.

She didn't see the gigantic, intricate web—a silver tapestry knit among pine limbs—or the encased body suspended in its sticky grip. Her left wing swept backward, colliding with the gluey mass. And it stuck.

"Migisi! NO!" I shrieked. She screamed back, thrashing to free her left wing. The wing was pinned, delicate dark feathers fused to slime. Now she was within lunging distance of the big cats. The smaller tiger, the one with hunt in him, crouched. He would be the one to take her down. His brothers had accepted this. He readied to pounce.

"Wait!" I screamed. "Look! Come for me! Look at my shitty wing!" I sprung forward as fast as I could, dangling my droopy wing as bait, hoping I'd get there in time, hoping I didn't have to watch them tear apart an adventure eagle.

My head darted, eyes searching the ground around me— *tools, MoFos use tools.* Rocks; there were rocks around. I snatched a sharp-edged stone in my beak, but it was no use. I was still too far away. The tiger was about to vault.

A deafening sound sliced through our skin. It sounded like a train scraping on tracks. We flinched. The tigers spun away from Migisi, ears flattened. We had company.

Strange creatures, neither MoFo nor arachnid, focused their hideous heads—those black eye holes—on the three big cats that paced in panic. Then the tigers stilled themselves. They lowered their bodies and I saw a ridge of fur rise on their backs. One let out a huffing sound, a low, shuddering warning. In response, one of The Weavers let loose a metallic scream. I hurtled to the western white pine and the horrible web that imprisoned Migisi. She thrashed violently, in danger of snagging her other wing.

"Stay calm! Don't thrash! Use your beak now. Quick, you have to bite at it, Migisi!" I yelled from the ground below her. She stopped flapping, hanging by her captured wing, raking at the tangled white mass with her knifelike beak. With a sharp rip, she slumped onto the grass next to me. A small snowing of feathers fell around her. Migisi righted herself, mouth open in a panicked pant, and stretched out her wings. The newly freed wing was fused with sticky web and wouldn't extend. Our eagle was flightless. She hopped helplessly. Her beak pecked desperately at the glue on her feathers. I looked over at the tigers creeping toward The Weavers, then snatched a stick from the ground.

"Don't move! Whatever you do, don't touch the web strands!" I told her. I lifted the stick in my beak to her wing, rolling it over the silver strings. They adhered to my stick in shiny sugar-spun wisps like the cotton candy cones at the Evergreen State Fair. I rolled the strand, teasing the last of the web from her dark plumage.

Migisi's wings spread like some great mythical creature, power in every pinion. She burst from the grass, snatching me up in those great black grappling hooks, lifting us up into the tree crowns. She perched on a thick branch with trembling legs and worked hard on her breathing.

And then came a fight. The tigers formed their formidable triangle as The Weavers launched toward them. They moved as spiders but with heads craned forward like sick MoFos, mandibles leaking fluid as they screamed their wrath. The tigers used their power, claw and tooth, to rip off limbs. The Weavers bit and swiped their angled legs and used their size to hold ground against the cats. The largest tiger brother took on two of The Weavers, standing on his hind legs as he delivered powerful blows, roaring to bring the sky down upon them. The Weavers outnumbered them—five I counted; their movements were mechanical and fast and they drove their mandibles into orange fur causing the cats to burst into frenzied attack. Three Weavers scuttled like great ticks toward the second tiger. One screeched, snatched the striped tail between its fangs and palps, bit down hard. The tiger bellowed, whirled, sank its teeth into the face of the hideous creature—right near those black, black holes—and the two other Weavers, waiting for their chance, leapt onto the great cat, knocking him to his side. They sunk their fangs into him mechanically as he thrashed and fought beneath them. One opened its mouth and let out a sound, a dental drill's wail. Then they lifted their dark abdomens where there were openings and out from those openings poured slimy silk. They moved quickly, wrapping their binds around the cat who fought and fought.

"No," I said, under my breath. "No, no, no..."

The three Weavers worked in unison, mimicking nature's mechanical engineers, wicked and strong with the prodigious powers of a spider.

But the tigers had something else. Two of the striped cats each pounced on a Weaver who spun a tiger in silks. With one vicious swipe, the largest cat tore a Weaver's face off, clean as sliced sushi. Migisi cried out, cheering on the carnage. The second largest tiger brother lunged, sending his claws to his brother's aid, driving the horrible creatures—one now faceless and twitching—away from his web-wrapped bulk. The bound tiger wriggled and roared, slicing himself free of slimy binds. He leapt to his paws, shaking off slime. His eyes filled with fire—cats fucking *hate* to be wet. His body tensed, readying to join his rescuers in their attack. The tigers had evolutionary advantage. And this is what I'd been banking on. They were masters, commanders of nature's killing instincts. The Weavers were new, underdeveloped, and were about to get ripped to shreds by their seasoned opponents.

We watched them getting dismantled, with their foul-smelling saliva and their sickly gray skin. I had learned about tigers from a National Geographic documentary that had triggered this whole bait idea, from a channel dedicated to MoFos' reverence of the natural world. Two million years of predatory instinct could not be denied and as a Weaver's head was swiped clean off its twisted body, I allowed myself an iota of relief. The power of instinct had killed my Dennis and now I was harnessing it to save our skins. Below, the mood changed. Where there was war, there was now a little playfulness, and as the largest tiger continued his work dispatching the faceless Weaver, his younger brother picked up a sickly, pallid limb, dragging it to the base of a pine trunk. He would dismantle it in his own time with the cool confidence of a cat.

Our work was done here. Migisi had rested enough to take to the sky once more, this time back to Dennis. Ghubari and Pressa close by, we swooped down, my heart chiming at the sight of the elephant herd, still in close proximity to Dennis, though no longer by his side. Now, they pulled the leaves off nearby trees with their trunks, their soulful presence a welcome zen. And I was about to disrupt it all. Ghubari and

Pressa screamed and squawked, raising the alarm. Great gray ears and powerful trunks lifted upward to take in the odd sight—a crow, an African gray, and a bald eagle being ridden by another crow (very handsome). Raccoons saw us, goats did, lascivious squirrels and moles and blue-bottomed flies. But they weren't who I was looking for. I was looking for the domestic dogs, who were all still there, milling around near Dennis where we'd left them on 164th Street. They all looked up to the sky with the other animals and cocked their heads at the cluster of birds and their cacophonous rally cries.

Migisi swooped right down in among the packs of dogs, Labradors, boxers, spaniels, and shepherds, brushing their fur with the tips of her flight feathers. I could smell their earthy doggy smell, which lit a fire inside me as I puffed out my chest and in my very best Big Jim voice yelled, "ZzzzZZZt! Good boy! COME!"

The first to leap to their feet were the shepherds, retrievers, a Doberman, and the collies. Fur along the ridges of spines stood to attention; black, wet noses lifted to the sky. Then, perhaps caught up in the excitement or by the familiar calls from another life they must have missed in their marrow, others leapt up and joined us. *Instincts.* Migisi, my fearless friend and majestic beauty, stayed low with the mass of slobbering canines, some lightning fast, others plodding but with that contagious fervor that is second nature to a dog. And I sang out the MoFo words, "ZzzzZZZt! COME! Let's go!" and they pounded after me with their moist panting and their irrepressible enthusiasm and hearts as big as blue whales.

We ran, with a sky full of cheering birds adding to excitement that already split up the sky with its lightning streaks. And it might be hard for you to imagine, but we ran like this—dog pack following low-flying eagle and crow speaking MoFo—for a long time. Migisi didn't give up. I—part MoFo, part crow, and proud to be caught in the middle of the two—didn't give up. The dogs didn't give up (well, some of them did, but French bulldogs and pugs have respiratory issues). More birds joined us in feather and spirit and more dogs trailed after the gargantuan pack. And eventually, we were at Bothell Landing.

The air at the park was dark with mobbing birds. New murders had joined our Sky Sentinels and were attacking The One Who Conquers from above. The orangutans had arrived at the park. The young ones threw rocks from the safety of the grand firs. Their mother was at ground level, advancing toward the wolves, the birds mobbing them, buying her time. The male orangutan bared his teeth and coughed out warning calls as he swung his weight behind his fist and struck a wolf across its muzzle. The wolf yelped and fell, springing back up to sink its teeth into its enemy—the long, ginger arm. The orangutan's hissing clowder of cats—streaks of ginger, brown, black, and white—arched their backs, swiping and lunging at predators many times their size without mercy. That insane tabby threw himself again and again at the wolves, evading the white menace of carnivorous canines, fueled by an endless ferocity. The wolf pack had done a lot of damage and the grass was littered with the bodies of fallen brethren.

I couldn't yet bear to look for Kraai. I had to focus. With one final, "ZzzzZZZt! Let's GO!" Migisi and I drew the pack into the clearing in the park and drove the mass of thundering domestic dogs into the wolf pack. And the wolves, who were so greatly outnumbered and sharp enough to recognize it, scattered. Migisi perched and we watched as the mass of domestic dogs—terrorizers of squeaky toys everywhere—chased away The One Who Conquers. Even the four snow-white sisters, tails tucked between legs, vanished into the tree line like distant moons.

CHAPTER 35

COMING UP FOR AIR
(THE SONG OF A HUMPBACK WHALE)

The soft prayer of seaweed; kelp fronds sway their salute
at the mercy of the waves.
Listen, their song holds the key to unlock living,
like brain coral's clever creases, its grooved wisdom
or the sparks from the sentimental skin of an eel.
Ocean's voice is old, graveled with salt,
crusty as a barnacle whose life was spent
dreaming of wings.
The whims of a minnow echo in dappled liquid light,
magnified one million times so that they flash and flaunt
like the spray of my breach.
There are no small splashes.
Our fins follow a journey made by a pulsing map
in the chambers of our hearts,
driftwood dreams of warmer waters
guiding us past a great garbage patch;
the last of Man's excess spilling into world of wave.

All is not lost.
Whoever forgets to come up for air
will wash up on shallow shoreline.
Beach.
Filling lung or gill is an act of faith;
swim forth come ripples of blue or ribbons of blood.
Baleen ballad and spume smile,
we will remember to count blessings like grains of sand,
and always come up for air.

CHAPTER 36

NOMADIC WANDERINGS ACROSS WASHINGTON
STATE, USA
(SHO'LEE`TSAH, FEMALE WOLF OF NOMADIC
BLENDED WOLF PACK)

There is a great change in the world and we feel a greater one coming. And so we must keep light, silent as the snakes that sway the grass. Watching you from the shadows, our golden eyes are filled with flame. We are led by the sisters, white as bone, who paint the land with their paws on borrowed time. We are hunted.

We sing by light of a Great Moon who dances in silver along the rivers and reminds the ocean how to breathe. We, all of us we, sing as one. Our song is for those who have left us, for those who are brave in their bones, for those who cannot sing. We sing to remember. We sing to celebrate a cloudy wisp of breath. And always, we sing for The Pack.

Howl out old pain. It is a soft and sonorous magic.

The Changed Ones are all around us, growing their packs. Swift on our paws, we must cover more ground and find refuge in the secrets the land has buried, listening to the wisdom of the water. The woods carry sounds in their slow rhythms, sounds that only a heart can hear.

Fight for your family. Protect the land that holds you.

We move as one because we are one. The code of wolf is family, The Pack is why we rise. We wander for miles, home in our hearts, guarding our pups with the fiery wrath of a sky storm. For our enemies, the end is swift and red. You will not see us coming.

But now, we are hunted anew.

We must roam, guided by the season's smell and the toothy gnaw of hunger. We are mountain wild and never lonely. The Pack will fight to thrive, for the dream of a den and the loud smell of a newborn pup. We all begin and end in blood, life's liquid. Roam, rove, conquer the land with our bodies. We are never lost and we never arrive, as The Pack seeks the journey. And as we protect The Pack from the hunters, we will fall in love with each moment, singing to a moon that has loved us since we were stars.

CHAPTER 37

❧✦❧

S.T.
DESTINATION UNKNOWN

We had been successful in driving off The One Who Conquers and, for now, had earned ourselves one of the luxurious moments of this life—stories shared by a fire I built (a match-in-the-beak party trick Big Jim taught me and now they all thought I was Hermione from fucking *Harry Potter*). We enjoyed each other's company, and a bag of marshmallows that we tore open and roasted on small twigs, as I extolled the virtues of MoFos, such as the varied histories of different cultures, the beauty in their physical differences, their creations, laughter, and love. I told them about how MoFos dedicate an hour to happiness every day with Pabst Blue Ribbon and heavily discounted tater tots. I told them about how even though MoFos weren't born with wings, they made their own and put them on airplanes and maxi pads, and about how they flushed all their poops out to *Echo*—the crows thought this was super hilarious. I explained birthday cake as a spongy mattress of awesome with hidden rivers of delicious goo to celebrate having stayed alive a whole year. I explained how MoFos measured time in German boobs and how their eyes rained when they were sad and also happy. I demonstrated—with a lot of flair—how moonwalking was different from walking on the moon. I had a hell of a time trying to explain Christmas, so I summarized it as "a fat MoFo in a red suit died and then came back and cached his treasures in a big red bag and sometimes MoFos went to the mall to sit on his crotch." I taught them commercial jingles and Seattle's signature song "Smells Like Team Spirit" and we practiced the "hello, hello, hello, heeelloooo" part. We practiced the impossible pronunciation of "rural brewery" together. I told them about dancing and the wonder of books and the world's greatest poet, Jon Bon Jovi. A favorite thing was when I talked about the food palace called Denny's and its magical dish of eggs and ham and cheese and sauce—man, they fucking loved that shit. Sometimes out of nowhere they'd just chant, "Moons Over My Hammy! Moons Over My Hammy!" Honestly, they became big MoFo fans; I'm pretty sure I converted them all. There were, sadly, some things that were just impossible to explain, like the plot of *Inception* and CrossFit.

We continued to roost at UW Bothell and its wetlands with an army of domestic animals starting their new lives in our vicinity. We all banded together—a necessary adaptation for survival. We were an odd and unprecedented bunch—birds and reptiles and great apes and cats and an ark-load of zoo animals—but a known adage of nature became our motto. Kraai once said to me, "We are more powerful when we work together because we look out for one another by being one. That is the code of murder." Kraai still said it all the time so it was easy to remember. We stockpiled food, grew in numbers, and collected MoFo things that the parrot pandemonium and I deemed valuable. We kept localized peace, even with some of the larger predators like the flamingo-snuffing snow leopard and the mama bear and cubs from the university public library who sought shelter from The Changed Ones. We all sought shelter. There were triumphs, like fending off The One Who Spits who showed up in many forms, and tribulations, like Orange the orangutan's beastly marital problems (they all stemmed from him discovering and coveting a healthy stash of Victoria's Secret catalogs). Kraai thrived in his role as the head of the Sky Sentinels. Pressa became a true MoFo apprentice, assiduously reciting MoFo words and, eventually, Bon Jovi lyrics. Ghubari became an unspoken leader, enlisting the help of the elephants to keep the peace, though even they were anxious around a short-haired tyrant named Genghis Cat. Migisi was the only living organism brave enough to mess with that cat. She was, after all, an adventure eagle.

There would always be dangers, especially with the ever-changing MoFos, but we focused on our present joy, which blossomed like a pink valerian flower growing through a crack in concrete. Perhaps the darker times made the good times sweeter, like the caramelized edge of a marshmallow, but it's hard to say. We were too busy living to dwell on these sorts of things.

One night, Kraai, Ghubari, Pressa, and a small assemblage of noble birds—a Steller's sea eagle, a northern harrier, and a sharp-shinned hawk—came to me (I now joined the murder as they met to socialize on the UW rooftops and roosted with them in the treetops of the north creek wetlands). It was an odd group of austere-looking birds of prey who said they had something to show me.

"We are going on a journey. You can tell *no one*," said the northern harrier with resting death face.

I had questions. "Where—"

"SHHHH!" They all shushed me in unison, this strange, sneaky conglomeration of feathereds.

"It has to be top secret," said the enormous Steller's sea

eagle. "We will not discuss any of this—not even among ourselves—until we have arrived." I looked at Pressa and Kraai for confirmation. Pressa nodded in agreement with the eagle and his terrifying beak that was roughly the size of a toaster.

"Trust us," she said.

Trust, that raspberry-flavored treat, was something I embraced, even cached, and though they didn't seem the most lighthearted of travel companions with their intense raptor expressions, I trusted Pressa, Ghubari, and Kraai enough to follow blindly. Once I had Migisi's promise to carry me, the matter was settled. And so, in the dead of night, we silently lifted into the sky. This was especially strange given that we were all diurnal birds and how much Ghubari loves his sleep.

The air had grown colder, breathing ice into our feathers. We headed due north, following a mind map delivered to Migisi in the utmost confidence. The journey was indeed a fucking long one. We slept in evergreens, and by day we flew over snowcapped mountains and rivers and streams that sparkled as if filled with loose diamonds. One morning, as *Aura* erupted around us, we flew over the crowns of trees that were draped in a giant netting of silver silks. I felt Migisi shudder beneath me and I knew that we were looking at the homes and damage of The Weavers. We pressed on, through rain and sun, choosing to focus on our secret mission instead of the darkness that spun its savagery below.

And I have to be honest with you here and tell you that I knew exactly what we were going for. It had been clear from the shine in Kraai's eyes, from the barely contained excitement that threatened to bubble out of the northern harrier, and the hawk's incessant talon taps, that this really *had* been a top secret mission just for yours truly. They had approached me in the manner Big Jim had when he had offered Tiffany S. a ring with three diamonds on it that we worked double shifts

to afford. And so I already knew as we left the safety of the
Sky Sentinels and the boundaries of our recently defended
territory that Kraai and this little circle of imposing birds had
located someone for me. I already knew, deep within my bird
bones, that when we'd land we'd be met by a small lump of
wrinkly folds. A slobbering codpiece of a canine who would
eventually chew through and ravage my sacred Cheetos® stash,
bay loud enough that little black fledglings would tumble from
low branches, and wreak general havoc on the college murder.
There weren't many bloodhounds in Seattle, so the long journey made sense, and to be honest, I wasn't thrilled about the
idea. How could any poor dog live up to my Dennis? I didn't
want a replacement, but I didn't know how to turn down this
elaborate gift, how to crush the excitement of birds with talons
like pocket *katanas*. So I tried to think about other things, but
found myself enjoying imagining what the pup might be like—
whether he or she would, like young Dennis, bark at mustard
bottles and have to overcome a fear of windshield wipers. I
kept it to myself and feigned total ignorance, concentrating on
the beauty of the flight, from the hairy musk oxen that grazed
happily on emerald hills to the pod of narwhals we skimmed
above, darting between their majestic horns as they whistled a
well-wishing song. What a surprise and a delight to see them
so far south. But the farther we flew, the more I felt my heart
quivering, the more I imagined a pair of stupid melted eyes,
and soon I found myself shivering with excitement. And I tell
you, eventually, I just couldn't wait to meet him. Listen, I knew
he wouldn't be Dennis, but I also knew I'd teach him all the
things I'd taught Dennis while he lounged around and licked
his nuts, terrorized salacious squirrels, or bulldozed the unruly
flower beds on the college grounds. I wanted to scream my
gratitude to Kraai and my new friends for the touching gesture.
It honestly took every ounce of my energy not to sing.

And then we flew over a devastatingly beautiful landscape. I suddenly recalled the words of a waxy monkey tree frog I'd once encountered...

Pass the moonstone river, he had said, and I heard his croaky voice on repeat as we sailed over a radiant river. Its waters looked exactly like the precious silvery white and icy blues of a moonstone gem.

"What is this? Below us?" I called out to Kraai.

While cruising below the clouds, he dipped his head to take in the breathtaking scene underneath him and said, "Moonstone river." I realized at that precise moment that the alpine carpet of trees were all pointing one branch north, guiding us forward and the skin under my plumage erupted into microscopic mountains. How had that weird little frog known I'd be here?

We eventually finished our avian tour with the Bering Sea and touched down to grass, surrounded by an abandoned village that had a sign that read "Welcome To Nunakauyak (Toksook Bay). We do not allow drugs/alcohol in our community. Violators will be prosecuted per our Nunakauyarmiut Tribal Codes." There was an abandoned yellow seaplane, presumably how MoFos flew to this remote village before the virus wiped everyone away. This had been the home of the Yup'ik, a First Nations people who were hunters and gatherers. A lineage of bloodhounds must live in this small village, tucked away in a sequestered envelope, an Alaskan sanctuary. We fluttered over to the top of a quaint little house, which sat next to a mud-splattered ATV resting peacefully for eternity. And across from the roof where we sat was a mural that stopped my pulse. On a brick wall, someone with great skill—the skill only a MoFo could have—had made a black ink drawing of a bird rising above an evergreen. In its beak, the bird held an eight-pointed star. Next to the bird was a perfect MoFo handprint. My skin rippled with bumps.

The bird was a crow.

This was the same depiction I'd seen at the horrible Seattle town house with the drug paraphernalia and a MoFo hanging by a rope and a litter of huskies that wouldn't have survived another day. I looked at my travel companions—raptors with eyes as sharp as a blade's edge—all beckoning for me to follow them to the open doorway of the tiny house whose roof I sat and shivered on.

I hopped back onto Migisi's chocolate feathers and we dropped to the ground. Dismounting, I shuffled up three wooden steps and through the frame of a green front door. Inside was chilly. There were cobwebs hanging over pots, and dishes littered the tiny kitchen sink. A charming old wooden stove, the likes of which I'd only seen on the History Channel, sat moodily, dreaming of hot stew. A pair of muddy boots rested lonely on the floor, calling out to be worn again. The northern harrier, sharp-shinned hawk, and the Steller's sea eagle all watched me. And surrounding the puppy, in front of the hawks and the eagle, in front of Kraai who gazed at them in awe, were five snowy owls. They had faces like perfect porcelain dinner plates, the alabaster plumage below their necks erupting into dappled black and white that looked like the salt and peppering of a thousand distant birds in flight.

The snowy owls were unsure. I could feel their uncertainty hovering like the motes of dust that danced through the cabin. It was written in their chatoyant yellow eyes. Kraai was facing my new friend, the little wrinkled pup with his droopy eyes, his fat little fawn belly and enormous spongy paws that he had yet to grow into. One of the snowy owls inched itself closer to the tiny puppy. Kraai looked back at me, his eyes full of expectancy. He was looking to me for answers. Pressa's eyes were wide and shiny. The eagles and hawks parted, giving way to me as I approached the bloodhound pup. And as I stood next to the five magnificent owls who held their breath in my presence, I realized that it wasn't a bloodhound baby. It was a MoFo baby.

The tiny MoFo was sleeping, bundled crudely in all sorts of material—kitchen towels, sheep's fleece, a paper bag, a pair of shorts. She was a little girl and her cheeks were flushed like blushing fireweed blooms, her tiny hands balled by her sides. And the moment I laid my beady little hybrid eyes upon you, my nestling, I was a goner. I fell in love with the smoothness of your skin and the roundness of your perfect little face that felt like discovering a new planet and a whole new beginning, a new chance at life. The owls had done the best they could, bundling you in their feathers to keep you warm, feeding you with what they scavenged—mostly water and drops of nectar and fresh wild honey—but you were starving and mal-nourished despite their efforts and so I vowed then and there, my nestling, that I would take over your care and I would be your guardian against this New World. I remembered how Pressa told me that all females are survivors and you are no exception. This is the moment I vowed to teach you everything I could about how to survive the sharp edges of where we now lived. I named you Dee after your Uncle Dennis, who I prom-ised to tell you all about and who lives on in everything we do. Uncle Dennis who floated away on the wings of a butterfly.

And my big journey, the one I slowly tell you as a bed-time story—along with *The Hobbit* because that's a goddamned classic—is how I know what I've told you is true. About how Mother Nature is not kind, but she is balanced. Every single one of us, from amoeba to blue whale to the tenacious bloom that dares to dream of tomorrow, have their own destiny-fulfilling journey as long as their minds and hearts are open. And how we are all connected by a web that looks gossamer but is stronger than a chain-link fence. And though Nature is tough, she is always conspiring for your success, encouraging you to evolve. You can even hear her if you listen carefully.

I am The One Who Keeps *you*, my nestling. I am The One Who Keeps us safe. I'm The One Who Keeps the stories alive. I'm The One Who Keeps up hope, staving off The Black Tide. I am not just one thing but a combination of them, peacock proud and imperfect. And I have kept my promise that I would tell you everything when you were old enough to understand. As an honorary MoFo, I'm here to be utterly honest and tell you what happened to your kind. The thing none of us saw coming.

And somewhere far away in a world we feel but cannot see, a bloodhound named Dennis now lives a dream where he chases rabbits in a field, trailing every last delicious smell to the ends of the earth and far, far, far beyond.

And somewhere in the ocean is a giant Pacific octopus. She pours forward, fluid and bone-free, on the tail of a current. Only she *is* the current, a magical liquid wonder and the fluid sum of Mother Nature's wisdom.

It is known.

ACKNOWLEDGMENTS

Thank you first and foremost to my superstar agent, Bill Clegg, for his incomparable brilliance, his vulpine instincts, and eagle eyes. This book was elevated in every possible way because of his guidance and literary finesse. I am eternally grateful. If Shit Turd got to Freaky Friday himself into a human, he would choose to be Bill Clegg.

My heartfelt thanks to all the incredible MoFos at The Clegg Agency—Simon Toop, David Kambhu, and Marion Duvert for shepherding *Hollow Kingdom* along its amazing journey. Many thanks to Chris Clemans. And special thanks to my wonderful film and television agent, Kassie Evashevski.

I am truly grateful to the Grand Central Publishing team. This book would not be what it is without my editor extraordinaire, Karen Kosztolnyik. Her ideas were sharp, funny, insightful, and Shit Turd–approved. Karen never even complained when she had to google a reference I'd made to water buffalo testicles. Thank you to Elizabeth Kulhanek, my Komodo friend, ally to animals, and genius editor. What an immense pleasure to work with you both. Thank you to Jarrod Taylor for my jaw-droppingly beautiful cover art and to Anjuli Johnson and Alayna Johnson, whose copyedit was so thorough it was a thing of great and humbling beauty. Thank you to my rock-star publicists, Andy Dodds and Jordan Rubinstein. Thank you to Thomas Louie, Andrew Duncan, Joseph Benincase, Alison Lazarus, Chris Murphy, Karen Torres, Matthew Ballast, Brian McLendon, and Ben Sevier.

To Douglas Wacker, PhD, our resident crow pro at UW Bothell. Thank you for the corvid counsel and the bird nerd chats. If you have a chance to listen to Doug give one of his excellent talks on crows—treat yourself.

Writers are solitary beasts, but I would be lost in the woods without my friends (literally—this has actually happened). They have shown endless support, whether it was listening to early drafts, joining me on research trips, hydrating me with prosecco, or watering their garden while wearing a crow mask in Shit Turd's honor. Thank you to Susan Urban, Stacy Lawson, Shoshana Levenberg, Corry Venema-Weiss, Randy Hale, Janet Yoder, Billie Condon, Susan Knox, Shelley Motz, Jennifer Fliss, Sharon Van Epps, Fredrika Sprengle, Vicki Olafson, Mark Michaels, Drake and Olivia Michaels, Paul China, Bergen Buck, Laura Wisk, Rebecca Wallwork, Sasha R. Moghimi-Kian, and John and Wendy Whitcomb. To Robin Quick, thank you for believing in me from the beginning.

A very special thanks to Karen Joy Fowler for her sage advice and an early read despite battling a bedbug apocalypse in Budapest. Thank you to Waverly Fitzgerald, who set me on the right path with her enthusiasm and generous spirit. To Monona Wali for the writing class that lit me up inside.

For help with translation, thank you to Dina Ayoub, Veena Lertpachin, Cynthia Large, and Duaa Al-Jassim.

Special thanks to Tree Swenson and Hugo House, Seattle's home for writers.

Thank you to Hedgebrook, an essential organization that supports women authoring change. To Nancy Nordhoff, who built a beautiful nest for women writers. Amy Wheeler, Vito Zingarelli, Lynn Hays, Cathy Bruemmer, Julie O'Brien, Harolynne Bobis, Denise Barr, Britt Conn, Evie Wilson-Lingbloom, and everyone I've met through Vortext. Your encouragement has meant everything.

Thank you to Erin, Simon, and Nathan Twine for all the love and support. Erin, thank you for always having the answers in life and literature. You are the sister I'd choose even if we weren't related.

To Em and Pops, who always encouraged me to follow my dreams, except the one about bringing home a twenty-foot snake. Thank you for my sense of adventure and devotion to animals. I think you knew I was an artist when I was knee-high to a fainting goat. Thank you for nurturing it—I would have made a horrendous accountant. I am so very proud to be your daughter.

And Jpeg, to whom this book is dedicated. Jpeg, who heard this book chapter by chapter as it was written and cheered it on like a fledgling along a branch. Jpeg assured me that dreams can come true. He was right. You're holding mine in your hands.

Though they may or may not read this, I'd like to thank the creatures great and small who have captivated me. Many species are in need of our help. Here are just a few spectacular organizations that deserve our support:

World Wildlife Fund
National Audubon Society
Oceana
The Jane Goodall Institute
The Nature Conservancy
Natural Resources Defense Council
Wildlife Conservation Society
Sierra Club
Woodland Park Zoo
Seattle Aquarium

To those who are advocates, champions, rescuers, and protectors of our animal friends—thank you. You are my heroes.

Thank you to my darling monstrous cats, and the two crows who inspired many of S.T.'s antics and attributes. And my bearded canine partner in crime, Ewok, who was by my side as I wrote *Hollow Kingdom,* fearlessly protecting me from the UPS man—good boy, buddy.

ABOUT THE AUTHOR

Kira Jane Buxton's writing has appeared in the *New York Times*, NewYorker.com, McSweeney's, *The Rumpus*, *Huffington Post*, and more. She calls the tropical utopia of Seattle home and spends her time with three cats, a dog, two crows, a charm of hummingbirds, and a husband.